About the Author:
"Timothy Diamond" is a pseudonym for my real name.
I Started writing between 1988 and 1994 I wrote multiple articles, and reports on recreational diving that were published in Scuba Diver Magazine, and the Gold Coast Bulletin. I also wrote the feature article 'The Round Trip' for Yachting Australia magazine in 2009.
My first foray into writing full length novels was in 2014 with the Catalyst Trilogy, which was loosely based around my own experiences.

Other books written are:
Playing with Fire: Catalyst Book 1
Divine Retribution: Catalyst Book 2
Last Man Standing: Catalyst Book 3
The Other Side of the Coin: a companion book to the Catalyst Trilogy
Ocean Gold
Chasing the Sun
The Tale of the MV Eagle Star
Kingdoms Bounty

Acknowledgements.

To Diane: Here we go again darling. Thank you.

The Ultimate Gamble

TIMOTHY DIAMOND

The Ultimate Gamble
Author: Timothy Diamond

National Library of Australia Cataloguing-in-Publication entry

Creator: Diamond, Timothy author.
Creator: Diamond, Timothy, author.

Title: The Ultimate Gamble / Timothy Diamond.

ISBN:(paperback) 978-0-6480117-7-4
ISBN:(Ebook) 978-0-6480117-8-1

Subjects: Historical - Fiction.
Action/Adventure - Fiction.
Naval Battles - Fiction.
War - Fiction.

Dewey Number: A823.4

A Note to Readers, from the Author.

Dear Readers: I know that I didn't know what my next book was going to be, after finishing Kingdoms Bounty, I had a lot of fun writing that, and so I have decided to continue that historical theme, with other members of the Fox-Davis/Tolcher clan.

I again contacted Andy, he sent me everything he had collected concerning his and Tom's forbears. After hours of going through everything he sent me, which included the individual Journals written by each family member. I decided to concentrate on members of the clan that had taken part in events that became pivotal moments in history.

The following story concerns not only one, but two members from each side of the clan, they both took part in what was a huge gamble, and has become known as one of the greatest naval battles of the modern era.

To all my faithful readers: I hope you all once again, enjoy the read.

Yours Sincerely,
Timothy Diamond.

Battle of the Nile Map:

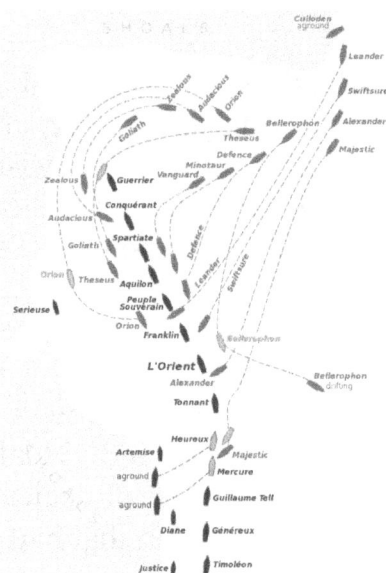

Taunton Manor

Trafalgar Plan of Attack:

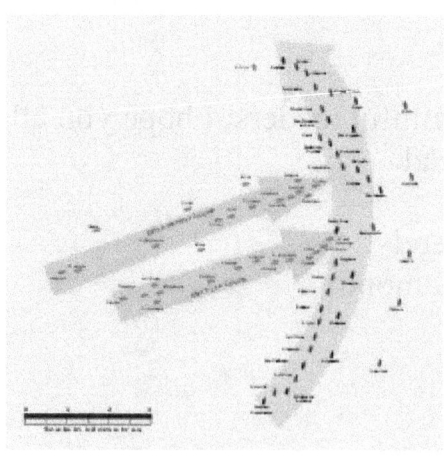

Preface.

The Battle of Trafalgar 1805.

The overwhelming victory over the French and Spanish fleet, off the Cape of Trafalgar on October 25, 1805 gave England's Royal Navy its most famous triumph, and confirmed a long tradition of naval supremacy.
The battle also immortalized the memory of Viscount Horatio Nelson, who was shot and died of his wounds, during the moment of his greatest triumph.

The naval campaign started as part of Napoleon Bonaparte's plan, to invade Britain in the summer of 1805. Napoleon needed to gain control of the English Channel to allow his Grand Armée to cross. To achieve this, he ordered the French fleet's three squadrons blockaded at Brest, Toulon and other ports to break out, meet in the West Indies, and then return as one fleet to gain control of the Channel.

In March the squadron of Admiral Villeneuve at Toulon, was able to evade the British blockade, joined up with a Spanish squadron, and left for the West Indies. Nelson learned of his departure on 10 April and was soon in hot pursuit. Villeneuve lost his nerve and immediately returned to Europe. After a minor battle off Cape Finisterre he was bottled up in Cadiz in Spain.

Knowing that the invasion was now impossible, Napoleon marched his Grande Armee, to meet the threat posed by Austria, and Russia in the east.

Nelson's fleet of 27 ships of the line, now waited for Admiral Villeneuve's force to emerge. The fleet was at high peak of fighting efficiency having been at sea blockading the French for almost two years. At the of September, Nelson revealed his plan to his captains; it was to be his ultimate gamble, the fleet would be split into two columns to break through the enemy line, and overwhelm the centre and rear sections of the enemy's fleet.

On 19 October a British frigate watching Cadiz spotted the Franco-Spanish fleet leaving harbour. It consisted of 33 ships of the line, including the 136-gun Santissima Trinidad, the largest ship in the world. Villeneuve's orders were to try to break into the Mediterranean.

The message was passed to Nelson's fleet, 48 miles off the coast and he ordered a general chase. By dawn on 21 October the British fleet was only 9 miles away from the enemy. At 11:48am, HMS Victory (Nelson's flagship) hoisted the famous signal 'England Expects That Every Man Will Do His Duty' followed by 'Engage the enemy more closely'. The two columns led by HMS Victory, and HMS Royal Sovereign, successfully pierced the enemy line, firing into the bow and stern of the enemy ships, as they passed between them.

The fighting was severe and much of it was at close quarters. Many of the British ships were damaged, some seriously, including the HMS Victory which engaged the French flagship Bucentaure and the Redoutable. But Nelson's faith in the superior gunnery and ship handling skills of the British crews was fully borne out with the capture of 18 enemy ships including the Santissima Trinidad. Villeneuve had surrendered at 13:45 (1:45pm) and despite renewed resistance by some Spanish ships the battle was over by 16.30 (4:30pm).

A great storm blew up on 22 October, and when it subsided only four enemy ships remained in British hands most having sunk. The total number of killed and wounded on both sides was about 8,500 whilst the British took about 20,000 prisoners. Nelson himself had been shot, by a musket ball at about 13:15 (1:15pm), and died around 16:30 (4:30pm), when victory was assured.

The era of British naval supremacy brought about by the victory at Trafalgar, lasted for a century until Germany's naval challenge in the third decade of the twentieth century.

Chapter 1.

Journal: Henry Robert Tolcher RN Captain.

October 25, 1805: I sit here in my cabin, alone with my thoughts, and my cousins' personal effects, these had been brought to me on the Victory this morning, when a captain's conference was called by Hardy. Until this time, I have been too busy to dwell on the fact, that my cousin and good friend, was killed during the battle in the most gruesome way.
Running my eyes over his possessions, I have noticed his now familiar journal had been brought to me among his gear, and I sadly get up and carefully extract it, sitting back, I open it and make for the last entry I had read.
From there, I have read through to his last entry with tears in my eyes, as I wipe the tears away, I have decided two things: The first, being that I will finish his journal, with an obituary of the first order, and try to do him proud. Second, the very next time I am given shore leave in England, I will personally take his possessions home to his wife Elizabeth, instead of just sending them to her, she has the right to know, how gallantly her husband had died, from one that witnessed his end during the battle
After I have brought this journal of mine up to date, I intend to visit once more, the early part of my life that has brought me to the present, with the hope in some way, that I have been able to emulate the bravery my cousin had shown during his life.

May 1794: As my time here at the Royal Naval College, ends, I have time to reflect on what my life has become so far. I was born in 1776 the only child of Elizabeth and Danyel Tolcher, and I grew up on the family farm in Devon, along with my parents and grandparents, pop Sam, and nanna Suzanna. I was never really interested in farm life, and yearned to see what was out in the world. To this end, after I turned twelve I would work in the nearby hamlet doing any job that would pay money.

You see I had decided to join the navy when I could, I could go to the Royal naval college at fifteen, and after three years would be made an officer, if I passed my exams, but to do this I had to earn as much as I could, so I could attend the college. Every penny I made from work went into a tin that my pop Sam kept for me, and I hoped that I could earn enough money for my keep in the three years leading up to sending in my application.

Even though father and mother didn't try to stop me, father would always want me to help him on the farm, but if this coincided any work that I would be paid for doing, he would let me go off to do it.

During the summer months, I was allowed to take the old draught mare to Cornwall, where one of Pop Sam's relations owned a copper mine, and I was soon at work being paid decent money as a miner, it was hard and dangerous work, but I revelled in it. Becoming an experienced mine worker quickly, the only real danger was the possibility of cave ins, but that was treated as an occupational hazard. At the end of the day my arms felt like lead, but this eased.

My body kept growing as a miner, and at the end of the first summer, I stood five feet six and had developed wide shoulders, and quite a muscular physique, some of the other older miners, had taken to teaching me how to fight, and in a boxing match, I was able to hold my own, against older, taller, and larger opponents.

At the end of that first season, I was told by my older cousin and wife who owned the mine, I would be welcomed back at any time. I thought this to be gracious, and told them that I had one more year before I could go to the college, and I would probably see them again the next summer. My cousin also hinted that I should go and see the Earl who was head of the family clan, and tell him of my expectations to see if he could help me.

During the ride home to our farm, I thought this advice over, considering it to be a sound move, and decided to ask father about our family connections when I arrived home.

Finally arriving at the farm after three days travel, my mother made such a fuss on my return, and went about clasping a handkerchief wailing about me being so grown up. When my father came in from the fields to find me home, he looked me up and down, nodded, and only said, "You've grown boy," That evening at dinner, I asked about our relations, and the present Earl as head of the clan, Poppa Sam asked why, and I told him about cousin Thomas recommending I go see the Earl and inform him of my plans about joining the navy.

Looking at my father, he seemed to think what I had said over, saying "Aye that seems to be a sensible thing to do. What do you think Danyel?"

My father looked up, stared at his father with disapproval on his face then looked at me, saying "I 'pose it couldn't hurt, but theys live way up in Taunton, Somerset twould take a week to get there by cart. You couldn't go alone, you'd need a family member to go with you, and I can't do it or your ma, so that's that boy."

The excitement that I had started to feel, felt like a rock crashing into the ground, as disappointment hit me. Then poppa Sam said, "Well I could take him, I'd like to see William again, it's been a long while since I saw him."

As my hopes started to rise again, I watched their faces closely, trying to see which of these two was going to win the byplay, father had no interest in what I wished to do, but my grandfather was willing to help me try to be a self-made man of my own choosing, whether he agreed with my decision to join the navy or not. He had once told me to runaway to sea was a fool's ambition, but a person had to learn that themselves, and a right to make their own choices.

Then help surfaced in the most unlikely corner, nanna Suzanna spoke, saying "You'll not be going without me Samuel, he is my brother after all."

My hopes soared, as my grandfather replied, "Of course dear, I wouldn't go without you."

Then mother looked at father saying, "Oh let them go Danyel, what harm can it do?"

Father looked at her, then at each of us around the table, growling, "Oh alright, take the cart, but don't you go blaming me if it turns out to be a fool's errand, and you get robbed along the way."
Pop clapped his hands together reached across and slapped me on the back, saying "Hah righto, we'll leave tomorrow morning, Henry best give me your earnings to go into the tin boy, sleep well tonight, tomorrow night we'll be under the stars."
Father glared at pop, and then mother, before saying, "I wish you good luck son, but that's all. Father you take good care of him."
The following morning, I had packed all my good clothes into a bag, before going down to breakfast, and as I entered the dining room, placed my bag on a spare chair, noticing that there was a case beside it. Father wasn't eating with us, he was already out in the milking shed. As we ate, mother told us this, and pop Sam said, "Aye he'll not stop his work, as is right, Henry after you're finished, go out and hitch Daisy up to the cart." I nodded with a smile on my face, and soon I was leaving the house to do just that.
When poppa Sam joined me he was carrying a larger bag, and I joined him in the barn as he was stuffing the bag full of straw, we filled it as much as we could cramming the straw in as tight as it would go, and when we finished, had a fine solid straw mattress which we put into the bed of the cart, then when our two cases and my bag were in the cart, cushions were thrown in, and I lashed the canvas covering into place.

Leaving a large accessible area at the front of the cart, behind the seat. Poppa Sam explained, this was in case nanna Suzanna wished to be comfortable in the wagon bed instead of sitting on the seat.
As all three of us were about to leave, we stood beside the cart, as mother was giving us all a last-minute kiss, then father came up giving Nanna Suzanna a hug and shook hands with pop Sam, and me, saying "Take care, and take this with you," with that he handed pop a flintlock pistol and a bag with powder and shot. Giving them to me, I placed them under the seat where I would be driving. We mounted the cart, first pop then nanna, and I followed up into the seat, with a flick of the reins I started Daisy walking.

Five days later, I guided Daisy into a sprawling manor house, and pulled up at the front door. Pop assisted nanna down from the seat, while I looped the reins around the brake handle, we were all dressed in our Sunday best, as we went to the door, and pop used the door knocker. The door was answered by a uniformed houseman, and pop said, "We're here to see the Earl, I'm Samuel Tolcher." The man replied, "Very good sir, please enter." Pop went first followed by nanna, then I followed. We were shown into a waiting room, and shortly, a door opened and another uniformed man, walked up to pop saying, "The Earl will see you now, if you will follow me please." Waving his arm in the direction to go, then we all followed. We were shown into a larger study, where two men were standing.

The first man was a little shorter than me, with grey hair, and would have been the same age as pop, the second was about my height, with black hair that was greying, and was probably about the same age as my father, both were dressed in very fine clothing, and had frock coats on, but unbuttoned. The older man came forward smiling, saying "Samuel, such a long time dear cousin." Embracing pop and they both slapped each other's backs as they hugged, then letting go of each other, he stepped back, looking at nanna, and said as he hugged her too, "Dear sister, it's so good to see you both after such a long time."

Then I moved forward to stand beside them, as I did the earl looked me up and down, asking "And who do we have here?"

Pop answered, "This is Henry, our grandson your grace."

I was about to bow to him, but he pulled me up, and shook my hand, saying "Now none of that airs and graces shit, from any of you, your family, excuse my language Suzanna."

Nanna laughed saying, "You used to be a lot worse when we were children brother dear."

"Oh, I still am sister, and, I've learnt a lot more words since then." As we all laughed.

Gesturing with his hand to the other man to join us, he said, "Let me introduce you to my son Albert, Albert, this is your Uncle Samuel, Aunt Suzanna, and your Nephew Henry."

Albert Shook hands with pop and me, and bowed to nanna, saying "Uncle, aunt Suzanna, nephew.

The earl then said, "Come let's all sit down you've all come such a long way," as we took seats facing each other, he turned to the servant standing by the opened door, saying "Refreshments please Jenkins." Who replied, "Very good my lord," as he left the room shutting the door as he went.

When he had left Sir William, faced us again, asking "So to what do I owe the pleasure of your company Samuel? And don't argue, you're all staying for a few days, I'll have rooms made up for you. Elizabeth will be thrilled."

Pop spoke up saying, "Well it's because of young Henry here William, he's been working the summer months with young Thomas at his copper mine in Cornwall, and he suggested to Henry that he come and see you."

"Oh, what this all about Henry?" The earl enquired as he looked to me.

I looked him in the eye, replying "Well you see sir…I told him everything that I wished to do, and the lengths I had gone to get enough money together.

My father's opposition to what I wanted to do, and up to my older cousin Thomas's… suggestion. I come and see you to tell you of my plans sir."

After I had finished, he looked at pop, then back at me, as he leaned further back in his seat saying, "Hmm I see, tis a noble ambition to serve one's country Henry, do you fully know what is required to enter the Naval College, apart from having the funds to sustain yourself while you are there, that means uniforms and such you know?"

Before I could answer him, the servant came back into the room with another carrying trays with fresh tea and the makings, along with cake and biscuits, while one of them served us, sir William, sent the other to ask Lady Elizabeth and Lucy to join us, who they were, I had no idea.

After being served my tea, cake and biscuits, I put down the plate, cup and saucer onto the table between us, and with a hard look said, "Sir William my answer to your question is, no sir, I'm not aware of what else I require."

He started laughing, and said, "Well Henry, you get a very steely look in those brown eyes of yours when you're angry, I take you are a trifle angered at my question, what do you think Sam?"

Pop replied, "Aye, he does tend to get that look in his eyes when his dander is up to be sure, and he's not one to trifle with then."

I threw a hard look at pop, but just then the doors were thrown open, and two older women entered the room, the older one exclaiming, "Suzanna, Sam, come here."

They both got up and exchanged embraces with her then she introduced the other, who was Lucy, Alberts wife, then getting up, I was introduced to both of them, the older was the earl's wife.

"Oh Jenkins," the earl said, "Our guest will be staying a few days, see to their rooms and belongings, that's a good chap."

"Very good my lord," Jenkins replied, as pop still standing said, I'll come with you to sort our stuff Jenkins." And they both left the room.

Having finished our tea and cake, the earl said, "Henry, Albert, let's leave the ladies to get acquainted, come."

With that we both followed him out one of the side doors to the patio, where he rounded on me angrily saying, "Now then, young Henry, let me tell you, it takes more than you think, to just get into the royal naval college, it takes grit and determination, which you have aplenty, it takes hard work, which I know you're not afraid of, it takes money, you may have some, but not enough, it takes schooling, yes, you may be able to read and write, but you have to be schooled as a gentleman, it takes the will to succeed where others have failed, and last of all, it takes a letter of recommendation from an influential person, if you think I'm wrong, just ask Albert here."

Albert chimed in saying, "Aye father's right young nephew, one of your cousins and my best friend is in the navy as an officer, he made it by hard work, as for the rest, they're all fops, popinjays, and milksops, that have never done a lick of hard work in their lives, that have come from landed gentry, or are related some way or another to members of the peerage. Yes, in a way like our family, but our family has always worked hard for what we've got, we don't shirk from the hard work that has to be done, our family goes back to the times of William the Conqueror and beyond. Our forebears worked damned hard from nothing and built everything you may see in the four counties of Somerset, Dorset, Devon, and Cornwall, they all comes to us as auspices under the Earldom of Straithhaven."

When they had finished, with what they were saying, my mind was whirling. *I was struck with everything I had to have to gain entry to the naval college, and what sort of people I'd by going up against, but I was still not going to let this stop me. I had just over a year to get what was needed.*

The earl and his son had stayed quiet while I let everything process in my mind, but were both watching my reactions, bringing my head up, I looked at the earl and Albert.

Then I faced the earl saying, "Sir, I have listened to you both sincerely, and heard what you have had to say, and I have two questions, one, do you know someone who can supply me with a recommendation to the college, and two, do you have a copy of our family history in your library?"

Chapter 2.

Earl William, smiled, passed a look to his son, and back at me saying, "Ahh, Henry, you remind me so much of your uncle, and his and your cousin, the answer to your first question, "Yes, I do know someone who can recommend you to the naval college. Now the answer to your second question is yes, I do have a copy of the family history, but it is quite a large volume and takes hours of reading, can I ask you why?"
I smiled saying, "Of course sir, while I'm here, I'd like to discover where I and my family came from."

He nodded saying, "When we go back inside, Albert will show you where it is. Now also I would like to see you and your grandfather in my study tomorrow at nine o'clock, in the meantime I want you to think over what you have learned in regard the naval college, can you do that for me please?"
I straightened up saying, "Nine in your study, and I can promise you I will think over what I have learned sir."
He smiled replying, "Good, now let's go back in."
"Excuse me sir," I asked, "Could you tell pop, I mean grandfather, about the meeting tomorrow please."
He replied and asked, "Of course I will, why?"
"Because I might start reading the family book sir."
He laughed saying, "Very well, but as I warned it will take hours, but that's your choice, now let's get back inside." Then we went back to the door inside.

I followed Albert to the library, and he got the family book for me, it was easily a foot thick, saying "That's volume one, volume two is beside where it came from, I'll leave you to it nephew. Good luck." As he smiled and left the room.

I took the large and heavy book to a comfortable chair, sat down and started reading. Next morning, pop came into the library, I was still there, I had been reading all the previous day and night, but still had half of volume two, to go.

"Have you been here all night?" He asked, then said, "Come on let's get you some breakfast before we go see William. I hope you are satisfied now, seems to be a lot of reading."

"It's bleeding fascinating stuff pop; do you know it all?" I asked.

"Nope, and have no need to, 'sides you know I'm not good at reading. And enough of that language." He said, and I laughed, as we went to the dining room for breakfast.

As we entered the dining room we were greeted by Albert and Lucy, Lucy exclaimed "Good Gratuitous Henry you look awfully tired, and your still in the same cloths, Albert can lend you something if you have no others, did you have a bad night dear?"

Pop interrupted saying, "Nah, he's been bloody reading all night."

Nanna exclaimed, "Samuel, that's enough of that language, right now!"

He replied docilely, "Yes dear."

As we all laughed, Albert asked "You've been reading all this time? What do you think of it?"

"Fascinating, but I'm only half way through volume two at present. I didn't know any of that, it's not taught in schools. That's if you go, I mean." I replied. Then tried a cup of coffee, I found it to be quite a stimulant, I liked the taste, and it cleared my sleepy brain. After breakfast was finished Albert asked if we were all done, and he was told we were, he said, "Well in that case we had best join father.

Albert kissed his wife, as did pop, we stood up, and followed albert to his father's study, which was the room we had met in the morning before. As we entered, we were greeted and bade to sit in the three chairs before the desk, behind which the earl sat. As we sat down, he mentioned to me, "You've some dark circles under your eyes Henry, rough night, thinking about what we discussed yesterday?" Albert interjected, saying "Reading all night father, uncle Sam had to pull him away for breakfast." The earl looked at me with a grin saying, "I did warn you my boy, fascinating stuff isn't it?" and I just nodded. "Well then, you probably didn't get much time to think over what we discussed."

"No sir, but I'd already made my mind up yesterday, I still intend to go to the college sir, and if I need more money, I'll just find work during any break that I get."

"Hmm, yes I guess you would, I like your spirit Henry, but are you a gentleman?"

I answered him, "I can be when I have to be sir."

"I didn't mean do you have manners, yes I know you do, but are you a gentleman, and can you, act like one?"

"I don't know sir, how does a gentleman act?" I
replied.

He smiled saying "Well that's just it you see, you
have to dress, act, think, eat, always think you're
better than the next man or those below your
station?"

I looked at him asking, "If you are asking could I
ignore poor people when I have means to help them,
then no sir, I consider myself no better than the next
man, either be it a lord or a farmer sir."

Sir William smiled and asked, "Can you use a gun,
or a sword Henry?"

Now it was my turn to smile, saying, "I am an
expert shot with pistol or rifle for shooting animals
around a farm, or for food sir, but no, I have not
used a sword."

He nodded his head, and asked "How much money
do you have Henry?"

Pop growled, saying "William you're treading on
dangerous ground here, the boy doesn't know
enough yet to work out you're insulting him, but I
do, and I'll not be taking it kindly!"

"Pray relax Sam, I'm merely trying to ascertain how
much help he really needs, and I would sooner cut
off my arm than insult family," the earl replied
calmly. "May I continue?"

Pop nodded, but was looking wearily all the same,
as I watched the byplay between them.

To stop the tension rising in the room any further, I
replied, to the earls last question, "I'm not exactly
sure how much I have, but poppa has been keeping
it in a tin for me, but I think it's close to thirty-eight

pounds sir."

Pop had calmed down a bit by now, and when he was asked pop produced the tin out of his shirt, and we all counted it. The money totaled thirty-eight pounds, sixteen shillings and ten pence.

Sir William told me that all up I had a good head for figures, considering I had never counted the full extent of my earnings as it went into the tin, or had counted it since. My estimation had been very close in the main with my correct count of the pounds, but the loose change was not to be sneezed at either.

Just then, we were interrupted as Jenkins knocked and came into the study, asking if we would care for morning tea. The earl told him we would, but before he left I asked for a small pot of coffee, instead.

Jenkins just smiled, nodded his head, and left. After he left, I was asked to wait, while the others had a quick discussion outside, they didn't come back in until the coffee and tea arrived.

Pop and Albert were smiling as they came in, but nothing was said as the tea was poured by Jenkins, and he left us, leaving the tray sitting on the side of the desk.
The earl then looked at me saying, "Henry you know what we were talking about yesterday, when you asked if I knew someone of influence that would recommended you to the naval college?"

I nodded my head.

As he continued, "Well if a person does that, they become what is known as a sponsor, now a sponsor is supposed to not only recommend you, but they also pay your tuition and fees at the college, for your clothing and uniforms this includes hats and a decent sword and other weapons, everything."

Taking another sip of his tea, he continued, "Now I like your spirit, in wanting to do this all on your own, it shows that you wish to be beholding to only yourself, and I commend you for this, but to do this on your own, I'm afraid is impossible. But toward what you wish to do, I am prepared to help you. I will make you a proposal, if you accept my offer, I will become your sponsor. If you decline, well I don't help you, and you probably won't make it past the doors of the college, all I ask is that you hear what I have to offer, then you give me an answer, what do you say?"

What else could I say? Of course, I was going to hear his offer, why else had we gone there? I looked him in the eye and trying act as adult as I could seem said, "Sir, I am quite prepared to listen to your offer, but reserve the right to think it over and get other opinions, before I make answer to your proposal."

He started laughing, and replied, "Very well said Henry, of course, you shall have all the time you need to consider my offer, but as I have to leave for London next week, let's make it not too long eh?"

I replied, "Sir if I hear your proposal now, I can assure you, you'll have my answer before tonight."

He laughed, saying "I should have known, splendid! Now my proposal is this…He went on to tell me that first, I would now keep my own money, and that I would now stay at his manor until the summer when I would go and work with Thomas, as I promised, then after a brief stop at home, return there.

Whist I was there, I would learn from a tutor what I needed to know in the way of schooling to pass into the naval college. I would learn the ways of being a gentleman from Albert.

Everything from ways of eating to dancing, Albert would also teach me how to fight with fists, guns and swords, all that would happen every minute whilst I stayed at the manor.
Everything I needed in the way of clothing I would pay for from my own money, if I needed a horse to go somewhere like Cornwall, I could rent one at a shilling a day…now your board and lodging will be at a rate of let's see what's fair, how about ten pounds a week (looking at Albert, who nodded)."

While he talked, *I wondered where I was going to get all this money, what I had was not going to last any longer than three weeks the way he was talking, truly I was starting to get agitated.*

After taking another drink of tea, and finishing his cup, he continued with what he was saying, "So while you are here Henry, you will be learning, learning, and learning some more, now for your time, I will pay you a sum of, what was the total of your money (looking at a pad)?

Ah, that's right thirty-eight pounds a week, but will deduct your board and lodging first, so you will receive twenty-eight pounds each week, if I'm not here, Albert will pay you Friday afternoon, and of course, I will supply you letters of introduction to the Commandant of the Naval College, there that's my offer, any questions?"

My mind was reeling I would be paid to learn!

I did have one question, saying, "Sir if I was to stay here from now, how could I escort my grandparent's home? I mean how can I be sure they get there safely?"

He laughed saying, "Yet again you rise higher in my esteem, for your thoughtfulness. I will have two of my men go along with them to make sure they reach your home safely Henry."

He was looking at me questioningly, as I returned his gaze, and said, "Thank you sir, I appreciate that. I would now like time to consider your offer, and talk it over with my grandparents, if you have no objection?"

He replied, "Of course not my boy, you've heard my offer, I leave it up to you, we'll say no more about just yet, meeting concluded good sirs, and it's almost lunch time, let us adjourn."

With that we got up, and made our way out of the study, Pop and I went to where our rooms were, showing me mine, I went inside and stripping off my coat and loosening my neckerchief I washed my face, with the cold water I poured into the washing dish from the pitcher on the small table in the room.

After freshening up, I went to my grandparent's room, and the door was open, but I still knocked on the door before entering. Pop and nan were seated in lounge chairs with a table between them, as I entered, they were discussing their next step, which was when they would return home, as I sat down, Nanna said, "Before you say anything my boy, Sam has told me about the offer my brother made you."

"And what do you think about it nanna?" I asked. She smiled saying, "I think it's better than you expected, considering you'll have the chance to learn everything you need to enter the navy, dear, and being paid to learn all that too, my brother must really have taken a shine to you dear boy, if I was in your place, I wouldn't even be thinking it over, I would have said yes straight away, that is if you really wish to join the navy?"
"Oh nanna, of course I do, you already know that, but I don't even get to say goodbye to ma and father, what will I say to them?"

Pop said, "You let me worry about that Henry, I'll smooth it over, and besides you could stop over on your way to Thomas in Cornwall on your way there, and on the way back, and before you ask me, you know I'd call you a fool if you turned down William's offer, as far as I'm concerned, you've done very well here, and should continue to do so, don't you worry about your grandmother and me, you heard William say, we'll be escorted by some of his men."

Then nanna said, "Goodness gracious, look at the time, come on you two downstairs for lunch, Henry help me up, ah there's a dear, thank you, now come on."

Downstairs in the dining room, everyone was seated as we made our way to the table, excusing ourselves for being late. During lunch, no business was discussed apart from the fact, that the earl informed his wife lady Elizabeth, that he had asked me to stay and help Albert while he was away in London.

Lady Elizabeth thought that a marvelous idea and said she looked forward to having me stay. I smiled and thanked her for her hospitality, and she replied, "Don't talk nonsense my dear it's been awhile since we've had anybody your age around her, hopefully you'll liven up the place, besides your family, you stay as long as you wish."

After lunch, I looked at the earl, and Albert then back to the earl, saying "Your lordship, do you mind if I talk to you and Albert for a while, if you're not too busy that is?"
He looked at Albert who shook his head to say he was doing nothing, and he looked back at me saying, "Of course dear boy, come to the study."

Chapter 3.

As we entered the study, I was waved to a seat in front of the desk, and Albert sat beside me as his father sat down behind it. Then the earl said, "Now enough of this your lordship, sir and title horseshit! From now on if I think you're going to tell us, what I think you, are you can call me uncle William, is that understood Henry?"
Before I could answer, Albert also said, "Same here, and you call me Albert." Then we all burst out laughing, and I replied, "Quite understood uncle William, Albert."
Then uncle William asked, "Well now Henry, what can I do for you?"
I immediately switched, from mirth to business, because that is what I now considered it. I replied, "Sir, allow me just this once more to call you that, from what I've heard you say, I can only assume that you are of the opinion that I'm going to accept your proposal, that we talked about earlier, and in truth, may I say that your assumption in regard this matter, is entirely correct, I do accept your proposal."
As I was talking, and framing my words, I had been watching his face, and had framed my words deliberately to make him think I wasn't going to accept the offer, as the smile left his face, and he looked crestfallen in disbelief, as he glanced at Albert. Inwardly I smiled at his reaction, as I wanted to make it plain in his eyes, to the fact I thought this, to be a business transaction only.

In case he thought, he was buying my friendship and allegiance.

He looked at me shrewdly before his face broke into a grin, as he replied, "Excellent! Oh, and Henry please remember, I consider you a member of the family, that I think, deserves the chance to make something of himself, don't for one minute, think that I'm trying to buy you in any way. You have a lot of learning to do, in such a short time, please don't make me regret my faith in you."

As he spoke, I thought, *the old fox, he knew exactly what I'd been doing.* As I replied saying, "Uncle William, your faith isn't misguided, I shall endeavour to do my damnedest to earn repayment of your faith, for you, the family, and my own sake, I will pass not only into the college, but all my exams first time. The only thing I need to ask, is when do I start?"

He laughed while he said, "Well I have some letters to write so I can find you a good tutor, but until we find one, you and Albert could probably see what you're capable of with some weaponry, but if you play with swords please do it outside, now off you go, and I'll see you at dinner."

With that Albert and I got up and left the study, He took me to another room that was next to the library, which reminded me to go in and tidy up from my all-night session with the family history, I put volume one back where it belonged, and put a marker into volume two where I had gotten up to, and left it on the desk, to pick up later. The next room had all manner of weapons hanging on three of the four walls, while the fourth held cabinets of guns and rifles of all make and size. As I looked around at the hanging weapons. Albert was saying, "Well you've already said that you're good with guns, so let's take a couple of swords with us and see what you've got."

As I looked over the displayed swords, my eyes fell on what I thought was a sturdy enough sword, it had a wraparound closure on the hilt that would protect the users hand on the hilt. As I lifted it down, I noticed that it wasn't too heavy or overly long, and that it was double edged, taking a couple of swings with it, I found it to be comfortable in my grip and I could wield it with either hand.

Albert watched saying, "Good choice, not as cumbersome as a claymore, but just as strong, let me have a look Henry." Passing it to him, he swung it in a couple of passes then felt it for its balance, and tried to bend the blade.

He passed it back to me saying, "Hmm, well balanced, sturdy blade, double edged, looks nice, not too delicate, a fighting man's weapon, over all a very good choice, grab the scabbard, it's yours now, let's go try it out." As he took down another sword and a thick curved one. Then we went out into the side garden.

After showing me a few moves, we faced each other and duelled slowly as he instructed me at the same time, an hour later we were duelling in earnest, and at speed, for each attacking stroke I would counter and block his blade, and attack, then he called a halt, so, we could catch our breathes and cool down.

Before we started again, Albert picked up the thick curved sword, saying, "Now this is called a cutlass, it's the main fighting sword used by men at sea, and according to Robin, he's seen quite a few officers swords broken by these, we're going to test that claim out, when we go again I will be trying hard to smash that sword of yours, so I'm going to be using all my strength, here go ahead, test it out before we start."

Taking it from him, I found it to be cumbersome and heavy, inspecting it, I found it to be very thick on the back of the blade, which only had one cutting edge, but pointed, and I could see how it would break other finer swords, also if stabbed by one of them, the wound would have a larger opening due to its broadness, I assumed that if stabbed by it to the full extent of its broad blade, the wound it caused would be death dealing.

Having been warned by Albert, I knew what to expect from him, and as I blocked blow after blow, I was fully expecting my blade to shatter, but it held firm, and after a further half hour of swordplay, Albert called it quits. Taking my sword to inspect, he told me, that apart from a few nicks in my blade it would hold up against any cutlass, so my choice had been a good one.

When we went back, into the house, and weapons room, I was about to hang up the sword, when Albert said, "No Henry, that is your sword from now on, my gift to you, as a fellow family member, you keep it in your room with your other belongings."

I was overawed by his generosity and kindness, but that did not stop me from trying to argue, and at least pay for the sword, and eventually he gave in, telling me, "Oh alright Henry, just to appease your stubbornness you owe me ten pence for the sword, you can pay me at dinner. You, stubborn country yokel."

I knew full well the sword was worth a whole lot more, but Albert, had given ground knowing I would not accept charity, likewise I had to give ground on my sense of fair play, and said, "Done."

That evening as we were all gathered for pre-dinner drinks in the dining room, I walked up to Albert, who was standing beside his father, and gave him the ten pence that I owed, saying with a smile, "I don't require a receipt, thank you Albert."

"What's this all about Albert?" Uncle William asked startled.

Albert looked at him without showing anything on his face said, "I sold young Henry a sword father."

Angrily, uncle William growled as his voice went up, "What! Why didn't you just give him one! You've cheated the boy, give him back that money this instant!"

I interrupter saying, "Oh No, uncle William a deal is a deal, and actually it was me that cheated Albert, you see he was going to give me the sword, but I finally won by getting him up to ten pence!"

As everyone digested my words, they all burst out laughing, Uncle Williams being the loudest, as he said, "That'll teach you to deal with country folk!"

"He's right their Albert, we'se pretty smart like that," poppa Sam said.
This started another round of laughter as we sat down to dinner.
Once we were all seated, poppa Sam said, "While we're all gathered here, I'd like to thank you for your hospitality, but Suzanna and I have planned to leave the day after tomorrow, if your men can be ready by then William?"
"Certainly Sam, we'll miss you both of course," Uncle William replied, "and I suppose I'd be best getting ready to leave also for the next sittings at Lords."
Then the chatter during dinner turned to other subjects as we ate.

Two mornings later, we were all bidding our farewells to my grandparents while four of Uncle Williams men dressed in plain cloths waited to be on their way. The pistol was back in the cart under the seat, as I helped nanna, onto the cart as I said my goodbyes to her, then pop shook my hand, as he said "Now don't you go worrying about anything Henry, your job here is to learn, and don't worry about your ma and pa, they'll be alright, 'sides, we'll see you as you pass through just afore the summer, and as always, take care lad."
I watched as the cart and horsemen disappeared from view around the gate of the manor house, then went with Albert and a couple of the housemen, as we took, pistols, muskets and rifles, along with powder and ammunition, food and water in a wagon,

out to the shooting range about a mile from the back of the manor house.

After an hour of practise with the long guns, Albert turned to me saying "Well Henry, I must admit I thought you were boasting when you told us you were an accurate shot with a muskets and rifle, but you've been making shots that make me look positively like a beginner, and I'm considered a fair marksman. After we have something to eat, how about we work with the pistols, there's a few things you need to know."

While we ate some, what are now called sandwiches we watched as the servants cleaned our long guns, placing them back into the wagon, at the back end of the wagon, they loaded six pistols and set them to half cock. This makes them safe and unable to fire, until they are brought to full cock before use.

After swallowing our eats down with some water, we moved to the wagon and each picked up a pistol, then walked to the row of targets that had been set up thirty yards from the firing line. As I gauged the heft of the pistol I was using.

I watched as Albert took aim slowly, bringing his body in line with his arm, as he aimed at the target, and fired, his shot was just on the edge of the bull.

As I walked to the firing line I brought the pistol to full cock, and as I brought it upright at waist height, I fired, my shot taking the bull dead centre.

Albert exclaimed, "What! How the bloody hell did you do that! You didn't even frigging aim!"

I smiled saying, "I can do that every time."

The two servants who had brought the other pistols over and placed them on the bench they were leaning on, smiled at my statement.

Albert looking at me incredulously, said "Now Henry, if that's not boasting, what is? But let's make this interesting, a pound for every time you can, but two pounds to me if you miss."

I smiled, shrugged my shoulders, saying, "Alright but let's make it fair, these pistols get reloaded, and I fire all six."

Albert, nodded and replied "Done!"

The two servants raced to grab our pistols and reload them, as they did, I picked up the next pistol, felt its heft again and repeated cocking it back to full cock as I got to the firing line, fired, with the same result. After three shots, I had to move to Albert's target, because the bull in mine had been shredded. This too was shredded by the time I was finished, and all three watched me in amazement. Albert tried to speak but couldn't for a few minutes, he was just shaking his head.

He finally asked, "Do you ever try to aim, like I did?"

"No," I replied.

"Have you ever tried?" He asked.

"Sort of," I replied.

As he turned purple, I thought he was going to collapse, and made ready to catch him. He rallied though, and said, "Sort of! What do mean by that?"

Shrugging my shoulders again, I replied, "Well I bring the gun up, point, and fire."

He stood there laughing silently shaking his head.

Then said in exasperation, "And what is usually the result?"

I laughed, and replied, "Albert, don't you know by now, I always hit what I'm looking at."

He laughed saying, "Well I'll be a whore's blanket, Henry, from now on I'll believe whatever you tell me. Though while we're here I have something to teach you"

Albert then explained and showed me the intricacies and rules of duelling. After he had explained all this, he asked, "Do you think you could shoot like that?" With honesty, I asked, "Right or left handed?"

"What!" He exclaimed. "You can shoot just as well with both hands?"

"Of course, here watch." I replied, going and getting two of the reloaded pistols. Then on the firing line fired first the right pistol, then the left, at the new targets both were bulls. Then I took the empties back and grabbed two more loaded ones, saying "Alright this time I'll try what you suggested, but I can't promise how it'll go." I moved my body into line as Albert had shown me and brought the pistol to full cock as I brought my right arm up into line and fired. It was a bull, then switching my position, I repeated the exercise, and fired again, and again another bull. I smiled as I thought, *well that's interesting I can still hit the mark no matter which way I shoot.*

Albert smiled, and said "Yes! Well Henry seeing all that, I can suggest that if you're ever challenged to a duel, choose pistols, you can't lose. Well done."

We spent the following hour, going through the techniques again and again until I had it down pat. After that, I gave Albert a lesson in firing two guns at once from a waist high position. Once the pistols were empty, they were cleaned and placed back in the wagon, as we headed back to the manor house.

At our pre-drinks time that afternoon, Albert entered with Lucy, and after getting her a drink, he came over to me and uncle William drink in hand, and counted out six pounds from his billfold, and gave them to me, saying, "There you go Henry, a bet is a bet, and thank you for the shooting display, father never, challenge this young man to a duel, because if he chooses pistols, I will be making your funeral arrangements."

As uncle William asked what this was all about, Albert filled in by detail our entire days shooting. After the tale had been told, uncle William asked, "How did you ever become so proficient with firearms Henry?"
I shrugged my shoulders, saying "Well growing up on a farm uncle William, my father taught me how when I was five years old, and I've been kept in practice ever since, I guess the rest is just a case of natural talent maybe."

Chapter 4.

The following morning, we all said our farewells to uncle William who was taking a carriage to London, before he stepped into the coach, he beckoned Albert and me to him saying, "I have the name of a suitable tutor, and I will see him first thing I'm in London, if I engage him, he should be here in a week or so, and he will ask for you Albert, right toodle pip." Then he stepped into the carriage, and the driver flicked the reins.

After he had departed, it was time for some sword practice, taking our swords out onto the balcony from the study, we practiced on the balcony.
After a couple of hours of continual practice, my body was automatically adjusting to the manoeuvres required for swordplay, and I think I was getting better. Albert remarked that my movements were becoming more fluid and some of my moves were becoming unpredictable, which was a good thing in a sword fight, because there was less chance for an opponent to strike.
When it was nearly lunch time, Albert called a halt to our sword play, as he said, "You're getting more graceful with your moves now Henry, I think your body is starting to adapt to this style of fighting, and the sword is moving a lot faster than the other day. Now I have some paperwork to do in the study for a while, before lunch, so you are free to do whatever you wish." Taking our swords into the study, he went to the desk while I made for the library.

In the library, I picked up the second volume of the family history, and took it back into the study, Albert was already hard at work at the desk, so I moved to one of the lounge chairs and took up reading where I had left off, instantly recalling what I had already read before I moved on. Perhaps it's just as well, I had done that, because I was so engrossed in the book, I hadn't heard Albert move toward me, to say that it was lunchtime, marking my place again, I put the book on the table in front of me, and stood up to go.

During lunch, Albert was talking lowly to the overseeing chief waiter, and I noticed him nodding with a smile, obviously Albert had given him some instruction, but what, I couldn't hazard a guess, but I was soon to find out.
After lunch was finished as we all rose, Albert told me to stay seated, as my plate and unused cutlery was taken away, as the women left the room, he came to stand beside me saying, "Now then Henry, it's time to learn the etiquette of fine dining."
As he did so, table staff started putting new cutlery in front of me, and different types of glasses, of course I knew what some of the cutlery was used for, but certainly not all, and the glasses, well, a glass is a glass, isn't it?" Once everything was laid out, Albert said, "Right let's start with what you already know," Then for the next two hours I learned and soaked it all in. What to use for what, and the correct way to hold the cutlery, the correct and polite way to eat.

At about three o'clock, we had moved onto the glassware, then as I stated I had it, Albert filled all the glasses asking which glass held which, and as I got them right, he would get me to drink, when I had them all right, he asked me to compare the different tastes, and seek my opinion as to the taste explaining why what went with certain portions of food.

After we had finished, he complimented me on how quickly I had learned, so I asked him, "So how do you know a good wine from something else that's the same. He smiled, grabbed about half a dozen bottles of white wine from the cupboard, and a couple of large glasses, bringing them to the table. Had me check the labels to make sure they were all the same sort of white wine. Then he opened one, and we each had a taste, it was bloody terrible, and sharp. Having already lined up the bottles, he opened the next one, it was slightly better than the first, but we able to empty the glasses without screwing up our faces. With each of the bottles, he explained the subtle differences, as the last one was opened, and we drank, it was superb compared to the first. We ended up drinking the whole bottle in appreciation of the taste. Then we repeated the exercise again with red wines, by the time we were joined by the ladies for pre-diner drinks, we were both absolutely drunk as lords. I went to stand up as they entered the room, and ended up falling flat on my face, and as I was down there, I rolled around laughing at how stupid I'd been, trying to get up like that.

Albert thought it quite hilarious as well, but at least he saved himself, by holding onto the chair he'd been in. Naturally that night we were not in the good graces of aunt Elizabeth, or Lucy.

The following morning at breakfast we had a lot of apologizing to do Aunt Elizabeth looked at me saying, "All well and good Henry, but I must ask you to refrain from swearing as much when you're like that, I thought your uncle could curse, but you Henry!"

I hung my head and apologized once more.

That morning, we both weren't feeling well enough, so instead of sword practise, we went to the stables, and Albert called the staff out, saying "Gentlemen, I need a sparring partner for my young friend here, he needs to learn how to fight, do I have any takers?"

One answered, saying, "what'll 'appen to us iffen he gets hurt master?"

"Nothing, I assure you, your jobs are all safe," Albert replied.

Cockily, I said "You won't need to worry about me, all you have to worry about is that you don't get too hurt!"

One of the larger ones said, "Cocky son of a whore, ain't you, I'll have a go," as he started stripping his shirt off.

As the men made a circle, I took off my shirt and neckerchief handing them to Albert, and he gasped as he took in my physique, then I turned to my opponent in the centre of the circle, and cocked my fists, the fight started as I landed a couple of punches, one to the midriff, and a left to the jaw, then he hit me with a right haymaker that came out of nowhere, and down I went. Getting up quickly, I avoided a left to the jaw, and lashed back with a flurry of rights and lefts to the midsection, as he started to buckle, I immediately switched targets as I set up his face with a left, then slammed a right into his jaw, and he went down as if poleaxed.

I waited for him to get up, but he was out cold, then one of the men that looked like a blacksmith, growled "You jumped up arsewipe, you're not getting away with hitting Teddy like that, you're mine now!"

I just stood looking at him, saying nothing, but beckoned him with my hand, as he took his apron off he rushed me, slamming me into the ground with him on top of me. Then it became a contest of strength, as I tried to lift him off me, and roll out of the way, I was finally able to do it, but not without smashing him full in the face first. As I got up, there was blood all over my face and singlet, but it wasn't mine, up on my feet my original opponent had left the circle, and was encouraging the new man, calling, "C'mon John smash him," as all the others were encouraging the blacksmith as well. Only Albert was saying nothing, just watching intently. When he was getting up, I appraised him, not only was he a lot older than me, he was strong and just as muscular as I, but I think I had the advantage, I would have put money on the fact that he was a wrestler and not a boxer, after my trying to get up I was tiring, and had to finish him quickly.

If I couldn't, I knew he was going to pound the daylights out of me. As he squared up again I went in fast, hammering left and rights to his face and midsection as fast as I could, evading his attempts to block my onslaught, but I was tiring fast, so I stepped in close and smashed with uppercuts, seeing he couldn't avoid my punches and was almost done, I put all the power from my shoulder into a vicious uppercut to the point of his chin, and as his head snapped back his eyes rolled, and he went over backwards out for the count. As I folded to my knees the men were all silent, as Albert stepped forward and helped me up, weaving to the closest horse trough, I plunged my head into it ignoring the screams of pain from cuts on my face and hands. Once I was aware of what I was doing again, I grabbed a bucket of water, and walked over to the inert body of my second opponent, pouring the water over him until he awoke, then I assisted him to his feet, shaking his hand, before meandering away, without saying anything. Albert soon followed with my shirt and neckerchief, caught me up, and took me to the patio door of the study, assisted me to flop into a chair, and poured me a glass of something, that he told me to sip slowly, then disappeared.

I almost gagged on my first sip, as the fiery liquid coursed down my throat, but it tasted nice. I leaned back as I slowly sipped the drink, it went to work healing and numbing my pains.

Then Albert returned with a female servant, and directed her to fix me up as best she could, and left the study again, as she knelt in front of me, she gasped, saying "Good lord sir! What has happened to you."

I winced in pain as I smiled saying, "You should see the other guy, and I'm not a lord or anything like that, just a plain ordinary old farmer at the moment you can call me Henry, and you are?"

She replied, "Joanna, s.. Henry, Joanna Yeoman, I'm one of the scullery maids, now hold still Henry." As she dabbed some stinging liquid onto the cuts on my mouth, and I took a sharp intake of breath as it stung. When she finished with my facial cuts, she started on my hands, as she said, "Looks to me Henry, as if you've been brawling."

I took another sip of my drink, this helped immensely, and replied, "Indeed I have Joanna, and after you've finished with me, you best go have a look at the blacksmith, I think his name is John."

She nodded her head, as I tried to pull my hand back from her grasp, wincing in pain from the liquid she was applying.

Albert came back into the study as she finished, as she said, "Right stand up and lift up your singlet, let's see what other damage has been done."

I complied as Albert freshened up my drink, and handed it to me, as she inspected my torso, every now, and then, a squeeze or light push, then she said, "Right Henry, those bruises will heal in a few days, if you take it easy, otherwise your good."

"Thank you, Joanna" I replied, "And please see to the blacksmith for me please."

She nodded and replied, "I shall, Henry, goodbye."

Then Albert opened the door for her, as she left with her tray. He turned back to me as he shut the door saying, "You, sly dog, trying to win one of the ladies, how's the scotch?"
I smiled saying, "Is that what it is, it's bloody nice, and can I help it if she was cute?"
He just laughed, and helped me on with my shirt.

For the next couple of days, I rested, without too much strenuous exercise, it was kept at a minimum of an hour's swordplay in the morning, the rest was of the day was made up learning more etiquette, my continued reading of the family history, and some horse riding. Joanna had indeed gone to the blacksmith, and when I saw him next he thanked me for it, and told me if I ever wanted to make some money, he knew of a place that held fight nights, and I could always make an extra bob betting on myself. I laughed and thanked him, the rest of the hands recommended lightning as well spirited horse to ride, whenever I went riding he was the horse for me.
The men that had escorted pop and nanna home returned, and reported to Albert and me, and I thanked them. Then on Friday morning as Albert and I went into the study where he asked me to join him at the desk, he counted out twenty-eight-pound notes, and handed them to me, and gave me a copy of the accounting, and had me sign the original, then said, "Well, I think we should go shopping today, so you and I old chum, are taking a carriage into town, where I will introduce you to the best gentleman's

outfitters shop outside of London, it's about time you had some more updated clothing, now you can keep the rest of your stuff, but a couple more outfits won't do you any harm, come let's go, the carriage is already outside waiting."

The carriage ride into Taunton was exhilarating, because we were in an open carriage. The driver stopped outside Howe's Gentlemen's Emporium, and Albert proceeded me inside.
As we went in, my eye fell on a counter that held pistols in the glass case, and as I stopped to view them, a man went up to Albert, greeting him and asked what he could for him.
Albert told him that he didn't require anything, but it was I that needed some new duds as Albert called it. Eventually after being in the store for an hour I bought half a dozen pairs of breeches of assorted colour (that needed tailoring, because they all needed to come up two inches), three new frock coats (that needed widening), four waistcoats, a top hat that albert convinced me to buy, and half a dozen new neckerchiefs. We also ran into a problem with shirts too, they would require being tailor made, so once more I was measured up, and he allowed for any extra growing I did, both in length and shoulder width then he asked what colours I would like, and showed me a bolt of Egyptian cotton, asking if I'd like them made out of that material, saying, "I have all the colours you wanted in the same material."
I nodded and said yes, then asked about fob watches, he took us to a viewing case that was beside the gun

case, as Albert chose the best one for me to look at, it was made of gold and the case would also hold a picture in the lid, and the chain was sturdy and thick. Nodding to the owner, I asked "How much it that all up please."

He did his sums, and told me that with the tailoring, everything came to two pounds sixteen shillings, and that when all the tailoring was done he'd also arrange delivery to the manor house free of charge. I nodded and paid him, as he placed the watch into its box, and started to fold up what we would take with us. Then I turned to Albert asking, "Do you think I need a brace of pistols Albert?"

Mister Howe, immediately said, "I've a beautiful set of Dance Brothers pistols, come in two days ago." And moved to the gun case and brought one out for me to see and feel. It was indeed nice, rose oak woodwork, with a silver butt cap, and inlaid filigreed silverwork in the handle and stock, an octagonal barrel with the rammer underneath. The mechanism worked smoothly, and it was very well balanced, and not too heavy. I tried it in both hands and liked it, then asked about holsters. He showed me the ones that came with them, and it fitted snugly and wouldn't drop out easily, then I asked for a black belt wide enough to go through the holster belt attachment, buying the lot for ten pounds. He placed the pistol and holster back into the case, and took it from the display cabinet, and placed the belt with my other purchases.

Then we bid him adieu, and went back to the manor.

Chapter 5.

During the ride home, I was wearing my new hat seeing Albert was wearing his, he and I discussed the wisdom of my gun purchase, he was in complete agreement with the purchase, but we debated the wisdom of not waiting for a later time. My argument was that for, one, it was better to get at the same time, to save buying a brace later, it would also give me a chance to practise with them, prior to not having had the chance to do so prior.

Getting the case out, we opened it and he picked one out, saying, "Well certainly looks fine, and has excellent grip, for something made in the American colonies, it feels quite fine, as though it is an extension of one's hand. What else is in the case Henry?"

Taking out the other pistol, I lifted the inlay for the guns, underneath this was the two holsters, which I took out, included was the cleaning kit with a small bottle of gun oil, a six-inch powder horn of bone and inscribed with the producers' name, wadding, and a dozen 50 calibre lead shots, a mould for making more shot, 6 spare flints, taking the powder horn out, I uncapped it to find it full of gunpowder.

Albert remarked, "Oh ho, everything you need it use them right away, my boy you have definitely made a very good buy."

After putting everything back in the case, we sat back to enjoy the rest of the drive to the manor. When we got there, after placing my purchases in my room, I returned to my reading in the study.

I finished my reading of the family history just prior to time for pre-dinner drinks, and once I had replaced the volume to its shelf in the library, I made for the dining room. There the main topic of our conversation with the ladies, was my little shopping foray.

After breakfast the next morning, it was planned for Albert and me to go back to the shooting range, this time however, instead of taking anyone along, we would reload the weapons ourselves, Albert brought two pistols and a bag full of powder and shot. I on the other hand took along my new belt, sword, and the case holding my new guns, as we were putting the stuff into saddlebags, I tied my sword to the saddle, and I was asked by Albert why I was bringing my sword along, I told him he'd see at the range, then with a laugh, I kicked Lightning into a gallop.

At the firing range, after securing the horses we unloaded everything onto the bench at the pistol range. Opening the gun case I took the top tray our, and reached for the holsters slipping one into place on the belt which was followed by my sword, and then the last holster, and fastened the belt around my waist taking each of the pistols and placing them in the holsters, the angle of the holsters sitting the pistol butt at forty-five degrees on upward on the belt on both left and right sides of my body allowing quick access to draw each pistol, I moved the loop for my sword scabbard into place behind the holster on my left, adjusting everything, so they sat perfect.

Then slipping the scabbard back, while Albert took the guns out of the holsters, while I made sure they didn't move, I got him to undo the belt for me, and while I made sure nothing moved we lay the belt on the bench upwards inside out.

All the while, Albert was looking perplexed, then realised what I was doing, when I drew out a pencil and marked where the holster loops were, onto the belt, and I also marked the holsters with a L and a R, then took the belt and holsters, back to the saddlebag on my horse, leaving them there, along with my sword.

Back at the bench we loaded our weapons, walking away from Albert, I fired off both pistols to make sure there would be no misfires or problems at all, but they worked perfectly, I reloaded again and took my place at the firing line, while Albert tacked up a couple of targets.

Then we fired both our pistols, my first two shots being each a little out of line, but still in the bull area.

As Albert stated, "Well my young nephew, I'm glad to see you're not infallible, you missed the centres."

"Aye," I replied, "But they were still inside the bull, enough to kill, come on, let's put some more targets up."

After that, now I had the feel of the guns, I was always in the centre of the bull, and I was extremely happy with my guns.

We spent an hour at the range before we called it a day, and started to clean our guns. Back at the stables, I went to see John the blacksmith.

Taking the belt with the holsters and sword scabbard with me, I explained and showed him what I wanted done, saying, "I'll come and see you Monday John, but please remember the alignment has to be perfect."

"Aye there, master Henry," he replied, "They'll be ready for yee and as perfect as you throw a punch sir." I smiled and nodded as I left him.

On the way back into the house, with my gun case under my arm, I asked Albert, "Could I get about a hundred rounds of shot to put in my case."

He passed me the bag of shot he was carrying, and said, "Here, there's probably more than a hundred in there, but it'll save me carrying them, there all yours."

In my room I put the bag of shot into the case, and went back downstairs, and that afternoon with Lady Elizabeth and Albert watching, I had my first dance lesson.

On Sunday, the following day, we were all going to church in the town for the ten am service, as we all met in the entrance hall, the new things I was wearing was one of the new waistcoats, my fob watch, and I was carrying my top hat. Once we were all gathered, I escorted lady Elizabeth, and Albert escorted Lucy, as we all went out to the open carriage, the ladies took the seat behind the driver facing backward as Albert, and I faced forward, and we had both donned our hats. At the cathedral aunt Elizabeth nodded to, and talked to other women she knew, as did Albert and Lucy, as we moved along.

Inside the church, I found the service to be boring, and actually fell asleep as the priest droned on. Not being an avid church goer, I couldn't get out of there quick enough. I was glad to be outside again, even if I did have to listen to all the towns ladies prattling on with endless small talk again after the service. When we all got into the coach to go home, aunt Elizabeth remarked "I really don't know why I bother going to church I get quite sick and tired of having to bother to talk to those boring women." I laughed, and Lucy said, "Because you have to be polite mama, but I know what you mean." The rest of the day I spent in the library reading a text book about navigation.

After breakfast the next day, before Albert and I were to start our sword practise, I went to see the blacksmith, but on my way through the back of the house and kitchen, I quite literally bumped into Joanna. Helping her back to her feet, and apologizing for my rush, I was able to talk to her without anyone around. Finding out that she was only a year younger than I, and her father was one of the stable hands, that lived on the property, and when I asked if see was seeing anyone romantically, she blushed, and answered in the negative. Unfortunately, our conversation was interrupted by her mother, who was one of the cooks, calling for her. Before she scuttled off, I asked if I could see her again, she blushed and nodded, and I smiled, then she was gone. I continued out through the back, heading to the blacksmithing end of the stables.

John saw me heading towards him, and called to the bench to see his handiwork. He had placed two studs through the belt and holster loop, for each holster making sure there on the belt position wouldn't change and smoothed down each side of the studs, so they wouldn't catch on my clothing, I told him he'd done an excellent job, and placed the belt on, and when I went to adjust the sword and scabbard, he said, "I noticed your sword was in need of some mending, because of a large nick in one of the blades master, so I took the liberty of fixing, and sharpening it for you, and gave it a quick polish."

As he handed it to me, hilt first with the blade held in a rag, I was overawed, it was positively gleaming, the hilt guard had been polished so much I could make out my face on the on each of the guard strips, and the blade edges had no visible nicks on them, and they were sharp, he had even polished up the engravings running down the centre of the blade, and it seemed a crime to handle in case one smeared the polished surface. I shifted the scabbard to behind the left-hand holster, also noticed the gleam on it as well, and I took out a shilling from my waistcoat pocket to give him, saying "John, this is extremely excellent work you have done, thank you, here, anymore work I may have, I will definitely be bringing it to you." Handing him the shilling piece.

He was flabbergasted to see how much I had given him, saying "Thank you, young master, but this is way too much."

I smiled, saying, "No John you've earned every penny, so let's not hear any more about it, once more thank you." With that I turned and walked back toward the house.

Inside I retraced my steps and headed for my room, in there I put the pistols into the holsters, trying everything for positioning, finding it all satisfactory, nodded at my mirrored reflection, then headed down to the study to join Albert.

With his comments about my being fully armed, I explained that I should practise with my sword, while fully armed to get used to movement with the added encumbrances, because that would most likely be the way I'd be fighting, if it came down to it.

He agreed with me, congratulating me on my sense of priorities, and forward thinking saying, "You've an old head on that young body of yours Henry, sometimes it's hard to comprehend that you're only fourteen, you think like a person twice your age. Right let's go practise!"

Outside, he made mention of the polished shine on my sword, and I told him the story of my session with John the blacksmith, he laughed remarking that he was going to put John to more use, after seeing his results, then we got into our practise. There was a difference in our practise now, Albert no longer instructed, as we duelled at full speed and effort, unless there was something wrong with my stance or swing, but that was usually after he would take advantage of my mistake, before explaining.

At one time, I was left sprawled on the ground with his foot in the middle of my back, as he kept me that way, as he explained my mistake, which was to overreach my balance, telling that if that happened in a real duel, I was likely to have my throat slashed open, or in the extreme, having my head taken off. That was one mistake I never made again, in fact most times he only needed to tell me once, and my mistakes were becoming fewer and far between, that's why we could now duel in earnest.

During our practise that morning, after an hour, Jenkins came outside, seeing him we both stopped what we were doing, letting him tell us that there was a gentleman waiting in the anti-room to see him. Albert said, "Very well Jenkins, bring him into the study please."
With that our practise ended and we both went inside wiping the sweat off our faces. Then I stood beside him as he took his place behind the desk. Unbuckling my weapons belt, I draped it over one of the arms of a nearby chair, as the door opened, and Jenkins announced the man into our presence, saying, "A mister Desmond Fox-Davis, your grace." Albert said with a laugh, "Hah, another family member, thank you Jenkins." Jenkins left closing the door, and as I assumed this to be another uncle, considering his age, came to the front of the desk. Albert, assuming the same as I, said "What can I do for you uncle Desmond?"
Uncle Desmond looked at me then Albert, saying, "I have come here, at the request of your father."

Albert glanced up to me, and back to uncle Desmond saying as he stood, "Well then uncle, please meet another of the family, this is Henry Tolcher, welcome to the house and we're pleased to meet you." As he put forward his hand.

Uncle Desmond, shook his hand and mine as I stepped forward proffering my hand, then Albert said, "Please uncle take a seat, Henry."

Uncle Desmond, sat down, and I took the other chair in front of the desk, as Albert sat as well. Then Uncle Desmond said, "As I have said, I'm here at the behest of your father, who has engaged me to tutor you, young Henry. Now let me explain why this is so. Most of my life I have been a teacher, but I haven't come from a school, until recently I have been an instructor and examiner at the Royal Naval College in Portsmouth, where recently I had the pleasure to instruct your cousin Robin Fox-Davis who serves on the HMS Majestic. It seems that now that I have retired, your uncle William has asked me to tutor you, in regard to first entering the college, and everything you're going to need to know whilst there, with the expectation of having you pass your officers examinations. There that explains my reason for being here. My wife Joy, who's a Fox-Tolcher will be joining me next week, as William told me we would live here until you leave for the college, apart from that, all I need is a room we can use for your schooling, I have everything that you will require with me, and to be shown to the room myself and Joy will occupy. Now, gentlemen it's back to you, before we discuss our working regime."

To say Albert and I were stunned, would have been a mere understatement, as we processed all the information he had imparted, it reminded me of my father, who would say things to me as if they were orders.

Albert cleared his throat saying "Well uncle Desmond, that was all forthright, let me inform you what sort of activities young Henry and I have been about while we have awaited your arrival, then Jenkins can show to your room and you can settle in. Give me a minute and I'll have Jenkins have your suite made up, in the meantime, Henry, please inform your new tutor of our routine." With that he left the study.

I turned to uncle Desmond, and filled him in, as to regard meal times, and our time to gather for pre-diner drinks. Then told him of what Albert and I usually did during the week, our sword practise each morning, my lessons in etiquette and behaviour, and about my dance lessons. I also suggested the library as my schooling room.

Then Albert returned to the room, and told him everything was being prepared. He asked to see the library, and after seeing it gave his approval, saying "Very well this will do nicely, now while I'm here both of you refer to me as only Desmond, drop the uncle, now let's talk about lesson times."

Chapter 6

"I agree that you keep up your sword training, but perhaps you cut it back to only one hour a day." Desmond told us, as we were seated back in the study. "I would also suggest that you might want to include firearms as well."

Albert held his hand up stopping him there, saying, "Desmond you haven't seen this boy shoot, trust me when I say that gun training isn't required."

"Humph," Desmond replied, "That remains to be seen, Henry has told me he's been schooled in etiquette and gentlemanly behaviour, dance lessons may continue, but limited to after dinner, so from ten am every day, except Sundays, you Henry will be in the library with me studying. Now I'm told I have until the end of May to get you ready, so our time together is going to be intense, are you up to that Henry, perhaps you can explain why I have only to then, the college intakes start in September?"

I told him that I was indeed able the handle the intenseness, and also explained about my promise to cousin Thomas to spend the summer mining.

"All well and good then," Desmond replied, "But I must say you're cutting it a bit fine, but I'll see what can be done."

As he finished speaking, it was time to make our way to the dining room for lunch, where Desmond was introduced to the ladies. They were looking forward to seeing his wife when she arrived. After lunch he settled into his apartments, and also prepared the library for his tutoring.

From then for the following eight months, my life was fully structured with swordplay from nine until ten each day, then my schooling from ten until four every day, except Sunday.

The following morning, I walked into the library, with my weapons belt hanging from my shoulder, and placed it on one of the coat hooks. Desmond came into the room and closed the door, he was carrying quite a few books, and as he put them down, said "I'm going to be teaching you a lot Henry, but let's see what I can whittle it down to? Now that we don't need, just the basics here, geography, that's a must, history also, spelling no, reading no, Maths yes of course. Alright here's what we'll be concentrating on, Maths, geography, history, and a little bit of basic science. These subjects will be all you require at the college, plus some navigational skills. Right ready to start?"
I nodded my head, and we started with mathematics.

Thus, started my education, which continued up to the beginning of May 1790. Amongst the back schooling I had missed out on, due to my father wanting me at the farm, Desmond would also tell me what I definitely required for life at the naval college. After hearing of my having read the book on navigation, he pulled it from the self, and he would show me at odd times what the phrasing referred to, and took it upon himself to teach me in the proper uses of navigation, so much so, that when I had a chance to ride into town, I went to Howe's.

There, I had asked mister Howe, to obtain a proper seagoing sextant and a good telescope with a belt case, and a compass. A telescope and compass he had in stock, but said he would make it his mission to obtain a sextant for me. While I was paying for the items, he enquired after upon opinion of the clothes I had bought and the tailoring.

I smiled saying, "Mister Howe they are excellent, and the tailoring was perfect, you take very precise measurements, now about the sextant, if you find a decent one, get it for me regardless of price, if you deliver it to the manor, I'll pay you then."

He smiled, saying, "Then I'll be seeing you soon."

Two months' after starting my education, uncle William returned from the sitting at Lord's until he was to journey there again a month into the future. During his first weekend back at the manor, he spent a lot of the time that was available talking with Desmond, and was quite pleased with me, obviously I assumed my work with Desmond was going well. Also in this time Desmond's wife Joy, had arrived and was now integrated well into our little band at the manor.

My dance lessons were progressing, and until uncle William had returned, we had moved from dances that required a set of four people, and even six, at most times my partner would be lady Elizabeth, though sometimes this would change. The entire group took part in my learning, with Albert calling what I needed to do, and also my current partner.

With the return of uncle William, this meant that sometimes one person would have to left out of a dance. Then I thought of a solution, to this, and one evening during drinks discussed my idea to rectify this with Albert. As he heard me out, he replied, "Yes, your idea has a lot of merit, and it also gives us the chance to work with four couple dances, but there's a few things that have to be overcome. First one being that, I don't know how the rest of the family will feel about your suggestion, but that won't be your problem, I can work on them about it. Secondly, you'd have to obtain permission from her parents, and thirdly, she'd have to wear proper dress."

Thinking about his reply about the second and third problems to my scheme, after pouring us another drink each, I asked, "Well if I can get her parent's permission, what say Lucy or one of the other ladies take her into town and get her outfitted properly, and I'll pay the bill?"

He mused over my question, and replied, "Well I can't see that being a problem, but again permission will be required. How will you go about getting that?"

"Oh, that's the easy part," I replied, "I'll just ask them."

He nearly choked on his drink as I answered him, and started laughing, then replied, "Yes, well, I suppose that's the best way, and when are you going to get the time to ask them."

Thinking that over, I smiled, saying, "Listen when I ask questions during dinner."

Looking perplexed, he just nodded, as he took another drink of his wine.

During Dinner, there was a lull in the conversation, and thinking to myself, *Well now's a good a time as any, in for a penny, in for a pound.* Then raised my voice looking at Desmond, I asked, "Just as a thought Desmond, I would like to know, if I am fulfilling your requirements as a student?"
Everyone stopped eating to hear his answer, fully aware of this, he looked around saying, "Well Henry you are making excellent progress, and you are far exceeding my expectations, but as yet I still have to see your marksmanship, before I give you full approval."
I smiled asking, "I see sir, and I thank you for your compliment, now seeing tomorrow is Saturday, if I may make offer a suggestion, what say we get out into the fresh air, and you, Albert and I, take a couple of servants and guns out to the shooting range, and we let you assess my ability?"
Uncle William interjected saying, "Well if you three are going, I'm coming too, besides, I've not seen you shoot yet either Henry. We can leave right after breakfast!"
Hah, I thought, *now that uncle William wants to go, Desmond has to agree, this is better than I thought.*
Desmond looked around, saying, "Very well, some fresh air will do us all good I think, good suggestion Henry."
Looking at Albert, he was silently laughing, and as he saw my look, he winked at me, and I nodded.

I thought to myself, *good, that's that taken care of,* *after dinner I'll go see Joanna's mother and* *arrange a time to see her and her husband* *tomorrow.*
Which was what I did, as I left the table, I pulled Boggs the chief waiter into the hall, asking him to take me to Joanna's mother, and asked her name, which was Alice. In the kitchen he introduced me to Alice, and then I asked for a good time to see her, and her husband together to discuss something. Being a trifle suspicious she told me the best time to see them both was a three in the afternoon, at their cottage. Asking and being told where their cottage was located, I said "Very well I'll see you and your husband at three, what's his name by the way?" She told me his name was Ted, and I let her go back to her work after thanking her.

After breakfast, the next morning, I grabbed my weapons belt from the cloths hook where I had hung it during breakfast, and followed everyone to the gun room. Two of the housemen took charge of the long guns placed in their arms, and the other two, took care of the pistols, powder and shot, taking everything out through the back door of the house to the prepared waiting wagon. While the rest of us went to the stables to mount the awaiting horses for us, by that time I had buckled on my weapons belt, then uncle William led the way to the range. As the housemen arrived two went to set up targets, while the other two started loading the muskets and rifles, laying them down at the back of the wagon.

My weapons belt had a new addition studded into place behind my right-hand pistol, which was my telescope case, cocked at an angle for easy withdrawal. Albert noticed the new addition and asked about and told him what it was. He said smiling, "No doubt about you Henry, you think of everything!"

As we moved to the firing line, I was holding a musket, and had made sure my targets had been set further back than the others by a hundred yards, after mentioning this fact uncle William and Desmond were told by Albert that I was giving myself a penalty of hundred yards due to my expertise, which was naturally scoffed at, after they had fired, it was my turn, then the targets were brought in, mine was the only one with a dead centre bull, as uncle William and Desmond stared in disbelief, I was handed a rifle, they wanted to see my result before they fired, uncle William exclaimed, "Bless me two perfect bulls!" As Desmond just nodded.

At the pistol range Albert announced, "There are twenty-four loaded pistols set out here on the bench, plus the two on Henry's belt, as you can also see there are twenty-six targets, Henry is going to give you a demonstration of his skill, and at the end, he is going to try something he hasn't done before, he will attempt to shoot this can out of the air with two reloaded pistols without aiming! Then all the targets will be collected for your inspection."

I stepped to the firing line with two pistols, in my

hands, and a houseman was standing beside me with two more. Setting myself, with an intake of breath, I started my demonstration, to everyone present of my skills with pistols, and every way I could fire. Then came the finale, both my own pistols had been reloaded and now sat in their holsters. Albert stepped up to the firing line with the can, looked at me to see if I was set, I nodded, and he threw the can into the air downrange, hitting it with my first shot, I changed its direction with my second, before it fell to the ground.

After I had fired I walked back to the bench, and asked for my guns to be cleaned. While this was being done my targets had been collected and given to uncle William, and after looking at each one, he passed them to Desmond.

Uncle William said, "Good God Henry, I know that Albert had told me how well you could shoot, but seeing it was something else entirely, absolutely fantastic, I've never seen a better display of skill, well done."

Desmond, stepped forward to shake my hand, saying, "I thought you were boasting, that was unbelievable and the results, are here in black and white, what superlative skill you have with long or short weapons, remind me not to take you on with a sword if you handle it as good as your firearms, I think you have proved your marksmanship beyond question."

Albert remarked, "He is as good with his sword, Desmond."

Then for the next hour they took time for some practise of their own, and I joined in as well.

At three pm that afternoon, using the direction given to me by Alice, I made my way to the Yeoman cottage. I was no longer wearing my weapons belt, and I was dressed wearing one of my new shirts, waistcoat and one of the new frockcoats, as I knocked politely on the door.

It was answered by the man that I had fought in the yard previous to John! This dashed my hopes a little, but I was determined to see this through, I said "Good afternoon Ted, I'm Henry by the way, and I was hope to speak with you and your good wife Alice."

He replied, "Aye she said you'd be coming, what's this all about?"

"Well sir," I replied, "That's why I'm here to speak to you both."

"Aye best come in then," he replied. And I followed him into the house, directing me to a seat in the lounge. I stood while he took his seat, but just then Alice came in, so I remained standing until she sat down, then took my seat, then started off by saying, "I'm sorry about our little mishap shortly after I got here Ted, but I must admit that idea about fighting wasn't my idea."

He smiled saying, "Aye, I thought as much, but you certainly hit hard, and I must admit you was telling the truth, and you made sure John was alright true enough."

I thanked for his candour, then leaned forward and outlined my idea for Joanna, telling them that I would look after, her and escort to and from dances, and that I would also pay the bill for the dresses she would be wearing, and that I would arrange for one of the ladies to take her to town to get them. Then I explained my full reason for being at the manor in the first place, and where I came from, and why I wanted to do this, and we had a bit of discussion over that, then Alice asked, "When is this likely to start sir."

I smiled saying, "Please don't call me sir Alice, I'm just a plain farm boy named Henry, and as for the other, well I'm not exactly sure Alice, Albert was going to ask his parents if it was alright, and to be honest with you, I'm not sure if they'll agree, but I hope they do, as yet Albert hasn't said anything, but he may be waiting to see if I get your permission as Joanna's parents first, before asking them."

Ted called, "Joanna, come here girl," then said, "It's alright with us, if its's alright with our daughter." Joanna appeared, and Alice explained everything to her, and she smiled and nodded her head, saying, "Oh yes please."

Ted said, "There that's settled, it's alright with us, and thank you Henry." He stood up, and shook his proffered hand, saying "Thank you, Ted, Alice, Joanna, I'll let you know as soon as I know." After that Ted showed me out, and I returned to the house.

Chapter 7

During our pre-diner drinks, I informed Albert of the
Yeoman's permission, and he smiled and let me
know that he had been working with Lucy, to
introduce my idea to the others in the household,
with the result that most thought it a sensible idea,
and that he intended broaching the subject during
dinner.
True to his word, the subject was brought up and
permission was gained, with the caveat that
everyone was to meet her. Summoning Boggs to the
table, Albert asked him to have Joanna join us, and
he left the room. As we finished dessert, he returned
with Joanna in tow, and she was introduced to
everyone, and asked to take a seat at the table, once
she was sitting, the poor girl was questioned by each
of the ladies, about everything to do with her life,
right up to how she had met me, including if she
knew how to dance.
After most of the questioning, uncle William,
"Joanna my dear, I think you are wasted in the
scullery, lady Elizabeth has been talking about
getting a hand maiden, haven't you dear (Elizabeth
nodded), now I think we may have found her one,
but it would mean, you would have to live here in
the main house, and your room would be next to my
wife's, pray tell me, would you be interested in such
a position?"
Nodding her head, Joanna smiled saying, I would
indeed your lordship."
Uncle William replied, "Excellent!"

After he took a drink, he continued, "I'll have Jenkins arrange everything tomorrow, and enough of the lord and ladyship garbage, I'm sir William, and my wife lady Elizabeth, now come and join us for some dancing."

Two hours later, at the Yeoman cottage, I was explaining everything about the night to Ted and Alice. After that Joanna became a permanent addition to the household. This gave me the opportunity to see her, morning, noon and night, as aunt Elizabeth insisted that she eat with us and join us for drinks, not that she was allowed to drink too much.

Tuesday evening, I was asked to the anti-room by Jenkins, who earlier during my stay, I learned was the household chief steward. I met Mister Howe in the anti-room, and he showed me a boxed brass sextant he had acquired, taking it out and inspecting it, I said "Excellent mister Howe, how much do I owe you?"
He moved in closer, and with a soft voice replied, "Just for you, young master, I'll sell it to you for what I paid, that being eighteen shillings, master Henry."
Asking him to wait, I rushed up to my room and withdrew a pound note from my billfold, then put the billfold back in its drawer, back in the anti-room I gave mister Howe the pound note, telling him to keep the rest, we shook hands, and he left. I took the sextant back into the dining room to show off.

My navigational skills increased dramatically, as I learned how, and when to take sun sightings, and I was able to pinpoint our position on a map, no matter where Desmond and I were, so much so that Desmond declared that he no longer need teach me anymore about navigation, I had learned everything he knew.

In the first week of May 1791, I had completed all my schooling with uncle Desmond, having learned, and been examined, on everything he had taught me. My etiquette, gentlemanly behaviour, and dance lessons, had all been learned, with the dancing, we now continued for fun without instruction, Albert and the rest of the family, having done their job well. My romance with Joanna was progressing, and by now everyone connected to the household knew I was courting her. Uncle William and aunt Elizabeth seemed to approve of my choice. I had made a purchase of a portmanteaux from Howe's, and this was able to hold, my gun case, sextant and all my newer clothing, footwear, in fact everything I owned, my canvas hold all only had my older style of dress, and my working clothes in it.

At the start of the second week of May, dressed in a set of my older clothes, with my weapons belt around me, and carrying my canvas hold all bag, I said goodbye to the household members for the summer, and grabbed my old tri-cornered travelling hat, as we all moved outside, to where Jenkins was holding Lightning already saddled, after placing my holdall into the nearest saddle bag, I said my final goodbyes, mounted and started lightning moving, as I turned to give a wave.

I was travelling light, and Lightning chewed up the miles, and I only had one overnight stop between Taunton and the family farm outside Dean Prior, which was in Chudleigh at a wayside inn.

I rode into the farmyard at midday, and I tying my horse to the fence rail beside the water trough, as my father came outside to see who had arrived, I strode over to him carrying my holdall, and he embraced me, then put his arm around my shoulder, as he led me into the house. As I said hello to everyone, I removed my weapons belt, hung it up and joined them at the table as my mother made up a place for me.

After a stay of three days, I mounted Lightning again and left for Seaton where cousin Thomas's mine and estate was located in Cornwall. After placing my holdall, in my room and freshening up, I joined Thomas and his wife for drinks before dinner, after they had told me that I had been missed, I told them what I had been doing up to the present time, at uncle Williams and that when I left them, at the end of the season, I would be making my way back to the Taunton manor, after a brief stop at the farm, and then going to the naval college.

The usual miners were glad to see me back again, as I went to work with them back in the mine, each Saturday I was paid thirty-two pounds by my cousin, and this went into my billfold. At the end of that my last season, I gave them my final farewells.

Back at the family farm, they knew I was not stopping long, and made the best time possible with me, before I left for my new life. Ten days after leaving Cornwall, my final goodbyes to my family long and difficult, I was hugged by all, as I finally mounted, and started back to Taunton, with a final wave, when I was out of sight of the farm, I wiped the tears from my eyes, and broke lightning into a run.

I was only at Taunton for a week, before I would accompany uncle William to Portsmouth, and he would go onto London for the next sittings of the House of Lords. I made that week count with all the family members, and especially with Joanna, the love of my life, who had bloomed into a beautiful woman.
Mine and uncle Williams goodbyes to my foster family were short, every significant thing had been said the previous night, but as I was about to mount lightning, Joanna ran into my arms from the entry and kissed me openly in front of everyone, who politely looked away, then we were away, with me riding beside the enclosed carriage.

It took us a week to travel to Portsmouth, and there we took lodgings in a respectable inn, close to the naval college.
The following day, we both went to the college in the carriage, and were shown in to see the commandant, Rear Admiral John Beckworth, as uncle William sat in front of his desk, I remained

standing, he looked at me, and then uncle William, saying "Alright young man, do you have your letter of recommendation?"

Uncle William interrupted, saying, "I believe you already have this man's recommendation sir, I am Sir William Fox-Tolcher, Earl of Straithhaven, I sent it to you three months ago."

The admiral replied, "Yes I seem to recall it, your lordship, about a certain Henry Robert Tolcher, I remember thinking yours to be a very fine letter sir."

"Thank you, sir," uncle William replied, "I also have this letter, that I have been asked to give to you." As he handed the admiral a letter, that I knew nothing about.

The admiral looked at it, then opened it saying, "Why this is from Desmond Fox-Davis, one of our old senior examiners! Let's see what he has to say." As he read Desmond's letter he would glance up at me, then said, "If your letter hadn't already been sent sir, this would have been enough to get young Henry admitted to the college, indeed a very glowing recommendation, I suppose he has also been tutoring you, young man?"

"Yes Sir," I replied.

He nodded saying, "Alright then, our fees are one hundred pounds a term, one hundred and ten if you require to stable a horse, this pays for your board and lodgings also, how would you like to pay that? By cash or letter of mark?"

I asked, "Would it be possible to pay for all three terms together sir, and I would pay cash and I will require stabling for a horse, sir."

Clearing his throat, the admiral said, "Yes you may pay for all your terms at once, which makes it three hundred and thirty pounds young man."
I took my billfold from my frockcoat, and counted out the three hundred and thirty pounds, and placed it on his desk, as I returned my billfold to my jacket. He was writing an address on a piece of paper saying, these are the best outfitters in town, take this to them and they'll supply all you require, I see you won't require weapons," as he finished writing the list, he continued, "Your term starts in ten days, at the end of term three, you will be able to sit your exams, unless you fall by the wayside, or get expelled beforehand. On your first day, you will report to the front office to receive your billet, and stable number. Good luck young Henry."
Then uncle William asked, "Admiral would it be possible for Henry to move into a billet and stable his horse tomorrow? You see sir I must be on my way to London for the next sitting of the house of lords."
The admiral rose from behind his desk, saying, "Please wait here sir, and I'll see what we can do." He also took the cash I had paid with him.
Ten minutes later he returned, with a receipt for my fees, and said, "Henry, you will return to the front office tomorrow at nine hundred hours where you will ask for a lieutenant Billingsly, he will then take you to your billet, and orientate you to the rest of the college, welcome to his majesty's royal navy."
I smiled and replied, "Thank you sir."
Uncle William stood up, and we were shown out.

The rest of the morning was spent at the marine outfitters as I was measured for my uniform needs, and all my supplies, which came to a sum of twenty pounds. I was informed my uniforms would be ready two days from then, in the afternoon.

The next morning, uncle William and I bid each farewell, as he said, "Remember Henry to come home to us at the end of each term, good luck my boy, though I don't think you'll need it."

He headed towards the road out of town to London in the coach and I rode my horse to the college with my portmanteaux and holdall.

I was shown my billet, and given the key, leaving my stuff in the room, I went for a tour of the college by Lt. Billingsly shown the eating hall and given meal times, all classrooms, everywhere around the college and lastly, he took me to the stables, after I had collected lightning.

I picked up my uniforms from the outfitters, and I took them back to the college, and to my room, which had a desk, cupboard, night stand a couple comfortable chairs, and my bed. I was ready to start term in a couple of days.

My intake of cadets, had six weeks leave at the end of terms one and two, and each year I returned to spend years end at the Manor house in Taunton being fondly received by my foster family, and Joanna each year. Whilst I lived there, I would visit my real family for one of the weeks, and they were always happy to see me, and hear how I was going.

June 8, 1794: I passed all my officers exams with honours, but at the time there were no officer billets available on sea going vessels, I was however, offered a billet as a midshipman on HMS Meleager, which was one of the blockading ships, attached to Admiral Jervis's Mediterranean fleet under the command of Captain George Cockburn.

I was also given to believe that my time as a midshipman, would quickly end, and I would be raised to officer status fairly quickly onboard one of the navy's fighting ships.
With this in mind, and the chance I might see some action so soon out of college, I decided to accept the admiralty offer. After giving the admiralty my home address as at uncle William's house, all I had to do was collect my belongings, horse and head for Taunton, and I was to be considered on shore leave.

I had been at uncle Williams manor house three weeks, when one morning a postal courier had arrived, with orders for me from the Admiralty.
I was to report aboard the HMS Avanti in Plymouth by the tenth of June, to be conveyed to my posting aboard the Meleager off Marseilles. Knowing my ships now, I remembered the Avanti was now a post ship, that had originally been captured from the Spanish.
Meleager was a forty-four-gun fifth rate ship of the line.
During lunch, I announced to the family that I had received my sailing orders from the admiralty.

Then told them where I had to leave from, and how long I had to get there, which was a week. The discussion turned to how I was going to get there, because I had decided I had no wish to take my horse, because there would have been nowhere to have him kept.

Uncle William said, "In that case my boy, take my carriage, that way the drivers can travel day and night to get you there, but even doing that you would have to leave by tomorrow morning, I'll arrange it for right after lunch."

After thanking him, I noticed that Joanna beside me, wasn't wearing the ring her mother had given her, which she wore on her right-hand ring finger, asking her about it she said it had spilt where it had been resized for, I had her give it to me, telling her I would have it fixed that afternoon. Asking Boggs to have my horse saddled, I left after lunch.

That evening during drinks, Joanna and I became betrothed, in front of the family, including her parents that had been brought in on my insistence, I had purchased an engagement ring at the same time I was getting her other ring fixed.

The following morning, I left for Plymouth in the carriage.

Chapter 8.

Journal Entry – July10 1804 Captain Robin Fox-Davis Royal Navy.
It is with joy that I know I will be spending this month on shore leave with my family. A short while ago myself and prize crew arrived at the Plymouth dockyards aboard the vessel Attica, which was captured by my vessel HMS Dreadnought in the Mediterranean Sea.

My ship is Admiral Collingwood's flagship and it was at his suggestion that I captain the Attica home and have a spot of shore leave, while waiting to re-join the fleet. Upon my arrival at the Admiralty, I was informed I would be captaining admiral Collingwood's new flagship back to the fleet. I would remain as Captain of the Dreadnought, while my 1st mate was promoted to flag captain. I smiled as I heard this news because Edward Rotherham's promotion was well deserved. I would be on fully paid leave while waiting for the new flagship to be ready, instead of only half pay.

Elizabeth, my darling wife was overjoyed when I arrived home at our manor at the start of the week, and the news I would be home for at least a month. Since then I have been spending time with my family, getting to know our children, the oldest being Adrian, still a toddler at age three, and my daughter Dorothy, who was born after my last visit home, and is barely a year old.

While the children sleep in the afternoon, and dear Elizabeth amuses herself in the garden, and prepares our dinner, I have taken to my study, with the purpose of bringing this journal up to date, something I have not got around to doing since my marriage to Elizabeth back in 1796, when I was newly promoted to 2nd lieutenant.

After looking at what I had previously written, I find it remiss of me, not to have had this Journal with me previously. If I am to keep my promise to father, I should include this journal amongst my possessions when I again go to sea. Oh, all those boring days at sea, when I could have concentrated on keeping my journal up to date! I must now make a start to catch up, therefore I am resolved to keep my afternoons free for this work, which I will start now. To my family descendants, who do not know what life is like in the navy, pray let me enlighten you.

Life on a sailing warship of the 18th and 19th Century, particularly the large ships of the line, was crowded and hard. Discipline was enforced with extreme violence, small infractions punished with public lashings. The food, far from good, deteriorated as ships spent time at sea. Drinking water was in short supply and usually brackish. Shortage of citrus fruit and fresh vegetables meant that scurvy quickly set in.

The great weight of guns and equipment and the necessity to climb rigging in adverse weather conditions frequently caused serious injury. Warships carried their main armament in broadside batteries along the sides. Ships were classified according to the number of guns carried, or the number of decks carrying batteries. The size of gun on the line of battle ships was up to 24 pounders, firing heavy iron balls or chain and link shot designed to wreck rigging. The Nile was a close fleet action. Ships sailed up to the enemy and in many instances anchored, delivering broadsides at a range of a few yards.

Ships manoeuvred to deliver broadsides in the most destructive manner; the greatest effect being achieved by firing into an enemy's stern or bow, so that the shot travelled the length of the ship wreaking havoc and destruction. During the Battle of the Nile, HMS Leander and Alexander positioned themselves to 'rake' the French Flagship L'Orient from its bow and stern quarters. The first broadside, loaded before action began, was always the most effective. To achieve maximum effect, the British ships held their fire until alongside the French ships, advancing in an ominous silence under the fire of the French Fleet and the shore batteries on Aboukir Island. Ships carried a variety of smaller weapons on the top deck and in the rigging, from swivel guns firing grape shot or canister (bags of musket balls) to hand held muskets, pistols and cutlasses, each crew seeking to annihilate the enemy officers and sailors on deck.

Wounds in Eighteenth Century naval fighting were terrible. Cannon balls ripped off limbs or, striking wooden decks and bulwarks or guns and metalwork, drove splinter fragments across the ship causing horrific wounds. Falling masts and rigging inflicted severe crush injuries. Sailors stationed aloft fell into the sea from collapsing masts and rigging to be drowned. Heavy losses were caused when a ship finally sank. Only 70 men survived the destruction of the French Flagship L'Orient, from a crew of 500 or more.

Ships' crews of all nations were tough. The British, with continual blockade service against France and Spain, were particularly well drilled. British gun crews fired three broadsides or more, to every two fired by the French. The French Navy still suffered from the loss of expert naval officers, executed or exiled following the French Revolution of 1789.

British captains were responsible for recruiting their ship's crew. Men were taken wherever they could be found, largely by the press gang.

All nationalities served on British ships, including French and Spanish. Loyalty for a crew lay primarily with their ship. Once the heat of battle subsided there was little animosity against an enemy.

Great efforts were made by British crews to rescue the sailors of foundering French ships. After the Battle of the Nile, some 200 sailors from the French crews were mustered into HM ships.

In the 18th century Royal Navy, rank and position

on board ship was defined by a mix of two hierarchies, an official hierarchy of ranks and a conventionally recognized the social divide between gentlemen and non-gentlemen. Royal Navy ships were led by commissioned officers of the wardroom, which consisted of the captain, his lieutenants, as well as soldier marine officers, all of whom were officers and gentlemen.

The higher ranked warrant officers on board, the Sailing Master, Purser, Surgeon and Chaplain held a warrant from the Navy Board but not an actual commission from the crown. Warrant officers had rights to mess and berth in the wardroom and were normally considered gentlemen; however, the Sailing Master was often a former sailor who had 'come through the ranks' therefore might have been viewed as a social unequal.

All commissioned and warrant officers wore a type of uniform, although official Navy regulations clarified an officer uniform in 1787 while it was not until 1807 that masters, along with pursers, received their own regulated uniform.

Next come the ship's three standing warrant officers, the Carpenter, Gunner and Boatswain (Bo 'sun), who along with the Master were permanently assigned to a vessel for the purposes of maintenance, repair, and upkeep. Standing officers were considered the most highly skilled seaman on board, and messed and berthed with the crew.

As such, they held a status separate from the other officers and were not granted the privileges of a commissioned or warrant officer if they were captured. 'Cockpit mate' was a colloquial term for petty officers who were considered gentlemen and officers under instruction and messed and berthed apart from the ordinary sailors in the Cockpit. This included both midshipman, who were considered gentlemen and officers under instruction, and master's mates, who derived their status from their role as apprentices to the sailing master.

A midshipman outranked most other petty officers and lesser warrant officers, such as the Master-at-arms. Boys aspiring for a commission were often called young gentlemen instead to distinguish their higher social standing from the ordinary sailors. Occasionally, a midshipman would be posted aboard a ship in a lower rating such as able seaman but would eat and sleep with his social equals in the cockpit (all Midshipman would be 'rated able' at some point in their service, it was a requirement for them to have been so before they could stand as a Mate, another requirement for promotion to Lieutenant). The remainder of the ship's company, who lived and berthed in the common crew quarters, were the petty officers and seamen. Petty officers were seamen who had been rated to fill a specialist trade on board ship.

This rating set the petty officers apart from the common seaman by technical skill and slightly higher education.

No special uniform was allocated for petty officers, although some Royal Navy ships allowed such persons to don a simple blue frock coat to denote their status.

Seaman were further divided into two grades, these being ordinary seaman and able seaman. Seaman were normally assigned to a watch, which maintained its own hierarchy consisting of a watch captain in charge of an area of the ship.
Grouped amongst the watches were also the landsmen, considered the absolute lowest rank in the Royal Navy and assigned to personnel, usually from press gangs, who held little to no naval experience. A final position on board ship was that of ship's boy, sometimes referred to as cabin boy. Normally between the ages of 8 to 12, ship's boys performed a variety of functions such as servants to officers, mess attendants, or as a powder monkey {officers' servants were usually 'young gentlemen' joining a ship at say 12 or 13, preparatory to becoming midshipmen; their prior service as a servant to an officer would be included in the Midshipman's recorded sea-service on going before the Lieutenants' Commission Board.

Promotion and advancement within the 18th and 19th century Royal Navy varied depending on the status of the sailor in question. At the lower levels, most inexperienced sailors began in the rank of landsman, those joining ships at a very young age were typically entered in the navy as cabin boys or officers' servants.
After a year at sea, landsmen were normally advanced to ordinary seaman. Three more years, with appropriate ability displayed, would see a sailor advanced to able seaman.
For the common seaman, this level is normally

where the career path ended, and many sailors spent their entire Royal Navy careers as able seaman on various vessels.

Advancement into the petty officer positions required some level of technical skill. Petty officer appointments were typically made by a ship's captain – sailors could also be rated on the books as a petty officer when a ship was in port searching for a crew. Honesty was implied, as a sailor falsely claiming experience to rate a billet on board ship would be quickly discovered once at sea.

Senior petty officers could also be rated as a standing officer, of which only three such positions normally existed (boatswain, carpenter, and gunner). Standing officers remained with a vessel during lay-up and maintenance, and were known to be highly valued due to their skill and experience.

Warrant officers were given their positions by various certification boards and had nearly the same rights and respect as commissioned officers, including access to the quarterdeck and wardroom.

Advancement into the commissioned officer grades required a royal appointment, following a certification by the lieutenant's examination board. Board eligibility was most often achieved by serving as a midshipman, although the career path of a master or master's mate also permitted this opportunity.

Once commissioned, lieutenants would be rated on board based on seniority, such as 1st lieutenant, 2nd lieutenant, and 3rd lieutenant, with the 1st lieutenant filling the role of executive officer and second-in-command.

Lieutenants, like ordinary sailors, were required to be signed on to various vessels due to manpower needs. If a lieutenant could not find a billet, the officer was said to be on half pay until a sea billet could be obtained.

Flag rank advancement in the 18th and 19th century Royal Navy was determined entirely by seniority. Initial promotion to flag rank from the rank of captain occurred when a vacancy appeared on the admirals' seniority list due to the death or retirement of a flag officer. The captain in question would then be automatically promoted to rear admiral and assigned to the first of three colored squadrons, these being the blue, white and red squadrons.

As further vacancies occurred, the British flag officer would be posted to the same rank in higher squadrons. For instance, a rear admiral of the blue squadron would be promoted to become rear admiral of the white, and then rear admiral of the red squadron.

When reaching the highest position of the rank (rear admiral of the red), the flag officer would next be promoted to the rank of vice admiral, and begin again at the lowest coloured squadron (vice admiral of the blue).

The process would continue again, until the vice admiral of the red was promoted to admiral of the blue.

The highest possible rank was admiral of the red squadron, which was synonymous with admiral of the fleet.

Some flag officers were not assigned to a squadron, and thus were referred to simply by the generic title admiral. Formally known as admiral without distinction of a squadron, the common term for such officers was yellow admiral. Still another title was port admiral which was the title for the senior naval officer of a British port.

Chapter 9.

The title of Commander was originally a temporary position for lieutenants placed in charge of smaller vessels. Successful commanders (who were known by courtesy on board their own ships as captain) could aspire for promotion to captain which was known as making post. Such post captains were then assigned to rated vessels in the rating system of the Royal Navy. Once a captain, advancement to admiral was strictly determined by seniority if a captain served long enough for more senior officers to retire, resign, or die, he would eventually become an admiral. One distinguishing element amongst captain was, however, determined by the rating of the vessel they commanded. The captain of a sixth rate, for instance, was generally junior to a captain of a first rate.

Royal navy vessels operated on many parallel hierarchies in addition to formal ranks and positions, paramount of which was the vessel's watch organization. Watches were stood 24 hours a day and divided into watch sections each of which was led by an officer of the watch, typically a lieutenant, midshipman, or master's mate. The captain and master did not stand watch but were on call 24 hours a day.

The heart of the watch were the watch teams, each led by a petty officer.

There were six watch teams on most Royal Navy vessels, divided into three deck teams and three aloft teams.

The aloft teams were manned by sailors known as topmen and were considered the most experienced men aboard. In all, the six watch teams were Aloft: Fore topman, main topmen, mizzen topmen, Deck: Forecastle men, waisters, afterguard.

The navigation and steering of the vessel from the quarterdeck was handled by a special watch team of quartermasters. Furthermore, the ship's bosun and his mates were interspersed amongst the various watch teams to ensure good order and discipline. The remainder of the ships' company, who did not stand a regular watch, included the ship's carpenter's crew and the gunnery teams (in charge of the maintenance of the ship's guns). Any other person on board who did not stand watch was collective referred to as an idler, but was still subject to muster when the "all hands-on deck" was called by the boatswain.

In addition to the standard watch organization of a Royal Navy vessel, additional organizational hierarchies included the division, headed by a lieutenant or midshipman, mainly for the purposes of mustering as well as messing and berthing; divisions were typically present only on the larger rated vessels.

The term Action Stations was a battle condition in which a Royal Navy vessel manned all of its guns with gun crews, stood up damage control and emergency medical teams, and called the ship's senior officers to the quarterdeck in order to direct the ship in battle.

British captains expected their ships to clear for action in 10 minutes. Cabin walls were dismantled; gun crews formed up; the gunner and his mates opened the magazine and distributed ammunition to the guns; decks were wetted and sprinkled with sand; the surgeon laid out his implements in the cockpit; the marines assembled to take post on the decks or in the rigging. The final act of preparation was for the gun ports to be opened and the guns run out, the truck wheels rumbling through the ship.

A sailor's action station was independent of their watch station or division, although in many cases groups of sailors manning the same action station were assigned from the same division or watch section.

Ships in the Royal Navy each had ratings as to the number of guns they carried. A first, second, or third-rate ship was regarded as a ship-of-the-line. The first and second rates were three-deckers; that is, they had three continuous decks of guns on the lower deck, middle deck and upper deck, usually as well as smaller weapons on the quarterdeck, forecastle and poop.

Notable exceptions to this rule were ships such as the Santisima Trinidad of Spain, which had 140 guns and four gun decks (the Spanish and French had, of course, different rating systems from those of Britain).

The largest third rates, those of 80 guns, were likewise three-deckers from the 1690s until the early 1750s, but both before this period and after it,

80-gun ships were built as two-decker's. All the other third rates, with 74 guns or less, were likewise two-decker's, with just two continuous decks of guns on the lower deck and upper deck, as well as smaller weapons on the quarterdeck, forecastle and if they had one poop. After a series of major changes to the rating systems the carronades carried by each ship were included in the count of guns. A first rate including all of the three-deckers adding in of their carronades meant that all three-deckers now had over 100 guns, the new second rate included all two-deckers of 80 guns or more, with the third rate reduced to two-decker's of fewer than 80 guns.

The smaller fourth rates, of about 50 or 60 guns on two decks, were ships-of-the-line until 1756, when it was felt that such 50-gun ships were now too small for pitched battles.

The larger fourth rates of 60 guns continued to be counted as ships-of-the-line, but few new ships of this rate were added, the 60-gun fourth rate being superseded over the next few decades by the 64-gun third rate. The Navy did retain some fourth rates for convoy escort, or as flagships on far-flung stations. The smaller two deckers originally blurred the distinction between a fourth rate and a fifth rate. At the low end of the fourth rate one might find the two-decker 50-gun ships from about 1756.

The high end of the fifth rate would include two-deckers of 40 or 44-guns, from 1690 or even the 32-gun and 36-gun ships of the 1690 -1730 years. Fifth rates at the start of the 18th century, were generally, 'demi-batterie' ships, carrying a few heavy guns on their lower deck, which often used the rest of the lower deck for row ports and a full battery of lesser guns on the upper deck. However, these were gradually phased out, as the low freeboard (the height of the lower deck gunport sills above the waterline) meant that in rough weather it was often impossible to open the lower deck gunports.

Fifth and sixth rates were never included among ships-of-the-line. The middle of the 18th century saw the introduction of a new fifth-rate type, the classic frigate, with no ports on the lower deck, and the main battery disposed solely on the upper deck, where it could be fought in all weathers.

Sixth-rate ships were generally useful as convoy escorts, for blockade duties and the carrying of dispatches, their small size made them less suited for the general cruising tasks the fifth-rate frigates did so well. Essentially there were two groups of sixth rates. The larger category comprised the sixth-rate frigates of 28 guns, carrying a main battery of twenty-four 9-pounder guns, as well as four smaller guns on their superstructures. The second comprised the post ships of between 20 and 24 guns. These were too small to be formally counted as frigates (although colloquially often grouped with them), but still required a post-captain an officer holding the substantive rank of captain as their commander.

The rating system did not handle vessels smaller than the sixth rate. The remainder were simply unrated.

The larger of the unrated vessels were generally all called sloops, but that description is quite confusing for unrated vessels, especially when dealing with the finer points of 'ship-sloop', brig-sloop', 'sloop-of-war' (which really just meant the same in naval parlance as 'sloop') or even 'corvette'.
Technically the category of 'sloop-of-war' included any unrated combatant vessel in theory, and the term even extended to bomb vessels and fire ships.

During the Napoleonic Wars, the Royal Navy increased the number of sloops in service by some four hundred percent. As it found that it needed vast numbers of these small vessels for escorting convoys (as in any war, the introduction of convoys created a huge need for escort vessels), combating privateers, and themselves taking prizes.

The rated number of guns often differed from the number a vessel actually carried. The guns that determined a ship's rating were the carriage-mounted cannon, long-barrelled, muzzle-loading guns that moved on 'trucks' (wooden wheels). The count did not include smaller anti-personnel weapons, such as swivel-mounted guns, which fired half-pound projectiles, or small arms.
For instance, HMS Cynthia was rated for 18 guns but during construction her rating was reduced to 16 guns 6-pounders, and she also carried 14 half-pound swivels.
Vessels might also carry other guns that did not contribute to the rating. Examples of such weapons would include mortars, howitzers or boat guns,

the boat guns being small guns intended for mounting on the bow of a vessel's boats to provide fire support during landings, cutting out expeditions, and the like. From 1778, however, the most important exception was the carronade.

Introduced in the late 1770s, the carronade was a short-barrelled and relatively short-range gun, half the weight of equivalent long guns, and was generally mounted on a slide rather than on trucks.

The new carronades were generally housed on a vessel's upper works, quarterdeck and forecastle, some as additions to its existing ordnance and some as replacements. When the carronades replaced or were in lieu of carriage-mounted cannon they generally counted in arriving at the rating, but not all were, and so may or may not have been included in the count of guns, though rated vessels might carry up to twelve 18, 24 or 32-pounder carronades.

For instance, HMS Armada was rated as a third rate of 74 guns. She carried twenty-eight 32-pounder guns on her gundeck, twenty-eight 18-pounder guns on her upper deck, four 12-pounder guns and ten 32-pounder carronades on her quarterdeck, two 12-pounder guns and two 32-pounder carronades on her forecastle, and six 18-pounder carronades on her poop deck. In all, this 74-gun vessel carried 80 cannons 62 guns and 18 carronades.

When carronades became part of a ship's main armament they had to be included in the count of guns.

For instance, Bonne Citoyenne was a 20-gun corvette of the French Navy that the British captured and recommissioned in the Royal navy, as the 20-gun sloop and post ship HMS Bonne Citoyenne. She carried two 9-pounder cannons and eighteen 32 pounder carronades.

One therefore needs to distinguish between the *established* armament of a vessel which rarely altered, and the *actual* guns carried, which might happen quite frequently for a variety of reasons. Guns might be lost overboard during a storm, or burst in service and thus useless, or jettisoned to speed the ship during a chase, or for a small vessel. The schooner HMS Ballahoo, lowered the centre of gravity by lowering her guns into the hold, and thus improve stability in bad weather. Also, some of the guns were removed from a ship during peacetime service, to reduce the stress on the ship's structure, which is why there was a distinction the *wartime* compliment of guns (and men) and the lower *peacetime* complement, the figure normally quoted for any vessel is the highest wartime establishment.

Well dear family, that is as much as I can tell you about life being in the navy, all of this has come out of memory, as most of the pertinent points are still there, after I learned all this from actual life at sea for the three years I waited to attend my officer's examinations. Some of what I have told you, I also had as examination questions at the Royal Navy College prior to being appointed a commission as a lieutenant. Then I had the interminable wait of three days to find out if I had passed or failed, because not everyone passes first time round. Especially those electing to learn at sea, rather than go to the naval college.

I must say that I was one of the lucky ones, there was a position open for me as 2nd mate aboard the Majestic.

However, others following my examinations would not have been so lucky, and would have either gone to sea as a midshipman, until an officers position became available, or would have remained ashore on only half pay until a vacancy became available.

As I have stated, I was lucky, I was ordered to Gibraltar just after my wedding to Elizabeth and a two-week honeymoon, I arrived there aboard the post ship HMS Orion during November 1796. As we entered the harbour, I caught sight of my new ship, and couldn't believe my luck, HMS Majestic was a third-rate ship of the line carrying seventy-four guns.

Later that evening, I met my new captain and his officers in the naval officer's shore mess. Captain William Cuthbert took a shine to me straight away, as his family and mine were distantly related through marriage. Majestic was the flagship for the admiral of the Mediterranean fleet, Vice Admiral John Jervis.

Chapter 10.

The following morning, I joined the Captain and other officers in the longboat, that was taking me and my possessions out to join the Majestic. Once aboard I took my gear sack to my assigned cabin, and settled in, before the scheduled officers conference in the captains' cabin. During this conference, I met the other officers and senior ratings that had not been at the mess the previous night due to watch rotation. Captain Cuthbert informed me of which watch rotation I would be taking over, which was the normal day watch as third in command.

As we stood around chatting, before we moved off to go about our business, letters arrived for the captain, myself, and a couple others of the officer's present. Reading the first letter he opened the captain announced, "Gentlemen before you go about your business, this has arrived from the Admiral. It seems his protégé, Captain George Grey will be arriving in the next couple of days, on Victory the admiral has sent me this, telling me he intends transferring his flag to Victory when it arrives. Now apparently Grey will be bringing Robert Calder with him, and he will be our new Captain of the Fleet. Knowing what a stickler Jervis is, I would suggest that we get the ship as ready as we can, to go to sea. Robin, get to know your watch hands before we do, the rest of you know what's needed, get to it!"

As he finished, we all chorused "Aye Sir." As we all left his cabin, I put my mail into my uniform jacket to read later.

Going out onto the quarterdeck, the 1st mate and my immediate superior 1st lieutenant George Blagdon said to me, "Come up onto the poop Robin and I'll introduce you to your watch captain," after we climbed the stairs onto the poop deck George took me to a petty officer dressed in a blue frock coat, he stood about five feet six with black wavy hair, and very broad shouldered and muscular, he seemed to have his eye on everything going on around the ship, aloft as well as on deck. George said, "Petty Officer Joe Dawson meet your new watch officer 2nd lieutenant Fox-Davis."

With that Dawson looked at us, and gave me a quick up and down glance gauging me in his eyes, as he replied, "Aye Sir," George moved off and left me to it, as Dawson continued placing his hand out, "Welcome aboard sir."

I shook Dawson's proffered hand and looked around before replying, "Thank you Dawson, and when we're alone make it Robin, you're Joe, is that right?"

A smile broke over Dawson's face, he looked around replying "Aye sir, I mean Robin."

I laughed and asked him about the hands on our watch.

He started pointing out the watch crew naming them one by one starting at the deck, then moving his arm aloft to the hands on the fore, main, and mizzen

masts, as he finished he said, "That's all of them, Robin, top hands all, and I don't allow any slackers in my crew, if'n you know what I mean sir."
I smiled as I nodded my head in understanding, and said "Good, that means none of the men will need any punishment, that sort of thing can ruin a watch crew, you can introduce them to me in a little while Joe, right now you and I have some business to discuss, come on over to the port rail." We stood side by side with our backs to the rail, as I informed him of the latest news concerning the admiral transferring his flag, and the captains' advice to make the ship ready to go to sea.

After I was finished, he whistled and said, "Hmm a hundred gunner first rate, ole Jervis must be expecting some action, and I know what cap'n Cuthbert means about him being a stickler Robin, he'll have the whole fleet out doing manoeuvres now he's got a new toy to play with, but beggin your pardon this old tub is as ready as she can be excepting victuals of course, but that's up to the quartermaster for that, not really our problem."
We both laughed as I said, "Right Joe, best you introduce me to the hands those on deck first, then we'll go aloft.
Then I want to meet the gunners on the upper gundeck seeing they'll be mine."
He straightened up, and replied "Aye, aye Sir, if you'll follow me."
The next couple hours took up meeting all the hands of my watch and all the gun crews that would be

under my responsibility on the upper gundeck most of them were already on my watch except the powder monkeys, those I would meet later.

When all the officers assembled in the wardroom for lunch, I was able to look at the letters that had arrived for me. One was from Elizabeth, and I smiled as I thought she must have written it the day after my departure, as it would have been aboard the post ship Orion, the very one that had brought me here.

The other bore the family seal, and rightly I assumed it had come from the Earl, William Fox-Tolcher.

Breaking the seal, I had time to peruse its contents before the first course was presented. Alberts was congratulating me on my marriage, and inviting us both to his manor for a few days when I next had shore leave. It also contained news of my second cousin Robert Henry Tolcher, he had entered the Royal Naval College and passed his exams as an officer by age eighteen. However, he had taken a berth on the HMS Minerve as a midshipman due to there being no officer ranks available at his time of passing the exams, in 1794 he joined Minerve with lieutenant Thomas Hardy and Captain George Cockburn.

Reversing his Christian names around, was known in all official papers as Henry Robert Tolcher.

I smiled as I thought this news over, and what I knew of the Minerve, knowing that this very year a man that was making a name for himself,

Captain Horatio Nelson, had become the new captain of the Minerve, and wondered if my cousin was still aboard, surmising that if he was, he was bound for glory under Nelson.

Captain Cuthbert had noticed my thoughtfulness and smile, and enquired, "I take it the news from was enjoyable Robin?"

I smiled replying, "It is indeed sir, the earl wrote to inform me that my cousin Henry had passed his college exams and is now aboard the Minerve."

He laughed saying, "Good fortune indeed for your cousin, that captain Nelson fellow likes a lot of action, and is going to go far! How are you getting on with your watch hands going well I hope?"

"Yes sir," I replied "Oh, and Dawson said we're as ready as we'll ever be for sea, except for provisioning of course. If I may make an observation sir, as the admiral is transferring to Victory, it's a first rate with over a hundred guns maybe we shall be seeing action ourselves sir."

My comment started a lot of talk about what may or may not come in the way of action.

The consensus of view was that Jervis may be looking to stir things up in the Mediterranean Sea. As all of the ten ships in the Jervis's fleet were all ships of the line, plus our ancillary frigates and sloops. Also before the lunch hour finished, the roll of who was eating at the shore mess and who would be sleeping ashore in the quarters, though I would eat ashore with all the other officers, I elected to sleep onboard in my cabin and have breakfast in the wardroom the following morning.

During the next couple of days, the entire crew practiced the call to action stations, it was expected of all ships of the line be cleared and ready for action within ten minutes. As all officers conferred on the poop deck after the first drill the timings weren't nearly good enough coming in at just under twelve minutes. Captain Cuthbert then called for all hands, on deck, and while we waited for the crew to assemble, he turned to me, saying "Right Robin, go give them the timings, and give them a bloody good tongue lashing!"

I replied, "Aye Sir," as I turned and walked to the rail of the poop above the wheel, and addressed the assembly.

"Right you slovenly rats, landlubbers can do better than that, it was atrocious for sailors in the royal navy.

You there! Carpentry gangs, and medical gangs, you took twice the amount of time you should have, so now the whole ship is going to know who is responsible for this stuff up."

With a quick breath, I continued, "From now, on until you lot of bilge rats get this time down to eight minutes you're going to bloody practice, and bloody practice again day and night."

I let this sink in before continuing as I glared at them all, "Next time the crew that takes the longest, will pay for it!

Every bloody one of you in that crew will receive

ten lashes! Now get out of my sight and on with your duties, go!"

As I returned to the captain and other officers, I found he was smiling, as he said "Well you've certainly given them something to think about, but ten lashes for each man in a crew! Surely five would have sufficed, you're a hard man Robin, but what's done is done, call the next practice during lunch."

"Aye Sir," I replied, as I returned to my watch station as they all dispersed to whatever they were doing prior to the drill. Soon I was joined at the rail of the poop by Dawson, turning to him, I said "Joe I want you to pass the word the next drill will be during lunch, but keep it quiet."

"Aye sir," he mumbled before ambling off and down to the quarter deck.

The next drill during lunch had us all excited as the whole ship was cleared for action in nine minutes with no crew lagging behind. Cuthbert was well pleased as he called for all hands-on deck, and waited for everyone to assembly on the quarterdeck. When everyone was there, he addressed the assembly this time as all the officers stood behind him, he said to them, "Well done boys this time you were already in nine minutes two seconds, very well done, that's the best you've ever done."

"Also no one requires a flogging! However, mister Fox-Davis has stated you are required to clear for action in eight minutes, so we will keep practicing, we still have tonight and tomorrow to go to satisfy him, return to your normal duties."

As the crew dispersed, George Blagdon asked me, "Robin isn't eight minutes a bit much, after all admiralty instructions only use ten minutes as the benchmark?"

Cuthbert interjected, saying "No mister Blagdon if our crew can be ready for action a full two minutes under the benchmark, we will be the best ship of the line in the entire fleet, keep it up Robin don't settle for less than the eight minutes you've asked for, but already what an improvement between the two drills! And already under the benchmark, well done Robin. Now gentlemen let's finish our lunch."

The topic of conversation in the wardroom as we finished our lunch, was the timings and the merits of calling for mass floggings of entire crews being late to be ready. There was another drill called at fifteen hundred (3pm) and this time, all our stop watches were stopped within a second or two at eight minutes twenty seconds.

I thought to myself, *Jesus that was excellent!* Everyone was once more surprised along with me, as the news was passed to the men before they returned to normal duties cheering, the crew were pleased with themselves as the officers were.

Before all the officers left the ship in the longboat that evening, those that were staying ashore for the night took their stopwatches with them at my request. When at dinner in the mess, I explained to them that I was going to call a drill in the morning as they arrived at the ship in the longboat.

Which started jokes about seeing how good the crew were first thing in the morning, as the jokes and comments died down I said to them, "Not only will it be first thing in the morning, they will be tired, because tonight back aboard I will call another drill at eight bells (midnight) just to see how they go." There were shouts about me being a slave driver and cracking the whip too often, but all were made in jest, then Cuthbert told me to let him know the results of that little exercise, during the morning drill, and I nodded that I would. After a few drinks in the mess after dinner, myself and the officers returning to the ship, made our way to the longboat, and were rowed out to the ship.

On the way to the ship, I told lieutenant Raymond Billings who would be the officer of the watch at the time I wanted, to call the drill just after eight bells. He nodded his understanding, and when we arrived at the ship we climbed aboard, and I went to my cabin and set the alarm on the clock for midnight, and lay on the bed fully clothed and went to sleep.

I awoke as the alarm went off, then heard Ray's yell to action stations, and his call to beat to station.
It wasn't long before I heard the melody of 'Heart of Oak' being beaten by the drummer boy. After nine minutes all the officers staying onboard were assembled on the poop, as we conferred over the timings, and the consensus settled on eight minutes thirteen seconds, we were all amazed as we compared times, this was unbelievable from dead asleep to ready to fight it was marvellous!

I called for all hands and as they mustered, I said "That was bloody well done, I hope no one was dreaming (there was laughter at my comment), well done boys go can go back to bed now!"

Then I hand went up, and a voice asked, "How'd we go Sir?"

I replied, "Oh, didn't I tell you eight minutes thirteen, still not under the eight yet, but I think that the quartermaster can find a tot of rum to put you back sleep, goodnight!

There were cheers and laughter as a lot of them shouted "And a goodnight to you too sirs."

Chapter 11.

The following morning, after I was dressed, because I didn't have a servant as some of the other officers did, I opened my cabin door and spied a passing seaman, and said "You there, summon petty officer Dawson to my cabin." With the typical "Aye sir" to an order the seaman rushed off.
I didn't have to wait long, and soon there was a knock on the door, as I answered "Come," Joe Dawson strode in, and I told him to close the door, and said, "Take a seat Joe, I'm giving you the heads up if you know what I mean, the next drill will be as the ships officers arrive, let's try to get under the eight, shall we? I can't promise that if we do, that will be the end of the drills, but I will certainly try to make it so. That's all now you can return to what you were doing, and I'll see you on watch."
He got up, saluted me saying "Aye sir, thank yee."

I nodded, and he left the cabin, then I too left my cabin and made my way to the wardroom, where those officers onboard were waiting for breakfast to be served, as we waited, the talk centred around the upcoming drill, I was questioned in regard to getting under the eight minutes, and whether that would end the drilling.
I replied with a smile, "I bloody hope to make it so, I'm getting sick of them." And everyone laughed.
After breakfast, I went to get ready for my watch knowing the longboat from shore would reach the ship, just after I started my watch.

As I went on deck, and was getting the report of activities of the previous watch, I noticed my watch hands were taking over from their watch positions, and after the report concluded I said, "Very well number four thank you, go and get something to eat, I have the watch." The previous watch officer left for some breakfast and I noted the changed of watch in the ships log.

Just as I finished writing in the log, I heard "Officer of the watch, longboat approaching starboard." I nodded and replied, "Very well, thank you Dawson," and went to the quarterdeck righthand rail to watch the approach of the longboat carrying the rest of the ships officers. As the captain started climbing up the ships side I turned and yelled, "Action stations, beat to quarter, action stations!" The captain stepped over the rail, saluted the flag, I saluted him, he returned the salute, saying "Carry on number two. Now let's see how much they've improved."

I replied, "Aye Sir," then went below to see how things were faring, as I reached the gundeck I saw a marine knock young midshipman Bryce sprawling, and when Bryce didn't do anything about it, as the soldier was about to pass me, I grabbed him asking "Name soldier?" He was trooper Barret R.E. Letting him continue, I looked at Bryce asking, "Why didn't you reprimand him Mister Bryce?" Bryce told me he didn't wish to interrupt the drill timing, I smiled bitterly, saying "Alright off you go and I'll see you on the poop deck."

After ascertaining all was going well, I returned

to the poop deck,to watch the remaining proceedings.

As all sections called in ready for action, we all stopped our stopwatches, and gathered to confer on our timings. The consensus being that the ship was cleared for action in seven minutes forty-six seconds which everyone beside myself found astounding.

The captain was in raptures, as he called all hands, on deck, and was about to step toward the forward poop rail, I stopped saying, "Sir, before you make the announcement there is a matter that needs resolving, may I suggest a conference of all ship officers including all those here, in your cabin after you announce to the crew the timings."

Looking at me angrily, and inquisitively in manner, he replied "Very well number two, gentlemen make it so." Then he continued to the rail saying, "Very well-done men, I'm highly pleased with your efforts, but we will have at least one more drill before sunset, now as to the time taken, seven minutes forty-six seconds, bloody well done, and for your efforts, quartermaster, an extra tot of rum for everyman, you may return to your duties."

Someone called "Three cheers for the captain!"

After the "Huzzahs," the captain bowed to them in response, as we moved toward the captain's cabin. Spotting Dawson I signed to him where I'd be, and he acknowledged with a nod.

Being last into the cabin all the senior officers were seated each side of the large table, with the captain at the head, one seat was vacant the one next to the captains left, which was mine. The rest of the lower rankings were required to stand, the captain then looked at me angrily asking, "What the bloody hells this all about Robin?"

I remained standing and reported the incident I had witnessed between the trooper and Bryce and the aftermath, then between exclamations of "What!" from the captain and the marine captain, I took my seat at the table. The captain pointed and shouted, "You there call the master at arms! Midshipman Bryce front and centre." As Bryce moved to the bottom end of the table, with his hat under his right arm, and standing at attention, he was questioned by both the marines captain and Cuthbert. At the end of his grilling by both, Cuthbert asked?" Do you know the prescribed penalty for someone striking an officer Mister Bryce?"
Before Bryce could answer, there was a knock at the door, and Cuthbert called "Come," the master at arms stepped in, and told to close the door and wait, then Bryce was told to continue. Bryce said, "Yes Sir, I do, thirty lashes for the miscreant sir, but I don't know what it is for a soldier, and he did only bump me out of the way sir."
The marine captain Stonington interrupted, saying "It's the same, and a bump means he as much as struck you lad, don't forget that." Bryce replied to him, "Yes sir."
Then Cuthbert said "Very well Bryce, any further questions gentlemen?

As he looked around the table, we all shook our heads, alright, you may return to your duties Bryce, and thank you, but the next time something like this happens, deal with it, or at least report it yourself, is that understood?"

Bryce saluted and replied "Aye, Aye Sir," before he left the cabin.

Then Cuthbert looked at each man starting at the table from the lowest ranked senior, to the highest, then to those standing, asking "Well sirs, your opinions?" The consensus of opinion was that the soldier be punished under the prescribed penalty. After that Stonington went with the master at arms to arrest trooper Barret and have him taken on deck for punishment.

The two of them left the cabin, then I was asked about the timings of the drill I had called at midnight, and a general discussion followed about the results then, and this morning's drill, with Cuthbert telling us the next drill would be after lunch and it would be the last one. Then he closed the conference and we all went on deck to wait for the punishment to be meted out to Barret, at the hands of the boatswain, as he was responsible to mete out the punishment floggings.

At this time, I will give you a brief rundown of admiralty rules and punishments in explanation. There were certain crimes aboard ship that were at the captain's discretion, but some crimes were deemed by the admiralty to be major, and there was a schedule of those considered to be major, and the punishment for said crimes. The worst case was being charged with treason or piracy, these carried the death penalty, those charged would have to face a court martial, if a person was found guilty of these by court martial they were to be hanged if the said ship was more than three months from return to home waters, if it was less than that, they would be incarcerated until reaching port and imprisoned while the admiralty reviewed the facts.

Striking an officer, above or below in stature, drew thirty lashes, stealing and drunkenness each drew twenty lashes, being drunk on duty, twenty-five, drunk on duty during wartime, thirty. Those were the significant ones with a prescribed punishment, any other rule breakage requiring punishment was at the captain's discretion, if the captain considered flogging of a miscreant, the number of lashes could not be more than the lowest disciplinary action considered by the admiralty. Which meant a captain could not have a person flogged by more than twenty lashes at any time unless the crime had a prescribed admiralty punishment. The captain could also use lesser punishments, such as loss of rank, forfeiture of pay, rum ration, being incarcerated on bread and water for minor infringements to maintain discipline.

Floggings by a captain was usually used as a last resort to maintain discipline, as the last thing they needed was to be a man down, as said person recovered from a flogging.

The ships doctor would usually keep men recovering from a flogging off duty for up to a week,

dependent on the severity of the flogging.
When a punishment by flogging was to be carried
out, it was done in public, by admiralty rules, all
hands were called on deck to hear the crime and
witness a punishment taking place, so that this in
itself served as a warning to others so inclined. In
other words, a preventative measure to maintain
discipline aboard.

As we all took our places on the poop deck we were
joined again by Stonington, who carried a rolled
scroll listing the crime, and punishment for the
accused, it being his duty to read it out as the
prisoner was a marine under his command, the
captain called for all hands, on deck to witness
punishment. As the crew came on deck they knew to
stay well clear of the area around the prisoner
secured to the rigging, as they had no wish to be
near where the cat of nine tails swung, in case they
were struck as well. The bosun was already standing
behind the prisoner with his shirt off, whipping a
person was hard work, and being bare above the
waist, also kept his shirt clean of flying blood.

When all was ready Marine Captain Stonington
went forward and stood beside the Captain.
He slowly raised his arms and voice as the scroll
rode open, saying "This trooper Barret R.E. has been
found guilty of striking an officer, he knocked
Midshipman Bryce over this morning during the
drill being performed, some of you may have
already seen this done (one could hear the growling

from the crew as Bryce was well liked).

Without further ado his punishment for this offence will be carried out as prescribed by admiralty rules of thirty lashes, bosun if you please!"

Johnson, the bosun had been watching the captain, and as Cuthbert nodded, he did in acknowledgement also, then set himself and the cat for the first lash, it wasn't until the fifteenth or sixteenth strike before the blood started spraying from Barret's back, but after that blood sprayed with every lash. Finally, it was over, and Barret cut down and taken below on a stretcher to the doctor's medical area. The captain released everyone back to their normal duties, while the officers went below, I stayed on the poop and was soon joined by Dawson as our watch continued.

He walked up beside me as I watched the other ships in harbour, he said "A hard business Robin, but he deserved it for knocking young mister Bryce sprawling."

I smiled despite myself, he knew what had happened even if he hadn't seen it, therefore someone of the crew had seen the incident, and it had been passed along through the ships scuttlebutt, it also told me how well young Bryce was thought of amongst the crew, as I replied, "More a grim business Joe, oh, six bells this afternoon by the way Joe."

"Thank yee Robin it'll be passed on, here, is that the Victory arriving into port?"

I looked up, and saw a warship of the line making its way to the harbour mouth, pulled my telescope from its pouch, opened it and trained on the arrival, passed him my scope, and slapped him on the back, saying, "By George you're right Joe, it's the Victory alright. Looks as if we'll be going to sea before the weeks out."

He passed my scope back, and smilingly said, "That be certainty sir," as he had spotted Cuthbert coming up the steps, which was enough to warn me.

Turning my head to Cuthbert, I said "The Victory's just arriving sir."

"By Jove, your right number two," he replied as he came to the rail pulling his telescope open, "Best go inform the others if you will."

"Aye Sir," I replied as I hurried below to inform the other officers, I wasn't gone long, but the poop deck was full of officers by the time I arrived back, most of them using their telescopes. Then we all watched as Victory came into the harbour proper, and found a spot to anchor. Then eight bells rang and we all went below to the wardroom for lunch.

The action stations drill went on at 1500(3pm) that afternoon with the ship cleared for action after seven minutes forty-four and the crew were again rewarded with an extra tot of rum. In the evening we all met the officers of the Victory in the mess, and after a fine dinner quite a lot of drinks were consumed, I was barely able to stand as I made my way to the longboat, out to the ship and to bed.

The next morning there was a conference in the Captain's cabin, and we were told we'd making for sea on Thursday's tide the day after tomorrow, luckily Cuthbert had foreseen this and had despatched the quartermaster to shore after lunch the previous day, to have our victualling list made ready for us today for pickup. This had us all smiling as we knew from experience, that having to get supplies at the last minute was always an uncertain achievement. This way we had guaranteed that we would get everything we had asked for, and wouldn't be going short. I was assigned the task to make sure the quartermaster had all the longboats he required to load our provisions and get them all back to the boat without anything being pilfered. The loading of our supplies took up the rest of the day.

Chapter 12.

The fleet sailing order, and Majestic was the third ship to leave harbour, by this time this time, Admiral Jervis had transferred his flag to Victory, and it now flew proudly from its main mast, along with the fleet, a couple of the sloops were to tow any derelict boats and any that were junk able rubbish cluttering up the harbour. Hearing this bit of news I immediately reported the fact to Cuthbert, and he smiled, he had surmised as I did, that Jervis was going to be using these derelicts for gunnery practise, He said to me, "Well it seems we might be going to get in some gunnery practise, Robin, pass this along to the gunnery officer, I don't want us looking like fools out there, I want perfect hits or as close to as we can get, and make it clear he understands that."

After making the traditional response I smiled and went to find Dawson who not only was my watch subordinate, he was also the ships Master Gunnery Petty officer, telling him what I knew and what the captain wanted he smiled answering, "That should not be a problem Sir, all gun teams aboard are all top hands, and I've trained them myself, the best of the best are up here on the quarterdeck, these boys can sink rafts on clearing shots, let alone the derelicts I've seen floating around this harbour, I'd bet money on it sir."
I smiled saying, "I hope you're right Joe, you could end up doing just that, carry on, and thank you."

On our third day out from harbour, the Med was as calm as a mill pond, but we had a light easterly wind that was blowing us along. Majestic was second in line behind the flagship, and from the flag signals, I knew we would soon be passed by three of the fleet frigates on our starboard side, then my attention was again drawn to signal flags hoisted on the flagship, as I read the flag message the captain also on the poop did the same, the message was for all captains to convene on the flagship. Cuthbert said, "Time to get the longboat in the water number two."

Looking toward the sailing master, I replied "Aye Sir, Dawson make ready the longboat, Jenner, acknowledge the message." They both replied in the usual way and went off to carry out their assigned duties as I watched Dawson and the crew get the longboat ready and manned. As the longboat lowered, I informed the captain, "The longboat is in the water sir."
Looking around Cuthbert dropped his voice, replying "Very well Robin, this shouldn't take too long, I think we're in for some gunnery action, inform George he has the ship."
I replied in the usual way, as he made his way to the main quarterdeck, then called to the closest hand, "You there, ask mister Blagdon to come up on deck." I was given the response, and my messenger rushed off.
Then I was joined once more by Jenner the sailing master, and shortly after by Lt. George Blagdon. Here a quick explanation is required dear family, the

sailing master is a hand that has usually risen through the seamen ranks to petty officer and when at sea he and his men are responsible to watch all flag signals and respond to them immediately, by acknowledging a signal to the ship, and to alert the command structure to the signal.

As to my message to Blagdon, whenever the captain leaves the ship the first mate is then in charge until his return.

The captain returned two hours later, and ordered reduction of sail to steerage only, then ordered an officers conference in his cabin, once everyone had arrived, he said "Gentlemen we've set sail to steerage only, because the admiral wants to reduce the speed of the fleet, giving the tow frigates time to set our targets for tomorrows gunnery practice. As you are all aware, each ship draws from a lottery of numbers, and this time we drew the first ship to show our virtues, with Victory coming up behind us in number two position."

He had a quick drink and continued, "Right George you'll be on the quarterdeck guns as usual, Robin, you have the upper gundeck, Tom as number three you have the main gundeck, and use young Bryce. Number four, Raymond, I'll sail straight towards the targets giving your forecastle guns a chance at them. Then I'll turn to get the broadsides in. Now there will be no waiting for a broadside order, you may fire as your guns bear giving each gun a go at the targets."

He continued after another drink, "Once the broadsides have been delivered, I'll turn us once again, so the rear gunners get a chance as well, any questions?"

I asked, "My number two sir?"

He smiled, saying "Well most of your deck watch are the gunners for the upper deck guns, therefore, petty officer Dawson is your number two Robin. Now Tom, I'm giving you Bryce as your number two, instead of Raymond, because it's about time he learned how to handle gunners in a fight. Any other questions."

There were none, so he continued, "Right now you all know how we are going to go about our business tomorrow, but I've got a little surprise planned for the admiral and Victory tomorrow, as we make our run at the targets, I'll increase sail, so we can move at optimum speed, hopefully the gunners will be able to get the range quickly enough, and with a bit of luck by the time we're finished with the targets there won't be much left for the others following us."

George laughed and said, "That won't make the admiral very happy with you sir, especially if we sink all his targets." Everybody laughed for a little while, then Cuthbert said, "Too jolly bad for him, as you all know I'll be retiring in a year or two, so I really don't care what he thinks of me."

Just then eight bells sounded, and he looked at me and number three Tom Higgins, saying "I believe you two have the watch to change, that's all gentlemen."

We all left his cabin, and Tom and I went to the poop deck and went through the watch change over, and as we were making our way below, I asked Joe Dawson to join me in my cabin. As we got comfortable I poured a couple of glasses of Madeira each, and passed one to him and told him what the conference had been about, omitting Cuthbert's remark about retiring.

After a minute or two, while he had a drink of the wine, he said "Aye Robin, our gunners can certainly hit the mark if the old man is going to do it that way, and firing as we bear tis a good way of doing a lot of damage, and will give time for a couple of shots from each gun, apart from the gunners on the Victory, I know our gunners are the best in the fleet. That's why Jervis used us as his flagship before getting the Victory, and I'll pass the word about going to action stations in the morning while I'm in the mess, we won't slacken our timings Robin, you can be sure of that."
I smiled and thanked him, then we discussed more of the day to day running of the watch while I was absent at the captain's conference.
He didn't have much to report, and after finishing his wine.
He said, "Well I best be getting below, have a good night Robin, and I'll see you in the morning, I'll also gee up the lads about tomorrow, thanks for the wine."
I replied, "The pleasure was mine Joe, see you in the morning and thanks." Then I showed him out.

When the ship is at sea, life onboard starts earlier that in a harbour with shore facilities, and breakfast for all officers in the wardroom was served at 0700(7am) or six bells, My normal day watch started at 0800 that didn't change, except there would be more of the officers up and walking around the ships quarterdeck or the poopdeck, most times after breakfast the captain would be on deck, that day was no exception, During the watch change I had asked if there had been any signals from the flagship, and there had been none.

At1000(10am) or four bells the flagship sent a signal to us saying, we could commence the exercise at our discretion, I immediately called "Action stations, beat to quarter, Action stations!" The ship came alive less than a second after my call, and I automatically set my stopwatch going, the captain came up to me saying, "Alright number two take your station, I have command." As I headed to my station, I heard him yell "Set all sail!"
On the upper gundeck this time all guns were being loaded for real, as Dawson shouted, "Ready for action!"
Going below to the main gundeck, Bryce was smiling, and said "A tenner says we strike first,"
I laughed, and in the excitement replied, "Make it twenty and you're on."
Bryce replied, "Done! It's a wager."
Then Tom Higgins called, "Ship ready for action!"
Going back up to the quarterdeck, I heard George yell, "Ship is cleared for action Sir!"

I again automatically stopped the stopwatch around my neck, the ship was picking up speed as the sails filled with air, and I returned to the upper gundeck. I moved to the most forward gun crews and waited with them. The Captain had stationed non-essential personnel on each gundeck to relay instructions, and we soon heard, "Starboard guns be ready." I got up and returned to the mid deck area and yelled, "Ten pounds if our guns strike hits first!" that way my gunners would share in my wager with Bryce, then I went back to the forward gun crew again.

Then we heard the forecastle guns below us open fire, and knew we were close, and the tension went up a notch among the gun crews. As I watched the target boat show through the gunport, the boom of the gun firing was deafening, then the next fired and the next, as the first crew were reloading and firing again, the smoke and noise was exhilarating! As the guns fell silent, except for the rear guns, as Dawson was telling everyone of our guns struck before any other gun on the ship, we heard the yelled "Port guns Ready!
I was laughing for two reasons, one I had won the wager, and two, I knew that the captain was zigzagging between the targets.
After the port guns fired, it would be the starboard guns again. As the forecastle guns opened up then go silent, I yelled "Get ready fire as you bear," just as I finished the forward gun fired, as did all guns along the deck, after two shots each, the rears started firing.

I yelled "Starboard be ready!" then came the yelled "Starboard guns Ready!" from the stairwell, as the forecastle guns started firing again. As they stopped firing my men knew they were next up, then they started firing in turn, reloading and firing again, as the rears started firing from the stairwell came, "All officers to the poopdeck!"

I literally ran the whole way to the poop, and as I reached the top, Cuthbert was laughing and waved his hand to the rear rail. I bounded to the rail pulling my scope out as I went, it was easy to see the last lot of damage, or should I say it wasn't, we had sunk the target and I could see the frigate crew hurriedly try to undo the tow rope from the rear capstan. Then I had to use my scope further down the rearward track to see what else we had done! The second target was now just an overturned hull, and we had also sunk the first target!

After seeing the result of our gunnery, we were all slapping each other on the backs and laughing loudly, as Cuthbert joined in hugging George, me, and Tom Higgins.

Saying, "Well done boys." Then going back to the forward rail yelled for the ship to come about, and all hands, on deck.

As the ship made its turn back to the way we had come, the hands had assembled, and Cuthbert told them all what a great job they had done, and ordered the quartermaster to issue an extra tot of rum to all gunners. The return to normal duties was called, but before this could be done, all guns had to be unloaded.

We passed in the opposite direction to Victory, as all the guns were cleared, and the walls reinstated on all decks, as we passed by, a message was run up for us, and the sail master passed along the message from the admiral, saying we should have left some targets floating at least, and we started laughing again.

Victory destroyed what was left of the second target, so the frigates were ordered to make up some targets for the rest of the fleet to practise with. During the rest of the day, the ship was back on normal watch, during my watch I was joined by midshipman Bryce and he handed me two ten-pound notes, saying "Remember to tell me not to bet against you again sir, I could lose a bundle doing that." I smiled and took the notes saying, "I shall indeed mister Bryce."

After he had left the poopdeck, I was joined by Dawson, and as he approached, I screwed up one of the notes, and cautiously, so no one could see, placed it in his hand.

Whispering, "Pass that out among the men please Joe." He told me he would make sure of it. At the end of watch, a new signal from the flagship came in, saying that all Captains and 1st mates were ordered to the flagship for a conference and dinner commencing at four bells (1800 or 6pm).

I had the drummer boy take the message to the Captain, and a copy for George, then went through the handover of the watch to Tom Higgins, then I went below to my cabin, poured a wine, sat down and got myself comfortably, then reflected on what the day had brought. Three bells (1730 or 5:30pm) hand rung as I walked into the wardroom all officers not on duty were assembled for pre-dinner drinks. The major topic of conversation being our show of gunnery to the fleet though not a lot of officers were astounded by our feat, they had already seen our gun crews in action.

I was asked why I was still wearing my stopwatch by Raymond Billings, it was only then that I hadn't even remembered I had it on. I looked at it and it was still stopped at the timing of the crew clearing for action, so I told them all the story, then passed it around for them to see the time. The crew had cleared the ship ready for action in seven minutes and eight seconds, needless to say everyone was astounded at the time. A few more drinks were had, then we sat down to a very fine dinner of roast pork and vegetables.

Chapter 13.

For the next week the fleet stayed at sea, and I suppose you could say that the admiral was looking for trouble. He would run half the fleet in close to the coast when we neared any French or Spanish port, hoping to entice some reaction. Near Marbello, a challenge was made, but the ship scuttled back into harbour, once they saw what they were facing. Soon after that the fleet made its way back to Gibraltar where we spent the Christmas and New Year period.

Two days after we made port, HMS Captain and Minerve, along with a small fleet of four ships under the command of Commodore Horatio Nelson had arrived for Christmas. He was on his way to the Italian peninsular, and I was able to meet with my cousin Henry for Christmas, and we enjoyed a family celebration together, he was now higher in rank to me, as he was 1st mate to captain Thomas Hardy and they both moved whenever Nelson changed ships.

Listening to him talk about Nelson, was as if he hero worshipped the man, but after meeting Nelson myself, I must say I changed my opinion, I too became an ardent follower of the man's genius, and his soft-spoken way of explaining things, making the complicated seem simple. Then the visit was over all too soon, but we were now in the same fleet at least, and had become firm friends.

Having received some news about the Spanish, we put to sea again on the twentieth of January 1797, for an infinite duration.

After the signing of the Treaty of San Ildefonso in 1796 allying Spanish and French forces against Great Britain, the British navy blockaded Spain in 1797, impairing communications with its American colonies.

The Spanish declaration of war on Britain and Portugal in October 1796 made our position in the Mediterranean untenable. The combined Franco-Spanish fleet of 38 ships of the line heavily outnumbered the Mediterranean Fleet of 15 ships of the line, forcing us to evacuate our positions in first Corsica and then Elba.

Early in 1797, the Spanish fleet of 27 ships of the line, which were supposed to join the French fleet at Brest lay at Cartagena, on the Mediterranean Sea, with the intention of sailing to Cádiz. Admiral Don José de Córdoba and the Spanish fleet left Cartagena on 1 February and might have reached Cádiz safely but for a fierce Levanter, the easterly wind, blowing between Gibraltar and Cádiz, which blew the Spanish further out into the Atlantic than intended. As the winds died down, the fleet began working its way back to Cádiz.

In the meantime, our fleet under Admiral Jervis, had sailed from Gibraltar with 10 ships of the line to try to intercept the Spanish fleet.

Admiral Don Joseph de Cordova, the Spanish commander, learnt from a passing American vessel that Admiral Sir John Jervis's Fleet, off Cape St

Vincent, comprised only 9 ships. De Cordova, with his 35 ships, including several of the largest battle ships at sea, resolved to take advantage of the enormous disparity, and attack us. However, after the American's sighting 6 further ships joined our fleet.

On 6 February, we were joined off Cape St. Vincent, with a reinforcement of five ships of the line, from the Channel Fleet under Rear-Admiral William Parker.

The knowledge that the Spanish Fleet was at sea, with the likelihood of a fleet action, brought Commodore Horatio Nelson hurrying from Gibraltar in the frigate Minerve to join Jervis.

On the night of 11 February, the HMS Minerve, under the command of Commodore Horatio Nelson, passed through the Spanish fleet, unseen thanks to heavy fog. Nelson reached our fleet off Spain on 13 February, and passed the location of the Spanish to Jervis. Unaware of the size of his opponent's fleet in the fog, Nelson had not been able to count them our fleet immediately sailed to intercept.

Unaware of our presence, the Spanish continued toward Cádiz, and early on the 14th, Jervis learnt that the Spanish fleet was 35 miles to windward. During the night came the sounds that we had been waiting to hear, the signal guns of the Spanish ships in the fog.

At 2:50am came the report that the Spanish fleet was some 15 miles distant. By early morning, at 5:30am, HMS Niger reported them to be closer still.

As the dawn came, it brought a cold and foggy February morning, in the increasing light, Jervis was able to see his fleet around him, formed into two lines of battle. He turned to his officers on the quarter-deck of Victory and said, "A victory to England is very essential at this moment." Jervis gave orders for the fleet to prepare for the coming action.

Captain Thomas Troubridge in Culloden was in the lead. At 6:30am, Culloden signaled that she could see five enemy sail to the south east, and then with Blenheim and Prince George turned toward the Spanish ships.

Jervis had no idea of the size of the fleet he was up against. As they loomed up out of the fog, a signal lieutenant in Barfleur described them as "thumpers, looming like Beachy Head in a fog."

As dawn broke, our ships were in position to engage the Spanish. On the quarterdeck of Victory, Jervis, Captain Robert Calder and Captain Benjamin Hallowell counted the ships.

It was at this point Jervis discovered that we were outnumbered nearly two-to-one:

"There are eight, sail of the line, Sir John."

"Very well, sir," Jervis replied.

"There are twenty, sail of the line, Sir John."

"Very well, sir," Jervis replied.

"There are twenty-five, sail of the line, Sir John."

"Very well, sir," Jervis replied.

"There are twenty-seven, sail of the line, Sir John."

"Enough, sir, no more of that, the die is cast, and if there are fifty sail I will go through them."

Seeing that it would be difficult to disengage, Jervis decided to continue, because the situation would only get worse if the Spanish joined up with the French.

Meanwhile, the Canadian Captain Hallowell became so excited that he thumped the Admiral on the back, "That's right Sir John, and, by God, we'll give them a damn good licking!"

As the light grew, it became obvious that the Spanish ships were formed in two loose columns, one of about 18 ships to windward and the other, of about 9 ships, somewhat closer to us.

At about 10:30am, the Spanish ships in the weather column were seen to wear ship, slow and turn to port. This gave the impression that they might form a line and pass along the fleet, exposing our smaller fleet column to the fire of the larger Spanish division.

At 11:00am, Jervis gave his order: 'Form in a line of battle ahead and astern of Victory as most convenient.'

When this order was completed the fleet had formed a single line of battle, sailing in a southerly direction on a course to pass between the two Spanish columns.

At 11:12am, Jervis made his next signal: 'Engage the enemy.'

Then at 11:30am, 'Admiral intends to pass through enemy lines.

The Battle of Cape St. Vincent had begun:

To our advantage, the Spanish fleet was formed into two groups and unprepared for battle, while we were already in line. Jervis ordered the fleet to pass between the two groups, minimising the fire they could put into him, while letting him fire in both directions.

Culloden tacked to reverse her course and take after the Spanish column. Blenheim and then Prince George did the same in succession. The Spanish lee division now put about to the port tack with the intention of breaking our line at the point where the ships were tacking in succession.

Orion came around, but Colossus was in the course of going about, when her foreyard and foretop yard were shot away. She was forced to wear ship instead of tack and the leading Spanish vessel came close enough to threaten her with a broadside.

Saumarez in Orion saw the danger to his friends and backed his sails to give covering fire.

As Victory came to the tacking point, another attempt was made to break the British line. Victory, however, was too fast and Principe de Asturias had to tack close to Victory and received two raking broadsides as she did so. "We gave them their Valentine in style," later wrote a gunner in Goliath.

As the last ship in our line passed the Spanish, our line had formed a U shape, with Culloden in the lead and on the reverse course but chasing the rear of the

Spanish. At this point the Spanish lee division bore up to try to join their compatriots to windward.

Had they managed to do this, the battle would have ended indecisively, and with the Spanish fleet running for Cádiz. The fleet ships would have been left harrying their sterns in much the manner of the Armada in 1588.

At 13:05, Jervis hoisted a signal: 'Take suitable stations for mutual support and engage the enemy as coming up in succession.'
Nelson had returned to his own ship, the Captain (a seventy-four), and was now towards the rear of our line, much closer to the larger group.

He must have concluded that the manoeuvre could not be completed to allow our ships to catch them. Unless the movements of the Spanish ships could be thwarted, everything so far gained would be lost. Interpreting Jervis' signal loosely, and disobeying previous orders, Nelson gave orders to his Captain Ralph Miller to wear ship and to take Captain out of line while engaging the smaller group.
As soon as the seventy-four was around, Nelson directed her to pass between Diadem and Excellent, and ran across the bows of the Spanish ships forming the central group of the weather division. This group included the Santísima Trinidad, the largest ship afloat at the time and mounting 130 guns, the San José, 112, Salvador del Mundo, 112, San Nicolás, 84, San Ysidro 74 and the Mexicano 112.

Nelson's decision to wear ship was significant. As a junior commander, he was subject to the orders of his Commander in Chief (Admiral Jervis); in taking this action he was acting against the 'form line ahead and astern of Victory' order and using his own wide interpretation of 'take suitable stations' in the later signal. Had the action failed, he would have been subject to court-martial for disobeying orders in the face of the enemy, with subsequent loss of command and disgrace.

At about 13:30 Culloden, was gradually overhauling the Spanish rear, and began a renewed but not very close engagement of the same group of ships. Jervis signaled his rearmost ship, Excellent, to come to the wind on the larboard tack and following this order, Collingwood brought his ship round to a position ahead of Culloden. After a few more minutes, Blenheim and Prince George came up behind, and the group of our ships prevented the Spanish from grouping together.

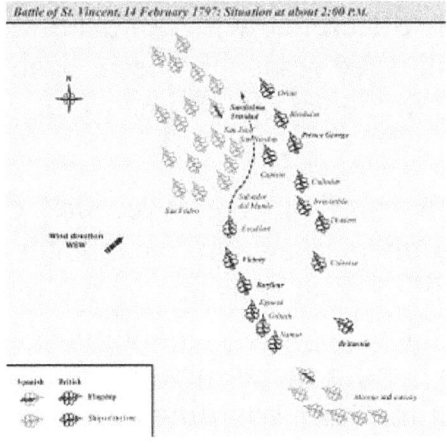

The Captain was now under fire from as many as six Spanish ships, of which three were 112-gun three-deckers, a fourth Córdoba's flagship Santísima Trinidad a 130-gun ship.
At about 1400, Culloden had stretched so far ahead as to cover the 'Captain' from the heavy fire poured into her by the Spanish four-decker and her companions, as they hauled up and brought their broadsides to bear. Of the respite afforded to her, the 'Captain' took immediate advantage, replenishing her lockers with shot and splicing and repairing her running rigging.
At about 1430, Excellent having been directed by signal to bear up, and edged away.

At 14:35 I could no longer watch the proceedings standing beside the captain on the poopdeck, George and I became embroiled in a fierce fight with the Salvador Del Mundo a 130 gun 1st rate. George directing his gunners on the quarterdeck from the poop yelled "Fire!" After a few minutes our guns were making the difference with our accurate firing and targeting, all three masts had been disabled, and Cuthbert turned to me saying, "Time to board them number two."

As I replied with a smile, "Aye, Aye, Sir!" George instructed his gunners to switch to cannister shot in attempting to kill or disable as many men on the deck of the Mundo as possible to aid in my boarding party. Sword in hand, I raced forward along the quarterdeck, yelling for a boarding party, soon I was joined by marines and sailors all armed to the teeth.

As my party got a gangplank rigged, I grabbed a line thrown down from above and with a wave to the topman, grabbed it and swung across to the deck of the Mundo. When I landed, with the grace of a cat, I swung my sword and slashed at the closest person, and continued on the attack, as more enemy raced toward me, I drew one of my pistols, and shot the officer leading the charge, as he went down, I switched pistols to a loaded one, and strode toward the command deck slashing at seamen as I went, a few seconds later, a crowd of my boarding party were fanned out beside me, keeping me in the centre.

The fighting could not be called gentlemanly, it was an ugly knock down, kill or be killed affair, then I was facing the captain in a sword duel, but as I knocked his sword aside and placed the point of my sword at his throat, he let his sword drop and surrendered, I had taken the ship!

Having their colours struck and replaced by one of Majestics pennants, claiming her as our prize, shouts of joy went up from the men aboard Majestic. As the crew was rounded up, I had the anchor laid, leaving the ship in the hands of the senior marine sergeant, and crossed back to my ship, my sword now in its scabbard, my clothing was covered in blood, thankfully, none of it mine, I was carrying the sheathed sword of the Spanish captain.

Chapter 14.

I received 'Huzzahs' from all the officers and crew as I made my way to the captain, and presented him with the sword of the Spanish captain, and was thanked by him as he gave me a hearty well done. Then he turned to the officers and men on the quarterdeck saying, "The battle's not over yet men return to action stations, and let's see if we can pick up another prize!"

I looked at the clock and found it to be 14:55 and realized that the fight on deck of the Mundo had only taken twenty minutes, it had felt like hours. With the ship moving again we took our place in the line, and returned to the fight, while I continued to watch all around to see what was happening, then I spied Nelson in an encounter, and continued to watch his engagement.

By about 15:00, 'Excellent' was already in close action with San Nicolás which, with foretop mast shot away, had been in action against 'Captain'. 'Excellent' fired broadsides into San Nicolás and then made sail to clear ahead.

To avoid 'Excellent', San Nicolás luffed up and ran afoul of San José, which had suffered the loss of mizzen mast and other damage. 'Captain' was by now almost uncontrollable with her wheel shot away.

At this point, her foretop mast fell over the side leaving her in a completely unmanageable state, and with little option but to board the Spanish vessels.

'Captain' opened fire on the Spanish vessels with

her larboard (port) side broadside and then put the helm over and hooked her larboard cat-head, with the starboard quarter of San Nicolás.

Both Spanish vessels were successfully captured. By that time Santísima Trinidad had struck her colours to surrender, Pelayo and San Pablo, separated from de Córdoba's group during action, having been dispatched by the commander the day before, sailed in and bore down on Diadem and Excellent. Pelayo's captain Cayetano Valdés warned Santísima Trinidad to fly her flag again under threat she would be deemed an enemy ship and raked.

The Spanish four-decker raised her flag. She was saved from being captured by the British.

By 16:00, the Spanish ship Santísima Trinidad was relieved by two of her escorts and made away from the scene. Admiral Moreno's squad put together the survivors of Córdoba's group and turned to assist the harassed Spanish sails.

Jervis signalled his fleet to cover the prizes and disabled vessels and at 16:15 the frigates were directed to take the prizes in tow.

At 16:39 the fleet was ordered to take station in line astern of Victory.

The battle was by now almost over with only some remaining skirmishing between Britannia, Orion and the departing Spanish covering Santísima Trinidad.

The captain of San Nicolas was in the act of surrendering to Nelson, after a vigorous struggle, when the crew of San Josef in the towering ship alongside opened fire on the deck.

Calling for reinforcements from 'Captain', Nelson boarded the second Spanish ship and took her, receiving the surrender from the captain.

This manoeuvre was so unusual, and so widely admired in the Royal Navy, that using one enemy ship to cross to another became known facetiously as "Nelson's patent bridge for boarding enemy vessels."

Nelson remained on board the captured Spanish ships while they were made secure and was cheered by the British ships as they passed. He returned to the Captain to thank Captain Miller and presented him with the sword of the captain of the San Nicolás.

At 17:00, Nelson shifted his pennant from the disabled Captain to Irresistible. The Battle of Cape St. Vincent had cost the lives of 73 men of the Royal Navy and wounded a further 227 (this figure only includes serious injuries). Casualties amongst the Spanish ships were far higher, aboard San Nicolás alone 144 were killed.

At 1800, the fleet lay at Lagos Bay, in Portugal, the Spanish prisoners received from the four prizes, numbering about 3000, were landed. The flagship signaled for all Captains, 1st and 2nd mates of all ships to convene aboard the Victory immediately. We had what was a great and welcome victory for the Royal Navy.

15 British ships had defeated a Spanish fleet of 27, and the Spanish ships had a greater number of guns and men.

But, Admiral Jervis had trained a highly disciplined force, and this was pitted against an inexperienced Spanish navy under Don José Córdoba. The Spanish had fought fiercely but without direction.

After the San José was captured it was found that some of her guns still had their tampions in the muzzles. The confusion amongst the Spanish fleet was so great that they were unable to use their guns without causing more damage to their own ships than to ours.
In the battle, Spanish casualties were about 1,000 men killed or wounded.

As we all gathered aboard the flagship, we were met personally by admiral Jervis, who shook our hands. Happily, I met my cousin Henry again, and he was just as bloody as I was, as he stepped aboard as part of Nelsons contingent.
Nelson himself was still black with smoke, with his uniform in shreds, he was wearing a frockcoat, that was too big (probably Henry's). When he was received on the quarterdeck by Jervis, who embraced him, and thanked him for the brilliant exercise of initiative that had led to such a success. When everyone was aboard we were ushered into the conference room by the admiral, and drinks were served to all of us, as Jervis made a toast, "Gentlemen, to victory!"
We all responded to the toast and drank heavily, and had our glasses refilled, as two secretaries sat down each side of the admiral, while we all remained standing. Jervis then said, "Now gentlemen as we go

around the room, your reports will be taken, we'll start with you, Commodore Nelson."

Nelson, said from where he was standing, with Hardy and Henry beside him, "Severely damaged two ships of the line, then took on the San Nicolas and the San Jose, in this action 'Captain' was severely damaged so I boarded the San Nicolas and captured her, then also boarded the San Jose and captured her also, losses to the 'Captain' four dead, and twenty-six wounded, ten of those severely."

Jervis interrupting said, "Yes, once again damned fine work Horatio."

As the reports continued being taken, it was soon our turn, and Cuthbert reported "We met heavy fire from the Salvador Del Mundo, and we engaged for some time, then 2nd lieutenant Fox-Davis took aboard a boarding party and captured the ship relatively intact, casualties to Majestic two slightly wounded in the boarding party."

Captain Troubridge growled "Damn you William, that should have been my prize!"

Cuthbert replied, "I don't see how Thomas, you only fired a couple of salvos and kept going, at least when I engage, I engage fully sir!"

Jervis stopped the argument, saying "Quiet! To claim a prize, you have to capture it though, well done lieutenant Fox-Davis."

I acknowledged by nodding.

When the reporting was finished, another round of drinks was served, Jervis remained seated with the secretaries, as we socialized with each other for awhile, then Jervis rose calling us to order, saying "Gentlemen The heavy damage to our ships and the presence of the unengaged 9 ships of the Spanish van has ruled out any pursuit so we have to be content and satisfied with the capture of 4 Spanish ships, 2 being first rates, it's a pity no other captain here had taken the initiative to capture the badly damaged Santissima Trinidad in the way Nelson had taken the San Nicolas and the San Josef. I'm sorry I can't raise you in rank Horatio, that can only be done by the admiralty, I'm afraid.

But, Cuthbert, for your work in capturing one of the first rates, I'm raising you to the rank of Commodore, Blagdon you are now made Captain, and mister Fox-Davis you are raised to 1st lieutenant, and I'll make damned sure the admiralty ratifies your promotions.

William your first order of business is to continue the blockades, with all the fleet ships still serviceable. While I and Nelson return to England with all the heavily damaged ships and the prizes. Any questions? Good, then let's have a few more drinks, then you're all invited to the wardroom for dinner."

The night was a long one and many of us were well and truly drunk by the time we returned to our ships, Henry and I spent dinner seated together at dinner, and he told me the tale of the fighting while boarding the two ships that were captured by Nelson, we congratulated each other on being alive. My promotion was congratulated, and we talked about our probability of seeing each other more frequently now that we would both be operating in the Mediterranean area.

During the following days, carpentry gangs were kept busy repairing ships, and making them seaworthy. Onboard the Majestic, ships captains came and went after being assigned the ports they'd be blockading over the coming months by the now Commodore Cuthbert.
George had given me a couple of his old spare uniform coats, and I now wear one to replace my blood soaked one that I no longer needed due to my increase in rank. Cuthbert had also done the same for George, and it was decided that the Majestic would make for Gibraltar, where all uniform needs could be looked after.
Tom Higgins had taken my spot as number two, Raymond Billings was now number three, and young Henry Bryce was promoted to lieutenant and made number four.

Several days later, the frigate HMS Terpsichore spotted the damaged Santísima Trinidad making her way back to Spain. The captain, Orozco, now commissioned by de Cordoba, had flown his flag in the frigate Diana. Terpsichore engaged but kept always out of range from the stern guns of the ship anytime Santísima Trinidad bore down on the English frigate. Terpsichore nonetheless was hit twice with those cannons in a sudden move, resulting in damage in her rigging, masts and sails as well as some impacts on her hull.

Captain Richard Bowen then ordered to keep the pursuit, but from a longer distance until the frigate vanished away.

After Bowen had made his report to the admiral, he was ordered to join Cuthbert's command. When all available repairs were carried out, both fleets made their way to the destinations, Admiral Jervis, Commodore Nelson (along with him my cousin), and all the damaged ships, and the captured prize ships were bound for Plymouth, while we made our way south. As we neared the Spanish ports to be blockaded on the Atlantic coast, the assigned ships would say their goodbyes and make toward them and patrol.

When we neared Gibraltar, the ships going with us, Espoir and Transfer, both lower rated fourth and five ships in that order plus two frigates, Eagle and Terpsichore made toward the harbour, while the rest continued their way to their assigned ports.

At that time the full aftermath of the battle of Cape St. Vincent was not known to me, but since then, the facts were made public knowledge, and this seems the best place to let you, that don't know, the full results of the battle.

Nelson was knighted as a member of the Order of the Bath. Nelson's promotion to Rear-Admiral was not a reward for his services, but simply a happy coincidence: promotion to flag rank in the Navy of the time was based on seniority on the Captain's list and not on achievement.

Admiral Jervis was made Baron Jervis of Meaford and Earl St Vincent.

The now Earl St Vincent was granted a pension for life of £3,000 per year.

The City of London presented him with the Freedom of the City in a gold box valued at 100 guineas and awarded both him and Nelson a ceremonial sword. The two swords awarded Jervis and Nelson were the first of their kind to be issued by the City of London.

St Vincent was awarded the thanks of both Houses of Parliament and given a gold medal by the King.

Jervis resumed his blockade of the Spanish fleet in Cadiz. The continuation of the blockade for most of the following three years, largely curtailed the operations of the Spanish fleet until the Peace of Amiens in 1802.

The containment of the Spanish threat, and the further reinforcement of his command, enabled Jervis to send a squadron under Nelson back into the Mediterranean the following year. That squadron, including Saumarez's Orion, Troubridge's Culloden, and the Goliath, now under Foley, re-established British command of the Mediterranean at the Battle of the Nile.

Many of the British severely wounded later died.

Jervis's plan, the forerunner of Nelson's aggressive attack at Trafalgar, was to take his fleet in line ahead through the Spanish formation, cutting the Spanish Fleet in two. The action was a decisive victory.

The Spanish Fleet failed to join the French in Brest in its threat to mainland Britain, remaining bottled up in Cadiz by Jervis's resumed blockade.
The captured Spanish ships were San Josef, Salvador del Mundo, San Nicolas and San Isidoro. All the officers and crew shared in the £140,000 prize money that was listed for the capture of the Salvador del Mundo.
The Spanish flagship Santissima Trinidad and several other Spanish ships were badly damaged. The Spanish admiral was arrested on his arrival at Cadiz, taken under military escort to Madrid, and dismissed by the Spanish navy by King Charles IV. and forbidden from appearing at court.
Several of the Spanish captains were tried by court martial and dismissed or reduced in rank.

The captured Spanish ships were taken into the Royal Navy, keeping, in accordance with tradition in most navies, their original names.

Chapter 15.

As we entered the harbour under steerage sail only, the harbourmaster, alerted to our condition, had boats waiting to take us in tow to the dock for repair. Then the Majestic was left with a skeleton crew, under the orders of the sailing and carpenter petty officers, all officers and crew were then given shore leave.

During the three months it took to complete all repairs, and return the ship to its former glory, the officers lived in the shore quarters pertaining to rank. The Commodore, George, young Bryce and I, all had our uniform needs looked after, and Cuthbert had his new Commodores pennant taken aboard, and flown on Majestic. I purchased a new hat, (mine was somewhere in the Atlantic Ocean), to go with my new topcoat. While there I also purchased a captain's frock coat and hat in the belief that I would someday become a captain before the end of my service.

A post ship had arrived from England, while we were there and along with letters from Elizabeth, there were two from the admiralty, one confirming my promoted to 1st lieutenant, and the second held a cheque and accounting for my share of the prize money for capturing the Mundo. I was astounded by the sum involved, and quickly made sure I deposited the cheque for the thirty-six thousand pounds into my bank account at the Gibraltar branch of the bank.

That evening in the mess, all the officers of Majestic celebrated our windfalls for the capture of Mundo, and many a toast was raised to me in particular. Whist in dock the Majestic had, had her hull scraped and a new sheeting of coppering applied just prior to her release from the dock, and we were towed to our harbour position upon release from the dock, by this time all the crew had been recalled to the ship, I had the watches reinstated, George as Captain, and I as 1st mate, we were now exempt from the watch rota.

The evening of our release from dock, Cuthbert called a meeting of all ships officers of his small fleet, telling us that we would leave harbour the day after next, and to provision for an extended patrol cruise, having already been warned, our supplies had been ordered from the providores that day by the quartermaster, and would be loaded in the morning.

Two days later, our little fleet sailed out of the harbour, making for the furthest Spanish port in the Mediterranean that was being blockaded by us. The plan being to visit each of the blockading mini fleets first in the Mediterranean, then back around to the Atlantic ports, before heading back to Gibraltar. The weather stayed mainly fine while we were in the Mediterranean, and the reports from the blockading ships were, that apart from the odd skirmish as the Spanish ships tried to breakout occasionally, all was going well, and none had escaped any of the ports. As we rounded into the Atlantic however, the weather turned foul, as we were met with blustery conditions and heavy seas. The conditions were so bad, that rope lifelines had to be strung and held onto, when on deck. The blockading fleet reports however, were the same as the fleets in the Mediterranean, but there had been a lot more attempts to break out, and the blockading fleets, were hard pressed at times to prevent a vessel slipping out to sea.

When we returned to Gibraltar, the harbour was a mass of ships of the line! Admiral Jervis had returned while we'd been at sea. After making the ship secure, the longboat was launched, George and I, accompanied Cuthbert to make our report to the admiral.

After arriving at the admiral's headquarters, we were shown into the admiral's office, he came forward to meet us and shook hands with us all, saying "Jolly good to see you all again, come let's sit at the table, and you can tell me what's been going on since we parted at Lagos Bay."

Cuthbert delivered his report, and made several recommendations that Jervis listened to, these being that the number of ships on the Atlanic coast be doubled, and the Mediterranean ships also be reinforced, plus all the blockading ships be relieved as soon as possible, as supplies were starting to run low aboard the ships. Nodding his head, Jervis went to a book on his desk, and brought it and writing essentials back to the table. Along with a letter from the admiralty for Cuthbert, as he put these all down, he handed the letter to Cuthbert, saying,

"William, I hope you forgive me, but I already know what the letter says, after I promoted you to Commodore, two vacancies in the lists occurred, you have been promoted to rear admiral of the blue along with Horatio Nelson, congratulations dear chap." Shaking Cuthbert by the hand, George and I also added our congratulations as well.

Then Jervis, started consulting his book, as he penned orders, and when he had finished, said "Hmm, that leaves me a bit short, but the other ships will be back soon, alright. (raising his voice yelled) Franklin!" A young lieutenant entered at his shout, and Jervis handed him all the penned documents, saying "Have these orders carried out immediately." The lieutenant replied, "Aye Sir," and left the room. Then Jervis said, "Now gentlemen, we have other grave things to discuss. There have recently begun rumblings of malcontent and mutiny amongst crews on ships of the line at home, and I don't wish it to spread here, therefore, I am engaged in drawing up certain reforms that I intend putting into practise in our fleet. They may seem a little heavy handed at first, but trust me, they will be for the betterment of all involved, officers, marines and seamen alike. Now before I let you go, is there any further business we need to discuss?"

Cuthbert looked thoughtful, and had been perusing his letter of promotion for some time spoke, saying "Yes Sir, as almost everyone knows, for some time now I've been contemplating my retirement, my, appointment to rear admiral was made longer than three months ago, therefore, it can't be rescinded, with this I can retire with enough money to last. Therefore sir, I wish to tender and announce my retirement from the service, and hope I can return home to England on the next post ship."

His announcement shocked us all, and we all started speaking at once, but Cuthbert put his hand up to silence us, saying "Nay I shall not be dissuaded, I leave the Majestic in the best of hands, and have done my duty to you sir taking control of the fleet while you were absent, truth be told gentlemen, I find myself getting too old for life at sea, John, please accept my apologies for springing this on you, but my mind is made up, nothing any of you say can change my mind, I've had a good run gentlemen, and now wish to spend what remains of my life with my family."

Jervis nodded, and looking sad, replied "Very well William, I will accept your decision, and you will be sorely missed." With that we stood, and Jervis embraced Cuthbert, saying "Good luck old friend." Then they each took a step back and saluted each other.

After that we left the headquarters building without saying a word, but made our thoughts known outside.

On our way back to the ship, Cuthbert told us that he would be packing his possessions when we got back, and moving to quarters on shore, therefore, George could move into his cabin after he left the ship that afternoon, which also meant I would move into George's cabin.

That afternoon, there was an emotional farewell for the Rear Admiral, from not only the officers, but by the whole crew, Cuthbert had been well liked and respected, and after his possessions were in the longboat, it took over half an hour for him to be able to leave the ship to a chorus of ongoing 'Huzzahs' as his longboat made its way from the Majestic.

During 1797 there was considerable discontent among the seamen of the Royal Navy. This discontent manifested itself at the Nore and at Spithead when the greater part of the Channel Fleet rose up against their officers. These mutinies were not overly violent, and the officers were put ashore and the heads of the mutinies established their own order and kept the ships under "committee" control until their collective demands were met. The mutineer's demands, ranged from discontent at cruel officers, to poor pay and long sea service without shore leave. There were other mutinies throughout the Navy that year, most notably HMS Hermione and HMS Marie Antoinette both on the Jamaica station. These mutinies resulted in the crews killing their officers and taking their ships into enemy held ports.

Jervis had the reputation as a disciplinarian and put in place the new system that would ensure that the men in the Mediterranean fleet did not mutiny. To begin with the admiral wrote a new set of standing orders. For example, Jervis divided the seamen and marines, then berthed the two separately, putting the marines between the officers aft and the men forward. Thus, he created an effective barrier between officers and potentially unruly crews. Jervis discouraged conversation in Irish though he did not ban it. He ordered the marine detachments to be paraded every morning and, if there was a band available, for "God Save the King" to be played. The marine detachment was then to remain armed always.

To keep his crews active and to ensure that the Spanish did not perceive that there might be discontent in the fleet, Jervis ordered the nightly bombardment of Cadiz in his own words to "Divert the animal."

The Admiral isolated the ships from one another to minimise collusion and the opportunities the men might have to band together in mutiny. St Vincent did ensure, however, that the men under his command were cared for.

When the stock of tobacco ran low the Admiral ensured that the supply was renewed from his own funds.

When the postmaster in Lisbon detained the letters and packets arriving from England for the men from fear that they would carry seditious communiques, Jervis set up a post office aboard his flagship, HMS Ville de Paris, to receive and distribute all the letters that arrived for both seamen, marines and officers. Jervis strictly adhered to the Articles of War and individual regulations that he had written for his fleet. Any infraction was dealt with harshly and he was renowned for treating both officers, and seamen with the same harsh discipline. As an example, one officer who allowed his boats crew to plunder a fishing boat was placed before a court martial and it was ordered that he be "degraded from the rank of Midshipman in the most ignominious manner by having his uniform stripped from his back on the quarter deck of the ship before the whole ship's company and to be further disposed of as the Commander-in-chief shall direct. To be mulcted of his pay now due to him for his services on board any ship of his Majesty's service and to be rendered incapable of ever serving as an Officer or a Petty Officer in any of His Majesty's ships."

Jervis later personally directed that the midshipman should have his head shaved, a notice hung around his neck describing his crime and that he should be solely responsible for the cleaning of the head (naval term for the communal toilets situated at the bow of the ship) until further notice.

In another incident, St Vincent instructed that two men aboard HMS St George who were tried for mutiny on a Saturday, were executed on Sunday.

The men were duly executed but Admiral Charles Thompson raised an objection to formal executions on the Sabbath and Jervis wrote to the Board of Admiralty demanding Thompson's removal, or that they accept his own resignation. The Board relieved Thompson. On 9 July 1797 Nelson wrote to Jervis congratulating him in his resolve, wholeheartedly supporting his decision to execute the men on a Sunday.

Jervis could also be exceptionally kind when he felt that the situation warranted it. On one occasion, while the fleet was becalmed the men of the flagship were ordered to bathe. The men leapt over the side to swim in a sail that had been lowered over the side. One of the men, a senior able seaman, jumped in wearing his trousers. In one of the pockets he had his prize money and back pay that he had been saving for several years.

The bank notes were destroyed by the water and when the man came aboard and discovered what had happened he began to weep. The Admiral saw the man and asked the problem. One of his officers told him, and St Vincent went to his cabin. When he returned he had the crew mustered and called the man forward. "Roger Odell, you are convicted, Sir, by your own appearance of tarnishing the British oak with tears. What have you to say in your defence why you should not receive what you deserve?" The man told him what had happened, and St Vincent replied, "Roger Odell you are one of the best men on this ship. You are moreover a captain of a top and in my life, I never saw a man behave himself better in battle than you did in the Victory in the action with the Spanish fleet.

To show therefore that your Commander-in-chief will never pass over merit wheresoever he may find it. There is your money Sir!" The Earl produced £70 of his own money and presented it to the surprised sailor "but no more tears mind, no more tears Sir".

When Nelson returned to the Mediterranean, St Vincent wrote to Earl Spencer, First Lord of the Admiralty: "I do assure your Lordship that the arrival of Admiral Nelson has given me new life, you could not have gratified me more than in sending him. His presence in the Mediterranean is so very essential." St Vincent detached Nelson to pursue Napoleon in his invasion of Egypt Rear-Admiral Sir John Orde who was senior to Nelson complained publicly and bitterly about what he considered a personal slight.

Jervis ordered Orde home. Orde requested that he be court-martialled in order that he might have the opportunity to clear his name. The Board refused. Orde then requested that St Vincent be brought before a court-martial. Again, the Board refused. The Board censured Jervis for not having supported his subordinates. Orde later challenged the ageing admiral to a duel. The challenge became public knowledge and the king ordered Jervis to decline.

When the men aboard the Marlborough refused to execute a man for mutinous behaviour and their captain did nothing, the Earl threatened the captain with replacement and had boats from the rest of the fleet armed with carronades surround the Marlborough, he then threatened to sink the ship if his orders were not carried out. The man was duly executed. St Vincent turned to an officer beside him watching the mutineer hanging from the yard arm saying, "Discipline is preserved, Sir!"

Between 1797 and 1799 alongside the suppression of mutiny Jervis set himself the task of improving the dockyards and defences of Gibraltar including building a new Victualling Yard and Water Tanks to replenish his ships. After the Battle of the Nile the dockyards, under Jervis' watchful eye, managed to successfully repair most of the fleet. Lady Lavinia Bingham, wife of Earl Spencer wrote to St Vincent to congratulate him for having provided the necessary tools for Nelson to have achieved the victory he did at the Nile.

"Never did disinterested zeal and friendship meet with a brighter reward than yours has reaped in this victory of your gallant friend."

Nelson commented that he had "never beheld a fleet equal to Sir John Jervis."

Having had great difficulty supplying the fleet with fresh water the Admiral arranged for large tanks to be built in Gibraltar.

On 14 February 1799 St Vincent was created admiral of the white.

Constant service and approaching old age meant that the admiral became increasingly unwell. Despite his failing health, St Vincent was reluctant to relinquish command and the Board reluctant to supersede him.

By 17 June 1799 he had no choice but to resign his command and return to England.

As his health had improved he was given command of the Channel Fleet. St Vincent was to comment

"The King and the government require it and the discipline of the British Navy demands it. It is of no consequence to me whether I die afloat or ashore. The die is cast."

Chapter 16.

June 12, 1794: I have been aboard the HMS Avanti, since leaving Plymouth on the night tide of the tenth.

I had arrived at the Plymouth navy docks on the afternoon of the ninth, after dismissing the carriage men to return home at their leisure, I took my portmanteaux and holdall aboard the Avanti, and was greeted by the officer of the watch, who escorted me to the captain's cabin. Entering the captain's cabin, I saluted Captain John Conn, and passed across my orders.

He sat down at his desk, saying "Ah yes, mister Tolcher, I was told you would be coming with us, and have a cabin ready for you. Let me explain what we are doing while at sea, we will be heading first for the channel fleet ships, then making our way to Gibraltar, before that we will visit each ship in the Mediterranean fleet north of Gibraltar, after leaving port in Gibraltar, we will round into the Mediterranean Sea proper, moving towards your ship. We should reach your ship by early August, dependent on winds of course.

Now Henry even though, you are technically an officer, you carry a midshipman's rating at present therefore, I'm afraid you will have to eat in the midshipman's mess, you are a passenger only this trip, and will not have any duties, you have the run of the ship while we are at sea, but please don't get in the way when we deliver our cargo to line ships. Any Questions?"

"Yes Sir," I replied, "May I ask when we leave tomorrow, as I would like to visit the bank ashore beforehand."

He laughed and smilingly replied, "You'll have all day tomorrow, we don't slip until the evening tide, Oh, whilst aboard ship, wear your uniform and weapons if you are on deck. That's all."

"Aye sir," I replied and left the cabin. Waiting for me was the purser, with my belongings, and he said, I'll show you to your cabin sir and also the way to your mess, them being on different decks and all."

I was shown to my cabin, and left my gear there, as the purser showing me the way to the mess told me that my cabin was a spare lieutenants cabin. I had memorized the way to the midshipman's mess on the way down, and gave the purser my thanks, and allowed him to go about his duties topside.

Back in my cabin, I went about unpacking what I would require for daily use aboard ship, and making myself comfortable. The cabin was furnished with a single bed, desk and writing chair, a smallish single seat lounge chair, and a bolted down wardrobe with a set of drawers one side and a hanging rail that went across the whole wardrobe. The bed and desk were set against the rear wall that had windows facing to the back of the ship.

I hung up my two lieutenants' uniform, which were on wooden bar hangers, the blue uniform breeches folded across the bar and my white waistcoats hanging inside of the blue frockcoats, the only difference to my present uniform frockcoat being, that my present frockcoat had a white-collar patch, and gold navy buttons. I hung my spare midshipmen's' uniform up as well, it being hung the same as my others my third hanger had my neckerchiefs draped across the hanger bar, then I hung my shirts up, and put my footwear into the bottom of the wardrobe with my holdall, after I had taken out my older work shirts, and placed in a drawer. My weapons belt was hung on a hook, inside the cabin door.

After getting myself settled and ship shape, I sat and opened my billfold, taking out all the different denomination pound notes my receipts for things bought and my accounting notes.

First, I checked to see if all my receipts had been entered on my accounting slip, they were, so I placed them into one of the side pockets of the portmanteaux, that was still open on the bed. Secondly, I counted all the cash that I had and compared the amount to my accounting sheet, and they both tallied. I thought for a while and decided to keep fifty pounds on my person, and bank the rest.

After all the money I'd been paid since going to uncle Williams' and all the money I had spent on my tuition, my personal and uniform items, Joanna's' dresses, and her engagement ring, I had one thousand two hundred, and ninety-five pounds left, a princely sum by any means. I reversed my original decision, and now decided to keep only forty-five pounds on my person and bank the one thousand, two hundred and fifty.

I then folded the notes over, and placed a small ribbon around the amount tying it securely, the other two twenties and the fiver I placed into my billfold Which went back into my inside jacket pocket, the folded amount, I placed into my breeches pocket until I went to the bank the following day. Then closed my portmanteaux, and placed it into the wardrobe, and shut it, turning the key in the lock.

That evening I met my fellow midshipmen in the cockpit (which is what the midshipmen's mess was called), there were only two of them, Peter and Mathew, from them over drinks and dinner I learned more about our captain and officers, I was also told that we were expected by the captain to wear our weapons everywhere on ship, due to the captain considering that a fair few of the crew were mutinous dogs. Apparently, Conn and a number of the junior rank officers were harsh task masters, Peter was able to back these claims showing me the whip marks on his back, he had been flogged for being late to his watch, though he had been held up getting to it, by the captain.
Later that night, as I lay on my bunk, I thought over what I had learned so far, and fervently hoped that that ship I was to join, was not like that, I couldn't for the life of me, approve of punishing a person unnecessarily.

The following morning, only Mathew was having breakfast, as Peter was sleeping after being officer of the watch on the early dog watch (4am to 8).

I had taken their warning to heart the previous night, and I hung up my gun belt on one of the inside door hooks, before sitting down with him.

After breakfast, I returned to my cabin and dressed in full uniform, went topside (The main deck), there I approached the officer of the watch, and logged myself off the ship, and asked him directions to the bank. Thanking him, I saluted him, then the flag as I made my way to the dockside across the gangplank.

Following his directions, I found the bank easily enough, but looking at my watch, I still had half an hour before they opened. Going to a nearby café and bakery, I ordered a mug of coffee and a jam tart, paying for them with the fiver. After being asked if I had anything smaller, I produced a ten pence piece, and was given eightpence change. Then I took my mug and tart, to a table beside the windows to await the opening of the bank.

The bank opened on time, and I made my way across to it. I opened my account given a receipt for my one thousand two hundred and fifty, and then had them change my twenties into two tenners and three fivers, four one-pound notes, and a pound of loose change.

After that was done, I left the naval station, going for a walk around Plymouth itself, then made my way back to the naval station, and back aboard ship, logging back aboard with the same officer of the watch I had encountered the day before. I noticed the activity aboard had heightened as last-minute loading, was being carried out.

That night, after dinner, and drinks I went topside as the ship was due to make to sea, on the top of the tide, which I calculated was near. At twenty hundred hours the mooring lines were slipped, and the Avanti moved away from the dock, and out to sea, I only went below to my cabin after we had entered the English Channel proper, and made the turn toward the French Coast.

August 3, 1794: Marseille, I have been aboard the HMS Meleager for four days now, after I was transferred aboard from the Avanti, this was done by use of a railed gangplank from deck to deck, the gangplank was at such an upward acute angle it was hard to climb up to the deck of the Meleager, without using the rope hand rails. I reported aboard after saluting first the flag, and then the officer of the watch, who welcomed me aboard, introducing himself as 2nd lieutenant Thomas Hardy, he then took me to my cabin where I stowed my gear, then took me to the captain to report.

Hardy was a round faced fellow with blonde hair, that stood about the same height as I did, and usually had a smile on his face.

He knocked on the captain's door, and on the command "Come," from inside he opened the door and we both went inside, he closed the door.

Captain George Cockburn stood about an inch taller than us, and had wavy pepper and salt coloured hair, after reading my orders, he welcomed me aboard, saying, "Welcome aboard Henry, you'll be the only midshipman on board, as our last one was killed."

He took a drink, before continuing, "Poor lad caught
a musket ball in the head last week, seeing you're
the only one aboard you may as well mess in the
officer's wardroom, and by the look of you, I'll be
promoting you to officer soon enough, I take it
you've passed your exams?"
"Aye Sir, I have," I replied.
"Good, good, Hardy here can fill you in on our
details, that's all for now, I'll see you at lunch," he
replied.
As we left him, Hardy suggested we go up to the
poopdeck, and he'd run over the ships situation with
me. He was a friendly chap, and always used
Christian names, even in front of the crew and other
officers, upon us discovering through talking about
his and my families, we were distantly related
through marriage, as one of his relations had married
a Fox-Tolcher. After that we became firm friends.
The ship's situation was such: It was part of a three-
squadron fleet blockading the port of Marseille, due
to the port being larger, it was constantly in action
trying to prevent the French and Spanish ships from
breaking out of port, and it saw a lot of action. My
watch would be as officer of the watch for the dog
watches (1600-1800 and 1830-2200), which meant I
had half an hour to eat during the watch. Because we
were in a constant state of war, we would be fully
armed whilst standing the watches.
At lunch that day in the wardroom, I met all the
other ships officers, and surprisingly enough, no one
complained about a midshipman joining the
officer's wardroom, according to Hardy, the captain

allowed this frequently if there was only one midshipman aboard, apparently, he didn't like the idea of someone eating alone. Speaking for myself, I liked his idea, but was unsure how this would go down if discovered by the admiralty.

August 16, 1794: Ha ha! Ten days after joining the ship, I saw my first action, and it all started during my watch. Nearing the end of my watch, I noticed a ship nearing the harbour mouth, inspecting it through my telescope, I was able to make out it was a Spanish ship of the line equal to a third rate in our navy, which meant she outgunned us. What drew my initial sight to it was the way it was constantly opening and closing her topsails, which to my now trained eye that is was definitely acting suspicious, as it passed a break in the breaking wall, I caught a glimpse of its name, which was Conquistadora. All that I had observed was written into the log.
As I handed over the watch to the fourth officer, James Upshot, I mentioned that he keeps an eye on it, saying, "I'd keep an eye on them Jimmy, I think they may be getting ready to make a run for it."
He smiled replying, "I'll do just that Henry, thanks, see you in the morning, if not before, goodnight."
At 0530, next morning I was awoken by the call to action stations, hastily dressing I grabbed my belt, and was fastening it on as I ran up the stairs to the deck.
Instantly taking the situation in, I saw the captain, on the poop with Jimmy Upshot, as they were joined by Hardy, looking forward I saw we were closing on

the Spanish ship that was off our portside (left), then I heard the captain yell, "Fire as you bear!" Then our port guns started to fire just before the Spanish fired a broadside, only one of their shots hit us, taking away the port forward railing. As we closed, our marines that were in the rigging started to fire their muskets, raking the deck of the Spanish ship.

Then I heard Hardy yell, "Grapples!" Knowing what would come next, I raced to about midships, and just as I was about to step up on the railing, called, "Boarding party to me!"

Leaping onto the railing, I bounded across to the deck of the Spanish ship with my sword out, I was confronted by two sailors with pistols, instantly drawing my right pistol, I shot the man then bounded forward lifting my sword, and slashed at the other, as he went down, I scooped up his pistol in my left hand, moving backward toward the command station without looking behind, then I was confronted by numerous Spanish, but I continued forward and engaged them, then help for me arrived. Many of our sailors and some marines swung into the group from Meleager, taking advantage of the respite, I looked left and right to find only ten men with me, and thanked god for the intervening boarding party, quickly we joined forces, continuously moving toward the command station.

I had fired both my pistols, and grabbed an unused belaying pin from its place, using it as a club and sword, then I was through the melee, and stood confronting the Spanish captain and 1st mate both had swords out and pointing in my direction, I brought the belaying pin up and threw it like a knife from my left-hand, it struck the 1st mate in the centre of his head, as he went down unconscious, I then confronted the captain, who immediately surrendered to me by dropping his sword. The ship was taken, and its colours struck, and replaced by the union jack. More members of Meleager swarmed aboard under the direction of our 3rd mate, I was ordered to return to Meleager, and report to the captain.

As I slowly left the Conquistadora, with the Spanish captain's scabbarded sword I looked at the time, it was only 0640. Reporting to the captain on the poopdeck of Meleager, I said, "The ship is ours Captain!"

Captain Cockburn replied, "Right very well done, mister Tolcher, come." As he moved me to the rear rail he faced me and dropped his voice asking, "Why in heavens name did you leave the ship without checking if there were hands to back you up, as it was, you and the ten men that followed you, could have been slaughtered for Christs sake?"

Clearly having been admonished, I didn't look for an excuse, instead I replied, "Well having been woken early, I decided that nothing builds an appetite like a good scrap, sir."

His head went back, and he started to roar with laughter.

Chapter 17.

During breakfast, I was congratulated on the taking of what now, became a prize ship. The captain, said to us all, "I've been thinking this over, and later we'll move in closer to the harbour, get their attention with a blank broadside salvo, and run up a flag of truce. We have sailors languishing in their goals, and I will propose a prisoner exchange, how many of the ship's crew do we have left alive, excluding the captain, number three?"

Martin Stroud, the 3rd mate, replied five hundred and three including seamen, boys and officers excluding the captain, sir."

Cockburn replied, "Very good Martin, at least this young hellion left some alive," he had looked at me, and everyone laughed. Then he continued, "Give me a proper accounting of ranks on paper later, now if the prisoner exchange happens, we'll fill all three of our ships with what personnel we've lost, and the rest can man the Conquistadora as a prize crew, and sail her to Gibraltar, with you as master and commander Martin. Mister Hardy, you are promoted to 1st lieutenant and mate, unfortunately Mister Grouse died earlier from his wounds, and you, young Henry, are promoted to 2nd lieutenant and mate for your heroism, and letting us all share in the prize money due to the ships capture. Martin, I will give you a letter to admiral Jervis and the admiralty to ratify these promotions I have just made. After breakfast number one, let's see what we can do to make the prisoner exchange work!"

During and after breakfast, my thoughts were in chaos, *bloody hell! Did he just make me a 2ⁿᵈ lieutenant! Shite, over the top of Jimmy Upshot too! I wonder what he thinks of that, I'll bet he's not happy about that, great. Let's take the time to work this out, aboard the Meleager only ten days, captured a third rate, been made a 2ⁿᵈ lieutenant, over another, who now probably considers me an enemy, all in only those ten, no eleven days, and I stand to make a lot of money from the capture, well Henry you certainly have come a long way!*

Later during the day, Thomas and I changed our cabins, as the truce became a day's ceasefire, as the prisoner exchange went ahead, and the Spanish captain transferred to a cell in our brig (jail). Hardy's old cabin was much larger than my old one, and was on the main gundeck, it faced the same way, but the furnishings had a larger bed, and two comfort lounge chairs, it also had two cannons and gunports. The wall and door were demountable, and the wardrobe was much closer to the door, giving gun crews plenty of space for action.

I have removed my white-collar patches from my two midshipman frockcoats, thus turning them into a lieutenants' uniform frockcoat. I had inspected the sword I had won, to find it made of fine Toledo steel, it was perfectly balanced, the hilt was made of gold, and had a fine gold filigreed hand guard, I have since had its scabbard attached to behind my telescope case on my weapons belt, by the sailmaker, and I now have the increased my fighting capability by adding another sword to the belt. After making my new cabin ship shape, I went topside to the upper gundeck, it was now my watch, as 2nd mate, I was responsible for the day watch aboard ship.

Thomas beckoned me to the poopdeck, and I was told that the first boatload of English prisoners was approaching the Conquistadora. He told me the arrangement was once they were safely aboard, the same number of Spanish would be released. He smiled at me saying, "Also, when the exchange was confirmed, the captain immediately sent for Upshot and promoted him to 3rd mate, and lieutenant to take Stroud's place, so don't go feeling too bad about jumping the ranks now.

The first load to be exchanged are supposed to be officers and midshipmen, the captain's clerk is aboard the Conquistadora now and will fill our vacancies first, before the other two in the squadron have their turn, the captains are meeting now."

I nodded replying, "Thanks for letting me know about Upshot, it's a bit of a relief, I thought for sure I had made an enemy."

He laughed, saying, "No need to worry about it, he knows you to be the better man and is pleased about yours and his promotions."

Just then, I heard the call, "Officer of the watch!" excusing myself, I made for the upper gundeck where there were a group of men standing by the gangplank on our deck.

Upon my query one officer, and three boys about my age, stepped forward, the officer was dressed in

A ragged frockcoat, as were the boys, the officer said saluting, "4th mate and lieutenant Cuthbert Knowles sir," I returned his salute, and he continued, "The midshipmen and I have volunteered to join your crew sir."

I introduced myself, and yelled for the purser, who joined us quickly, as I ordered, "4th Lt Knowles and these midshipmen have volunteered to join our crew, please show them to quarters and see if you can replace their rags."

The purser replied, saying, "Yes sir, if you'll follow me gentlemen."

As they moved off, Hardy joined me, as I addressed the other officers saying, "Now gentlemen, what can we do for you?"

One of them stepped forward saluting and saying, "2nd lieutenant Harris sir, your clerk asked us to come aboard to be introduced to the captains aboard."

Hardy moved forward saying, "Then you'd best follow me gentlemen, and I'll take you to the captain's cabin, I'm 1st lieutenant Hardy."

They all saluted, and Hardy led them off toward the entrance to the captain's cabin.

The prisoner exchange went on throughout the day, and I had sent for the gunner who was my watch second in charge, bosun, carpenter, armourer, caulker, master at arms, and sailmaker, to sort out the able seamen and seamen into where in the crew they would be going. Having done that, it was almost time for lunch. After telling Jackson the petty officer guns, where I would be, in the wardroom.

I entered the wardroom, and it was full, as I divested myself of my weapons belt, I was handed a drink, as the captain said, "Ah, here he is now, gentlemen a toast, to Lt. Tolcher, the man that has made all this possible."

After the toast, I was introduced to those I didn't know by Hardy, then we all took our seats at the table which had been expanded and more chairs brought in.

As my watch was ending, the prisoner exchange was still going on, and Jimmy Upshot came to take over the watch, he was smiling and personally gave me his congratulations on the promotion, as I did the same to him. Then I had told him what had been arranged with the petty officers, and signed off watch in the log.

At 1400, the other two captains left, the Meleager in longboats, along with the new officers going with them. The captains clerk, already had a list of the seamen they required.

That night at dinner, the captain told us, that the following day Martin Stroud would leave with the prize ship, he had two junior officers, a midshipman, and a prize crew made up out of the prisoners, as he left, he would go to the HMS Amphitrite first and drop off her consignment of seamen and pickup any despatches for Gibraltar or further, then he would proceed to the HMS Blanche doing the same, before making for Gibraltar. Cockburn announced this so that if any of us had mail we wished sent, everything could go together with his dispatches.

August 18, 1794: During my watch, a fleet of six ships was sighted during my watch, and they were bearing in our direction. After they came closer, I was able to see they were flying the union jack, they were ours! Watching the lead ship, I saw her preparing to launch a longboat, which pulled away from the ship, as they rowed toward us, with an officer onboard.

I had the captain summoned, and as the longboat was secured to the Meleager, he and Hardy joined me at the rail, to greet the captain from the longboat. Once on the deck, he saluted the flag then us, we returned his salute, and the captain led him toward his cabin. Hardy stayed on deck with me, as we watched the squadron circle back toward us.

One hour later, signals had been sent to our other two ships, we were to make for Gibraltar, as we had been relieved, while newer squadron took up our blockade. After saying farewell, to our relieving captain, Cockburn ordered all sails set, and soon we were pulling away with our course set towards Gibraltar. After arriving in port in the early afternoon of our fourth day at sea, whilst I saw to setting our anchoring, and having the longboat launched, for the captain to go ashore and report to Admiral Jervis, Hardy had been searching for sign of the Conquistadora. Once the captain had left the ship, he remarked that she wasn't anywhere in port, and we wondered if she had either run afoul of other Spanish or French ships, or had she been sent onward toward England, by Jervis.

Surmising that we'd find out either way when Cockburn returned, he went to his cabin, while I continued my watch.

As I was handing over my watch to Upshot, the captain arrived back aboard, and upon seeing me, said, "Henry, can you get mister Hardy and the both of you join me in my cabin please."

I replied, "Aye sir," and went off to get Thomas. Having been given the 'come' command as Hardy knocked on the captains' door, we both entered removing our weapon belts, hanging them up on the door hooks, and seated ourselves before the captain as directed.

As we sat, he said, "Good news gentlemen, the admiral sent young Stroud on toward England, after he was reprovisioned, so hopefully our prize money will come sooner than expected. Also, your promotions have been ratified, here are your admiralty confirmations. Now at dinner I intend to announce that the whole ship's compliment, has been granted three weeks shore leave. However, I have been given command of the newest fifth rate, the HMS Minerva, and you two, are coming with me! So, pack your possessions before tomorrow morning, we'll move aboard her before we commence our shore leave."

August 24, 1794: In the company of Captain Cockburn, and Tom Hardy, we were rowed to the Minerve, when we got there, the captain presented our orders to the officer of the watch, Petty Officer Guns, George Michaels, and we moved into our new cabins, and after settling in, I put some of my clothes into my holdall, along with this journal, I was then ready to join the captain and Hardy, as we were rowed ashore to begin our leave.

November 12, 1794: There has not been too much for me to comment on, of late, but will update this journal where I left off.

After finishing our shore leave, we returned to the Minerve, and during a captain's conference with all Officers, and Petty Officers, the captain was appraised that the crew of the Minerve, mainly a new crew, with only a limited number of seasoned able seamen aboard, only the petty officers, and their subordinates were veteran sailors, and out of the officers and midshipmen the captain, Hardy, and myself were the only ones with sea going and battle experience, even though mine was only over the last few months aboard the Meleager.

Cockburn was furious, and instituted a series of drills to be practised day and night, saying, "By god if they don't perform to standard, we'll have to whip them into shape! All of you from now on will wear stopwatches, and time all drills, gentlemen we will drill and drill, and drill some more until this ships' crew come up to standard, and can exercise these drills with their eyes closed! That goes for officers and men, anyone who can't perform their duty, will be demoted and flogged, is that understood?"

The entire compliment answered, "Aye aye sir!" in chorus.

"Right," said Cockburn, "Assemble the crew on the

upper gundeck, so I can address them all, get to it!"
With that the conference broke up, and left the
wardroom, Cockburn turned to me and Tom, saying
as he raised his eyes and shook his head, "Well, a lot
of this is going to fall on your shoulders you two, so
I expect you to work hard with these men, and
hopefully it will pay off in the long run. Alright let's
head to the poopdeck," I opened the door letting
Cockburn and Hardy past, then closed the door and
followed them.

For three months the drilling had been going on, day
and night, and I must admit, I was starting to feel
drained. My style of dress had changed to the now
local tradition of not wearing a neckerchief, and
leaving my shirts unbuttoned at the top, this allowed
air to circulate around ones' neck and throat,
keeping me cooler, in the warm temperatures.

All the drilling, had brought dividends, or perhaps it
was due to an incident where the bosun, was found
to be unfit for his duty.

His punishment for this breech had already been
stated by the captain, in front of the crew, he was
restrained and stripped of his rank, his position
passing to his immediate subordinate. The entire
crew having been called on deck to witness his
punishment. He was then made to kiss the gunners'
wife (held down along one of the cannon and tied
into place), his shirt torn open, as he received ten
lashes. Though I didn't like the idea, it had the
desired effect, the crew could now complete all
operations required for a ship of the line crew, in
record times.

After everything was going well with the drilling, petty officer Michaels my watch subordinate, came to me on the poopdeck during our watch, and I asked, seeing the concern on his face, "Alright George (I had also taken to calling him by his Christian name when we were alone), what seems to have you in a tizz'?"

He smiled saying, "Well mister Tolcher, all this drilling is doing wonders, the only thing that now bothers me, is that I don't know what my gunners are capable of, I've never seen them work, and have no idea if they can hit a target or not, or whether they are able to outfire the enemy, sir."

Thinking his concern over, I said, "Hmm, you're right George, that is a concern, I'll bring it up with the captain for you."

His face took on a smile, as he replied, "You will? Thank you, sir."

Chapter 18.

That night in the wardroom, over dinner I brought up George's concerns with the captain and other officers, which resulted in a discussion about how our chances of getting in some gunnery practice were, and if so, where?

I saw that my concerns about the gunnery crews, had struck home with the captain, and he sat there thinking while the discussion took place around the table.

Next morning, Captain Cockburn let us know that, that morning he was going to call upon the admiral, and asked me to make sure the longboat was ready for him to go ashore. I told him, that I would see to as soon as I took over the watch.

He returned from ashore just prior to lunch, and there he announced, "Gentlemen, last night number two gave me food for thought, when he brought up the concerns from the guns petty officer. This morning as you know, I saw the admiral, and a solution has been found to our problem, Christmas you know is not far away, and after the turn of the new year, we have permission to join the blockading fleet at Cadiz, where we will practise our gunners, whilst also hitting the enemy at the same time. We will make for sea on the morning of January two, this will also give us time to recover from the Christmas and New Year Balls, that all officers are to attend, in your best uniforms, of course. However, the admiral has ordered, no weapons need be worn for the occasion, any questions?"

There were none, then looking at me, he said "Henry when you resume your watch, would you be so kind as to send guns to me please?"

"Aye sir," I replied.

Then he slipped a couple of envelopes out of his jacket, and passed one to me, the other he gave to Thomas, saying, "I think you'll both enjoy this mail."

Noticing they were from the admiralty, I placed mine in my jacket pocket, while Thomas opened his, and laughed, saying "Well bless my soul." Placing the envelope into his jacket.

After lunch, I had passed on the message to George Michaels, and once the message had been delivered, while he went off to see the captain, I went to the poopdeck and opened my letter, it was an accounting notice, and a cheque made out to me for twenty-seven thousand pounds! Being my share of the prize money for the Conquistadora.

During the following week both Hardy and I, got the opportunity to slip ashore and deposit our cheques into the bank. The purser and guns were busy with loading stacks of powder and shot, for our cannons, and it took almost a week before all our gunnery supplies, had been loaded, our stocks had been increased tenfold, and I assumed that guns feared the worst, and was making sure we had more than enough supplies, to keep training the gun crews to the standard he wanted.

At the first ball, on Christmas Eve, I became the centre of attraction for quite a few ladies, wanting to dance with me, and also try their feminine wiles on me, in regard romance, but were all exasperated, as I continually explained that I was already engaged to another at home. Not that some didn't try talking me around, with the premise, that they were here, and available, where she wasn't.

Not giving into temptation though, I think I may have broken a few hearts, but it also made the next ball on New Year's Eve, easier for me to be able to dodge any further advances.

March 12, 1795: The Minerve slipped out of Gibraltar on the morning tide, the second of January, with instructions and despatches for the eight men of war blockading Cadiz harbour, all the way from Gibraltar, until we reached Cadiz, George had been merciless with the gun crews, conducting exercise after exercise.

Once our despatches had been delivered, and the fleet made aware of what we would be doing, we started our gunnery practise for real, using the harbour of Cadiz as our target.

The captain would pick a target, and it was up to the gun crews to obliterate said target. Our practise wasn't only kept to daylight hours, as we would also pound the Spanish at night also. It was only after, all gun crews could fire three shots, accurately, in the space of a minute, did George Michaels consider them good enough, it had taken two full months, before he, the captain and all officers, agreed that we now had gun crews worthy of merit, and to that end, Cockburn ordered all gun crew personnel, be issued a double ration of rum, for three days, due to their improvement, since we had started their exercises.

Having our gun crews all fully trained and capable, our next mission was to collect any despatches going back to Gibraltar, and make for our home port. Our supply of powder and shot was close to being exhausted by this time, and the captain and all of us, hoped that we didn't run into any problems, during our voyage home.
After arriving back in our home port, all despatches had been delivered, and the ship's crew was busy reprovisioning our food and all needed supplies, and of course, our gunnery supplies.

November 14, 1795: Since our reprovisioning back in late March, Admiral Jervis, had the Minerve join a fleet of six other ships of the line, one of these was our sister ship the HMS Blanche, our mission was to relieve the blockading fleet off Toulon.
After taking our station, we found that there wasn't a week go by without some action, as the Spanish ships were constantly trying to break out of port. Then our fleet was relieved, and we returned to Gibraltar for some much-needed shore leave, and reprovisioning, before we would move back to Cadiz, and take up station to replace our blockading fleet there.

November 1796: That whole year we would patrol different ports as a relief, blockading which port we were assigned to by Admiral Jervis.

Then we too, would rest before, continuing the blockades, whilst on station our gun crews were into action faster than any of the other ships, which made Cockburn extremely happy.

In mid-September, admiral Jervis ordered us to escort two captured prize ships, back to Plymouth, and once delivered safe and sound, our entire ships compliments were to have six weeks paid leave, before returning to Gibraltar. Whilst at Plymouth both ships would have their bottoms scraped and coppered, and any other maintenance carried out. This was indeed good news, and everyone aboard went about the voyage home with smiles.

Arriving in Plymouth, our ships were moved to the work docks, and the crew were released from the ship. I only took my weapons belt and holdall, as I went into the town to buy a horse and saddle, then by the evening, I was riding into the family farm at Dean Prior.

My father stabled my horse, as I went to see my family, and they were happy and surprised to see me, and a little taken aback by my now weathered face and body, I was no longer a boy anymore, but a full-grown lieutenant in his majesty's Royal Navy.

As we sat down to dinner, pop, asked, "Well Henry, you've been gone awhile now, what have you been up to since we saw you last?"

I laughed saying, "To tell you all that, will be thirsty work, so if you'll pour me a mug of cider, I'll start…" The meal was over by the time, I described my capture of the Conquistadora, everyone, including father was hanging to my every word, as I talked, and as I got up, to collect the Spanish sword to show them, their eyes followed my every move, and as I placed my sword on the table. Father picked it up saying, "Aye tis a handsome blade, is this gold?"

I smiled, as I replied, "Aye that it be father."

He stared at me for a short time, before saying, "Henry my boy, I hope you'll forgive me, but I really thought your idea to join the navy was just a pipedream, but it seems you've proved me wrong, and look at you now! You have made something of yourself and are truly a man in your own right, I'm proud of you boy."

For the three days at the farm, I was constantly asked more and more about my exploits, but I could only tell them what had been done up till then, and about the long periods of boredom that was only livened up if action came our way.

During dinner of my final night at the farm, I told them of my plan to visit uncle William, and his family, plus also see my love, Joanna. But I told them I'd be calling back there on my return journey to Plymouth.

Early the following morning, I was up and had breakfast with my father and mother, before my grandparents got up, after saying my goodbyes to mother, father and I went to the barn, where I saddled my horse, and we shook hands in farewell, as I placed my holdall into the saddlebag.

With a wave, to my mother, I rode out of the farm, and made for Taunton, at a casual pace. After spending an overnight stay at Broadclyst, in a wayside inn, I continued to Taunton the following morning, arriving in the early afternoon.

Instead of my usual practise upon arrival of rushing into the manor, I knocked on the door, and turned my back to it, as I heard uncle Williams voice saying, "It's alright Jenkins, I'm here." As the door opened, I refrained from turning until uncle William asked, "Yes lieutenant, what can I do for you, I hope it's not bad news about Henry?"
I said, as I started to turn, "No sir, in fact quite the opposite."
His faced turned into a smile as he rushed forward and clasped me in an embrace, saying "Oh Henry, it's so good to see you, come on in my boy."
Taking my hat off, I was ushered into the study, then Jenkins was called for and told, to set another place for dinner, look to my horse, tell no one else I was home, and to get another bottle of scotch.
After divesting myself of my weapons belt, we sat opposite each other at the desk, as uncle William remarked as he poured two generous glasses of scotch, "I see you added another sword, which is what confused me at the door, no doubt you're going to tell me how you acquired it, it seems to be a fine blade."
I tossed a mouthful of the fiery alcohol down my throat, as I replied, "Of course I am Uncle."
He laughed saying, "Well don't rush into it boy."

As he took a pull of the scotch, before continuing, "Just take it step by step from the beginning."
We had been talking for, or rather I did the talking while uncle William listened, for over an hour, every now and then, he would pour us each another drink.
Then I heard the door open behind me, and a voice remarked, "Hah I'd know that belt anywhere!"
Stopping mid-sentence, I got up, turning at the same time, as Albert came forward to embrace me, saying, "Welcome home cousin, why haven't we been told you were here?"
Uncle William interrupted saying, "Because I decided to keep it mum as a surprise for everyone, when they came down to drinks. Henry is on leave for a few weeks, and as you can see, he's been promoted, that happened only after twelve days on his first ship, but he can tell everyone the story later, come sit and join us, Albert."
Albert joined me in the other chair across from the desk, and as he took a sip of the whiskey, he'd been poured, said "I noticed you have added to your arsenal, why and where did it come from?"
I repeated the story of my dilemma aboard the Conquistadora, when I faced two men with swords, and I having only one, and my pistols being empty, he laughed uproariously when I told him of the use I had put the belaying pin to, and got up to have a look at my new sword. Drawing it from the scabbard, gave it an intense inspection, checking the balance and blade, and hilt, before making a few moves, and swings testing its combat effectiveness.

Then said, "Ho, Toledo steel, no one makes a finer blade than the Spanish, though our people are getting better and better, it's a good sword Henry, that captain must have been very rich, well done." Replacing the sword into the scabbard, he finished his drink, he continued, "Now back to business, while you two must have been discussing your exploits, I came in to collect you father as the women, have made their way to the dining room, so time for drinks father, and we'll have Henry join us last, keeping with your surprise, the ladies will be besides themselves, and glad to see you home Henry!"

When he had finished uncle William and I, drained our glasses, as he said, "Oh very well Albert, Henry we'll continue this later, right now, we best go surprise the women, otherwise we'll get merry hell for holding them up."
As we walked to the door, our entry was decided upon, and as we approached the dining room, I hung back waiting for my que.
I didn't have to wait long, after the ladies had been served drinks, I heard Albert ask, "Father, are we expecting another guest? It seems there's too many places at the table set."
While this byplay was taking place, Boggs had been sent to the doorway to announce my arrival into the room, and with a smile, waited until I gave him the nod.
Uncle William, replied to Albert, saying, "What?"

Taking a drink, uncle William continued, "Oh, yes, I'm expecting an old friend, that we haven't seen for quite some time, he should be here soon." With that he looked toward the door, saying "Oh good, here he comes now."

I gave Boggs the nod, and he announced, "My lord, ladies and gentlemen, lieutenant Henry Tolcher!"

As I walked in through the door, everyone had been looking toward the doorway, so I was the centre of attention.

I noticed Joanna's' face light up with a beaming smile as she placed her glass down, then rushed into my arms, flinging her arms around my neck exclaiming, "Oh Henry!"

Chapter 19.

After Joanna, had made her leap across to me, aunt Elizbeth came toward me with a smile on her face, Joanna was still clinging to me, as aunt Elizabeth said, "Joanna my dear, you should know not to act so shamelessly in public, now let Henry go, and act like a lady, allow me time to greet my nephew." Joanna blushed and let me go, hanging her head in shame, as she was reprimanded by my aunt, saying, "Yes marm, please forgive me, but I'm so glad to see him."

"As are we all, my dear." She replied with a smile, "But you don't see the rest of us acting so shamelessly." Turning to me, she said, "Henry, it's so good to see you home safe and sound dear." As she embraced me and kissed me on the cheek, saying, "I've missed you terribly, along with some others," as she glanced to Joanna.

I smiled saying, "It's really good to be back aunt Elizabeth, but I fear it will be only for a short while."

Lucy came and embraced me in turn, telling me she was glad to see me home.

Albert passed me another drink, and uncle William said, "A toast, to lieutenant Henry Tolcher RN, to his skill and heroism, in capturing the Spanish ship Conquistadora, during combat in the Mediterranean, and the prize money he received."

Amongst queries and questioning looks, I was toasted, then everyone wanted to know the full story, relenting, I gave them all a very brief version.

Uncle William, said "He is being too modest and brief family, I will give you all the full details during dinner, but I will say this now, that what he has told you, took place after only eleven days of him joining his ship!"

During dinner, uncle William gave a full accounting of my exploits to date, after which I was bombarded by questions, as to how I rose to 2nd mate so quickly, if I had been paid my share of the prizemoney, and how long I was home for.
I answered the questions in detail, explaining my rise in naval status, and letting them know what my share of the prize money came to, they were astounded to say the least at my good fortune.
Then I told them when I had to report back aboard the Minerve, and that it would be returning to the Mediterranean fleet under Jervis, once we left port.

For the following few weeks, I spent as much time with Joanna, as was possible, as our love for each other continued to grow. I also spent quite a deal of time with Albert, and in confidence, he disclosed the fact that his father's health, was indeed failing, so much so, that each time uncle William went to London, Albert feared that it could be his last, each time he went, uncle William would spend days afterward here at home recovering from the ill health it caused to his father. Then he asked me, "Henry while you're here can you spend a bit more time with him, he keeps himself in that study of his from morning to night, doing god knows what."

Taking a breath, he continued, "He loves and admires you Henry, as do we all, but he has taken a particular liking to you, and I would be remiss if I hadn't told you all this, because I greatly fear, that when you go back to duty, you may never see each other again."

I told Albert that I had, had no idea of uncle Williams illness, because he always seemed jovial and fit, every time we saw each other, and Albert remarked "Yes, he certainly perks up when you're around, but cousin, don't let this fool you, he is sicker than he seems, and you know how he likes to keep things hidden, even I had the damnedest all of a time getting this out of him, and I had no idea either. It wasn't until a week before you arrived home, that he told me, after telling me that he was taking steps to have the family title transferred to me, it was only then that I got any inkling as to his ill health."

I promised Albert that I would keep his confidence, and spend more time with uncle William, then he thanked me and asked, "Henry I would like to ask you for another favour, I know that you will be seeing your grandparents on your way back to Plymouth, if I send the carriage and some men with you, could you please have them return here, because your pop Sam and he are such good friends, and I know he'd like to have his sister here too, they will be welcomed here, and should be here with him, no matter how long it takes?"

I hung my head, so that my tears weren't visible, and nodded, asking "It's that serious Albert?"

"Yes nephew, I think it is," he replied earnestly. After wiping my tears away, I lifted my head, saying "In that case uncle, I will write them a letter today, and you can have the carriage and men sent to them tomorrow."

He was stunned and stammered a thank you, and told me that was a terrific idea, then said he would arrange for them to leave first thing in the morning. When we finished our swordplay, he went to arrange the carriage and men, while I took to the library, and started to compose the letter to my grandpop Sam and nanna Suzanna. Once the letter was written, I addressed it and sealed it with the family seal, and placed it in my jacket pocket.

Just before lunch, Albert informed me that he had arranged the carriage and men to leave at first light, and that Joanna's father Ted would be in charge of the group. I smiled and told him I would go see Ted after lunch, and give him the letter to take with him.

When I had finished eating, I excused myself from the table explaining that I had an errand to run, and left the room. Going through the back of the manor, I made my way to Ted and Alice's cottage, and caught them both before they returned to their duties.

I was let in by Ted, and we shook hands, and I gave Alice a kiss on the cheek, by this time they were used to me, having visited them many times either in Joanna's company or not. As I said my hellos to my prospective in-laws to be, I asked Ted for a minute of his time, and we both sat in the lounge room.

When seated, I said, "Ted I came to you, because I know you're going with the men and coach tomorrow, so I have a couple of things for you." Reaching into my jacket pocket, I produced the letter he was to take, and a mud map to help him with directions to the farm, saying "This letter, I want you to give to my grandfather Sam only, what he tells my mother and father is up to him, this will also be your best time to meet my father and mother, before Joanna and I get married."

He laughed saying, "Aye tis what I was thinking too, and I'll be sure to give the letter to your grandpa Sam only, Henry. When do yee go back to sea, if I may ask?"

I smiled saying, "I think that by the time you return, I'll only be here a night or two more, before I have to leave for Plymouth and my ship. I will have time to say my goodbyes to you and Alice before I go though."

He laughed, saying "Mind you bring Joanna along too, we don't git to see her much now she's liven' in the big house."

Smiling, I replied "I'll make sure of it Ted." Then got up and we shook hands, and we both left the cottage at the same time, but in different directions.

During pre-dinner drinks that day, I was able to get Joanna alone, for a little while, and informed her of my uncle's condition, and what was being done, and that if she didn't think I was spending enough time with her, it would be because I would be with uncle William. She also confirmed Albert's assessment, from things that my aunt would hint at, from time to time, I thought, *so aunt Elizabeth is also aware of uncle William's health condition, that makes what Albert and I have done a little easier. When the time comes at least she'll have Sam* and *Suzanna here, to help her through his passing.*

The next afternoon, I walked into the study, and uncle William and I spent the afternoon, chatting about anything he wished to raise, and that became my pattern for the rest of my leave before returning to Plymouth, we would either talk, or sometimes we would sit and play chess.

Ten days later, the men and carriage returned with pop and nanna, and uncle William was overjoyed having been told by pop, they thought they would visit for a while, which was what I had asked him to say if questioned. Even though I kept up my routine with uncle William, my time at the manor was growing short, with only three days left before I had to depart for Plymouth. At least now, he would have pop's company when I was gone.

The second last evening before I left, Joanna and I spent with her parents, and Ted was all happy and smiling, as we talked about his time at my parent's farm, and how much he enjoyed their company. Of course, my last evening was spent with my family, and after breakfast the following morning my goodbyes were said, as they came out to see me off and on my way. With a last embrace and kiss from Joanna, I mounted, and rode off with a final wave.

After selling my horse, I finally boarded the Minerve, to find Hardy and Cockburn already aboard, as I looked at the ships in the harbour, Tom told me that they were part of Commodore Nelson's fleet heading for the Mediterranean. The following afternoon, during our provisioning of the ship, I was called to the arrival of Commodore Horatio Nelson, as he made his way aboard. After he saluted the flag, I then saluted him, and welcomed him aboard.
As I took in his appearance, he was a small man about three inches shorter than my five feet seven, with blondish hair poking out from under his hat, and he seemed to be blind in his right eye. As I escorted him to the captain's cabin he asked my name, and upon hearing it remarked "Well I've certainly heard of you Henry, wasn't it you who took the Conquistadora off Marseilles?"
I smiled, with remembrance of the event, as I replied, "Aye Sir, here we are sir," as I knocked on the cabin door.

Turning to leave, Nelson said "No Henry, stay please," as I open the door on the command from inside. I opened the door, then made way for Nelson to enter, both Hardy and Cockburn came to attention, though didn't salute as they were bare headed.
As he approached the desk, Nelson said "Gentlemen I have asked mister Tolcher to stay, as I wish to speak to the most senior officers aboard, which are you three. Please sit while I outline what we're about to do."

As we took our normal places at the conference table, Nelson sat and removed his headgear, letting his overgrown blonde hair flop down. Then he said, "No doubt that you know, the other ships in the harbour, apart from the Blanche, are all my fleet, we are being provisioned in turn to head to Gibraltar, same as you and Blanche. Now the only two ships that will be ready to leave tomorrow, is the Blanche and yours George. Therefore, I'm going to transfer my pennant to the Minerve, and we will leave on the morrows tide with Blanche. I will be calling a conference tonight at 1700, and I will return at 1600 George, to settle in, any questions? Good until later gentlemen!"

With that he rose, as we did too, placed his hat on, and headed for the door, as I rushed to open it for him. Then followed him to the gangplank, and he left the ship.

He returned that afternoon just before I was about to go off watch, but waited for our 3rd mate Dan Culverhouse to welcome him aboard as officer of the watch. I went to the gangplank as this happened, and seeing me, he passed his pennant to me asking, "Mister Tolcher could you have this run up for me please?"

Passing the pennant to Dan I said, "Aye sir, Dan see to it please."

Dan Replied, "Aye Sir," and went to get it hoisted onto the mizzen mast, as I escorted Nelson to his quarters.

During the next hour, Culverhouse was kept busy, welcoming the fleet officers aboard.

The starboard side stateroom that Nelson occupied as Commodore was larger than the captain's cabin in the centre of the ship, with Hardy's cabin being on the portside.

Nelsons stateroom included a larger conference table that was big enough for everyone to sit. As Nelson outlaid his plan to go ahead to Gibraltar, and wait for his fleet to join him there, then they were told that the Blanche and Minerve, would leave with the morning tide.

After the conference, all the officers were able to be accommodated in the wardroom, and we had drinks prior to dinner, which was served at 1800.

December 24, 1796: As we made our way closer to Spain, on the morning of the nineteenth, two Spanish frigates were sighted, and we chased and engaged them in combat, the Minerve went for the Santa Sabina, while Nelson ordered the Blanche to attack the Santa Ceres. The Sabina surrendered after being boarded by me, Hardy, and fifty men.

When the Spanish crew had been locked in the hold, and the Captain of the Sabina, Don Jacobo Stuart, transferred to the Minerve. Nelson had Thomas and Dan Culverhouse, take a prize crew aboard, then all three ships continued toward Gibraltar, after the Ceres had gotten away.

Imagine our surprise when we sighted a larger Spanish squadron, including two more frigates and the huge 112-gun first rate ship of the line Principe de Asturias coming after us! All we could do was run, and hope we could outrun them. Tom Hardy took in the sight and immediately turned to starboard and drew the Spanish away from us, as he started firing. We watched as he kept firing until his ship was dismasted, and captured.

Nelson ordered us to put about, and have a truce flag raised. The truce was accepted by the Spanish, and as we closed with them an exchange of prisoners was arranged through the bullhorn.

We got Hardy, Culverhouse, and the prize crew, as we released Don Jacobo Stuart, and his crew. Then we poured on all the sail, so we could to get away. With two fast enemy ships pursuing us, Cockburn ordered more sail. During this operation, a topman fell overboard. The ship hove to immediately, and a boat with Hardy in it was lowered to search for the missing mariner. As the enemy ships were closing fast, Cockburn thought it prudent to withdraw, leaving the longboat that had recovered our man, to the Spanish, but Nelson overruled him yelling "By God, I'll not lose Hardy, back that mizzen topsail!" This confused the Spaniards who checked their own progress, allowing Hardy time to return to our ship and we escaped.

After meeting up with Blanche again, we both sailed into Gibraltar on December 23, well in time for the Christmas festivities.

Chapter 20.

Upon reporting to admiral Jervis, the following morning, Christmas Eve, Captain George Cockburn was assigned to another ship, but this time however, Hardy and I couldn't go with him, because Nelson wished that Tom be promoted to captain of the Minerve, and I was to become 1st mate and lieutenant.

Admiral, Jervis approved our promotions, telling us that he would make sure, that the admiralty would ratify our promotions. Before we left his office, he told Nelson to report to him first thing, on the morning of the second of January for orders.

After leaving his office, with me reeling from my rapid advancement to 1st lieutenant, both Hardy and I made for the uniform shop, while Nelson and Cockburn made for the ship, promising to send the longboat back for us.

After purchasing more shirts and vests, with my old frockcoats I had enough, clothing for my new status, plus if I was ever made a captain I had at least one captains frockcoat and hat.

After Hardy had completed his purchases, we made our way to the quay, where the longboat was waiting for us.

Back at the ship, we said our farewells to captain Cockburn, as he wished us good luck in the future, he had been the only captain I had known, and I would miss him, Hardy too had been with Cockburn for a long time, so our goodbyes were quite a deal emotional for all of us, then he left the Minerve.

Once he had left, both Hardy and I moved quarters once again, but because we were now used to moving like this, it really took no time at all, and half an hour later, all my possessions had been stowed into their correct places.

After the officers joined Captain Hardy and I in the wardroom, Hardy sent for one of the midshipmen, Charles Denman, and promoted him to fourth mate, as he advanced Dan Culverhouse, and Mathew Markham up to 2nd and 3rd mate respectively.

That afternoon, knowing my cousin Robin, to be aboard the Majestic, I had myself rowed across to her, and boarded. Robin was the officer of the watch, and after saluting the flag, he saluted me, due to my being higher in rank than he was.

Naturally he didn't know who I was, and I, him, until we introduced ourselves, then we both had a chuckle, as he led me to the poopdeck, where he could keep an eye on things going on around the ship. When we were alone, we talked of family matters, and I informed him of uncle Williams condition, warning him that we may be notified at any time of his passing. It was then that he disclosed, that without uncle Williams help, he would not have made into the navy.

After hearing this, I disclosed my own relationship with uncle William, and how it was he, and his entire family that had made entry into the navy possible. Robin said, "Aye that's the sort of man he is, and believe me Henry, he will be very proud of you, as am I, you have achieved so much so soon."

I laughed saying, "That dear cousin is only because of luck, and falling in with the right people, like George Cockburn, and Tom Hardy, I don't think I would have made it so far so quickly without their help. I made a gross mistake once, and would have died if they hadn't of sent help to me, when I was aboard the Conquistadora."

"Ah yes," he replied, "I heard about you doing that." Then he laughed and continued asking, "How about you tell me all about it, and what was the mistake you made?"

I told all about the action with the Conquistadora, mentioning my blunder about not checking if any of the crew had followed me aboard. He laughed heartily about that, and we joked about what could have happened to me, as he said, "Well Henry, I'll wager you won't make that mistake again, and after your warning, I'm not likely to either, but you survived it, and made quite a name for yourself from what I hear, and I'm not surprised, looking at the way you're dressed, with your weapons, you look downright ferocious."

Then he told me of the usual festivities, that we as officers of the line, were expected to attend, with number one being the ball the following night, and urged me to arrange to secure a room in the officer's quarters ashore, having already had that done by Hardy, I told him that they were already arranged, and we both laughed. Then we conspired to have our places at the mass dinner to be changed so that we could sit together.

Sometime later, after shaking hands, and saying our

farewells until the following evening, I left the Majestic, and was rowed back to the Minerve.

January 3, 1797: Robin and I met as arranged, at the Christmas eve gala, and I was able to introduce him to Nelson and Hardy. Nelson was quite taken with Robin, and wished him success during his career, Tom also switched his placing, and we sat together during dinner, prior to the ball. Our dinner conversation centred mainly around all our different family connections, and Hardy was able to fill Robin in with details of how we were all distantly related.

We all had a great evening, and made our way to our quarters, close to 0100 on what had become Christmas day. Meeting again at breakfast, after a few hours' sleep.

The New Year's Eve gala was literally a repeat of the Christmas eve one, except that the party went through the entire night. The longboats at the quay leaving for different ships after breakfast each held quite a few officers suffering hangovers, so I wasn't alone with my indisposition. Tom Hardy didn't look too well either.

Nelson had stayed ashore, because he was meeting with admiral Jervis the following day to receive his orders. Returning to the ship, he called Hardy and myself to his stateroom, and informed us, that he had been given HMS Captain as his flagship, and that we, were assigned as part of his squadron, he had been given independent control over all the blockading ships in the western Mediterranean, the other ships that were leaving with us, apart from his squadron, would be sailing to join admiral Cuthbert Collingwood in the eastern part of the Med.

The following morning, we slipped out of Gibraltar on the morning tide, we looked a fine sight, with twelve ships of the line in all, of those, six were part of our squadron, which included the Captain, flying Nelson's pennant, Blanche, Orion, Theseus, Audacious, and us of course in Minerve.

The other squadron, were those going to join admiral Collingwood, Leander, Goliath, Defence, Bellerophon, Swiftsure and Zealous.

We formed into two columns, with the ongoing ships off our starboard side, and our column on the leeward side to them. We would sail in station like that until it was time for the ongoing fleet to peel off and go their separate way.

January 18, 1797: Today we have been at sea for fifteen days, and are getting close to the point where the ongoing squadron will depart. A fishing smack has been sighted, and it was making its way to the Captain, then it went alongside, its captain went aboard, and was there for nearly a half hour.

Keeping my scope trained on the flagship, I saw the fishing captain leave the ship, and Nelson talking to his captain. Then I noticed a longboat being prepared, and looked to the signal flags, reading that we had been ordered to heave to (stop). The next messages run up were to order squadron two, to proceed to the east, and join Collingwood.

After that, the next signals ordered the rest of our squadron to proceed to the rendezvous point with the blockading ships and await further instructions, and that Captain and Minerve were returning to Gibraltar at all speed.

Knowing something was amiss, by our ship slowing, Hardy came to me asking "Alright Henry what's happening?

Still keeping watch on the flagship, I answered him, explaining everything I had observed. He took out his scope and we both kept the flagship under observation, and we both saw Nelson's pennant lowered, as he made to the side of Captain and climbed down into the longboat, and a bundle, presumably his pennant was thrown down to him, as Tom muttered, "Well we'll find out what's happening soon, here he comes."

Soon the longboat from Captain was alongside, and pushed off back toward the Captain as soon as Nelson had climbed onto the Minerve. He was assisted over the rail and we went to join him as he ordered "Hardy bring her about and head back to Gibraltar, and get us there fast!"

Tom nodded, and I went about turning the ship, as he and Nelson moved toward his cabin. Once the ship was on course with all sails set, I left control of the ship to Dan, and headed to the captain's cabin and knocked on the door, I heard the order to come and, made my way into the cabin. Both Tom and Nelson were standing as I entered, and Nelson said, "Ah good, Henry, now we can proceed." Passing me a drink of sherry, and continued saying, "I've just had some information passed onto me, gentlemen the Spanish fleet has broken out of Cartegena, and at this moment making for Cadiz, I don't need to tell you what will happen if that occurs, so we are going to warn Admiral Jervis, I can sense a battle coming, and it's going to be a big one! I have transferred to your ship Hardy because it is the fastest, and Captain will follow, at its best speed."

That is the summation of today's events, and I only hope that I have the chance to bring this journal up to date after, what will assuredly be a great battle.

Journal: Henry Robert Tolcher RN 1st Lieutenant.

February 20, 1797: By the grace of god, I have survived, what is now being called the Battle of Cape St. Vincent. Let me explain events as they unfolded from my last entry.

We reached Gibraltar on the evening of the fifth of February, to find an empty harbour. Nelson immediately had us berth at the sea dock, where he went ashore, and we could be reprovisioned first thing in the morning.
He returned to the ship an hour later, and informed us Jervis was out patrolling toward the north of Spain, the intelligence about the Spanish fleet under the command of Admiral Don Jose de Cordova escaping out of Cartegena was known and a message had been sent to find Jervis, with the news.

It had been arranged for the supplies we needed to be available first thing the next morning, and with a bit of luck, we could be out of the harbour before the afternoon. Then he told us where Jervis was supposed to be, and consulted the charts, with a lot of summation considered, where we were most likely to intercept Jervis, if indeed he had got the news about the Spanish fleet. Using our best guesses, it was determined that we should come across Jervis, near the cape of St. Vincent on or near the twelfth or thirteenth of the month.

Having made our assumptions, I plotted the course toward the cape. Leaving Gibraltar behind us, we sailed northward along my course. On the eleventh of the month, for some unknown reason, I started to become wracked with the jitters, past experiences had taught me that something was about to happen, but I knew not what. I don't know why, but I had the ship slowed by reefing in the topsails, then just on dusk, the top lookout called "Sail Ho, out of the west south west!"
Nelson and Hardy came on deck immediately, Tom asking me why I had reefed the topsails, and I quickly explained what I had felt, and Nelson who had been watching the ships in the gloom, heard me and said, "Henry, you just keep acting on those impulses, that's the bloody Spanish fleet! By god man well done. We'll be able to slip in amongst them during the darkness, keep all lights out on deck, and only bare minimum below decks, and no noise."

I turned to the 3rd mate, Mathew Markham, saying, "Make it so Mathew."

He replied with a smile saying, "Aye sir." As he left to make the instructions happen.

With all windows in the ship blackened out, that night, we had a subdued dinner in the wardroom, and Nelson asked me, "Henry tonight when we're fully amongst the Spanish fleet, do you think you could get a star sight, and determine our position, and their course?"

I thought about it for a minute before answering, and said "Aye sir, we're in the dark of the moon, so it would have to be a star sight, off Venus, but I'm not sure how accurately I could give you our position, but as to their course, that won't be a problem, but I'll need time to work it out, sir."

He laughed saying, "Good lad I know you'll be able to handle it. Now remember men, we'll be in their midst soon, so definitely no noise, or we're likely to be blown to kingdom come, we're on our own, no help will come to us, stealth is the way this night gentlemen."

Through the night, there was no bell to tone out the time, and I was relying on my fob watch. At midnight I made my way on deck, Charlie Denman and I took the sightings required, as he whispered the calculations to me.

After the sightings were taken we looked around, and in the gloom, we could make out the shapes of ships all around us, as the ship weaved in and out between the ships of the Spanish fleet, also amazed at how quiet the ship was, even with men on watch.

By the time I had made all the calculations, and determined our position and marking it on the chart, I then started on the Spanish fleet course, marking it on the chart also, and drew a line along their course. Their course line, and admiral Jervis's assumed course intersected, just off Cape St. Vincent, this was where the two fleets should converge, on our present course, we should reach the admiral the next afternoon, and be ready to attack the Spanish the morning after that.

After making my report the following morning to Nelson and Hardy, we were now well clear of the Spanish fleet, Hardy ordered all sail to be used to speed us up, as we made for the wardroom and breakfast.

Having had a rather sleepless night, after breakfast was done, I went to my cabin, and slept until lunchtime.

Chapter 21.

Admiral Jervis's fleet was sighted at 1300, and we had closed with them, and were within rowing distance to the flagship by 1500. Earlier as we got closer to them the top lookout had identified the HMS Captain as being with the fleet.

Mathew had the longboat launched on our portside, and myself, Hardy, and Nelson clambered over the side to be rowed over to the Victory, Jervis's flagship.

Reaching its side, our launch was secured to the side by a rope line that had been lowered, and the three of us climbed up the starboard side, I was clutching the waterproof tube that held the chart I had used, in the earlier hours of the morning.

We were greeted at the rail by Jervis, and went immediately to his stateroom, at Nelson's insistence. Inside the cabin, Nelson announced, "Sir, we have matters of great import regarding the Spanish, last night with great stealth the Minerve, manoeuvred amongst and through the Spanish fleet, determining their course."

Jervis immediately took more note of Nelson, saying, "Did you by god, damned well-done Horatio, come show me."

Having been given a nod by Nelson, I moved forward to the table, taking the chart from the tube, and spread it out on the table, weighting it down with items already on the table, so it didn't roll back into place again, facing the admiral, explaining the marks and course lines I had made the previously.

Admiral Jervis was studying the chart as I made my explanation, then turning to Nelson from his still bent over position, asked, "Well Horatio, you stand by this?" Waving his hand at the chart.

Nelson smiled and replied, "Yes Sir, Henry is most arguably, one of the best navigators in the fleet, and I'd wager my life on his knowledge, sir."

Jervis looked at me, then back to Nelson, and back to me asking, Well, mister Tolcher, would you, too gamble your life away on your calculations?"

I straightened up to attention, and replied, "Sir these calculations were made just after midnight, on a moonless night, using Venus as a star sight, and are only approximates, but yes Sir, I stand by this, as my best guess."

Jervis straightened up, and replied, "Hmm, in that case mister Tolcher, we are all going to be gambling our lives on your best guess, gentlemen, I will convene a conference for 1800, followed by dinner, now Horatio, do you have any idea how many ships we face?"

Nelson came to attention, saying, "No sir, I'm afraid not, it was dark, and a mist had rolled in."

Jervis replied, "Very well, leave this chart here please, so I can study it, and I'll see you at 1800, Horatio, move back to your flagship, there's a good chap."

Nelson replied, "Aye Sir."

With that we exited the cabin and made our way back to the Minerve, where Nelson's pennant was struck, and he was then rowed to the Captain. The longboat stayed in the water for Hardy that evening.

As we closed to the intersecting point during the night, we started to hear the signalling guns of the Spanish ships, and at 0530, Jervis signalled for all ships to close and form line for battle.

February 14: The dawn broke on a bleak overcast and foggy morning at 0630, as we waited in line, the Culloden under Troubridge was first, and signalled that she saw five enemy sail to the south east, and turned in their direction, followed by Blenheim and the Prince George.

1030: The Spanish ships in the weather column were seen to wear ship and turn to port. This gave the impression that they might form a line and pass along the weather column of the British fleet, exposing our smaller column to the fire of the larger Spanish division.

1100: Jervis signalled his orders, form in a line of battle ahead and astern of Victory as most convenient. When this order was completed the fleet had formed a single line of battle, sailing in a southerly direction on a course to pass between the two Spanish columns.

At 11:12 Jervis made his next signal: Engage the enemy! then at 11:30 Admiral intends to pass through enemy lines. To our advantage, the Spanish fleet was formed into two groups and was unprepared for battle, while we were already in line. Jervis ordered the fleet to pass between the two groups, minimising the fire they could put into him, while letting him fire in both directions.

Culloden tacked to reverse her course and take after the Spanish column.

Blenheim and then Prince George did the same in succession. The Spanish lee division now put about to the port tack with the intention of breaking our line at the point where the ships were tacking in succession.

Orion came around, but Colossus was going about when her foreyard and foretop yard were shot away. She was forced to wear ship instead of tack, and the leading Spanish vessel came close enough to threaten her with a broadside. Saumarez in Orion saw the danger to his friends and backed his sails to give covering fire.

As Victory came to the tacking point, another attempt was made to break our line. Victory, however, was too fast and Principe de Asturias had to tack close to Victory and received two raking broadsides as she did so.

13:05: Jervis hoisted a signal: Take suitable stations for mutual support and engage the enemy as coming up in succession.

Nelson on Captain (a seventy-four) and was now towards the rear of the British line, much closer to the larger group. He concluded that the manoeuvre could not be completed to allow us to catch them. Unless the movements of the Spanish ships could be thwarted, everything so far gained would be lost. Interpreting Jervis' signal loosely, and disobeying previous orders, Nelson gave orders to Ralph Miller to wear ship and to take Captain out of line while engaging the smaller group. As soon as the seventy-four was around, Nelson directed her to pass between Diadem and Excellent.

Running across the bows of the Spanish ships forming the central group of the weather division. This group included the Santísima Trinidad, the largest ship afloat at the time and mounting 130 guns, the San José, 112, Salvador del Mundo, 112, San Nicolás, 84, San Ysidro 74 and the Mexicano 112.

13:30: Culloden was gradually overhauling the Spanish rear and began a renewed but not very close engagement of the same group of ships. Jervis signalled his rearmost ship, Excellent to come to the wind on the larboard tack and following this order, Collingwood brought his ship round to a position ahead of Culloden. After a few more minutes, Blenheim and Prince George came up behind and the group of British ships prevented the Spanish from grouping together.

The Captain was now under fire from as many as six Spanish ships, of which three were 112-gun three-deckers and a fourth Córdoba's 130-gun flagship Santísima Trinidad.

About 1400, Culloden had stretched so far ahead as to cover the Captain from the heavy fire poured into her by the Spanish four-decker and her companions, as they hauled up and brought their broadsides to bear. With the respite given to her, the Captain took immediate advantage, replenishing her lockers with shot and splicing and repairing her running rigging. By about 1300, Excellent was already in close action with San Nicolás which, with foretop mast shot away, had been in action against the Captain. Excellent fired broadsides into San Nicolás and then made sail to clear ahead. To avoid Excellent, San Nicolás luffed up and ran afoul of San José, which had suffered the loss of mizzen mast and other damage. Captain was by now almost uncontrollable with her wheel shot away. At this point, her foretop mast fell over the side leaving her in a completely unmanageable state and with little option but to board the Spanish vessels. Captain opened fire on the Spanish vessels with her larboard (port) side broadside and then put the helm over and hooked her larboard cat-head with the starboard quarter of San Nicolás.

While I was watching the Majestic with Robin onboard, I saw him about to lead a boarding party onto the Del Mundo, my attention was diverted as Hardy told me he was going to run in and close with the Captain to help with their steering, and suggested I lead a boarding party to reinforce Nelson, because it looked like he was going to board the San Nicolás.

Making my way to stand beside one of the cutlass barrels on deck, I called "Boarding party to me!" Fifty of our sailors and marines, were ready to follow me, the sailors grabbing cutlasses from barrels as they came.

As Tom brought the ship to Captains rail, I yelled, "Follow, me hearties!" As we swarmed across Captain's deck to join Nelson's boarding party. Nelson smiled saying, "Glad to have you Henry, ready to go to work?"

I smiled and nodded, as he yelled "Westminster Abbey or a Glorious Victory!"

Then we swarmed onto the San Nicolás. We immediately were engaged with the fight for possession of the ship, with Spanish sailors and soldiers as we moved toward the captain and officers.

Having used up my pistol shots, I drew my second sword and with Nelson beside me, we surged forward clearing a line along the ship toward them, slashing and killing or maiming as we went, they surrendered to Nelson, and our men, as I led a party up to the poopdeck killing any one that looked like not surrendering, I struck their colours, the ship was ours!

Then we immediately came under fire from men aboard the San Josef, as pistol and musket fire poured tore into the poop and upper gundeck. Yelling to my party to find cover, I dived over the forward rail, and landed and rolled onto the upper gundeck, winded by the fall, I lay there as shots tore into the deck around me.

Seeing my precarious predicament from the cover of a doorway, Nelson ran to me and grabbed one of my out flung arms, and pulled me to safety. At the same time, he yelled for our marines to open fire at the San Josef. As I regained my feet, I saw a new detachment of marine's board from the Captain, and they helped turn the tide of rifle fire, while I loaded both my pistols again.

While I was doing this, Nelson waited, and when both were reloaded, He said with a grin, "Henry, what think you about being a trifle audacious, and we take another ship?"

Looking around at how many men we had in view, I laughed, replying, "I think that would be a splendid idea sir."

He was still grinning and replied, "For the glory then, ready?"

Grinning also, I replied, "Aye Sir! For the glory."

He clapped me on the shoulder, raised his voice and yelled, "At them lads!"

We broke cover, and started running toward the San Josef, the survivors of our initial boarding party, joining with the marine detachment as we leaped onto the San Josef, going into action straight away, but in this case the fight was over quickly, as nearly all the Spanish we neared started surrendering. On the poopdeck I struck their colours, and stood there with my pistol hanging in my palm unfired, and I holstered it then sheaved my sword.

As I glanced over to the upper gundeck, the captain and officers were surrendering their swords to Nelson, he was covered in blood and gore, and most of his uniform was in tatters.

Shrugging out of my bloodstained frockcoat, I noticed that my shirt was also as bloodstained as my jacket, going down to the gundeck, I walked to him at the railing where he was observing the last of the battle, I passed him my jacket, saying with a laugh, "Here you go sir, this should fit you for the time being."

He laughed as he pulled it on, saying "Thank you Henry, for everything. You know what I mean, not just the coat, god I wish I was as broad-shouldered as you are, but at least it's warm."

After that, we went about putting the two captured ships in order, and having prize crews placed on both. Ralph Miller was placed in command of the San Josef, and his 1st mate were placed in command of San Nicolás.

While the Captain was made secure, rafted against the Minerve, with myself staying onboard the Captain. Nelson stayed aboard the San Josef, as we sailed toward the flagship in line, Nelson was cheered and saluted by every ship and crew we passed, as we sailed along.

1700: as our mini procession passed by Majestic, I stood on the poopdeck of the Captain, and saluted the gathered officers on the poopdeck of the Majestic, Robin, Blagdon, and captain Cuthbert returned my salute.

As we neared Victory, signals were run up ordering Nelson to shift his pennant to the Irresistible, then the next signal ordered the fleet to take station in line astern of Victory.

An hour later, we were ordered to make anchor in Lagos bay in Portugal, the prisoners were to be disembarked on the beach, and all captains, 1st and 2nd lieutenants were ordered aboard the Victory.

Tom and I boarded her at the same time as Nelson, who was still wearing my frockcoat, admiral Jervis came toward us and embraced Nelson saying, "Thank you Horatio, that was a brilliant exercise of initiative, and has led us to a tremendous success and victory."

When we were all gathered in the wardroom, each

of us were handed a glass of fine Madeira as Jervis raised a toast to victory, after the toast each captain gave his individual reports of the action. While Captain Cuthbert was giving his report, an argument ensued with Troubridge from Culloden, which was silenced by Jervis, and for their capture of the Mundo, Cuthbert, Blagdon, and Robin were all promoted a grade in rank, making Cuthbert a Commodore, Blagdon a captain, and Robin a 1st lieutenant, making him equal in rank to me.

All ships are being repaired as best they can be to make them seaworthy, the plan being that some will return to duty under Commodore Cuthbert, and the rest will return to England for necessary repair, the steering has been repaired to a fashion of the Captain, and I will be her master and commander during the return to England, Hardy will also be one of the escorting ships. Back in England we will be on paid leave until summoned by the admiralty.

Chapter 22.

Journal Entry Continued – July15, 1804:
Captain Robin Fox-Davis RN.

June 20, 1797: Majestic, was still in port at
Gibraltar, and waiting for orders from admiral Jervis
after Rear Admiral William Cuthbert, had departed
the Majestic, we still saw him, and he would join us
in the mess or at dinner, whenever we went ashore.
Two days later, a post ship arrived, and the
following day mail was delivered to the Majestic,
and amongst it were letters for George and me.
Having received our mail, we both went to our
cabins, to catch up with news from home.
There were three letters from Elizabeth, one bulky
letter from my cousin Henry, and one from the
admiralty.
The one from the admiralty, I opened first, and it
held the ratification of my promotion to 1st
lieutenant and mate. The one from Henry was really
two letters in one, a short note from him, it read:
Dear cousin Robin, I hope my letter finds you in
fine health, but it is with a sad heart, that I must
disclose, that what was feared about William Fox-
Tolcher has come to pass, and he died, two days
before my arrival home at his house in Taunton,
Albert, now the new Earl, has enclosed a letter to
you with mine, I remain your friend and cousin,
Henry.
Then I opened the letter from my friend and other
cousin Albert, that carried the family seal.

Breaking the seal, it read: Dear friend, and cousin Robin, it is with heavy heart that I write to inform you of the passing of my father William, we had received reports about Henry's and your actions during the Battle of Cape St. Vincent, and thank god that you both survived, and promoted into the bargain. Henry is now at home and will attend father's funeral, but Henry has informed me you will be unable to attend, due to your duties. I wish you every success with your new duties, and expect to see you and Elizabeth here during your next leave, take care dear friend Robin, yours Albert, Earl of Straithhaven.

After reading both letters, I stopped for a time, as I reflected upon my time in Albert's fathers company at my home and at the manor house, it was he, who had vouched for me, when I had enlisted in the navy, and even now I still consider him a great man. My letters from dear Elizabeth, I have no need to mention, as they are of a private nature, but after I had finished reading, and drew writing material to answer my mail, writing to both Albert and Henry care of the manor, then I started answering my wife's letters, and was half way through this when George Blagdon entered my cabin without knocking, as was his right, as Captain of the Majestic.

He said, "Come on Robin we've been summoned to the admiral's office, it seems we may finally have some orders, this sitting in port, isn't doing us any good at all, do you think the old man will be going home on this post ship? It'll probably leave at the end of the week."

I laughed and replied, "Most likely, at least we won't have to put up with his grouching anymore if he does. I wonder what Jervis has up his sleeve for us, ok I'm ready let's go, sir." We both had a hearty laugh.

Then he said with a growl, "Enough of that, sir shite, when we're alone."

I smiled a reply, "See, you're already starting to sound like the old man." We both chuckled as we headed out on deck, making for the longboat.

We entered the admiral's headquarters, and waited to be shown into his office, then a secretary came out, and bid us to enter.

As we did Jervis left his desk and came forward with his hand out, shook our hands, saying "Ah George, Robin, good to see you, sorry it's taken so long, but I've been juggling where to send all my ships, we seem to have an abundance now, after St. Vincent."

As he made his way back to his desk we followed, and seated ourselves, after he waved us to chairs, then he sat down as well.

Holding up a piece of paper, he said, "I've been asked by the admiralty, to assign a small squadron to the Jamaica station, to give Sir Peter Parker a hand, for a while until they can send more ships out there, after those bloody incidents with the Hermione, and Marie Antionette."

After taking a sip from his water glass, he continued, "So I've decided to send him, you, Orion under Saumarez, Minotaur under Louis, and Zealous under Hood, but I have no Commodore to take command, therefore, George I'm making you the squadron commander, now I expect that you should only be out there for a year at the maximum, after that I want all four of you back here."

Blagdon replied, saying, "Yes Sir."

Jervis went on saying, "I will call you all to a conference in two days, you might want to start thinking about your supplies in the meantime, because you leave on the morning tide, Monday next. That's all until the conference, any questions?"

Blagdon replied, "No sir, not until the conference."

Jervis said, "Very well gentlemen, that's all."

Having been dismissed, we stood up and left his office.

Outside George said, "Bloody hell, what have we done to deserve this, bloody Jamaica, nothing but mosquitos, pirates, and mutineer scum!"

I laughed saying, "Cheer up George, its only for a year at most, besides we may have more of a chance of ship captures out there."

He grumbled saying, "Knowing our luck they'll sink before they get back to England, bugger!"

Back onboard we made the purser aware of our sailing, and he scuttled off to start getting a supply list together with the quartermaster. Back in my cabin, I finished my letter to Elizabeth, informing her off our new destination, and the expected duration of our time out there, so it didn't look like I'd be getting home leave anytime soon. Which I was hoping for, after our capture of the Mundo during St. Vincent, a bit of rest and recreation at home in blighty would have gone down a treat.

Two mornings later, we were rowed ashore for the officer's conference at the admiral's headquarters, in my jacket was the letter I had finished to Elizabeth, because knowing the post ship was due to leave in a couple of days, I wanted to get it posted, which I did on the way to headquarters.

We all knew each other, and though there were captains more senior to George present, ours was the last ship to have had a commodore aboard, therefore, George was considered the senior captain of the expedition.

Jervis explained everything he expected us to do while we were on station, stating that if any of us had the chance to retake the Hermione or the Marie Antionette, he expected us to do it, if we captured any of the mutineers, they were not to be taken for trial, but hanged immediately upon capture, as each was under a death sentence from the admiralty.

If any had already been caught, we were to give notice of their sentence to Sir Peter, and we were to notify the admiralty at once, if he failed to exercise the sentence.

We were also told, that any captured ships would be held in harbour under guard, until they could safely be transferred home, by tow or prize crews.

He finished the conference saying, "Gentlemen with the amount of activity in the Caribbean, you should be able to earn quite a deal in prize money, good luck and god speed!"

After the conference we all made for the mess for some socialising and a few drinks, while we waited for lunch to be served. Admiral Cuthbert was in the mess, and told us that he was leaving on the post ship, and had already placed his possessions aboard her, we told him where we were headed for, and he gave us a hearty well done, telling us we should be able to pick up some prize money out in the West Indies, telling us some of the best places to make captures, we also arranged to meet him the following night in the mess for a final farewell before he left for England.

Our squadron made our way out of the harbour, the Majestic flying a command pennant that the petty officer sails, had found among the signal flags, by dinnertime that evening we were well out in the Atlantic, and on course for Jamaica.

As we sailed south, with a fair breeze pushing us, we were out to sea, off the American colony of New York, when a sail was sighted, sailing north a little southeast of our position, George immediately, signalled Zealous and Minotaur to go full out to cut her escape to the south as we sailed toward her.

As we drew nearer I noticed she wasn't flying any flag, and through my scope just made out her name. I yelled, "By god, that's the Hermione!"

George called out immediately, "Action stations, beat to quarters, action stations! Pour on the sail!" As more sail increased our speed, signals were sent to Orion informing them of our intentions.

As we closed, George said he was going to head for her leeward side, so I yelled, "Forward and port guns, fire as you bear!"

The forward gun salvo, fired two minutes later, taking away her forward guns, and some foremast rigging, then the port guns opened up, and her foremast was broken at deck level and crashed backward against the mainmast, sending bodies falling to the deck. Orion's starboard guns fired a broadside, as Saumarez swerved at the last minute, his salvo wrecked half of the upper gundeck cannon, and did a fair amount of damage to her main gundeck, from the debris that was thrown into the air.

I yelled, to the upper gundeck crews, "Cannister, rake their deck with cannister!"

Looking back to Blagdon, he nodded and had Majestic turned toward them, as I got ready to give my next order, as I grabbed a cutlass from one of the barrels, then yelled "Grapples! Boarding party to me!"

The gunners threw the grapple hooks and started hauling on them to bring her closer, as the boarding party readied itself, when we could leap the gap, with a pistol in one hand and cutlass in the other, I gave the order, "Boarding party away!" And leaped to the rail, and jumped onboard the Hermione followed by my crew, anyone in our way was killed.

As we made for the poopdeck where the ships commander was, once my pistol was fired I tucked it into my belt and drew my other sword, as I ran forward slashing, cutlass in one hand, and my sword in the other. Our boarding party were now old hands at this style of fighting, splitting up, one group with Bryce went forward, while my group made for the back toward the ships commander.

Eventually I came face to face with the captain and we duelled for a short time, but he stood no chance while I was armed with two swords, and I cut him down after five minutes. Having seen him go down the rest of the crew started throwing down their weapons and surrendering, we had taken her.

As we waited for Zealous and Minotaur to return, Orion, rafted up to the Hermione's other side. Captain Saumarez, smiled as he made his way aboard, and clapped me on the shoulder, saying, "Well done Robin, I'm going to talk to your captain." As he continued across to Majestic. While the clean-up was going on, I saw Saumarez and George talking on the poopdeck of Majestic.

After all the enemy sailors and officers were locked up below, under guard, leaving Bryce in command, I went back aboard the Majestic, and up onto the poopdeck where all four captains now stood.

Watching the ship, I saw our carpentry gang board the Hermione, and they were joined by a gang from Orion as they both started clearing away the sails, rigging and debris of the foremast, as I was called to the captains' discussion, they had started to fashion a new foremast, though much shorter than the original.

As I joined the discussion, it seemed as if an accord had been struck, as they were all nodding their ascent. I was told, Saumarez and Orion would take the Hermione back to Gibraltar, then return to Jamaica and join our group again. I asked, "And the prisoners?"

Saumarez answered, "Don't worry Robin, I'll find out if any the mutineers are onboard, and carry out Jervis's orders, the rest can rot in the brig until we make Gibraltar, also I will testify that Majestic was responsible for her capture, all the prize money will go to her."

I was dumbfounded and stammered, "But Orion helped in her capture, surely she should share in the prize money?"

Saumarez laughed saying, "Nay Robin, you had her dead to rights, and caught her by surprise, she would have been yours, even without the damage I did to her starboard side, but, you better give me a chance to win some of the prize money off you at cards, when we join up again."

I laughed a reply, "Aye you can count on that Juan."

Blagdon said, "Alright Robin clear our men from Hermione, and we'll get back under way."

Fifteen minutes later all our men were back aboard Majestic and the lines holding us against her, were loosed, and we slowly drifted apart, the other captains had returned to their ships, when there was enough distance, our sails were hauled open.

Juan Saumarez was carrying a despatch from George to Jervis, with a last wave to Orion, our small fleet once more set course for Jamaica.

When Orion re-joined us a month later in Jamaica, we were given the latest news by Saumarez, out of the five hundred crewmen left alive on the Hermione, after our engagement, four hundred of them had been amongst the original mutineers. Saumarez had tried his best, but there were still one hundred and twenty, that were left to be hanged by Jervis, by the time he made port in Gibraltar.

The Hermione was sent back to Portsmouth, before Orion had left Gibraltar again, to join us in Jamaica, Jervis had wanted him to tell the tale of how he had to wait to see all the mutineers hung, before he was allowed to leave port.

Chapter 23.

During the month, we waited for the return of Orion, when we first arrived in Jamaica, George and I reported to Sir Peter Parker the Commander in Chief of the Jamaica station. He was happy to see us, and explained the current local situation for us, and he was quite happy for us to operate as an independent squadron, whilst there.

The local situation, was the Caribbean was rife with pirates, and his ships also contended with Spanish convoys, as well from their central American bases. His ships crews weren't a happy lot, and sedition was rife amongst the crews of his ships, which had led to the mutinies aboard the Hermione and Marie Antoinette.

He was happy to hear of our recapture of the Hermione, but not the punishment, that had been ordained by the admiralty, however, should we bring him any of the mutineers, he would obligingly do his duty, and hang them without trail.

After the situation had been explained, over drinks of sherry, Sir Parker, dressed in the height of splendour as governor in light breeches, colourful shirt, and a gold laced waistcoat under his tan frockcoat, and wearing an extravagant neckerchief, asked, "So Captain Blagdon, what do you intend doing while you wait for the Orion to join you?"

I still stood looking over the governor as George contemplated his answer, Sir Peter stood about five six, with salt and pepper hair under his white wig, and at one stage, he would have been muscular.

Life in the tropics, had taken its toll, and he was going to fat, from lack of exercise, he had a jovial manner about him, but what else would you expect from politician?

George answered, "Well Sir Peter, I shall split our ships and patrol the nearby islands, and see what we can scare up, do you have any intelligence that does concern the present whereabouts of the Marie Antionette, I would dearly love to recapture her whilst my ships are here?"

Sir Peter replied, "The last report I had sir was that she was still in Port Au Prince harbour on the island of Haiti. If anything, further comes to light, I shall have you informed immediately."

After thanking him, George, and I left the Governor's mansion, returning to our ship, then had signals run up calling the captains and 1st mates of our squadron to a conference aboard the Majestic.

Once they were all onboard we went to the wardroom for our conference, where a map of the Caribbean was spread out, both ships would sail together, and patrol off the South American coastal Islands of Aruba, Curacao, and Bonaire, seeing if they could scare up any action, but they were forbidden to go anywhere near Tortuga, which was the main base area where pirates congregated.

He said, "Once we have Orion back, this will be our main target, but not until then. Allow yourselves a two-week patrol, before, coming back to Kingston, I will be doing the same, but I also have some scouting to do, any questions?"

There were none and he continued, "Then I think it's time for drinks while we wait for lunch."

Over our drinks, Louis from the Minotaur asked, "And may we enquire, what you will doing while we're out patrolling, George?"

Laughing, George replied, "You certainly may William, I have been made to understand that the Marie Antionette is in harbour at Haiti, I therefore, intend to find out if this is true, and if it is, when Juan gets here we're all going after her."

There was laughter and cheerfulness after his answer, and during lunch. After that they went to make their ships ready for sea again.

Four days later, as we neared the island of Haiti, which was French territory, George explained what he had in mind. He was going to slip into the Sainte Marc channel at night getting as close, to shore as he could where I and a select group of men would be given a longboat to make shore, it was going to be up to us, to get as close to the harbour as we could, and find out what we would face, and find out if the Marie Antionette was actually there. He would return to the channel on the third night, and the following two nights, if we weren't picked up the first time. But after the third night, of us not showing up, he would consider us captives, and leave.

Luckily, it didn't come to that, and we made the rendezvous with Majestic during the second night. The day after that, having had some sleep, I joined George in his cabin to report what had been found in the harbour.

The Marie Antoinette, was indeed anchored in the harbour, along with two more French fourth rates, but I added that all the ships, seemed to only be manned, by skeleton crews. Then I proposed a scheme that had him laughing in raptures.

As he said, "By god Robin, that would be positively unheard of, but what a coup it would be, do you actually think we could pull it off?"

I nodded saying, "I do, with the right amount of men."

After telling me that he would give it some thought, no more was said about my scheme, until an officers conference back in Kingston harbour. Majestic was back in the ramshackle harbour of Kingston four days later, all around the harbour, and streets are the jerry made huts of the families that live here, they have made their homes out of anything that has been scrounged and often look mismatched and unsightly, with gaps where pieces of wood or canvas have been joined, though these gaps allow ventilation in this year-round tropical paradise.

The main style of dress being open necked short, sleeved shirts and wrap-around cloth for the men and the women just wear wrap-around cloth in the shape of dresses.

During the midwatch, two days later, Zealous and Minotaur returned, the Minotaur was towing another ship, that looked like a fifth rate. George had been called on deck, and we both observed the ship under tow, counting the gunports, I determined she was of fifth rate class, and her name was the Sea Lion. As we watched, the Sea lion made anchor between across our rear, while Minotaur, and Zealous turned to port, so that they were facing to the harbour mouth, like we were. Then their captains were rowed over to us as their crews furled sail, and made the ships ready for life in harbour. Once William Louis of Zealous, and John Hood of Minotaur, were aboard, we made for the captain's cabin, and we all sat around the larger table as they proceeded to give their verbal reports, as George's clerk made notes.

They had come across the Sea Lion, just north of Aruba, and she had made a run for it, so they chased her, and a fight ensued, until she was boarded and captured. As they gave their reports, they were dressed in the same manner as George and me, with open necked shirts, and uniform waist coats that were unbuttoned. When we arrived in Jamaica, George had prescribed the manner of dress at an earlier conference, and due to the heat, we only wore our frockcoats, during official occasions.
Asked why they had given chase and engaged the Sea Lion, John stood, unfurling a flag that he spread across the table, saying, "Because they were flying this flag!"
It was, a black flag emblazoned with a skull and cross bones, the infamous Jolly Rodger, flown by pirates. He went on to say, "Against the two of us they really didn't stand a chance, with our superior gunnery, and we poured broadsides into her from both sides, before I had the grapples thrown, and

they surrendered soon afterward."

Then he produced two pages of paper, saying, "Here's a list of the names of those still alive, imprisoned below decks."

Taking the sheets, George said to the clerk, "Check these against the names of the mutineers Percival." Then we all had drinks, and toasted their good fortune in the capture, whilst the clerk was looking at the lists, and comparing them. He interrupted George whispering in his ear, then George answered, "Are there, by god?" Right, John, have these men taken aboard your ship, William take the Sea Lion to the dock tomorrow and have the rest marched to the prison, and charged with piracy. There are ninety-five mutineers amongst them, in two days, we will have all ships witness punishment, John have twelve at a time hung from each of the yardarms, and leave them hang overnight before feeding the bodies to the sharks. I will call on the governor tomorrow and explain my actions."

Then the news of our expedition was imparted, and the results, and we settled down to talk about our options, of a recapture, my suggestion, wasn't broached at this time, and as I was about to put forward my plan of action, George gave me a look and shake of his head, that meant, 'don't say anything', so I kept silent.

After a relaxed lunch, both captains returned to their ships, and Hood went about having the prisoner transfer take place, as ten fettered prisoners were transferred at a time.

The next day, George left to call on the governor,

and returned two hours later, in a jovial mood. The Sea Lion was still moored against the dock when he returned, and I was asked how long they had been there, which had only been half an hour, and an hour later, I watched as she pulled away from the dock, making her way back to where we were anchored, and turned into line ahead, as the rear anchor was set, and the sails furled by the crew handling her.

At the tenth hour, the following morning, hands on all ships were summoned to witness punishment, this time all officers were in full uniform, the accused were brought out from below decks of the Minotaur. Each of the Majestic and Zealous had been rowed closer to Minotaur, and all were rafted together, as John Hood read out the list of names of the prisoners, then said, "All of you have been found guilty of mutiny by the admiralty, and there being only one penalty, you are all sentenced to death by hanging! Bosun have the sentence carried out as you will."

Each of the prisoners, were all moved into place around the deck of the Minotaur, to where ropes with nooses were slung over all available space over yardarms, each rope had a gang of six men standing with the loose end of the ropes, As the nooses were placed around the necks of the prisoners, the rope slack was taken up by the hauling gangs, as the last prisoner had his noose placed around his neck, the bosun turned to the captain, saying, "Ready to carry out the sentence sir!" Hood nodded, and the bosun, turned toward the bow yelling, "Heave, Heave!"

At the bosun's direction, the rope crews hauled the prisoners to the top of the makeshift gallows, and the ropes secured in place by belaying pins, after the executions, all ships companies were dismissed to go back to their duties, as Majestic, and Zealous were turned loose from the Minotaur, and the anchorage lines hauled in, taking them back to their original positions.

Each time I glanced at Minotaur that day, it was a gruesome sight, with bodies hanging from the yardarms, in plain sight of everyone in Jamaica.

Sir Parker, had a message sent to Blagdon, showing it to me before he took it back, the governor had asked, not ordered though, that the bodies be taken down from sight, George just growled, balled up the message and threw it overboard, commenting, "To hell with him and his sensitive views."

A week later, Orion sailed into the harbour, and made anchorage beside us. George called for all captains and 1st mates to make for the Majestic, and a daylong conference.

As we all sat around, the table in Georges cabin, we were all in a relaxed state, as drinks were placed on the table, and each of us poured our own drinks, as Saumarez brought us up to date with the goings on back in Gibraltar.

Once comments and remarks were exchanged about his news, George turned the conversation to the state of affairs here in the Caribbean, mainly for Juan's knowledge, then talk turned to our finding of the Marie Antoinette, and where we she was situated. As plans for her recovery were again discussed. Typically, Juan, as was his style suggested sailing into the Port Au Prince harbour, all guns blazing, and take her from them. George and I smiled, as this had already been suggested, by Hood a week prior. After letting the discussion take its course, without getting anywhere in the way of a firm decision, George looked at me, and nodded, given his permission, I said, "Gentlemen, since our last discussion on this subject, I have given this a lot of thought, and have come up with a plan that may lead to the success of not only recovering the Antoinette, but the other two French fourth rates as well!"

Immediately all discussion ceased, as I became the centre of attention, I excused myself to go to my cabin, and got my maps and intelligence I had collected during my stay on Haiti, and returned with them to the table. As I sat all eyes came back to me as I said, "What I propose is somewhat simple and audacious at the same time, each of the ships are manned by light to medium skeleton crews, it would be my intention that each of our ships, Zealous, Minotaur, and Majestic tow four longboats full of prize crews, to this point (pointing to my mud map), where we will then row into the harbour.
Each ships longboat will make for a targeted ship, board and take them, then make them ready for sea. Then our four ships form up and indeed invade the harbour targeting the defences, once the

bombardment commences, the captured ships will make good their escape, once they're out of the harbour, our squadron disengages and leaves."

Saumarez laughed saying, "Hah that'll get up the frogs' noses, you certainly have balls Robin, what a brilliant idea!"

The other two captains and all the junior officers agreed with the idea, then George asked, "Well gentlemen, there's a plan on the table, all in agreement, a show of hands please?"

All agreed, so George said, "Very well, in that case let's get into the specifics of the raid, Robin carry on please."

The next couple of hours was spent going over all the details of the planned raid, Minotaur's crew were to target La Contessa, Zealous the Danseur D'Onde, while I took the Marie Antionette.

Chapter 24.

The raid took place, a week later during the dark of the moon. We had slipped out of Jamaica during the night, without anything said to anyone, mainly for security reasons, not wanting the French prewarned. Four nights later our ships were in position down in the Sainte Marc channel near where George had left my boat crew a few weeks earlier.

Where our longboats were launched and roped nose to tail as the boarding prize crews climbed into them, then with they're top masts bared so they wouldn't show we made our way down to the harbour mouth in line astern, with Orion as the last ship keeping the longboats covered against any surprise.

Then I made the signal to untie from Majestic, and each other, as I cautioned the rowers for silence, as we rowed into the harbour, making for our target ship. The tow ropes were reattached to the longboats as we snuck onto the Antoinette, and this gave the opportunity to see the progress of the other raiding parties.

The skeleton crew were no match for my men, and each of them were silenced and gagged before being locked below. Then my men went about making the ship ready for sea, men were all in the rigging ready to release sail, and men on the capstan ready to bring the anchor up, before I gave the prearranged signal to our ships outside the harbour.

As I watched they sailed in under full sail and started opening up with broadsides to the fortifications as I yelled, "Up anchor and release the sails, gun crews be ready!"

The Antoinette started moving slowly at first, but built up speed as the sails were set, then I looked behind me, to see our longboats following astern followed by the other two ships. Our squadron ships were creating havoc everywhere with their broadsides, and the harbour mouth defences didn't challenge our departure, after they had been reduced to rubble in the first salvos. After having the course set, I looked back toward the harbour to see our ships coming out of the harbour still with their guns blazing, we had made it clear! With no ships to chase us, as they were now in our hands.

After dawn, the longboats were hauled out of the water as the squadron formed up around us, and we all sailed for Jamaica, but there were many a signal raised congratulating us on the raid, and comments passed to and through. Also during the voyage back to Jamaica, the names of our prisoners, were collected, apart from three French officers that had acted as the captains of the skeleton crews, all the rest were English, and part of the mutinous crews from Antoinette and Hermione.

We drew quite an audience as we sailed into Kingston harbour, with Sir Parker arriving at the dock in his carriage, and he was rowed out to where we were taking up our mooring positions. Being first aboard he congratulated us on our captures and demanded an explanation.

Being told of our raid, and how it came about, the

governor said, "Very well-done Captain Blagdon, in the short time you have been here, you have made a significant difference to our interests here."

Taking a mouthful of his wine, he continued, "And I will be passing a favourable report along to the admiralty, please pass along my congratulations to your other captains, now is there anything else before I leave?"

George answered, "Yes Sir, apart from the three French officers, we captured, the remaining, two hundred and sixty are all English sailors that took part in the mutinies aboard the Antoinette and Hermione, and who are still under admiralty orders to be publicly hung!"

Parker, took a deep breath and let it out, and in resigned expression came over his face, as he said, "Very well captain, have them all transported to the prison, and I will make sure the sentence is carried out in the town square."

The following morning, after a raucous celebration by all the captains and officers that night, as many toasts were made and drunk to me and Blagdon, along with all the prize crews that had taken part in the captures, all the prisoners were placed aboard the Orion and Saumarez delivered them from the dock, in chains to the prison. The French officers weren't chained, and were treated with the respect they were due.

Two days later, the executions were started in the town square, twenty a day, until all of the mutineers had received admiralty justice.

A month later, we were patrolling south west of

Jamaica about approximately one hundred and fifty miles north of Barranquilla on the South American continent, when we encountered a small Spanish fleet, made up of two large galleons that sat low in the water, and four, forty cannon frigates. George looked at me and asked, "What do you think Robin?"

I took a closer look through my scope, before replying with a smile, "Well the big ones are sitting low in the water, which means they have full loads of treasure aboard."

He smiled saying, "My very thought, Signals! Hoist Engage the enemy, Minotaur and Zealous the frigates, Orion the other galleon. Action stations, beat to quarters, action stations!"

Because the small fleet was travelling slow, we were able to close with them, the frigates tried to lead us away from the transports, but they were soon engaged by Minotaur and Zealous, as our gunnery superiority showed the difference between us and the Spaniards, the transports were one hundred guns first rates, but no match for Orion or us, in the gunnery stakes as we fired three broadside salvos to their one.

Our first salvo took away or destroyed all upper gundeck cannon, and created hell for the Spanish, as man and guns were blasted off their ship by our double shotted cannon (which is to say each cannon had been loaded with two balls instead of one, this was a favourite opening gambit with us English), Then our main gundeck thirty-two pounders, did massive damage as we closed with them, killing, maiming and blowing away cannon, then it was time to board, and we swarmed aboard.

After some fierce hand to hand combat that lasted nearly forty minutes, I eventually gained the upper hand, as the ships' captain surrendered.

Once the ship was ours, I took time to see how Orion was doing and, I saw Saumarez leading his boarding party, with the same result, only in his case he killed the captain during their duel.

Three of the frigates had struck their colours, and as I watched the fourth started sinking.

As was tradition with the capture of treasure ships, once I had the keys to the treasure holds, I called George, the sergeant at arms, and the purser aboard, then we went below to the treasure hoard, while the sergeant at arms stood guard at the door, both George and myself grabbed two sacks from the pile near the door, and started filling them. I concentrated on coinage and gems, filling a sack with each, and exited as the purser grabbed one sack. As George made his way out, the sergeant at arms took his sack. Once both had finished, they placed their sacks in a place no one else would take, and both stood at the doorway.

When I made it to the upper deck, I had the boarding party, one by one go to the treasure holds, each man was allowed one sack only, once the boarding party had taken their share the rest of Majestics crew lined up behind the officers, until each man had returned aboard the Majestic with their booty.

Officers were allowed two sacks, while each crewman was allowed one.

Whatever was left remained aboard to be part of the prize money paid to the ships responsible for the capture.
Each member of the crews shared in these spoils, for the capture of the ship. Once the Majestics crew had their share of the booty, I signalled Zealous to replace us rafted to the treasure ship and the process was repeated. Taking my sacks and putting them in my wardrobe, to be examined later.

After all ships hands had, had their pick of the booty, and the holds relocked and sealed, it was time to have prize crews allocated to each ship, so we could sail back to Kingston. The patrol had indeed been profitable, with two first rates, and three frigates, now amongst our tally of captures.

During the voyage back to Jamaica, I had time to examine my booty, and found that keeping to smaller items had indeed been fortunate, apart from the gold coinage, half the sacks were full of Diamonds, Rubies, Emeralds, Sapphires, and fine jewellery pieces, I only had a rough idea of the value of my booty, but figured I had close to a million pounds worth of jewels alone, without the gold coins, and I was staggered by my calculations. I could retire from the navy, and enjoy a very comfortable life indeed! I dismissed the thought as soon as it came to me though, because I was enjoying my life.
By the time we made Kingston, I noticed a post ship had arrived and was alongside the dock.

Our little anchorage was now getting a little crowded, as each ship was anchored, the captures in their own area.

While our squadron remained a little away from them. This time however, we had to have marines keep guard aboard the treasure ships twenty-four hours a day.

Once we were anchored, George concentrated on writing up all the despatches he wanted sent to the admiralty. Taking a longboat to the quay, I went to the post office, and enquired about mail for all four of our ships, and was given a large sack for each ship, marked with their name. Then I enquired how long the post ship was in port for, and told that it would be sailing a week later, and last post the day before it left. Hoisting two sacks across each shoulder, I made for the longboat and threw the sacks down to the waiting seamen.

I was rowed to each ship, and hailed the officer of the watch on each, having a line passed down which I secured to the sack, so it could be hauled aboard, but when we finally reached the Majestic, we stayed in the longboat as it was hauled up to the rail.

Calling the purser, I gave him the mail sack, and went to see George.

After telling him that the post ship was in port for a week, a knock came upon the door, and after calling "Come" the purser entered with all the mail for the both of us.

Glancing through mine, I had one from the admiralty, which I opened, and four from Elizabeth, the one from the admiralty held an accounting of the prize ship Hermione and a cheque for twenty-eight thousand pounds.

Showing George my cheque, he showed me his. I was a little dumbfounded as I questioned the amount, his was only two thousand pounds more than mine, which I queried telling him he should have got more than that.

He laughed shaking his head, and saying, "No Robin you led the boarding party, so you get a lion's share, but it's all prorated to the responsibility, of the action itself, read the section on prize ships in the manual, and you'll see what I mean."

That was one of the many sections in the admiralty manual, that I hadn't bothered to read as yet, and decided to look it up and read the whole section, not that I was really worried about it, the admiralty accountants would be sticklers for adhering to the correct rulings, in regard the sharing's of prize money.

After leaving him to his despatches, I went to my cabin and looked up the section on prize ships, and discovered that each man in the boarding party upon capturing a vessel received, bonuses for the capture.

Our next patrol a month later, produced the capture of two more, fifth rates, both pirate vessels, the first being taken a little west of Aruba, the Conqueror, aboard her we found the last of the mutineers, all except one had been found.

The second was taken between Curacao and Tortuga, named the Vanquish, another fifth rate.

Then low on supplies we returned to Jamaica. Our,

captures now numbered eleven, soon we would have to send some back to England, as space was now becoming limited. But fate was soon to take a hand. After nine months in the Caribbean, we had captured, two first rates still with treasure aboard, three fourth rates, three fifth rates, and three frigates. Then a fleet of ten ships under Commodore Wilson arrived in Jamaica to relieve our squadron.

George made the decision to have, the two first rates and the Marie Antoinette tow the frigates, back to England, and prize crews would be placed on the others, and we would all sail home together.

Six weeks after leaving Kingston our little fleet, arrived in Portsmouth, where each of our captures were taken to the back harbour, now all our ships with our full crews aboard were placed side by side on finger docks. All Captains and 1st mates were summoned to the admiralty headquarters building, where we told to wait as George lodged his full report.
An hour after that, a captain approached us, and asked us to follow him, and he took us to a large office, and asked us to wait.
Then the door was opened again, and an officer in a vice admiral uniform entered, we immediately came to attention, and we were each introduced to the First Naval Lord, Vice Admiral Sir Hugh Palliser, he was there to congratulate us on our keeping the peace in the West Indies, he talked to each of us in turn, and we even lunched with him.

Back in his office, we were all given a month's shore leave along with our crews, at full pay, before we had to report again on the 1st of June to be sent back to the Mediterranean.

His final words to us were, "Good luck on your leave gentlemen, and happy hunting when you resume your duties."

Back aboard the Majestic, I packed my gear, and the booty from the treasure ship, then went and hired a coach to take me home, which was a two-day trip, but I had more than enough money to warrant the expense of a carriage.

Elizabeth was so glad to see me, and the first night at home we talked, or rather I talked about my adventures, and my time in the Caribbean, while she just listened and asked questions. When she asked about what happened to the gold and jewels, I went to the hallway bringing back the two sacks, and upended them on the bed. And we laughed heartily, before she helped me gather them up, and place them in the safe, before we went to bed to make love to each other, something we had been unable to do for such a long time.

Chapter 25.

Journal: Henry Robert Tolcher RN 1st Lieutenant.

May 10, 1797: Naval headquarters, Portsmouth. I had arrived as ordered, to be told that Captain Hardy and I had been assigned to HMS Mutine, as the Minerve was undergoing maintenance that wasn't finished, but our old crew had also been assigned to Mutine. We would sail in ten days, as part of a convoy proceeding to Gibraltar.

However, before telling you about this, let me bring my journal, and you up to this present time:

When we reached Portsmouth after the battle of Cape St. Vincent, we were all placed on leave with pay, until directed otherwise by the admiralty. I arrived home at Taunton to find the household in mourning, Uncle William had succumbed to his illness and died two days prior to my arrival.

Not the sort of homecoming that I had imagined, as I joined Albert in the study, where he welcomed me home and told me in detail what had occurred. I told him that Robin and I had met on a couple of occasions, the last being after the battle.

He looked at me asking, "What! He was there too, thank god you both survived, how is he?"

I smiled saying, "Oh he's fine, and he was even promoted to 1st lieutenant after the battle, because it was he that captured the first rated Salvador Del Mundo, so we're now both the same rank, I think he may have been a little miffed when we first met, because I was already a 1st lieutenant by then."

Albert asked, "Miffed, why should he have been miffed?"

I smiled replying, "Well he had been in the navy longer than I had, and here I was, rising faster through the ranks than he was, but I did explain that it was due to falling in with the right people, like George Cockburn, Tom Hardy, and now Nelson."

Albert exclaimed, "Nelson! By god now there's a man that will lead you to glory… or death, you look after yourself Henry!"

I told Albert that I was, and told him about my leave, so I was home until a letter arrived calling me to duty again. Then said, "Speaking of Robin, he and I discussed uncle Williams' illness, so I had best write him a letter, because there's no way he can make the funeral, he had to go back to Gibraltar and the Mediterranean with Commodore Cuthbert."

Albert nodded his head, saying, "Yes, do please Henry, but don't post it I'll give you one of my own to go with it." Then we both started to write the letters, mine was short and to the point, because I knew Albert's would go into detail.

I was unable to see any of the other family members, except Lucy who joined us for lunch, aunt Elizabeth and Joanna, had taken to the habit of having breakfast and lunch served in aunt Elizabeth's room, and wouldn't know I was home until dinner that evening when they both came down.

When she saw that evening, she launched into my arms, then hovered between me and Elizabeth, during our drinks, during dinner Elizabeth chided her, saying, "Joanna dear, now that Henry is home, you have much more to do than look after a crotchety old woman, we don't know how long Henry will be here, perhaps he can enlighten us, but you are to spend as much time with him as you can, don't worry about me dear, I can look after myself, so don't bother arguing."

She looked at Elizabeth with a sad smile, and replied, "Yes marm."

Then I said, "To answer everyone's question, about my return to duty, even I have no idea, all I can say is that I'm on leave until I'm instructed to return, but the way things are going with the war, I expect it to be sooner rather than later."

Albert asked me to recount the story of my exploits that he already knew, and some he didn't as I entertained the family for the rest of dinner, telling them what I had been doing since I was last home. Joanna joined us for breakfast, the next morning, and we organised to go riding for a few hours that morning.

While she went to change, I had Jenkins organize our horses for us, and when she came down again, we exited the house, through the back, saying hello to her mother on the way through.

After riding for a while, we were both laughing and having fun, then stopped and walked together, with our arms around each other, and I proposed a journey for us, saying, "Joanna my love, do you think that after William's funeral, we could go away together for a little while, we could go visit my parents at the same time my grandparents go home, and I'll see if Albert will allow your parents to go with us as well, that way you can meet them, and they you."

She laughed saying, "I think it would be wonderful darling, and if my parents came I think your aunt would let me go, anything to be out and away from the house right now, it seems as if all the cheeriness has left it, do you think it will ever return Henry?"

I nodded grimly, and replied, "Yes I think I know what you're saying, the place is like a grave yard, now that William has gone, but I think the cheery atmosphere will return… slowly maybe, bit by bit after the funeral."

"Oh, I do hope so," she replied.

When we returned to the house, it was close to lunchtime, while Joanna was changing, Albert informed me, "The funeral will be tomorrow at ten, Henry, and I rather think father would like to have you in your uniform, if you would please."

I nodded grimly, and replied, "Certainly Albert, will it be at the cathedral in town?"

He nodded saying, "Yes, and I've already arranged for both carriages, the women will travel in the coach, and your grandfather, you, and I will be in the open one, and I'll explain this to everyone at lunch, before I inform mother after that."

After nodding my assent, I broached the subject of taking Joanna to meet my parents, and he thought it a marvellous idea, and gave permission to let her parents accompany us, as he said with a smile, "At least that'll take care of the necessary protocol of having chaperones."

"I know what you sailor types are like, by the way, have you decided on a wedding date yet?"

I replied, "Well I was hoping to get married during this leave, but with what's going on I didn't think it appropriate, and haven't even brought it up to Joanna yet."

He laughed saying, "Well let's think this through properly, and as far as this being inappropriate, nonsense old man, a wedding will bring back the cheer into this place! Now here's what I think you should do…" Then he suggested leaving my nan and pop there, but taking Joanna and her parents with me not to stay there, but to bring them back to Taunton with us, he would talk to the bishop about the ceremony at the cathedral, and the wedding reception would be held at the manor.

He would also get Jenkins to have my rooms changed to a suite for a married couple, and he would look after all the arrangements, which would include disclosing the facts to other members of the household and he finished with, "Now by the way do you have a best man picked yet?"

I laughed saying, "Yes, it's going to be you Albert."

I smiled saying, "Well in that case old man, I humbly accept your invitation to be your best man." We both laughed out loud, then he called for Jenkins, giving him instructions for my change of rooms."

Jenkins replied with a smile, saying "I will arrange it personally my lord, and all your things, you will find in their correct places in your new suites master Henry."

I thanked Jenkins, then Albert laughed saying, "Come Henry, time to give everyone the sad news." He put his arm around my shoulders and guided me to the dining room. Everyone was seated for lunch, as we walked in with him still guiding me, after seeing me seated, he moved to the head of the table, which was now his position, as head of the clan, but before sitting, he said, "May I have everyone's attention please, I have some sad bits news to depart to you all, first father's funeral will take place at ten am tomorrow at the cathedral, ladies will travel in the coach, and gentlemen will ride in the carriage. Secondly, the morning after that, Henry and Joanna will leave with her parents for Dean Prior, Sam and Suzanna, unfortunately you will not be going with them. When they return, they will be bringing his parents back with them, now thirdly, the saddest of all news, Henry will be leaving the state of bachelorhood behind, and will marry Joanna soon after returning, it is with great sadness I give you a toast to Henry and Joanna."

The toast was drunk to us, then everyone started talking and querying his announcements at once, as Joanna dug me in the ribs, saying, "You haven't even discussed this with me, why not darling?"

With a bewildered look on my face, I smiled, saying, "Because I only found out two minutes before we came in here, unless you don't wish to go ahead?"

She had a pitying expression on her face, as she replied, "Oh, of course I do, but…"

Then she hugged me to her, after I had just shrugged my shoulders in bewilderment, as she said, "Trust Albert, he's just like his father." And we laughed. After lunch, Albert excused himself saying, "Excuse me, but right now I must inform mother of what is happening, I leave poor Henry to your further inquisitions." He laughed and left the room.

To avoid any questions, I didn't have the answers to and looking like a complete idiot, I grabbed Joanna by the hand, and had her stand with me, as I said, "You'll have to excuse us too, Joanna and I have to see her parents."

I marched her with me out of the room, before anyone could stop us. As we got to the Yeoman cottage, I kept knocking on the door until Ted opened it, dragging Joanna along with me past him into the lounge, with a quizzical look on his face, he closed the door, and followed us into the lounge. As I said, "Sorry about this Ted, but we both need to tell you and Alice what's happened, Alice!

Alice came rushing into the lounge at my call, and Ted indicated we all sit.

Then I disclosed the whole story of what had happened at the lunch table, Ted was laughing as I explained everything, and Alice had her hands across her mouth, with a bewildered look on her face.

When I was finished telling them the whole story, Ted still laughing, said, "Hah aye, that master Albert is definitely his fathers' son alright, well mother, you'd best be packing some clothes, we're going on a trip."

Alice laughing also around her hands asked, "So when are you to be married?"
As all eyes turned to me, I shrugged my shoulders. And they started laughing again, then Ted said, "It'll be after we get back of course, but whenever it be, I know our Joanna, will have a fine husband in master Henry."

The following morning, after facing the music with the family at drinks the evening before, where Elizabeth announced she was well pleased with the forthcoming arrangements, and that she was happy for the both of us, luckily Albert had been there to fend off questions, only he had the answer to. When Lucy asked about Joanna's wedding dress, Elizabeth stated that she would wear her wedding dress which could be altered to fit when we returned from Devon. At the same time announcing she would be Joanna's maid of honour, and Lucy her bridesmaid.

We all gathered outside beside the carriages, at 0915, all the women wore black, and hats with black veils, both Albert and Grandpop, wore black frockcoats and white shirts with neckerchiefs, and grandpop was using my black top hat, and Albert wore his also. I was dressed in full dress uniform and hat, and my weapons belt. The coachmen were also wearing black, and I noticed Ted would be driving our carriage. Once everyone was in the coaches we set off toward town.

Along the way Albert Told Ted about the trip he and his wife were taking, and that they would be taking the enclosed coach, I interrupted him saying I wanted two riding horses and saddles to go also in case I felt like riding.

Albert quizzed me on how long it would take to get to Dean Prior on the way in and I figured out that we would be back in seven days at the latest, and asked why, but he just told me he was wondering about it.

The cathedral was packed with townsfolk, and members of the house of lords, politicians, and everyone moved outside after the service to the graveyard where a plot had been dug to receive my uncles coffin, looking around at the honour guard I noticed that there were only six members, upon having a word to the sergeant in charge I found out one of the guard had taken ill, so I volunteered to become the seventh man in the salute.

As it became time for the casket to be lowered I joined the honour guard in a final salute to my uncle, as I emptied one pistol, then the other, which I reloaded for my third shot.

Mourners then gathered and talked amongst themselves and the family after the graveside ritual, Albert was deep in conversation with the bishop who had officiated during the funeral, and they went off together.

Once he came back, and joined us, many of the mourners joined the procession back to the manor with the family being the lead coaches.

During the wake, Albert was in discussion with

members of the house of lords, and upon nearing the conversation, I heard more than one urging Albert that it was time to take his seat in the house.

To save any embarrassment to Albert, I excused myself into their conversation, saying that as yet, no agenda and instructions had been sent to Albert.

This took the heat off Albert as the members started to discuss this appalling lack of procedure. Albert thanked me, as I steered him away from them.

Finally, after everyone had left, it was family time, over dinner we discussed Joanna's and my trip the following morning. Before we all retired early for the night.

Next morning after breakfast, they all came out to see us off, Ted and Alice were already in the coach, as we joined them, I noticed that there were two saddled horses tied to the coach one was lightning, and the other a fine bay mare.

After two overnight stops, I was riding lightning while Ted drove the coach into the yard at my parent's farm.

Chapter 26.

After all the introductions had been made, we entered the house, and spent the next couple of hours discussing what was to take place.

My father's main argument against going back to Taunton with us was, that he had no one to look after the milking of the cows.

I suggested that he ask his friend Jack Poulson on the next farm to have it done, and he seemed uncertain about this, so, used to ordering men my senior around I finally said, "Right there's two horses saddled outside, come on we'll ride over and see if he will do it for you."

Not used to being ordered around, he looked at me, then finally nodded his head, and followed me to the horses. Ted followed us out and asked, "Would you prefer me to go with you master Henry?"

I replied, "No Ted, this is my problem to fix."

He answered, "Right you are then sir." Giving me a wink that was unseen by my father."

My father had heard, and seen the way Ted deferred to my judgement, and I could see him trying to work out how I could earn a man like Ted's respect. On the ride to Poulson's he asked how I could expect respect like that, and I answered, "Father, I'm an officer in the navy, I lead men older than me into battle to do that, you first have to prove your ability to command." That's all I said, and let him chew that over and work out for himself. There was no problem with Poulson looking after the milking, after father told him to keep the milk for himself.

Back at the farm, mother was having a great time with Joanna and her family, and father and I joined in when we got back, dinner was made by both Alice and mother, and we had a relaxed meal with drinks, I was asked what time we would depart for Taunton and I told them after breakfast and the dishes done. Joanna asked me if she could ride for a while the next morning, and I told her she could, and this pleased her.

As we rode ahead of the coach next morning, we talked about our upcoming nuptials, and I asked if she was happy to wear Aunt Elizabeth's wedding dress instead of a new one. She told me that she had seen it, and that it was beautiful and was more than happy to wear it, besides it would give Elizabeth so much pleasure to see her in it. I nodded, then we heard shrieks of laughter coming from the coach, and surmised everyone was getting on well. As we looked at each other and smiled, then continued riding. She was taking in a lot of the scenery, and asked me about places she pointed out, and I answered her the best I could.

That night we stayed at a wayside inn at Exminster, while we were there after dinner, after everyone else had gone to bed, my father joined me while I was having a quiet scotch at a table in the bar, I bought another two scotches, and after a sip he asked, "Your new father in law was telling us a few things, that he has heard and seen you do today while we were travelling, how come you have never told me all the things you can do boy? Things like your shooting, fighting ability, of how you have captured enemy ships, and having survived great naval battles, and your promotions? Why haven't I heard about these things?"

I looked at him and replied, "Because father, when I've tried you, were always too busy to take any notice of what I had to say, or didn't even want to know, you never have taken the time to really listen to what I was saying or suggesting, you always knew better, if it wasn't about the farm, you didn't wish to hear it, even when I begged you to let me join the navy, you never once gave me any help, if it hadn't been for Grandpop, and uncle William, I'd have got nowhere, which is where you wanted me, you wanted me to be a farm boy, everything else wasn't important, as long as I learnt everything about farming. Well, I've made something of my life, thanks to grandfather and William and his son, I command men in battle, and walk beside great leaders and heroes, like Jervis and Nelson, they all know and respect me for who I am, which is not what you wanted me to be, but it was what I wanted!"

He was taken aback at my vehemence, as I slugged down my scotch and indicated another, to the barman. As it was brought to the table, I took a handful of gold coins out of my pocket, and placed them on the table, as the barmaid picked out what she wanted, then I looked at him again saying, "You want to know something? My mother knows more of what I can do, and have done, than you ever will, you saw the money I fished out of my pocket, that is nothing, I have more than enough money, from

my life so far in the navy, that I could buy your whole farm ten times over, and still have plenty of money left, and you wanted me to be just a farmer? I'm glad I struck out on my own."
Finishing my drink, I got up and left him at the table, as I went up to my room.

The following night we stayed at White Ball, and arrived at the manor before lunch the following morning. Since the night at Exminster, my father had said nothing to me, and from what I could make out, hadn't said much to anyone. As the coach pulled up in the drive near the door, Albert, Lucy, pop and nan, and even Elizabeth came to see us home, after everyone was introduced we went inside, Albert also asked Ted and Alice to join us for lunch.
During lunch, as everyone was getting to know each other, I turned to Albert, saying, "Albert, I'm in need of some exercise after lunch, are you up for it?"
He smiled, saying, "Oh ho, with pleasure Henry."
Father looked us questioningly, but didn't say anything, then pop, said "I'll come and watch, so will Danyel."
Again, father looked confused, but didn't say anything.
As Elizabeth said, "Well you boys can go and play your silly games, we ladies have some alterations to make, and we don't wish to be disturbed."
All the men looked at her questioningly, as she smiled, like father we said nothing, as they giggled.

On the way to the study, Albert said, "Let's make this a little interesting," and diverted to the sword room, we all followed, and while Albert picked another sword, and I buckled my weapons belt around my waist, father was taking in the swords, and asked permission to pull one down, Albert gave his permission as we left toward the study, father bringing the sword he had pulled down. As we passed through the study, albert picked up his own sword and we went out onto the terrace.

As we faced off, both of us with a sword in each hand, he asked, "Ready."

I nodded, and he attacked, but I could see that he wasn't used to fighting with two swords, and went at him concentrating on his off hand, and eventually I disarmed him of his second sword, with a couple of quick deft moves from my offhand then, let mine drop, as his went sailing through the air.

Albert didn't let being disarmed of one sword deter him, and he attacked in a flurry, each of which I deflected, as I went back on the attack, both smiling we kept up our sword play for close to an hour, before I again disarmed him and placed my sword point at his throat, then took it away again.

We were both laughing as he picked up his sword then went to get the other one. As I placed both of mine into their scabbards.

Father asked, "You care to give me a try?"

Dumbfounded, I looked questioningly at him, saying, "You just saw how I defeated Albert, and he's a very accomplished swordsman, he taught me all I know."

Albert interjected saying, "Thank you for the compliment Henry, but I didn't teach you everything, a lot you have learned yourself. But he's right Danyel, I am quite accomplished with a sword, but not as good as your son with his shooting, are you sure you wish to try?"

Father nodded saying, "I'm game if Henry is?"

I nodded my head, and answered, "Alright."

As we moved away from pop and Albert, I heard pop say, "Sit down Albert, this should be interesting."

Puzzling that remark over, I stood ready as I easily parried my father's attack, then started my own, after a few minutes we were going at it hammer and tong, and I quickly reassessed his ability, he was good, which was a surprise, then we started trading attack and defence rapidly as if we were both in a combat situation, he was good, no, he was bloody good! We had been going for nearly forty minutes, when at last I found an opening, and I disarmed him as I turned with a stroke that would have taken his head off, had I have let it land, my blade was actually touching his neck as I stopped it, it must have looked very close, because Albert was on his feet yelling, "Henry stop!"

Father stood there with a smile on his face, as he wiped at his neck after I removed my sword, and said, "You have indeed learned well boy."

After placing my sword back in its scabbard, I asked, "How?"

Father finished my question, "How do I know how to handle a sword that well?"

I nodded, as we all stood together, and he continued, "I wasn't always a farmer son, I spent time in the cavalry as a sergeant, I've seen what war can do, and I had no wish for you to grow up and be placed in that sort of danger, I wanted for you to stay alive, and not be harmed, that's why I tried to keep you from getting in harm's way, but it seems you went and found it anyway, it's probably where you get your shooting ability from too."

Before anything more could be said, Albert said, "Well that deserves a drink, care to join me gentlemen?"

We all went into the study, and Albert poured everyone a tumbler of scotch, as father took Alberts second sword and his back to the weapons room, and he returned, after I had hung up my weapons belt, and turned to pop asking, "You knew about this pop?"

Father came back into the room and answered the question, "Aye he did, but I swore him to secrecy, even your mother doesn't know, I was going to let you know in my own time, but I never got around to it, before you left son."

Then he came toward me and embraced me, then held me at arms-length, and continued saying, "And now look at you, all grown up and about to marry, I'm proud of you, my son."

Then we all sat and took sips of the fine malt scotch, as we arranged to go out to the shooting range the next morning, so father could assess my shooting abilities, as Albert said, "You know Danyel, I think your son will surprise, even a trained man like you."

Then talk drifted to other matters to do with the wedding, and other general matters., And I was also asked to give my view of the Battle of Cape St. Vincent by my father.

Giving everyone, my impression of the battle and Robin's capture of the Del Mundo, I then told them what had occurred aboard the San Nicholas, and San Josef, as Nelson and I boarded both, even detailing how Nelson had saved me from being killed, after my idiotic dive for cover, this gave them all a good chuckle, but father said, "You did the right thing Henry, but you be wary of Nelson, he's a reckless type of officer, that could get you killed, if you're not careful, I've seen his sort before."

During lunch, Elizabeth asked, "So Henry, what will you be wearing at your wedding?"

As everyone looked at me, I had no answer, as I said, "I haven't made any decision yet aunty, but I was going to go into Howes, and buy a new suit, why do you ask?"

She replied, "Well your wedding is in three days you should be thinking of that by now, but also the ladies, and I have all come to the firm conclusion that you should wear your uniform, you looked so handsome in it at Williams funeral, but don't wear that belt with all your weapons, surely you have a fine sword you can wear?"

Her suggestion had reminded me of something I was going to do, but I was side tracked by the funeral and had not thought of it since, so I replied, "Yes I have Aunty, and I will be led by your suggestion."

She smiled in victory as she looked around the table as each of the women smiled and nodded slightly, obviously she had won a point with them.

Once lunch was finished, I had all the men join me in my new rooms, as I laid out all the swords, that had been handed to me in ship surrenders from the case I had put them in.

Then I asked them for their opinion, as to which one I should wear, they all pointed to the one I had received as the price of victory, from the dying admiral of the San Josef. It was a superb blade, made of Toledo steel and the hilt was surrounded by a hand guard of pure gold and shaped exquisitely, the scabbard also was made with gold tendrils running up and down the length of it and around it also, in a fine display of design.

Then I had father choose a sword he liked, as I said, "Father the one you choose will go home with you as my gift as a memento of my adventures, the rest will stay here and be added to the weapons room, if that is alright with you Albert?"

Albert with surprise showing on his face replied, "My dear nephew, you honour me sir, and I humbly accept your generosity."

I smiled saying, "Good, hopefully they will repay your generosity, because you're not getting the sword you sold to me back. It's too much of an old friend now."

He and I smiled, and we embraced each other with claps on each other's backs.

Once the picked swords had been moved away from the array of swords, Jenkins was summoned.

He was told what was to be done with the swords, and he said, "Your instructions shall be carried out master Henry." As he started picking up the swords with reverence, and took them from my rooms. Before he left my rooms, Albert told him of our plans for the morning, telling him to have all the pistols taken, and four each of the muskets and rifles, and too make sure of plenty of powder and shot.

Taking my new dress sword with me, we all went to the back of the house and made for the stables, as four horses were saddled and brought out for our use. While the others waited, I went to John and asked him to have the sword and scabbard polished for me, and was told he'd take care of it for me. Then the four of us rode into town, and to Howes shop.

Chapter 27.

We dismounted outside the store, and all trooped in, then Albert announced, "Gentlemen, anything purchased today will be put on my account as my gift to you all, so don't hold back, now uncle Samuel, surely you will need a new suit, you too Danyel?"

Grandfather nodded, and made to look at the suit rack, while father said to Albert, "No I won't need one cousin, I know I can still fit into something that will be a surprise for everyone, but possibly a couple of new shirts and a new sword belt."

Mister Howe was helping grandfather, with a new suit, and while he was trying his choice on, Mister Howe came to me, and I ordered a dozen white shirts, made to my measurements in the Egyptian cotton, and after father asked me about them, mister Howe showed him some already made, after trying one on loved them and took half a dozen of varying shades. Then both he and I chose new wide sword belts each.

Grandfather, came out to show us his choice and was rewarded by Albert on his choice, then he went back to change into his other clothes, Howe moved to take and wrap his new suit, for him, then he had a new black top hat added to his purchases, Albert bought a new suit and top hat as well, then everything was added up and placed on Alberts bill. Before we left the shop, Howe told me that when my shirts were ready, he would bring them out to the manor himself.

After we arrived home, I took my belt with me to John to measure and secure the scabbard of my new dress sword and belt into place. Father had followed me and watched with interest how we measured and marked the place for the site of the scabbard, and watched as John fixed the scabbard loop into a permanent place on the belt, remarking that it was a fine idea, and asked John if he could do the same for him. John told him he could, so he went off to get his new sword, while I tossed a schilling piece to John asking if that would cover the price for all his work on both belts. John smiled, saying "Of course it will master Henry, its more than enough." I tossed him another schilling telling him that was for all his help.

Father returned with the sword and a repeat of the performance was made to his belt, then we left John to get on with work, and went back inside.

While we were having our pre-dinner drinks, that evening, Boggs came to me and waited until I had stopped my talk with Joanna, and whispered in my ear, "Sir, the blacksmith would like to see you and your father, so I had him wait in the weapons room." I told him very well, and looked toward father and Albert, who had been in conversation, but had stopped to watch what was going on.

Excusing myself from Joanna, I inclined my head to them which meant for them to follow me, and as they started moving toward me, I headed for the door, then we all went to the weapons room, where John was waiting for us, and he bowed to Albert as he waved his hand to the finished sword belts.

Both of them were highly polished, and as pulled my blade, I noticed John had added his usual ministrations to the blade and edges, and it shone like a mirror, father was looking in awe at John, after he too had pulled the blade out.

As we both thanked him, he bowed again saying, "Nothing but the best for you, master Henry, if'n you're happy, I'll be going now sir."

Father said in wonderment to Albert, "My advice to you cousin, never let that man go, his work is exquisite."

Bypassing the dining room, father and I took our swords to our rooms and I hung mine up, Albert had gone back to the dining room, and father and I re-entered shortly after, to take up our drinks again.

Next morning, after breakfast, we took to our horses, as the women went to do whatever they do. Ted was driving the wagon himself, so he could actually see how good he had heard I was.

At the firing range, pop just watched instead of shooting, and after finding himself outclassed, Albert soon gave up, as a competition developed between myself and father. It was only after the targets had been shifted back to five hundred yards, that I was able to triumph.

Then we moved to the pistol range, where instead of going shot for shot, I gave them a demonstration of my ability, which was old hat for Albert, so he assisted by throwing tins and glass into the air, as I perfected my moving target alignment, not that it was really needed.

Father was impressed with my ability, and told Albert he had been right, I had surprised him with my abilities with a pistol, and he congratulated me on a fine demonstration, telling me that to get accuracy out of a pistol over a distance of forty yards was a feat in itself, let alone the fifties I was able to achieve.

That night during dinner, Elizabeth said to me, "Take a last look at your intended, because tomorrow you two are not to see each other, until after the wedding, us ladies will keep to ourselves tomorrow, and the morning of your wedding day, we will be spending the time at the Yeoman cottage, and poor Ted will just have to put up with us, however the married ladies will return for dinner, and breakfast, Albert I suggest you start entertaining Ted amongst you all." Her instructions put a bit of a dampener on the rest of the evening, as I had counted on seeing Joanna the following day, but orders were orders, and I was used to those.

The following afternoon, while all five of us were in the study after lunch, having a quite drink, a post rider arrived at the manor with orders for me from the admiralty, opening the despatch, I read: Henry Robert Tolcher, 1st lieutenant, RN. You are required to attend the general office of admiralty headquarters at 1000hrs on May 10th, 1797, to receive sailing orders. It was signed by the placements captain John Russell. Sighing, I said, "Well looks like I'll be having a short honeymoon."

As the letter was passed around, and I asked Albert to pass it onto Lucy, so Joanna would know.

The wedding was set to take place at 1300, and we had to be at the cathedral an hour beforehand, we were to be taken there by the open carriage, which would return for the bride and her father, which would follow the ladies into town in the coach.
I was bathed, shaved, and was getting dressed as father came into my rooms, dressed in his old cavalry dress uniform which was adorned with his service medals. I stared at him and nodded, as I said, "Mother is going to have a fit when she sees you dressed like that father."
He smiled saying, "She already did son, when she saw me lay them out, so naturally I had to tell her the whole story. Come on, let's get you finished dressing."
Helped me into my jacket, then I buckled my sword around me, as he did the same, then picking up my hat, we marched downstairs, and into the study.
Albert and grandfather were already there having a bracer, as we entered Albert, poured us each a tumbler, and passed them to us. He was dressed in his new suit, and had his sword belt buckled on, with his sword gleaming like mine and fathers, pop was in his new suit and holding his new hat in one hand, the tumbler in the other, we all stood silently as we took each other in, and in silence we all clinked the tumblers and took a pull of our drinks. We heard the carriage on the drive, we all smiled, drained our drinks, and placed the empty tumblers

on the table, and proceeded outside to the carriage, once in the carriage we all put our hats on, as the drive to town started.

Outside the cathedral, invited guests had started to arrive, and I passed the wedding rings to Albert, before they approached to start chatting with us. Guests were making their way into the church, as we waited to catch site of the coach before making our way inside. Albert and I went in to stand and wait, as father and pop waited to join their ladies, then they would come in and take their seats.

Father escorted both mother and Alice in, then as we stood waiting I heard a rustle and murmur go through the attendees, and Albert and I turned side on to watch the doors, first came Elizabeth and Lucy, followed by Ted, with Joanna on his left arm. I nearly buckled as I took in the sight of Joanna, she was beautiful, and that was an understatement of great proportions, but it is hard to describe as I took in the sight of her.

As they joined us, Ted put Joanna's hand in mine, and with a wink at me, retreated and took his place beside Alice.

Standing side by side, and looking at the Bishops' beaming smile as he started the service, Albert placed our rings on the bible and I took Joanna's and placed it on her finger as I completed my vows of marriage, and she did the same with my ring, when her's were completed. The bishop then concluded the wedding service, before we kissed, and were introduced to the guests as mister and misses, Henry and Joanna Tolcher.

After receiving kisses from Elizabeth and Lucy, and a handshake from Albert for me and a kiss for Joanna, we started back down the aisle to receive congratulations and applause from everyone present that we passed by.

Outside we were showered with rice from all the well-wishers, after receiving kisses and handshakes from all the family members, I helped Joanna into the waiting carriage, as I joined her, on the ride back to the house.

Arriving there, with a few minutes in front of everyone else arriving, we went up to our rooms, and after taking off my sword belt, and hanging it up, we really kissed for the first time as husband and wife, she took her hat into her bedroom, and lay it on the bed, then checked the drawers and wardrobes, all of her stuff had been moved in while we'd been away, after looking there she went for a look in my bedroom, and looked in the wardrobes and drawers again.

Hearing noises that announced the arrival home of family, we went and called on everyone, before they went down for the wedding breakfast, that was to take place in the ballroom. After going back to our rooms, I poured us a glass of sherry each, as we sat for a quiet drink together, before we made our down to the breakfast, then with a kiss, we walked hand in hand downstairs, and into the ballroom.

This part of the day became long and drawn out with speeches, and toasts. We surprised those not in the know, with our dancing, before meals were served first to the head table, and eventually everyone else.

Everyone had a great time and Joanna and I danced in different sets for different dances, before joining Albert and Lucy for a very fast dance for two couple sets, and we were applauded by everyone not dancing.

Eventually at roughly ten that night, we left the party and went up to bed. Then we had to decide which bed to sleep in, but because Joanna wanted to see what her bed was like, we disrobed each other, throwing the clothes anywhere, but we were both shy as to what was to do next as we explored each other's bodies, before making love to each other. Unfortunately, Joanna's pleasure, turned to shame as she spied the sheets that were stained with virginal blood, she had me help her, strip the bed so the mattress wouldn't get stained also. The effected bedclothes were left in a pile on the floor, as we went to my bedroom, and after enjoying each other once more, we passed into sleep, in each other's arms.

We were almost inseparable after that, except for the time she spent with Elizabeth.

A week after our wedding, my grandparents and my parents said their goodbyes, as they were leaving to go back to the farm, Albert sent them home in the coach with a couple outriders, after wishing them well.

I think that during his time here, my father and I have been able to mend our thoughts of each other, and in my case, I have learned to respect him, and I hoped that he has learned to respect me more, it had seemed his attitude toward me had changed a lot.

The following week, I started preparing to return to duty, Albert was going to accompany me to Portsmouth in the coach, as he was going to London, to be invested into the house of lords. Mysteriously, his paperwork had arrived not long after the words I'd had with the lords, that arrived for his father's funeral. We'd had many a joke over that issue before my wedding.

Joanna was prepared for my departure, though she clung to me the morning I had to go, she didn't wish me to leave my bed, but knew we had to get up and ready for breakfast, after which, Albert and I would leave. Taking my portmanteaux, holdall, and hat with me, I took them down to the front door on the way to the dining room, Joanna, deciding to help me looked quite a funny sight with my weapons belt wrapped around her, as I took it off her and hung it up. I was dressed in one of my seagoing uniforms, my new shirts from mister Howe, were already packed in the portmanteaux, with older ones in the holdall.

Three mornings later after saying goodbye to Albert, I walked into the office at admiralty headquarters. After having sent for a carriage, the placements Captain and I, waited outside the office building, when it arrived driven by a sailor, the captain told him where I was going, he and shook hands in farewell, as he wished me good hunting.

Arriving at the Mutine, I walked aboard as the sailor carriage driver, carried my bags. As the officer of the watch was called, I saluted the flag, then him

as he arrived and saluted me. Stating my orders, and asked, "Is the captain aboard yet number two?"
He replied, "No sir, he's not due until tomorrow sir."
"Very well, show me to my cabin please," I replied. In my cabin, I told him to sit after putting my stuff on the large bed, and started to unbuckle my weapons belt, I asked, "So what's your name number two?"
He answered as I hung up the belt on the door hook, "Noakes sir, Christopher Noakes."
I sat down, and looked him saying, "Well then mister Noakes, you and the rest of the crew, had best be on your toes tomorrow, there better not be any lacksidaisical efforts like today, you should have been at the gangplank to meet me, not having me wait like I did just now. If Captain Hardy isn't happy, I'm not happy, and shit runs downhill if you get my meaning! Dismissed!"

Chapter 28.

After settling in, I've brought my journal up to date, and now intend to tour the ship, and try to get the lay of the land before Tom gets here tomorrow. Buckling on my gun belt, bareheaded I went exploring the ship, what I found below decks, and on the main gundeck, didn't impress me much, and then I went topside, taking in everything with a trained eye, the upper gundeck, was a little in better condition, than what I saw below deck, but all in all not up to fleet standards as far as I was concerned, and not for the first time, I wished I was back on the Minerve.

That evening, I introduced myself to all the ships senior officers, and asked them their ages, not one of them was younger than twenty-five, or been at sea much let alone take part in battles, and I said, "Well gentlemen, I'm only twenty-one next month and if you don't like being ordered around by someone younger than yourself, either get used to it, or request a transfer! Not one to big note myself, but I captured my first ship at seventeen, and she was the Conquistadora, a first rate, since then I've taken part in many engagements with the enemy, my last being with Nelson at St. Vincent. The same can be said for your new captain Thomas Hardy, who I've been with since leaving the college. Now I've looked around this scow, and what I've seen, is a bloody disgrace! Now something else you should know, I didn't get here through any family connections, I got here by determination, and I rose through the ranks."

Taking a drink, I looked around as I continued, "A lot of that determination comes from self-discipline gentlemen, something all of you lack! How do you expect to discipline others, if you can't discipline yourselves? If I go through this ship one more time, and find rust on cannon barrels, papers strewn around, grime and grease everywhere, it won't be the sailors who pay the price, it will be one of you! So, unless you like the idea, of a public flogging, you will shape up, and look carefully into your areas of responsibilities, or face a flogging! Am I understood?"

They all came to attention chorusing, "Aye, aye Sir!"

Lowering my voice to normal, I said, "Good, because I won't be saying this again, you will dress properly, until I say otherwise, and what is the standard of dress during wartime Mister Purser?"

The purser, snapped to attention, replying, "Full uniform, plus swords and weapons, sir."

I smiled and asked, "And were you wearing your weapons today sir?"

"No Sir, and no excuse sir," he replied.

I looked at him, and around all of them, as I said, "Very well, I will forget it this time, but you should all think about that from now on, now someone pour me another drink, you've all had enough of a dressing down for now."

As they all visibly relaxed, I was asked if I had truly been with Nelson, at St. Vincent. I answered the question with honesty, and remarked, "If any of you are ever looking for cover, don't dive from a higher deck, the bloody deck is frigging hard." Looking around my story was putting them at ease, and using the dive story, gave them all a laugh.

That night I slept fitfully, as I missed being with my new wife, opening my fob watch, I looked at her likeness, that I had, had placed into the face cover, then drifted off to sleep again.

May 12, 1797: The following morning, after breakfast, I went on deck to find a lot of bustle taking place, as I made my way to the poopdeck, to have a look over the ship. I was pleased to find that there were work crews scurrying all over the upper gundeck, and the cannon crews were all paying attention to their guns maintenance. Obviously, my little pep talk in the wardroom, had the desired effects. All officers were in correct uniform and wearing their weapons. Glancing upward, I saw the topmen attending to tears and holes in the sails, I watched as one on the top most foremast was refurled, and the next one down was let out for inspection, this was taking place on all three masts at the same time. With a smile on my face, I went below, to find the same amount of feverish activity, as I toured the ship on each deck. Then made my way back topside, to the poop, and looked around the front harbour, where we were situated.

As I looked I observed an open carriage, similar to the one I had used the day before, it held a familiar figure, and I smiled, because I was glad to see my friend and captain again.

At least Noakes had smartened up, as he remarked,

"Looks like we're about to have company sir, if you'll excuse me?" As I smiled once more and nodded.

As Hardy was being greeted by Noakes, I made my way down and toward Tom, as he stepped forward and we saluted each other, then shook hands, as he said, "Glad to see you again Henry, come and show me to my cabin." The sailor that was carrying Hardy's possessions, followed us as I took Tom to his cabin, he entered, and I stood back to let the sailor come in as Hardy told him to place them on the bunk, then he left with a "Thank you sir," as I closed the door.

Tom said, "Take a seat Henry, while I sort all this out, and you can fill me in, on the state of the ship, there seems to be a lot of work being done?"

I laughed saying "Aye Sir," as he moved around stowing his gear, I gave him the full story after my arrival aboard, including the dressing down I gave the senior officers the night before.

He laughed heartily, remarking, "Hah, I'd have loved to have heard it, I've seen and heard you on many an occasion, remember. Alright to summarize, we've officers that have seen minimum sea time, and no action. I think it's about time to find out about the rest of the crew, don't you? Go and get the hands mustered, I'll be along shortly Henry."

Leaving his cabin, I went up to the poopdeck and ordered Noakes to assemble the whole crew, and as they were assembling, Hardy joined me at the forward rail, with all officers and midshipmen, standing in a line behind us.

All eyes were on Hardy, as he raised his voice, He introduced me and himself, announcing the orders for the ship, telling them that after our stopover in Gibraltar, we would be joining a squadron, under Captain Thomas Troubridge off the French port of Toulon.

Then he told them that, he and I, had served on ships a number of years that were considered to have the best crews at everything, gunnery being number one. Then he told them the expectations of the admiralty for all ships of the line toward clearing for action, and rates of gunnery fire and accuracy, then said, "However, mister Tolcher and I expect more, this ship, I expect to clear for action in eight minutes or less, and gunners your rate of fire is to be three rounds a minute, with ninety percent accuracy or better, make sure you take note! Now I want a show of hands, how many of you have been under sail continually for a month or more?"

Only a quarter of the assembly put their hands up. Hardy continued asking, "How many of you have seen combat at sea?"

Less than fifty men put their hands up, and I grimaced.

As Hardy said, "In that case, gentlemen, we are going to design some exercises to get you ready for what we face as a blockading ship, where you could be called to duty anytime of the day or night, and I want you to remember the number of hands that I saw, that went up during my last two questions, when you start gripping, which you no doubt will, but rest assured it will be done with the main aim of keeping as many of you as I can, alive! Any slackness on your parts will be dealt with harshly, is that understood!"

The whole crew chorused, "Aye, aye Sir!", Then he released them to their duties, and called for all officers to meet in the wardroom.

In the wardroom, I explained the exercises, and ordered the purser issue stopwatches to every officer and petty officer. Then I said, "Once everyone has a stopwatch, you are to report to me purser, then gentlemen, I will tell you when, and what exercise will be conducted. I want a meeting of all senior and junior officers and petty officers in here tomorrow morning a nine, therefore you will all have had your breakfast by eight at the latest, or you will go without! Any questions?"

There were none, and I dismissed them all, after they had left us alone, Tom said, "Henry, drive them hard, then drive them some more, otherwise we'll lose half of them in our first engagement."

After my conference with every senior and junior officer from every part of the ship, where I outlined their responsibilities, it was during this conference when the purser issued everyone with a stopwatch, as I finished the conference saying, "Right you are all aware of your responsibilities, the training will start in earnest anytime from now until we reach our blockading station, dismissed!"

I called for the first exercise at 1400 that afternoon. I had already expected it to be terrible, but it was more dreadful than I had imagined, with the last station reporting ready after twenty-one minutes!

Naturally, I gave the entire crew a dressing down, that had many hanging their heads and counting the deck boards.

June 25, 1797: Today we reached, and joined with captain Thomas Troubridge's squadron, and took our place amongst the blockading ships.
From my last entry, the crew slowly started to improve, then went ahead in leaps and bounds, by the time we were half way to Gibraltar, the ship could clear for action in eight minutes. By the time we arrived in Gibraltar, the gunnery crews were getting in nearly four shots to the minute, and their accuracy rate was close to ninety-five percent, every member of the crew was happy, and this included me and Hardy.

December 20, 1797: After joining Troubridge's squadron, we went to action within three days, as the squadron came under heavy attack from ships trying to break out of the port, this attack lasted almost three days, before the French ships retreated back to the harbour, but unfortunately two of them were able to get away during the battle. During the respite Troubridge called a captain's conference, at which reports were taken, though our ships sustained damage none of it was severe, and we lost no men. Troubridge, then gave us a report that made us all think, the attempts of breakout had slowly been increasing, and was now becoming a weekly event, and we were the only ships in the Mediterranean since it was abandoned the year before.

Troubridge was determined, to fulfil his orders, and was hoping for a relief force to arrive.

Three months later, no relief had been forthcoming from Jervis, and our ships were starting to run short on all supplies, and rationing was implemented among the crews, but the straw that broke the camel's back, came during another particular concentrated attack that lasted with breakout attempts continually over seven days, during this time two of our ships ceased fire, due to running out of munitions.

After hearing this Troubridge, signalled all ships to break station, we were sailing back to Gibraltar.

We arrived there in mid-November, where repair work to our ships was started immediately. There was only room in the docks for two ships at a time, and the rest of us had to wait our turn, but we were able to give our crews shore leave.

One morning the officers of the squadron were summoned to the officer's mess, where we were addressed personally by Admiral Jervis, letting us know that he was sorry, he had been unable to send any relief, but that there would no longer be any forays into the Mediterranean until otherwise ordered. And once all our repair work could be completed, we would be either be stationed in port. or relieving other fleets blockading the northern ports.

Today sees the Mutine moving into the dock, for our repair work to be carried out over the month.

Once the work is carried out, the ship will be completely re-stocked by the time we leave dock, ready for sea.

January 2, 1798: Last night was a surprise for both Tom and I, we met with now Admiral Horatio Nelson, once more, it was a shock to both of us though, that he now only had one arm! Drawing us away from the reception area of the New Year's Eve ball, toward a side room where we could sit and hear his tale.

It was about the Battle of Santa Cruz de Tenerife, that took place on the twenty second of July the previous year in 1797.

"The battle plan called for a combination of naval bombardments and an amphibious landing. The initial attempt was called off after adverse currents hampered the assault and the element of surprise was lost.

Though I immediately ordered another assault, but this was beaten back, and I prepared for a third attempt, to take place during the night.

Although I personally led one of the battalions, the operation ended in failure, the Spanish were better prepared than I had been expecting and had secured strong defensive positions.

Several of the boats failed to land at the correct position in the confusion, while those that did were swept by gunfire and grapeshot. my boat reached its landing point but as I stepped ashore I was hit in the right arm by a musket ball, which according to Eshelby fractured my humerus bone in multiple places. Naturally I was rowed back to Theseus to be attended to by Thomas Eshelby. Arriving at the ship I refused to be helped aboard, telling them to, Let me alone! I have got my legs left and one arm.

I was taken to surgeon Eshelby, and instructed him to prepare his instruments, because the sooner it was off the better. Most of my right arm was amputated, but I was back to issuing orders to my captain's half an hour later Hardy. Now what have you two been up to?"
Hardy told him what we'd been up to and what ship we had, and about her still being repaired.

Nelson said, "Alright leave it with me, I've been given, Vanguard as my flagship for now, with Edward Berry as my flag captain. French activities in the Mediterranean theatre are raising concern with the Admiralty. Napoleon has been gathering forces in Southern France, but the destination of his army is unknown. I've been dispatched to reinforce the fleet, and investigate into the Mediterranean. I'll get rid of Berry soon enough, and I'll get you two back with me again!" Then he started laughing before saying, "Let's all go get a drink."

Chapter 29.

March 30, 1798: Nelson left with his fleet two weeks after New Year, and nothing has been heard of him since, but before he left port, Thomas and I were often joined by him in the mess, each time we were altogether was a joyous time for us, as we swapped stories, of what Thomas and I had been doing in the interim period.

When talked turned to me, I told Horatio (which was the way he wanted us to address him, when we were alone), about my marriage, and showed him the likeness of my sweet Joanna, he congratulated me heartily.

He told us of his mission, then said, "God! What I'd give, to be able to have a larger fleet, we could chase the frogs all over the Mediterranean then bring them to heel, and annihilate them once and for all." Then he told us how he was going to get us transferred to his ship, he would send Berry off in our ship with despatches, and have us come aboard as captain and mate, as he said, "I intend to do this the next time we are joined again, I haven't worked that wrinkle out yet, but when we meet again be ready for it to happen, my dear friends."

Repair work on the Mutine was finally completed at the end of February, and all officers and crew reported back aboard, to take her out of the work dock, to our anchorage.

A week later, another fleet twenty ships strong sailed into harbour, one of them being Majestic.

Needless to say, my cousin and I were able to spend a great deal of time together, swapping news while he was in port., I laughed as he told me of his windfall capturing the treasure ships, as he said, "So while I was on leave, I had the gems valued in London, and I learned that from them alone, my family and I will never want for anything again, because the booty I picked out came to an overall value of one and a half million pounds! And on top of that, my share of the captured ships was nearly two hundred thousand pounds! Oh, that reminds me, Henry, I need to warn you of something, now you're a married man."

Seeing we were in his cabin aboard the Majestic, he pulled down his copy of the admiralty standing orders and manual, at one of the pages he had earmarked, by folding over a corner. He showed me what was written about monies in accounts held in the naval bank. Then said, "What this means, is that if you haven't switched the money in the account to another bank, they take the money back if you're killed! It isn't paid out to your widow or family! If you're smart, do what I have done, I now leave a minimal amount in the account, say a hundred pounds, and I've taken the rest out in cheque form, sent it to Albert to bank, and keep in trust for me, that way the admiralty can't take it all if I die."

In alarm at this news, I thought of all the money that was in my naval account, and decided to do something about it.

The day following Robins warning, all captains and

1st lieutenants were called to a conference at admiral Jervis's headquarters. There was plenty of room for us to sit around the huge table and Robin and I sat with Hardy and Blagdon beside each other. Jervis, stated his concerns about not hearing from Nelson, and asked for ideas, after an hour of discussion, it was decided to send a fleet into the Mediterranean to look for him, or at least try to pick up word as to where he maybe, from the numerous ships that navigated those waters. A force that was not too big to draw too much attention, but also not too small should they encounter the French, and have to make a fight of it.

He decided that captain Troubridge would lead a fleet of ten ships of the line, plus four frigates for despatches, after that he named the ships to go, and Majestic and Mutine were amongst them, and that we would all stock up on provisions, and leave in a week from then.

As we left headquarters, it was decided that Robin and I would inform our pursers via our longboat crews, and they would return for us after lunch. On our way to the mess to re-join, Blagdon and Hardy, I called into the bank, to determine my finances, after learning my balance was two hundred thirty-seven thousand, six hundred and fifty-six pounds, which was made up of prize money paid into my account and wages. I made a cheque withdrawal, leaving only the fifty-six pounds in my account, with the cheque made out to Albert.

Before leaving harbour, I would write to him enclosing the cheque, which he could keep in trust for me and letting him know that at times I would send more amounts. Then Robin and I continued to the mess for drinks before lunch.

Now the ship is already for departure, and we sail on the morning tide, all the officers in the wardroom that night, were jovial, and like me, couldn't wait to way anchor and be on our way, we had been in harbour for too long, it was time to be at sea again! This will be my last entry until we locate or hear some news of Horaito.

May 21, 1798: Nelson has been found, as he was making his way back to Gibraltar, he has signalled for a conference aboard his flagship for all captains and 1st mates. The Vanguard was soon surrounded by secured longboats as we attended the conference, which was started by him asking, "So gentlemen, to what do I owe this honour?"
Troubridge answered, saying, "Sir because we haven't heard from you, Earl St. Vincent sent us to find you, and I also convey new orders for you."
Nelson smiled answering, "Do you by damn, let's see them, and I tell you what has befallen my fleet."
Troubridge passed them over to him, as he started to tell his tale.
As his squadron had approached Toulon, it was struck by a fierce gale. "Vanguard lost its topmasts and was almost wrecked on the Corsican coast. The remainder of the squadron was scattered. When I found my ship's, they were sheltered at San Pietro Island near Sardinia."

"My frigates were blown to the west and have failed to return. After the storm, we made hasty repairs, and after finding Toulon empty of the frogs, I was heading toward Gibraltar, where you found us. Now let's see what this has to say," he said. As he opened the orders envelope.

We waited while Nelson, read the orders, then he threw them onto the table, saying, "Damn it to hell! Gentlemen, the orders are to pursue and intercept the frogs, but although we now have enough ships to challenge the French fleet, we suffer two great disadvantages, one, no intelligence regarding the destination of the frogs, and secondly, no frigates to scout ahead of our force.

Troubridge said, "We do now sir, I have four of them amongst the fleet."

Nelson jumped to his feet saying, My God man, why didn't you say so before, that's bloody good, but I would like to have a few more. Any suggestions gentlemen?"

Hardy said, "We could call at Elba, or go onto Naples, Sir Hamilton may be able to shed some light on where they may have gone."

Nelson replied, "Excellent idea Hardy, we'll do both, Troubridge send two of the frigates to Elba, we'll keep the other two out front scouting, and head to Naples, sailing order gentlemen, two columns of seven, line astern of my flag, Troubridge you lead the other column, Hardy you will come in behind me, Right gentlemen, let's form up and keep going, dismissed!"

With that we made our way to our longboats, and back to our ships, as the sails were set to give steerage, I navigated Mutine, so that it pulled in behind Vanguard, as the four frigates raced past the fleet, and I watched as two, peeled off toward Elba. Later during the day, a signal was sent to us from the flagship, telling us to secure the floated line. Going forward, to the bow I watched as a line was thrown and played out from Vanguard just forward of the poopdeck.

Ordering an able seaman to grab a long boathook, I had him climb over the railing, and down as far as he could go without falling, expertly he snagged the line with a float attached, and walked along the port combing rail until he was near the rail entrance, and he passed the line to me, I secured it with a belaying pin. Having acknowledged its receipt, I watched some more line played out between both ships.

The next signal read: Guiding line for longboat, then I knew exactly what was happening.

An hour later, I smiled as I read the signal flags, inviting Hardy and I to dinner, and I had sails send back: Would be our pleasure.

Then I went and let Tom know about our dinner invite.

In his cabin, I told him about our dinner invite and my reply, he sat back laughing, and said, "No doubt about Horatio, he does enjoy good company at dinner, go tell him we'll join him for drinks at 1700, that should give him a chuckle."

I had message run up, when I was back on deck.

May 30, 1798: The fleet has reached Naples, along with the two frigates that had been assigned to go to Elba, so, we were back up to full strength again, and we have anchored for the night. I expect Horatio will go and see the ambassador Sir William Hamilton during the morning, to shed any light in regard to the French fleet. But he didn't do that, instead I was quite surprised to see him leave, Vanguard in a longboat as soon as it was anchored.

August 4, 1798: A lot has happened between my last entry, and now, so I will start from where I left of three months ago.

Horatio, returned to Vanguard, a little before lunch and had flag signals run up convening a captain's conference for 1400, and I passed on the message to Thomas as we gathered for lunch.

After lunch was over, I had Noakes launch the longboat, and have it ready for Hardy. Tom left the ship at quarter to the appointed hour, and I followed his progress to Vanguard from the poopdeck, at the same time, I observed that other longboats were heading towards her as well.
Hardy returned to Mutine, an hour and a half later, and ordered the longboat taken out of the water, then asked me to follow him to his cabin. Once inside and the door shut, he said, "It seems that Sir William has had news of the French Henry, he reported to Horatio, that the fleet has passed by Sicily and were headed toward Malta. We're leaving port tonight!"

Following the conversation in the captain's cabin, I had the ship made ready for sea, and consulted the tidal information almanac as to regard the tidal information, for the port of Naples, after checking the variance table, I determined that the high tide was at1840 that evening, at 1845 a signal was hoisted from Vanguard reading, away all ships, take up sailing stations.

On the twenty-second of June, a brig was sighted, and Nelson slowed the fleet, and sent one of the frigates to parley with the captain and crew. After what seemed an age, I saw the brig and frigate part company through my scope, and turned my attention to the signals being run up from the frigate, and they read: Sailing from Ragusa, the brig reported the news, that the French had sailed eastwards from Malta on 16 June.

Immediately after, Vanguard hoisted signals for the fleet to slow to steerage sail, the next signal was calling all captains and mates to a conference. Ordering the longboat readied, the longboat crew, Hardy and me, were in the boat as it was lowered over the side, and were soon aboard the flagship. Once all the officers were present, Horatio who was sitting at the head of the table, said "Gentlemen we now know that Napoleons fleet was headed east after stopping at Malta, any guesses as to where?" Putting his hand up, Robin was acknowledged, as he said, "Egypt, most likely Alexandria sir."

Horatio smiled, saying, "I think you right, mister Fox-Davis. I think we can assume we're about a week behind him, now we can make up some time."

After taking a sip of water, he continued, "Here's what I propose, we sail directly to Alexandria, and catch the bloody frogs unloading, and unable to manoeuvre, what say you?"

Then a discussion ensued over the wisdom of this move, here I would like to inform you, Horatio's assumption and ours was later to prove incorrect! In actuality, we were only two days behind them. If we had of gone into Malta we would have found this out, and caught Napoleon, by surprise as Horatio predicted. So, this action proved to be costly. But back to what DID happen.

There was argument as to the wisdom of Nelson's proposed course, but the majority of us agreed with Horatio.

Troubridge from Culloden asked, "But, what if you're wrong sir?"

Horatio was stubborn, yelling, "In that case, Thomas, I'll be wrong! Berry make direct course to Alexandria, and that's the end of it gentlemen, dismissed!"

Back onboard Mutine, the sails were set once more, and we made rapid time on a direct route, our fleet reached Alexandria on 28 June and discovered that the French were not there! This was disappointing to say the least.

After anchoring, all captain and mates were rowed ashore, along with Horatio, on the beach, we had a meeting with Alexandria's very suspicious Ottoman commander, Sayyid Muhammad Kurayyim, and some of his men, and discovered that the French had not been sighted at all, nor were there any reports of him landing anywhere in Egypt. Troubled by this Horatio ordered the fleet to the north, With the frigates out scouting, we reached the coast of Anatolia on the fourth of July, then we turned west, heading back toward Sicily, as the search went on.

We reached Syracuse in Sicily on the nineteenth of July and took on essential supplies. By July twenty-fourth, the fleet was resupplied and, having determined that the French must be somewhere in the Eastern Mediterranean, Nelson had us sail again in the direction of the Morea.
28 July: We've arrived at Coron, where we finally obtained intelligence describing the French attack on Egypt. We turned south across the Med, as fast as we could go.

Our scouts, sighted the French transport fleet at Alexandria on the afternoon of August one.

Chapter 30.

Journal Entry Continued – July18, 1804: Captain Robin Fox-Davis RN.

January 10, 1798: During my leave, a naval dispatch rider arrived at my cottage, with new orders from the admiralty, extending my leave, due to the planned maintenance on our ships, not having been completed, my new reporting date back at Portsmouth was now to be January eight, and I was wished a merry Christmas.

Having read the dispatch, I smiled and went inside to tell Elizabeth that I was going to be spending Christmas and the New Year at home this year.

We were both overjoyed at this news, as she grabbed me by the breeches and pulled me upstairs with her to our bedroom, not that I held back at all. Once there she started to unbutton my shirt after dragging it out of my breeches, and I got into the spirit, by spinning her around as I undid her bodice. In a short time, we were both naked, as I picked her up and placed her on the bed. She had locked her arms around me, pulling me down upon her, as she spread her legs to receive me. I entered deeply inside her, and her giggles were replaced with moans of joy and ecstasy, as I plunged into her, she groaned in joy each time she was wracked with a climax, and shrieked in joy as my seed poured into her. After our lust had been fulfilled, she said, "Just as well the nanny and children are in the garden."

I laughed at her comment, asking, "Would that have made any difference to you dear heart?"
Laughing as well, she replied, "Not in the slightest, my good captain."
Our cottage was a happy place that Christmas, as we entertained her mother and father, who spoiled our children, showering them with presents.
On New Year's Eve, Elizabeth and I celebrated, our own way, by drinking Champagne and taking each other's bodies, as the midnight bells rang out Elizabeth's shriek of fulfilment, mingled with them.

I arranged a seat on the passenger coach leaving for Portsmouth on the sixth, which arrived in the early hours at Portsmouth. I walked into the admiralty office at the appointed time, and was directed to Majestic, at number thirty on the eastern dock.
Arriving aboard I was greeted by James Holloway the number two, and he informed me that Blagdon was already aboard, he had arrived an hour earlier than I did.
After, stowing my gear, and making my cabin habitable, I went to George's cabin, and we both sat with drinks, as I was informed that Majestic would be part of a large convoy fleet heading to Gibraltar.
He said, "Well Robin, finally we once more get to go to sea, what we'll be doing after Gibraltar, god only knows, but I would assume that Jervis will have something for us to do. From the scuttlebutt I've been hearing about the French, don't be surprised if we're off to the Mediterranean, I heard that Nelson was headed that way, a few months ago.

During dinner in the wardroom, I determined if the ship was provisioned and ready for sea, with all crew aboard, which it was.

Three days later we moved from the dock, out to the sheltered waters of Spithead, where the fleet would assemble prior to sailing, when we anchored, I looked at some of the already assembled ships, and everyone was a ship of the line, there were a couple of fourth rates, but the majority were two and three rates, and a couple of days later two first rates joined the assembly.

The fleet was led by rear admiral Cuthbert Collingwood, as we wayed anchor getting underway, Collingwood was taking three first rates and two second rates and a third rate to the Jamaica station, but Collingwood was to call into Gibraltar, and reprovision, all the other ships in the convoy were to become, part of Admiral Jervis's Mediterranean fleet, Majestic amongst them.

On the fourth of March, we sailed into Gibraltar shortening sail to steerage only, as signals, were passed to each ship from the harbourmaster directing them where to make anchor. As Holloway directed our anchoring, I had been looking at the names of the ships in harbour, and discovered the Mutine, my cousins latest ship was also in port, and I smiled, as I thought, *well Robin looks like you'll end up getting drunk with your cousin in the mess tonight.* Which is exactly what happened, as we met each other in the mess, and brought each other up with the current news, of family and friends, and we arranged for him to visit the Majestic the next day.

During a discussion I had with George over prize monies paid by the admiralty many months, prior, and after looking at the particular section concerning these matters, to relieve the boredom at sea, I had taken to reading in detail, other sections, of the book present on all naval ships, Admiralty Instructions and Manual.

Among this manual, I had come across a section that dealt with monies paid into naval bank accounts, and in particular, what happened with distribution of said monies upon death of the account holder. I discovered that detrimental to the account holders' family or heirs, the monies held in trust, are returned to the bank and navy.

Which meant that an officer like me, who really hadn't gone through the manual with a fine comb, and on the face of it, find it boring. Any monies accrued, from wages and prize money over their career, if they expected that these monies would be paid to said family of the person concerned upon death, were sadly mistaken, and their family could become destitute.

After discovering this, I took steps to have my future wages paid into the bank where my household account was held, instead of the small allotment I had earlier allocated. Then I was determined to check my naval account balance regularly, particularly if I knew of any prize monies, that may be forthcoming into my naval account. I then emptied my account, only leaving one hundred pounds in it as a floating balance. The money I withdrew, was made into a cheque.

Made out to our family clan Patriarch, in this case Albert Fox-Tolcher, I sent a letter and the cheque to Albert explaining what I was intending, and that the sum would be held in trust for me, or my family, should the unthinkable occur.

Since then, I have made it my mission, to inform everyone I come across as to the particular section in the admiralty manual. What they do after learning that, is only their concern.

I explain this, because the next morning during my time with Henry, I disclosed that same fact, and the look of surprise on his face, was not the first time, I had seen this look, after disclosing this little tidbit of information hidden in the manual.

Henry told me of Nelson being here at New Year, and his leaving in early January, plus the fact, that since then no one had heard from him, and the mood amongst the officers of the fleet, was one of unrest, as many would like to take to the sea, and find him. I too was not happy about his news, because three months of not hearing from a fleet, in this day and age, of fast frigates, is unheard of.

The day after Henry had spent a few hours with me aboard the Majestic, flag signals were sent to all ships, summoning all captains and mates to a conference at headquarters immediately, the message was relayed to me in my cabin, and I asked, "Has the captain been informed?" the response was, "Aye sir, and the longboat lowered."

Nodding my head, I stood up from my desk and going to my wardrobe, pulled out my frockcoat, and reaching the door I buckled on my weapons belt, grabbing my hat, I left my cabin, and made my way to the railing, and waited to be joined by George.

In the admiral's conference room, the reason for conference was explained, I think even the admiral heard the sighed remarks of "Finally," but if he did, he chose to ignore it. George and I were seated beside Henry, and captain Hardy, and their voices were among the many that had murmured.
We learned that Mutine and Majestic were going to be part of the fleet under Troubridge, that would depart the following week, in search of Nelson.
After this, the conference broke up, and as George, Hardy, Henry and I, went outside, it was decided that Henry and I would inform our longboat crews, to go back to our ships, and have the pursers start making a list of provisions, then return for us after lunch.
While we made off to do that, George and Hardy would wait for us in the mess. After delivering our instructions to the longboat crews, I joined Henry, as he made for the naval bank branch. He had taken my warning to heart, and was doing something about the substantial amount he had in his account, and he told me he would enclose the cheque with a letter to Albert.
Then we joined George and Hardy in the mess, having a few drinks, while we waited for lunch to be served, being joined by several officers we knew.

A week later, after being fully provisioned, the fleet sailed out of Gibraltar on the morning tide, and formed up in two loose columns, with the frigates ranging out in front of us, Majestic led the second leeward column, while Troubridge's Culloden led the other.

On the twenty-first of May Nelson's small fleet, had been found, and a conference took place onboard Vanguard, Nelson's flagship, after all sail had been reduced to steerage only.

Nelson explained to us that his fleet had been struck by a huge gale, and after having to make repairs, and his frigates had never returned, they were on their way back to Gibraltar, when we came across them. After reading his new orders from Jervis, that were given to him by Troubridge, we split into two columns of seven, with Nelson leading one, and Culloden would come in front of Majestic, as our column lead ship. Then we started a search of the Mediterranean Sea for the French fleet.

To explain why we were doing this, you need to understand the situation that had developed through ideas that Napoleon had, and why our naval campaign ranged across the Mediterranean during the next three months, as a large French convoy sailed from Toulon to Alexandria carrying an expeditionary force under General Napoleon Bonaparte.

Bonaparte's victories in northern Italy over the Austrian Empire helped secure victory for the French in the War of the First Coalition in 1797.

Great Britain remained the only major European power still at war with the French Republic. The French Directory investigated a number of strategic options to counter British opposition, including projected invasions of Ireland and Britain and the expansion of the French Navy to challenge the Royal Navy at sea.

Despite significant efforts, British control of Northern European waters rendered these ambitions impractical in the short term, and the Royal Navy remained firmly in control of the Atlantic Ocean. However, the French navy was dominant in the Mediterranean, following the withdrawal of the British fleet after the outbreak of war between Britain and Spain in 1796.

This allowed Bonaparte to propose an invasion of Egypt as an alternative to confronting Britain directly, believing that the British would be too distracted by an imminent Irish uprising, to intervene in the Mediterranean.

Bonaparte believed that, by establishing a permanent presence in Egypt (nominally part of the neutral Ottoman Empire), the French would obtain a staging point for future operations against British India, possibly in conjunction with the Tipu Sultan of Seringapatam, that might successfully drive the British out of the war.

The campaign would sever the chain of communication that connected Britain with India, an essential part of the British Empire whose trade generated the wealth that Britain required to prosecute the war successfully.

The French Directory agreed with Bonaparte's plans, although a major factor in their decision was a desire to see the politically ambitious Bonaparte and the fiercely loyal veterans of his Italian campaigns travel as far from France as possible.

During the spring of 1798, Bonaparte assembled more than 35,000 soldiers in Mediterranean France and Italy and developed a powerful fleet at Toulon. He also formed the Commission des Sciences et des Arts, a body of scientists and engineers intended to establish a French colony in Egypt. Napoleon kept the destination of the expedition top secret, most of the army's officers did not know of its target, and Bonaparte did not publicly reveal his goal until the first stage of the expedition was complete.

Bonaparte's armada sailed from Toulon on 19 May 1798, making rapid progress through the Ligurian Sea and collecting more ships at Genoa, before sailing southwards along the Sardinian coast and passing Sicily on 7 June.

On 9 June, the fleet arrived off Malta, then under the ownership of the Knights of St. John of Jerusalem, ruled by Grand Master Ferdinand von Hompesch zu Bolheim. Bonaparte demanded that his fleet be permitted entry to the fortified harbour of Valletta. When the Knights refused, the French general responded by ordering an invasion of the Maltese Islands, overrunning the defenders after 24 hours of skirmishing. The Knights formally surrendered on 12 June and, in exchange for substantial financial compensation, handed the islands and all their resources over to Bonaparte.

This included the extensive property of the Roman Catholic Church on Malta.

Within a week, Bonaparte had resupplied his ships, and on 19 June, his fleet departed for Alexandria in the direction of Crete, leaving 4,000 men at Valletta under General Claude-Henri Vaubois to ensure French control of the islands.

Before Bonaparte had sailed to Malta, the Royal Navy entered the Mediterranean for the first time in more than a year. Alarmed by reports of French preparations on the Mediterranean coast, Lord Spencer at the Admiralty sent a message to Vice-Admiral Earl St. Vincent, commander of the Mediterranean Fleet to despatch a squadron to investigate. This squadron, consisting of the flagship and three other ships of the line and three frigates, was entrusted to Rear-Admiral Sir Horatio Nelson.

Chapter 31.

Although initially disappointed that the main French fleet was not at Alexandria, Nelson knew from the presence of the transports that they must be nearby. At 14:00 on 1 August, lookouts on the Zealous reported the French anchored in Aboukir Bay, its signal lieutenant inaccurately describing 16 French ships of the line instead of 13. A conference convened aboard Vanguard before moving to there in pursuit.

When seated, Nelson said, "Hardy I want you to move in close to the stern of me, when we attack, and Henry, you're to muster all men that can be spared, and be ready to take one of the ships, I'll tell you when from my poopdeck. As for everything else gentlemen, the plan will be as we discussed on our way back here, don't forget your lighting. Before this time tomorrow I shall have gained a peerage or Westminster Abbey."

Both hardy and I smiled, as I had heard Horatio say something similar at Cape St. Vincent, and referred to the rewards of victory and the traditional burial place of British military heroes.

Nelson ordered the fleet to slow down at 16:00 to allow his ships to rig 'springs' on our anchor cables, a system of attaching the bow anchor that increased stability and allowed our ships to swing our full broadsides to face an enemy while stationary. It also increased fast manoeuvrability and reduced the risk of coming under raking fire from our enemies, and developed by Sir Francis Drake many years ago.

When we had discussed the attack plan, Nelson had no charts of the depth or shape of the bay, except a rough sketch map, Swiftsure had obtained from a merchant captain, an inaccurate British atlas from Zealous, and a thirty-five-year-old French map from Goliath.

Nelson turned to Sam Hood saying, "Sam it will be up to you to establish the safest course into the harbour.

Hood replied, "Sir, I will take careful soundings as I advance to test the depth of the water, and that, If you will allow me the honour of leading you into battle, I will keep the lead going."

We all smiled at his comment, knowing that he always liked to be the first into battle.

The plan was to advance on the French and pass down the seaward side of the van and centre of the French line, so that each French ship would face two of our ships and the massive Orient would be fighting against three. The direction of the wind meant that the French rear division would be unable to join the battle easily and would be cut off from the front portions of the line.

To ensure that in the smoke and confusion of a night battle our ships would not accidentally open fire on one another, Nelson ordered that each ship prepare four horizontal lights at the head of their mizzen mast and hoist an illuminated White Ensign, which was different enough from the French tricolour that it would not be mistaken in poor visibility, reducing the risk that our ships might fire on one another in the darkness.

Admiral François-Paul Brueys d'Aigalliers sent the Alerte ahead, which passed close to the leading British ships then steered sharply to the west over the shallow shoal, in the hope that the ships of the line might follow and become grounded. None of Nelson's captains fell for the ruse and the British fleet continued undeterred.

At 17:30, Nelson hailed Zealous under Hood, to be the first to fire on the French. Shortly afterwards, Nelson paused to speak with Hardy on Mutine. Hardy yelled to him, "Sir I have seized some maritime pilots from a small Alexandrine vessel.

Nelson laughed and yelled back, "Then pass them over Hardy!" as Vanguard came to a stop.

The following ships slowed, and this caused a gap to open between Zealous and Goliath and the rest of the fleet. To counter this effect, Nelson ordered Theseus under Ralph Miller to pass his flagship and join Zealous and Goliath in the vanguard.

By 18:00, our fleet was again under full sail, Vanguard sixth in the line of ten ships as Culloden trailed behind to the north, while Alexander and Swiftsure hastened to catch up to our west. Following the rapid change from a loose formation to a rigid line of battle both fleets raised their colours; each British ship added additional Union Flags in its rigging in case its main flag was shot away. At 18:20, as Goliath and Zealous rapidly bore down on them, the leading French ships Guerrier and Conquérant opened fire.

Ten minutes after the French opened fire Goliath, ignoring fire from the fort to starboard and from Guerrier to port, most of which was too high to trouble the ship, crossed the head of the French line. Captain Thomas Foley had noticed as he approached that there was an unexpected gap between Guerrier and the shallow water of the shoal. On his own initiative, Foley decided to exploit this tactical error and changed his angle of approach to sail through the gap.

As the bow of Guerrier came within range, Goliath opened fire, inflicting severe damage with a double-shotted raking broadside as his ship turned to port and passed down the unprepared port side of the Guerrier. Foley's Royal Marines and a company of Austrian grenadiers joined the attack, firing their muskets. Foley had intended to anchor alongside the French ship and engage it closely, but his anchor took too long to descend, and his ship passed Guerrier entirely.

Goliath eventually stopped close to the bow of Conquérant, opening fire on the new opponent and using the unengaged starboard guns to exchange occasional shots with the frigate Sérieuse and bomb vessel Hercule, which were anchored inshore of the battle line.

Foley's attack was followed by Hood in Zealous, who also crossed the French line and successfully anchored next to Guerrier in the space Foley had intended, engaging the lead ship's bow from close range. Five minutes later, Guerrier's foremast had fallen, to cheers of our approaching ships.

The speed of our advance took the French captains by surprise; they were still aboard Orient in conference with the admiral when the firing started. Hastily launching their boats, they returned to their vessels. The captain of Guerrier shouted orders from his barge for his men to return fire on Zealous. The third ship into action was Orion under Saumarez, which rounded the engagement at the head of the battle line and passed between the French main line and the frigates that lay closer inshore. As he did so, the frigate Sérieuse opened fire on Orion, wounding two men. The convention in naval warfare of the time was that ships of the line did not attack frigates when there were ships of equal size to engage, but in firing first French Captain Claude-Jean Martin had negated the rule. Saumarez waited until the frigate was at close range before replying.

Orion needed just one broadside to reduce the frigate to a wreck, and Martin's disabled ship drifted away over the shoal. During the delay this detour caused, two other ships joined the battle: Theseus, which had been disguised as a first rate, followed Foley's track across Guerrier's bow.

Hardy steered Mutine through the middle of the melee between the anchored British and French ships until he encountered the third French ship, Spartiate. Anchoring to port, Mutine opened fire at close range.

The next three ships, Vanguard in the lead followed by Minotaur and Defence, remained in line of battle formation, and anchored on the starboard side of the

French line at 18:40. Nelson focused his flagship's fire on Spartiate, and after ten furious broadsides yelled to Hardy, "Send Henry Now!"

Hearing the yell, I got my men ready as Thomas swung us in close, and the grapples were released, then, I yelled, "Boarding party away to me!"

My men followed me, and we swarmed aboard the Spartiate, as a furious fight without quarter ensued for control of the ship.

Audacious under Captain Davidge Gould crossed the French line between Guerrier and Conquérant, anchoring between the ships and raking them both. Orion then rejoined the action further south than intended, firing on the fifth French ship, Peuple Souverain, and Admiral Blanquet's flagship Franklin.

While Captain Thomas Louis in Minotaur attacked the unengaged Aquilon and Captain John Peyton in Defence, joined the attack on Peuple Souverain.

With the French vanguard now heavily outnumbered the following, ships Bellerophon and Majestic, passed by the melee and advanced on the so far unengaged French centre.

Both ships were soon fighting enemies much more powerful than they, and began to take severe damage.

Captain Henry Darby on Bellerophon missed his intended anchor near Franklin and instead found his ship underneath the main battery of the French flagship.

Majestic also missed his station and almost collided with Heureux, coming under heavy fire from

Tonnant. Unable to stop in time, Blagdon's jib boom became entangled with Tonnant's shroud. During this time my boarding party was having to make a real fight for it as the night began to close over us. We had almost taken half the ship, but the French were hardier men than their Spanish counterparts and we had to fight hard, then at about 19:00 the deck beneath our feet started to shake as the Audacious had swung her guns to the Spartiate, and were firing at the guns below deck, to where we were standing.

Deciding this wasn't the place to be, I encouraged my men and we doubled our efforts to wrest control of the ship. Finally, at 19:30 I was face to face with the French Captain Maurice-Julien Emeriau, after a short duel, and mortally wounded, he ordered his colours struck, and passed me his sword, we were now in control of the ship. As my men supervised the collection of weapons, Hardy brought the Mutine in close and rafted up to Spartiate as I placed the four lights on the yardarm to show her as one of ours.

My uniform coat was in tatters, and my shirt soaked with blood and gore, and my face was grimed with used gunpowder and cannon smoke, as I took account of my men, I had lost ten of my men, and fifteen were wounded. There were still skirmishes aboard ship as we found pockets of resistance that wouldn't surrender, and had to be killed before the ship was truly ours, and it was past 21:00 before that happened, and I was able to rest. I was watching the battle going on around the French flagship, Orient.

Then I noticed that our ships Swiftsure, Alexander, and Orion start to move slowly away from the Orient, and in the gloom of their lights, I saw them closing their gunports, and wetting down their ships. Puzzled by this, I kept watching, and saw other ships moving away from Orient, both ours and French ships.

Taking my watch out, and noting the time, I had just returned it to my pocket, and was looking at the Orient, when suddenly, the night was turned into daylight briefly, quickly follow by two simultaneous explosions of huge proportions, so much so that I was knocked off my feet by the resultant shockwave. Like all the fires of hell had erupted! Bewildered and without thought, all I could do was sit there mesmerized by the sight, as bits of debris and body parts fell all around the bay.

I was shocked out of my reverie, by a leg thumping onto the poopdeck not a foot, from where I had been sitting!

For ten minutes after the explosion there was no firing; sailors from both sides were either too shocked by the blast or desperately extinguishing fires aboard their own ships to continue the fight. During the lull, Nelson gave orders that boats be sent to pull survivors from the water around the remains of Orient.

At 22:10, Franklin restarted the engagement by firing on Swiftsure. Isolated and battered, Blanquet's ship was soon dismasted and the admiral, suffering a severe head wound, was forced to surrender, due to combined firepower of Defence and Swiftsure.

More than half of Franklin's crew had been killed or wounded.

By midnight only Tonnant remained engaged, as Commodore Aristide Aubert Du Petit Thouars continued his fight with Majestic, and fired on Swiftsure when the British ship moved within range. By 03:00, after more than three hours of close quarter combat, Majestic had lost its main and mizzen masts while Tonnant was a dismasted hulk. Although Captain Du Petit Thouars had lost both legs and an arm he remained in command, insisting on having the tricolour nailed to the mast to prevent it from being struck and giving orders from his position, propped up on deck in a bucket of wheat. Under his guidance, the Tonnant gradually drifted southwards away from the action to join the southern division under Villeneuve, who failed to bring these ships into effective action.

Throughout the engagement the French rear had kept up an arbitrary fire on the battling ships ahead. The only noticeable effect was the smashing of the Timoléon's rudder by misdirected fire from the neighbouring Généreux.

As the sun rose at 04:00 on 2 August, firing broke out once again between the French southern division of Guillaume, Tell, Tonnant, Genereux, and Timolean, and the battered Alexander and Majestic. Although briefly outmatched, our ships were soon joined by Goliath and Theseus.

As Theseus briefly came under fire from the frigate Artémise. Miller turned his ship towards Artémise, but Captain Pierre-Jean Standelet struck his flag and ordered his men to abandon the frigate. Miller sent a boat under Lieutenant William Hoste to take possession of the empty vessel, but Standelet had set fire to his ship as he left and Artémise blew up shortly afterwards.

After rising early, I donned a new uniform, my leftover rags from the day before, were in the pile I'd left them in before my bath. Wrapping my weapons belt around me, I went on deck to view the state of the fleets.

God! What an awful sight it was. The whole bay was covered with floating dead bodies, mangled, wounded and scorched, not a bit of clothes on them except their trousers.

Chapter 32.

As we entered the main battle area at 20:00, I heard Blagdon yell, "Mister Fox-Davis, we're coming in too fast, furl the mains quickly!" While she was slowing, George at the wheel himself, swung hard to port and we avoided a collision with the Heureux which was our target.

However, coming under heavy musket fire from her. We all dived for cover as the deck was raked by their fire, from my place beside a cutlass barrel, I saw George hit by five musket balls, and I raced to the wheel, ignoring the shots whipping around me. Reaching George, I saw my friend and captain of many years was dead! Gritting my teeth, I grabbed the free running wheel, and brought the ship under control, but I was unable to prevent our jib boom becoming entangled with Mercure's shroud, which swung us broadside on, and our guns let loose. Medical men were removing the dead and wounded from the deck, as the bosun took the wheel.

As our ships parted, I had the anchor dropped as we started trading broadsides with Mecure, then went up to the poopdeck to direct our fight.

After half an hour under our guns, the Mercure struck their colours, placing a prize crew aboard with a lighted union jack and some candles were lit on the yardarm. Then I moved Majestic to between Tonnant and Heureux, and started a battle with Tonnant.

To the north Bellerophon was in serious trouble as the huge broadside of Orient pounded the ship.

At 20:10 the mizzenmast and main mast both collapsed, fires broke out simultaneously at several points. Although the blazes were extinguished, the ship had suffered more than 200 casualties. Captain Darby recognised that his position was untenable, and ordered the anchor cables cut at 20:20, and his ship drifted away from the battle.

The French flagship, Orient had also suffered significant damage and Admiral Brueys had been struck in the midriff by a cannonball that almost cut him in half. He died fifteen minutes later, remaining on deck and refusing to be carried below. Orient's captain, Luc-Julien-Joseph Casabianca, was also wounded, struck in the face by flying debris and knocked unconscious, while his twelve-year-old son had a leg torn off by a cannonball as he stood beside his father.

To support the centre, Captain Thompson of Leander abandoned the futile efforts to drag the stranded Culloden off a shoal and sailed down the embattled French line, entering the gap created by the drifting Peuple Souverain and opened a fierce raking fire on Franklin and Orient.

I was still directing our battle with Tonnant at 22:00, when suddenly there was a tremendous explosion, like a hundred thousand Guy Fawkes bonfires igniting as one, and my hearing was silenced, as I turned to witness the Orient exploding, the shockwave nearly threw me over the forward poopdeck railing, then body parts, blood, bits of wood, and burning cloth rained down around me, as I quickly tried to protect my head, after my hat had been blown off my head with the shockwave. Falling wreckage started fires on Swiftsure, Alexander and Franklin, although in each case, teams of sailors with water buckets succeeded in extinguishing the flames, despite a secondary explosion on Franklin.

It has never been firmly established how the fire on Orient broke out, but one common account is that jars of oil and paint had been left on the poop deck, instead of being properly stowed after painting of the ship's hull had been completed shortly before the battle.

Burning wadding from one of the British ships is believed to have floated onto the poop deck and ignited the paint. The fire rapidly spread through the admiral's cabin and into a ready magazine that stored carcass ammunition, which was designed to burn more fiercely in water than in air.

Alternatively, Fleet Captain Honoré Ganteaume later reported the cause as an explosion on the quarterdeck, preceded by a series of minor fires on the main deck among the ship's boats. Whatever its origin, the fire spread rapidly through the ship's rigging, unchecked by the fire pumps aboard, which had been smashed by British shot. A second blaze then began at the bow, trapping hundreds of sailors in the ship's waist.

Captain Aristide Aubert Du Petit Thouars continued his fight with our ship, and also fired on Swiftsure when she moved within range. By 03:00, after more than three hours of close quarter combat, my ship had lost its main and mizzen masts, but Tonnant was a dismasted hulk. Although Captain Du Petit Thouars had lost both legs and an arm he remained in command, insisting on having the tricolour nailed to the mast to prevent it from being struck and giving orders from his position propped up on deck in a bucket of wheat. Under his guidance, the battered Tonnant gradually drifted southwards away from the action to join the southern division under Villeneuve, who failed to bring these ships into effective action. The surviving French ships of the line, covering their retreat with gunfire, gradually pulled to the east away from the shore at 06:00. Zealous pursued them, and was able to prevent the frigate Justice from boarding Bellerophon, which was anchored at the southern point of the bay undergoing hasty repairs.

For the remainder of 2 August our ships made improvised repairs, boarded and consolidated our prizes. Culloden especially required assistance. Troubridge, having finally dragged his ship off the shoal at 02:00, found that he had lost his rudder and was taking on more than 120 long tons (122 t) of water an hour.

Emergency repairs to the hull and fashioning a replacement rudder from a spare topmast took most of the next two days. On the morning of 3 August, Nelson sent Theseus and Leander to force the surrender of the grounded Tonnant and Timoléon. The Tonnant, its decks crowded with 1,600 survivors from other French vessels, surrendered as our ships approached while Timoléon was set on fire by its remaining crew who then escaped to the shore in small boats. Timoléon exploded shortly after midday, the eleventh and final French ship of the line destroyed or captured during the battle.

British casualties in the battle were recorded with some accuracy in the immediate aftermath as 218 killed and approximately 677 wounded.

Although the number of wounded who subsequently died is not known.

The ships that suffered most were Bellerophon with 201 casualties and Majestic with 193. Other than Culloden the lightest loss was on Zealous, which had one man killed and seven wounded.

The casualty list included Captain Blagdon, five lieutenants and ten junior officers among the dead. Admiral Nelson, Captains Saumarez, Ball and Darby, and six lieutenants wounded. Other than Culloden, the only British ships seriously damaged in their hulls were Bellerophon, Majestic, and the Vanguard. Bellerophon and Majestic were the only ships to lose masts: Majestic the main and mizzen and Bellerophon all three.

Nelson, who on surveying the bay on the morning of 2 August said, "Victory is not a name strong enough for such a scene," remained at anchor in Aboukir Bay for the next two weeks, preoccupied with recovering from his wound, writing dispatches, and assessing the military situation in Egypt using documents captured on board one of the prizes. Nelson's head wound was recorded as being "three inches long, with the cranium exposed for one inch". He suffered pain from the injury for the rest of his life and was badly scarred, styling his hair to disguise it as much as possible. As Nelson recovered, our men stripped the wrecks of useful supplies and made repairs to our ships and prizes. Throughout the week, Aboukir Bay was surrounded by bonfires lit by Bedouin tribesmen in celebration of the British victory. On 5 August, Leander was despatched to Cadiz with messages for Earl St. Vincent carried by Captain Edward Berry.

My cousin Henry, had been made a Captain, and Hardy made Fleet Captain and they were now both aboard the Vanguard. I had also been promoted to Captain, and moved to the Dreadnought along with the remainder of my men that had survived the battle.

Over the next few days we landed all but 200 of the captured prisoners on shore under strict terms of parole, although Bonaparte later ordered them to be formed into an infantry unit and added to his army. The wounded officers taken prisoner were held on board Vanguard, where Nelson regularly entertained them at dinner. Henry recounted to me later, that on one occasion Nelson, whose eyesight was still suffering following his wound, offered toothpicks to an officer who had lost his teeth and then passed a snuff-box to an officer whose nose had been torn off, which caused a lot of embarrassment. On 8 August our boats stormed Aboukir Island, which surrendered without a fight. The landing party removed four of the guns and destroyed the rest along with the fort they were mounted in, renaming the island 'Nelson's Island'.

On August 10, Nelson sent Lieutenant Thomas

Duval from Zealous with messages to the government in India. Duval travelled across the Middle East overland via camel train to Aleppo and took the East India Company ship Fly, from Basra to Bombay, acquainting Governor-General of India Viscount Wellesley with the situation in Egypt.

On 12 August the frigates Emerald under Captain Thomas Moutray Waller and Alcmene under Captain George Johnstone Hope, and the sloop Bonne Citoyenne under Captain Robert Retalick, arrived off Alexandria. Initially the British mistook the frigate squadron for French warships and Swiftsure chased them away. They returned the following day once the error had been realised. The same day as the frigates arrived, Nelson sent Mutine to Britain with dispatches, under the command of Lieutenant Thomas Bladen Capel, who had replaced Hardy after the latter's promotion to Fleet Captain of Vanguard.

August 14, Nelson sent Orion, Majestic, Defence, Bellerophon, Minotaur, Audacious, Theseus, the Franklin, Tonnant, Aquilon, Conquérant, Peuple Souverain, and Spartiate to sea under the command of Saumarez. Many ships had only jury masts and it took a full day for the convoy to reach the mouth of the bay finally, sailing to open water on 15 August. August 16, we burned and destroyed the grounded prize Heureux as no longer fit for service and on 18 August also burned Guerrier and Mercure.

August 19, Nelson sailed for Naples with Vanguard, Culloden, Alexander, and my ship Dreadnought.

leaving Sam Hood in command of Zealous, Goliath, Swiftsure, and the recently joined frigates to watch over French activities at Alexandria.

Saumarez's convoy of prizes stopped first at Malta, where Saumarez aided a rebellion on the island among the Maltese population against the French. He then sailed to Gibraltar, arriving on 18 October to the cheers of the garrison. Saumarez wrote that, "We can never do justice to the warmth of their applause, and the praises they all bestowed on our squadron." On 23 October, following the transfer of the wounded to the military hospital and provision of basic supplies, the convoy sailed on towards Lisbon, leaving Bellerophon and Majestic behind for more extensive repairs. Peuple Souverain also remained at Gibraltar: The ship was deemed too badly damaged for the Atlantic voyage to Britain and so was converted to a guardship under the name of HMS Guerrier.

The remaining prizes underwent basic repairs and then sailed for Britain, spending some months at Gibraltar, and joined with the annual merchant convoy from Portugal in June 1799 under the escort of a squadron commanded by Admiral Sir Alan Gardner, before eventually arriving at Plymouth. Their age and battered state meant that neither Conquérant nor Aquilon were considered fit for active service in the Royal Navy and both were subsequently hulked, although they had been bought into the service for £1,803,000 each as HMS Aboukir and HMS Conquerant to provide a financial reward to the crews that had captured them.

Similar sums were also paid out for Guerrier, Mercure, Heureux and Peuple Souverain, while the other captured ships were worth considerably more. Constructed of Adriatic oak, Tonnant had been built in 1792 and Franklin and Spartiate were less than a year old. Tonnant and Spartiate, both of which later fought at the Battle of Trafalgar, joined the Royal Navy under their old names while Franklin, considered to be 'the finest two-decked ship in the world,' was renamed HMS Canopus. The total value of the prizes captured at the Nile and subsequently bought into the Royal Navy was estimated at just over £11,720,000.

Both parliaments gave unanimous votes of thanks, and each captain who served in the battle was presented with a specially minted gold medal and the first lieutenant of every ship engaged in the battle was promoted to commander. Troubridge and his men, initially excluded, received equal shares in the awards after Nelson personally interceded for the crew of the stranded Culloden, even though they did not directly participate in the engagement.

Before Nelson and my cousin sailed for Naples, the surviving Captains and senior officers of all ships were treated to a party aboard the Vanguard, and some of the officers that had previously been missed in the promotions immediately after the battle, had their rank status changed with promotions.

As a token of our esteem for Nelson, the finest of all the captured swords, had been engraved with the names of all officers of the ships present at the battle of the Nile, and presented to Nelson, through Thomas Hardy, who was our spokesman for the presentation.

Nelson drew the sword to see all the names that were engraved into the blade, and stood holding the sword high, and close to tears, said, "We happy few, who remain, you and I will always be brothers, a band forged in battle, that will never be broken, we are a band of brothers for all time. I thank you heartily for this fine gift, that I will treasure unto death." Then raising a full glass toasted, "Our band of brotherhood!"

We all repeated the toast and drank with him. Since then a Nelsonic Band of Brothers, formed of high quality officers has been present in the Royal Navy.

Chapter 33.

Journal: Henry Robert Tolcher, Captain RN.

December 26, 1798: We have finally reached Palermo, after sailing through heavy gales.
After leaving Aboukir bay, with me in a command of my own, Vanguard was mine, luckily, I had, had good teachers in both Cuthbert and Tom Hardy. Using their examples was a godsend, with captaining the Vanguard, as I got to know her, and it served for my apprenticeship, while I still had Tom close by.
We set sail for Naples on the nineteenth of August, and arrived there at the end of the month. Our fleet entered the harbour to the cheers and applause of the citizens that saw us coming into the harbour. Our welcome to Naples, did in some ways make up for what Horatio considered a slight when he was only appointed a baronetcy, after hearing about it, he would often remark, "That he would rather have received no title than that of a mere barony."
He was however cheered by the attention showered on him by the citizens of Naples, the prestige accorded him by the kingdom's elite, and the comforts he received at the Hamilton's' residence. While our ships were being repaired, there were long periods that we didn't remain aboard ship, and wherever we went in the city, Hardy, Robin, Sam hood and I were treated like heroes, in the hotel where we stayed we were given the best rooms they had, and we were often invited to aristocratic balls.

Horatio made frequent visits to attend functions in his honour, or to tour nearby attractions with Emma, with whom he had by now fallen deeply in love, and she was almost constantly at his side.

Orders arrived from the Admiralty, to blockade the French forces in Alexandria and Malta, not wanting to leave Naples, he assigned the task to his captains, Sam Hood and Alex Ball.

Despite enjoying his lifestyle in Naples, Nelson would often ask me, "How long before the ship is ready Henry?" Confiding in me that he was beginning to think of going home to England.

King Ferdinand of Naples, after a long period of pressure from his wife, Maria Carolina of Austria and Sir William Hamilton, finally agreed to declare war on France. Nelson had agreed to assist the Neapolitan army, which was led by the Austrian general Mack. We sailed the fleet into Rome, and retook it from the French in late November.

But the French regrouped outside the city and, after being reinforced, routed the Neapolitans. In disarray, the Neapolitan army fled back to Naples, with the pursuing French close behind.

Nelson hastily organised the evacuation of the Royal Family, several nobles and the British nationals, including the Hamilton's. The evacuation got under way on 23 December and sailed through heavy gales before reaching the safety of Palermo in December.

Hardy did not altogether approve of Lady Hamilton who had once tried to intervene on behalf of a boat's crew. Hardy had the crew flogged twice, once for the original offence of swearing, and again for having petitioned lady Hamilton to intercede on their behalf.

After leaving Palermo, Nelson had the fleet make for Gibraltar, where we arrived on the twenty-fifth of January 1799. On the eighth of June of that year, Horatio transferred his flag to the HMS Foudroyant, of course Hardy and I went with him.

At the end of June, the fleet led by Nelson on my second ship, landed marines in Naples to assist with the overthrow of the Parthenopean Republic so allowing Ferdinand's kingdom to be re-established. Due to ill health Thomas Hardy, officially handed command over to me of Foudroyant and transferred to the fifth rate Princess Charlotte on the October 13, 1799, and returned to England.

Nelson returned to Palermo in August and in September became the senior officer in the Mediterranean after Jervis' successor Lord Keith left to chase the French and Spanish fleets into the Atlantic, Nelson spent the rest of 1799 at the Neapolitan court but put to sea again in February 1800 after Lord Keith's return.

On February 18, Généreux, a survivor of the Nile, was sighted and I gave chase, capturing her after a short battle, which won Keith's approval. Nelson had a difficult relationship with his superior officer, and he was gaining a reputation for insubordination, having initially refused to send ships when Keith requested them, and on occasion returning to Palermo without orders, pleading poor health. Keith's reports, and rumours of Nelson's

close relationship with Emma Hamilton, were also circulating in London, and Earl Spencer wrote a pointed letter suggesting that he return home:
You will be more likely to recover your health and strength in England than in any inactive situation at a foreign Court, however pleasing the respect and gratitude shown to you for your services may be.

The recall of Sir William Hamilton to Britain was a further incentive for Nelson to return, although he and the Hamilton's initially sailed from Naples on a brief cruise around Malta aboard the Foudroyant in April 1800. It was on this voyage that Horatio and Emma's illegitimate daughter Horatia was probably conceived. After the cruise, Nelson conveyed the Queen of Naples and her suite to Leghorn. On his arrival, Nelson shifted his flag to HMS Alexander, but again disobeyed Keith's orders by refusing to join the main fleet. Keith came to Leghorn in person to demand an explanation, and refused to be moved by the Queen's pleas to allow her to be conveyed in a British ship.
In the face of Keith's demands, Nelson reluctantly struck his flag and bowed to Emma Hamilton's request to return to England over land.

Lord Keith came aboard Foudroyant, and we spoke in my cabin, during questioning by Keith regarding Horatio's behaviour while Lady Hamilton was aboard, he asked me, "Do you condone admiral Nelson's conduct while said lady was aboard captain Tolcher?"
Being married myself I must admit that I didn't like

Horatio's antics especially by cuckolding Sir William. So, in answer to lord Keith's question, I replied, "No sir, I do not."

Lord Keith then informed me, "I will be taking this ship and the rest of the fleet back to Gibraltar where you will become part of my fleet, but I do have my own flagship, so you will be an independent captain again, do you have problems with that captain?"

With a smile, I replied, "None whatsoever Sir!"

He smiled also saying, "Good, we'll leave day after tomorrow Henry, please pass that onto the other ships."

"Aye sir," I replied. Then he left my ship for the time being.

Nelson, the Hamilton's and several other British travellers left Leghorn for Florence on 13 July. They made stops at Trieste and Vienna, spending three weeks in the latter where they were entertained by the local nobility and heard the *Missa in Angustiis* by Haydn that now bears Nelson's name. By September they were in Prague, and later called at Dresden, Dessau and Hamburg, from where they caught a packet ship to Great Yarmouth, arriving on 6 November. Nelson was given a hero's welcome and after being sworn in as a freeman of the borough and received the massed crowd's applause. He subsequently made his way to London, arriving on 9 November. He attended court and was guest of honour at several banquets and balls. It was during this period that Fanny Nelson and Emma Hamilton met for the first time.

During this period, Nelson was reported as being cold and distant to his wife and his attention to Emma became the subject of gossip. With the marriage breaking down, Nelson began to hate even being in the same room as Fanny. Events came to a head around Christmas, when according to Nelson's solicitor, Fanny issued an ultimatum on whether he was to choose her or Emma. Nelson replied:
I love you sincerely, but I cannot forget my obligations to Lady Hamilton or speak of her otherwise than with affection and admiration. The two never lived together again after this.

June 1, 1801: Since the fleets return from Naples, our duties have been varied, and included patrolling from the Atlantic coast of France and Spain, around into the Mediterranean and their ports there. I must admit that after the constant battles over the past few years, it was boring while the peace lasted.
I have been informed by Keith that he was sending Foudroyant back to Plymouth, and I was to take a year's leave at home, and await further orders.
This was great news, a whole year with my wife and family, and I couldn't wait for the day to leave Gibraltar. The thing about being in port quite a few times, was that I Robin and I saw each other every few days, and we had both had confirmation of our Captaincies, and all the band of brothers were awarded the admiralty gold medals for the Battle of the Nile by Lord Keith. I was informed by Keith that my years leave was to be on full pay, due to my service at the Nile, also mail was frequent.

Battle of the Nile medal. Normally worn from a wide Blue ribbon. In 4 grades awarded by rank: Gold to Nelson and his Captains, Silver to lieutenants and Warrant Officers, Copper and Gilt to Petty Officers, Bronzed Copper to ratings and Marines.

All the accountings for our prize ships payments came in a bulk letter from the admiralty, and with the accounting, came a cheque for Three hundred and forty-six thousand pounds (£346,000). In disbelief I looked again at the covering letter, and found that I had been paid bonuses for two ship boarding's and as a captain. Knowing I wasn't a captain at the time, again I looked at my rank confirmation, in wonder, I silently thanked god for Horatio, the dispatches he had made listed me a captain, as of the thirty-first of July, and I laughed for nearly fifteen minutes.

That day I met Robin in the mess, he dragged me away from everyone and whispered, "Henry, Nelson actually post-dated my captaincy from the end of July."

I laughed saying, "I suppose you found that out, when you checked your prize money cheque?"

"Yes, Why?" He asked looking bewildered.

I smiled saying, "He did the same for me, and I'd say most of the others he likes, my advice cousin, the admiralty accountants know what they're doing, so let it lie and take the windfall." Then we both burst out laughing.

The day for Foudroyant to leave Gibraltar arrived, and we finally, sailed into Plymouth this morning, after packing my possessions, and with my weapons belt on, I left my ship in the capable hands of my officers. My first stop was at the naval bank, and I enquired as to my balance, then withdrew everything except one hundred pounds, in a cash cheque form, the cheque went into my Jacket pocket along with the prize money cheque.

My next stop, was to a livery, where I bought a horse and saddle, and saddle bags, and after placing my holdall into one of them, I secured my portmanteaux, with my dress sword strapped to it, across the back of the saddle. After riding slowly through Plymouth, I kicked the horse into a gallop, and reached my father's farm at Dean Prior during the mid-afternoon.

As I rode into the yard, my mother came racing out to greet me, followed by my grandparents, they told me that father was up in one of the far paddocks, but was due to return soon. Mother immediately wanted to know all the news from Taunton, believing that's where I had come from.

Laughing I said, "All I can tell you is from Joanna's letters, I've come up from Plymouth, this is my first time home, since I left after my short honeymoon."

As I was saying this, father came into the yard, and embraced me, then we shook hands. Mother explained to him where I had come from, and he gave me a hand to unpack my gear from the horse, telling me he would put it into the barn later.
Once we were all inside the house, I started to tell them what I had been up to since the last time we saw each other at my wedding. Mother was shocked to know that I had taken part in the Battle of the Nile, saying, "Oh dear, I'm glad you're safe, the reports here were full of horrendous reports of so many dead and wounded. In the thousands, how terrible it must have been. What are you going to do now dear?"
I smiled as I replied, "Well, I'm on leave for a year now, after spending some time with Albert, Joanna and I will probably go looking for a house to buy."
Father interrupted asking, "Will you have enough money, son. If not, you can both come and live here you know?"
I smiled, reached into my jacket pocket then produced the admiralty cheque and showed him, saying, "That's my share of the prize money from the Nile alone, and I still have more to come from captures since then, yes I think I have enough to buy a house and live comfortably."
My father shared the cheque around the table, and gasps of astonishment came from all my family members, and chuckles from both father and pop. After staying with them, for a few days, I then made my way back to Taunton and the homecoming embrace of my wife, and family there.

After being home for a week, I had not forgotten Robin's warning, and in Alberts company, I opened a bank account with a reputable bank that had many branches and one each in Plymouth and Portsmouth, should I need them. The account was opened with all the monies I had sent to Albert, and with the admiralty cheque, bringing my balance to well over six hundred thousand pounds, naturally I was now considered a very important person, and there was nothing they couldn't do for me. I opened a second account with my other cheque, and this would be for everyday living expenses, and I asked to have all the details written down, to pass onto the admiralty, as the new account for my wage deposits.

I also kept abreast of naval affairs, and read what I could find, on the progress of my two friends, and Robin.

Chapter 34.

Journal Entry: Captain Robin Fox-Davis RN.

January 8, 1805: Today I reported back to Portsmouth to take command, of HMS Royal Sovereign, a one hundred-gun first rate, and have been aboard for the last eight hours, meeting the officers and crew. Again, I have noticed that I need to bring my journal up to date from my last entry.

Since watching my cousin Henry, sail to England for a year's shore leave, on Foudroyant on June 1, 1801, Dreadnought has stayed active with patrolling and blockading duties, in the Mediterranean and Atlantic. Since then our fleet admirals have changed a couple of times, Lord Keith was succeeded by admiral Cornwallis, for a short duration, the admiral of the Mediterranean fleet is now our old friend Horatio Nelson, and his second in command is vice admiral Cuthbert Collingwood, and I and my trusty ship Dreadnought are part of his fleet.
Royal Sovereign, which I now command is to be his new flagship.
With nothing else to relieve the boredom of constant patrolling, I scoured the naval newspapers, that come to us every now and then, for tidbits of news about Thomas Hardy, and Horatio Nelson.

Recovering his health after a year of shore leave, Hardy had gone to Plymouth in December 1800 to take command of the first-rate HMS San Josef.

The San Josef was the ship Nelson and my cousin Henry had captured during the battle of Cape St. Vincent, and had just finished being refitted. Shortly after his arrival in England Nelson was appointed to be second-in-command of the Channel Fleet under Lord St Vincent. He was promoted to Vice Admiral of the Blue on 1 January 1801, and travelled to Plymouth, where on 22 January he was granted the freedom of the city, and on 29 January Emma gave birth to their daughter, Horatia. Nelson was delighted, but subsequently disappointed when he was instructed to move his flag from HMS San Josef, to HMS St George, of course he took Hardy with him in preparation for a planned expedition to the Baltic.

Tired of British ships imposing a blockade against French trade and stopping and searching their merchantmen, the Russian, Prussian, Danish and Swedish governments had formed an alliance to break the blockade. Nelson joined Admiral Sir Hyde Parker's fleet at Yarmouth, from where they sailed for the Danish coast in March. Having been sent to force the Danes to withdraw from the League of Armed Neutrality.

On their arrival, Parker was inclined to blockade Denmark and control the entrance to the Baltic, but Nelson urged a pre-emptive attack on the Danish fleet at harbour in Copenhagen. He convinced Parker to allow him to make an assault, and was given significant reinforcements. Parker himself would wait in the Kattegat, covering Nelson's fleet, in case of arrival of the Swedish or Russian fleets.

On the night of 1 April 1801, Hardy was sent in a longboat to take soundings around the anchored Danish fleet. Hardy's ship drew too much water and so took no part in the Battle of Copenhagen the following day.

Hardy's work proved to be of great value. The only two ships that went aground, the third-rates HMS Agamemnon and HMS Bellona, were taken in by local pilots and did not follow Hardy's recommended route.

On the morning of 2 April 1801, Nelson began to advance into Copenhagen harbour. The battle began badly for the British, with Agamemnon, Bellona and HMS Russell running aground, and the rest of the fleet encountering heavier fire from the Danish shore batteries than had been anticipated.

Parker sent the signal for Nelson to withdraw, reasoning: I will make the signal for recall for Nelson's sake. If he is in a condition to continue the action he will disregard it, if he is not, it will be an excuse for his retreat and no blame can be attached to him.

Nelson, directing action aboard HMS Elephant, was informed of the signal by the signal lieutenant, Frederick Langford, but angrily responded: "I told you to look out on the Danish commodore and let me know when he surrendered. Keep your eyes fixed on him."

He then turned to his flag captain, Thomas Hardy, and said "You know, Hardy, I have only one eye. I have a right to be blind sometimes." He raised the telescope to his blind eye, and said "I really do not

see the signal." The battle lasted three hours, leaving both Danish and British fleets heavily damaged.
At length Nelson dispatched a letter to the Danish commander, Crown Prince Frederick, calling for a truce, which the Prince accepted. Parker approved of Nelson's actions in retrospect, and Nelson was given the honour of going into Copenhagen the next day to open formal negotiations.
At a banquet that evening, he told Prince Frederick that the battle had been the most severe he had ever been in. The outcome of the battle and several weeks of ensuing negotiations was a 14-week armistice, and on Parker's recall in May, Nelson became commander-in-chief in the Baltic Sea.   As a reward for the victory, he was created Viscount Nelson of the Nile and of Burnham Thorpe in the County of Norfolk, on 19 May 1801. In addition, on 4 August 1801, he was created Baron Nelson, of the Nile and of Hillsborough in the County of Norfolk, this time with a special remainder to his father and sisters.
Nelson had sailed to the Russian naval base at Revel in May, and there learned that the pact of armed neutrality was to be disbanded. Satisfied with the outcome of the expedition, he returned to England, arriving on 1 July.
Hardy stayed on as flag captain to the new fleet commander, Vice-Admiral Charles Pole, until August 1801 when he took command of the fourth-rate HMS Isis.
In France, Napoleon was massing forces to invade Great Britain.

After a brief spell in London, where he again visited the Hamilton's, Nelson was placed in charge of defending the English Channel to prevent the invasion.

He spent the summer reconnoitring the French coast, but apart from a failed attack on Boulogne in August, saw little action.

On 22 October 1801 the Peace of Amiens was signed between the British and the French, and Nelson in poor health again, retired to Britain where he stayed with Sir William and Lady Hamilton.

On 30 October Nelson spoke in support of the Addington government in the House of Lords, and afterwards made regular visits to attend sessions. The three embarked on a tour of England and Wales, visiting Birmingham, Warwick, Gloucester, Swansea, Monmouth and numerous other towns and villages.

Nelson often found himself received as a hero and was the centre of celebrations and events held in his honour.

In 1802, Nelson bought Merton Place, a country estate in Merton, Surrey where he lived briefly with the Hamilton's until William's death in April 1803. The following month, war broke out again and Nelson prepared to return to sea.

Nelson was appointed commander-in-chief of the Mediterranean Fleet and given the first-rate HMS Victory as his flagship. But Victory wasn't ready for sea, there he found Hardy.

In July 1802 Thomas Hardy had been appointed captain of the fifth rate HMS Amphion, his first mission, was to take the new British Ambassador to Lisbon, and return.

At Portsmouth, in May 1803 he met Nelson, who promptly, transferred his flag to the Amphion and set sail for the Mediterranean. Nelson and Hardy finally transferred to Victory off Toulon on 31 July 1803, and I had to laugh when I heard that it was under my cousin, Henry's command! They would have had a high old time the night he took Nelson and Hardy onboard.

March 10, 1805: The last few days have been hectic to say the least, I arrived in Gibraltar on the first day of the month, and handed over command of the Royal Sovereign over to Edward Rotherham, and vice admiral Collingwood, the following day. Then I went back aboard the Dreadnought, where my new number one John Conn was in charge.

A few days later, we were charged to relieve a squadron of the blockading ships off Brest in the company of five other ships of the line.

As we made our way north, with the squadron, we encountered a huge gale, that scattered us, the weather was so severe, I had lifelines rigged for the watch crews, and shortened the sails.

At one stage it looked as if we might lose her, as we got stuck in a trough between two huge waves, I was assisting the bosun with the wheel, and we had to fight to bring the ship around into the wind, so our bow was facing the wave bearing down on us. Seeing what was coming at us, I only had enough time to yell, "Hold for your life's!"

Then we were hit by the wave, the bosun and I were flung sideways as the wheel broke with a terrible snap, both of us ended up slamming into the starboard side deck railing, the bosun was knocked unconscious, and I was also on the point of losing consciousness, as I felt the Dreadnought heel over. As water poured over the side of the ship, it wiped the fogginess engulfing my head, and I watched as the ship fought back of its own accord, and righted itself. Quickly, I got to my feet and raced below, calling for help as I went.

Racing to the emergency steering station, below decks, I had crewmen attach the tiller to the runaway rudder, and with the help of the bosun, still bleeding from a head wound but back in control of his faculties, and his mate, we took back control of the rudder, and returned to our course, I made sure there were sailors to relay course instructions to the bosun, as I went back on deck to watch and steer the ship, having my instructions relayed below decks to the bosun.

My 1st mate John Conn, had crewmen manning the pumps to get rid of all the water that had come into the ship, while I was re-establishing steerage control, and between our efforts, and those of my fast-acting crew, Dreadnought was saved from a watery grave.

However, we didn't exactly escape unscathed, after the storms had abated, we were able to assess all the damage, we had lost rigging, and all the sails that I had up were in tatters, the wheel station was irretrievably damaged, and would need to be refitted whilst in a dry dock, all our powder was useless due to the drenching in all the water that came inboard, and likewise all our food provisions. Therefore, I had no other recourse, but to limp back to Gibraltar. While the assessment, of all the damage was carried out by John, I sailed the ship from the poopdeck, with my instructions being relayed to the steering crew below.

The rest of our scattered squadron started to reassemble, and all were soon close enough to my position, to be able to read my flag signals to them about the predicament I found myself in, and my intention to return to Gibraltar. As they once again turned northward, I set course to the south, and Gibraltar.

After three weeks, we were in sight of our base, and I ordered the flag signals be run up informing the harbourmaster of our predicament. Shortly four longboats came to greet us and a small sailing tug, it was their mission to take us straight into number three dock, and to turn us, as the ship needed to go into the dock stern first. Once in the dock, the mooring lines were set, and gangplanks moved into position. Then a gang of dock workers closed the dock gates and the water we floated in was pumped out by big seesaw pumps. There were still longboats around our hull, and they positioned stays under the combing rail to keep the ship upright, as the rest of the water was pumped out. Every now and then instructions were relayed backwards and forwards between the longboat crews and the shore pumps.

Then the yard shipwright came aboard, to receive my report, and make his own evaluation. He reported to me that the Dreadnought would be in the dock for at least six weeks, and suggested, the crew be given shore leave, and the officers move to shore quarters. After consulting a calendar, I had the crew assembled on the upper gundeck and addressed them, giving them all shore leave, and they were to report back aboard, no later than August 1.

Once the crew left the ship, I gave orders to my officers, to move into shore quarters, and after dismissing them, I went to pack my belongings. After settling into my shore quarters, I reported to headquarters to inform the admiral of the Dreadnought's disposition, then he heard the rest of my report and I was dismissed. On my way back to my shore quarters, I called into the fleet post office, and there were letters there held for me.

In my quarters, I sorted my mail, and separated the admiralty one from my letters from my sweet Elizabeth, then opened the one from the admiralty, and it was an accounting of the prize money for the Attica, that had been captured by Dreadnought prior to my leave, and in it was a cheque for a further twenty-six thousand pounds in prize money. Placing it aside, I started to read my mail from my darling Elizabeth, in her first letter she informed that she was now pregnant again with our third child, and was blaming me for being too amorous while I was last home. This made me smile, as I reached for the next letter, reading it, the smile was taken away from my face as she informed me that our third child had been stillborn due to complications during its delivery, but had been another son. I was crying as I read the rest of the letter, as I felt her anguish and pain at our loss.

To distract my thoughts, I went out to the naval bank and cleared my account of any wages and commissions, it wasn't all that much in the balance, because my wages were now being sent to my household account. I had the cheque made out to cash. This I would send to Albert along with the prize money cheque, in a letter that would go on the next post ship back to England. Along with the letter I would write in reply to Elizabeth's letters.

Chapter 35.

Journal: Henry Robert Tolcher, Captain RN.

November 12, 1802: This morning was the day, that Joanna and I left Taunton to spend some time in Plymouth, where it has been decided that we will live. We said our goodbyes to friends and family, and took the coach, as I didn't intend to be in Plymouth all that long, we were going to see what we thought would make a good home.
Albert's lawyers had been in touch with lawyers in Plymouth, and one had found what maybe suitable properties were available, there were five in all.
Lucy was going to look after our first daughter, Eliza, while we were gone from Taunton, and though Joanna fretted about her, she was pleased to make the journey with me, as this was the first trip where she had ever left Somerset.

Bypassing my family farm, we went straight to Plymouth, we had plenty of time to visit on the way back to Taunton. We were shown the properties available, but we decided on the one that was shown to us first. It was on Mount Wise the highest point of Plymouth, and the house was a sprawling two level manor, that included stables and two carriages, like Albert's one open, and one enclosed coach. It also over looked the Tamar river, the naval port, and the southern main harbour entrance. The manor was part of a deceased estate, and I was able to purchase it for twenty thousand pounds, lock, stock, and barrel.

While in Plymouth, I employed ten house staff, whose job it was, to get the place habitable so we could move into it just after the new year. We came away from Plymouth both feeling very pleased with my purchase.

We did stop at the farm on the way back to Taunton, and we spent the night there, as we informed them that we had purchased a house in Plymouth, and they would be welcome there anytime they wanted to visit. During our trip home, Joanna also informed me she was pregnant again, and as I did the math, I was disappointed that I would be at sea, when my second child was born.

Being told about my purchase, Albert gifted me two, four horse carriage teams, and six riding horses that would go with us to Plymouth in the new year.

Ted and Alice were also going to move with us to oversee things whilst I wasn't at home, especially after Joanna told them that the manor had three caretakers' cottages, and that they could choose which one they moved into. Christmas came, and though we all had a joyous time, it was also a sad time as soon, Joanna and my family would be leaving.

On the day we left, all our clothing and possessions were in the coach, along with Joanna and Eliza, and Alice, while Ted drove one the wagons full of his and Alice's possessions and furniture, with the carriage horses tied to the wagon, while I rode lightning, pulling the string of riding horses along. We reached Plymouth, and the house a week later, and over the following week, before the rest of

Albert's men returned to Taunton, Ted and Alice had been moved into the cottage of their choice, and the stables had been cleaned out and made ship shape, along with the two carriages, then we said goodbye to the coach and wagon, and Albert's men as they headed back to Taunton.

Alice took to overseeing the household staff, and cooks, and Ted was now the head stableman and caretaker, of our home.

Two weeks after we had moved into my new house, I rode down to the naval yard and visited the admiralty office, to inform the admiralty of my change of address. The yellow admiral (a non-seagoing, and in charge of port flag officer), took me into his office saying, "Well your change of address is most fortuitous, as your next command is here having all its work done, and should be ready for you by the time you come off leave, anyway I'll pass your details along, thank you Captain."

Though not in uniform, I stood to attention, and replied, "Aye sir, and thank you. Could you give me the name of my next command sir?"

Smiling, he said, "Of course captain, you will be commanding the HMS Victory."

My mind was reeling, *I was to command the victory, what an honour, a one hundred-gun first rate!* I stammered my thanks, and as I was about to leave, he said, "I'll see you when you report in for duty captain Tolcher, dismissed."

My excitement must have shown as I entered the parlour where Joanna was with Eliza, and she asked, "What's got you so excited Robert?"

Taking her into my study, I walked her to where the was a telescope set up on a tripod, and I quickly scanned the dock yards, finding the Victory, then had her look at it, as I said, "That dear heart is my next ship, the Victory!"

All she said was, "That's very nice dear, its big isn't it?"

Exasperated, I replied, "Yes dear heart, and it's the most famous ship in the entire fleet!"

She replied, "Well I hope you enjoy your games with it, can I go back to my sewing now?"

My excitement took a dive in cold water, and I cursed under my, breathe thinking, *Women! They've got no bloody idea!* As I gave up and said lowly, "Yes dear."

A month later, an admiralty despatch rider arrived to hand me my new orders, my return from leave was still the eighth of June 1803, but now, due to my change of address, I would be reporting to Plymouth headquarters, to take command of the Victory. Whilst on leave, I had taken a leaf out of Horatio's book, and visiting the naval tailors in town, had my service medals for St. Vincent and the Nile embroidered onto my working frockcoats, for everyday use aboard, while the originals stayed pinned to my full-dress frockcoat. I also had them contact Howes in Taunton, requesting another dozen shirts and waistcoats, for me.

As the day neared for my return, I packed my gear, strapping my dress sword around my portmanteaux, and instead of using my holdall, I used saddle bags.

These were packed with my older everyday wear for aboard ship. Then each day, I would look towards Victory in the dock area, and watched its progress on the morning of the fifth, as it was moved from the docks to the main wharf, where it was secured, and two gangplanks put into place, fore and aft. Over the following couple of days, I watched as an endless stream of powder and shot was loaded aboard, along with other provisions and supplies. The night before my departure from home, I arranged for Ted, to drive me to the naval yards the following morning in the open carriage.

June 10, 1803: This morning, the Victory left the port of Plymouth, we are bound for Gibraltar, to meet up with Horatio and Thomas Hardy, as admiral of the Mediterranean fleet, and Fleet captain respectively.

After breakfast on June eighth, I farewelled my heavily pregnant wife, as she walked out of the house with her mother, once I was ready in the carriage, Ted flicked the reins and started it moving out of the yard, and down the hill toward the naval yard. Reporting for duty to the admiral, I left his office with the crew manifest and supply ledgers, Ted took me to the ship. He carried my possessions as he followed me aboard, where I was challenged by a familiar officer of the watch, as he saluted, and I returned his salute, I asked, "I know you, don't I, Dawson isn't it?"

He replied, "Aye sir, we met aboard the Majestic when your cousin Robin, twas a 2nd lieutenant."

I smiled, as I recounted the first time I had seen him, then said, "Ah yes, now I remember, can you show me to my cabin please Dawson?"

He was smiling also, and replied, "Aye sir, iffin you'll follow me."

He showed Ted and I to my stateroom, and opened the door for us then left, to go back to his duties.

After Ted had put my belongings on the bed, we said our farewells, shook hands, and he exited the cabin, closing the door and left the ship to return home.

After stowing my belongings where they needed to go, leaving the ledgers and my journal on the desk, I went on deck, and made my way to the poopdeck, and calling Dawson across, I told him that there were a lot of familiar faces amongst the crew, he let me know that the crew compliment was made up of veterans from the Majestic and Minerve crews that had survived the Nile, and a few other ships, but all were fine seamen.

Then I asked, "What about officers Joe, why aren't any aboard?"

He smiled and replied, "Apparently, they're not due to report until this afternoon, but no doubt you'll probably find them in the officer's mess sir, a couple have come to the ship while our loading was being done by the quartermaster and purser."

When we were finishing our talk, four midshipmen had come aboard, and the officer of the watch, being Dawson was called.

Following him, all four saluted me and I returned their salutes, one came forward, and I knew him.

His name was George Clark, and I said, "Very good to see you again mister Clark, care to introduce these others please?"

He replied with a smile saying, "Aye sir, this is Monty Davis, Arthur Billings, he's no relation to 2nd lieutenant Billings sir, and Tom Bronte, and we'd like permission to come aboard sir?"

I smiled saying, "Permission granted gentlemen, when you stow your gear, mister Clark will show you where, then I want all of you to inspect every part of the ship, so you know her from stem to stern, no use being on a ship if you don't know where everything is, is that correct mister Clark?"

"Aye Sir," he replied, and I made him senior midshipman.

Turning to Dawson, I told him, I would be in the mess ashore, then left the ship and crossed to the officer's mess.

Inside, I spotted my officers at a table playing cards, and walked over to them. As I was spotted by Ray Billings, he said something, and they all stood to attention, as I addressed them saying, "Well hello you lot, I suppose you know I'm your captain, so who's what amongst you, hello mister Price, nice to see you passed your exams."

Dan Culverhouse, spoke saying, "I'm, your 1st mate sir, Ray is 2nd officer, Charlie's your third, and Pricey here is your fourth, captain." We all shook hands, and renewed our bonds, as each of them had been present on different ships, during the battle of the Nile. Joining them, a drink was brought to me, as I was telling them that the crew aboard were all from ships they had manned in some way, so all the crew would be familiar with each of us, and I joked with Ray Billings about, now having two mister Billings to worry about.

We all had lunch together, and afterward, I said, "Well gentlemen, thanks for the company, but some of us have work to do, I'll be aboard, and consider yourselves reported in, I'll see you aboard."

Later that evening, during drinks in the wardroom, I met the only new face aboard, that being the captain of marines, David Forsyth, and the rest of us renewed our acquaintances, it was nice to see that we had a competent surgeon aboard in the form of doctor William Beatty, the Purser was Walter Burke from the Minerve, and the chaplain Alexander Scott from Majestic, it was nice to see he had survived the Nile. Sometimes he, Robin, and I had many heated arguments over theology, but took them in the spirit they were meant to be, as different viewpoints.

The following morning, I had the entire crew mustered on the quarterdeck, and had Mister Price mark the ships roll, then he turned to me saying, "All ships compliment aboard sir," and saluted.

I returned his salute, then moved forward to the poopdeck railing, and addressed the crew, "Well me blood thirsty hearties, we meet again (laughter), you all know me and my officers, and what we expect. For those of you that have had your head in a bucket for the last year (laughter), the frogs are at it once more, it's up to us to kick Napoleons' arse again!"

Letting the cheers and laughter die down, I continued, "Our ships mission is to become the flagship for Admiral Lord Nelson, and we will take him onboard either at Gibraltar, or at one of the blockaded ports. You've all served under him, and know that he only expects you to do your duty, when it's our time to kick the frogs and Spanish, back to where they came from, with as much butt kicking we can give them, hopefully enough so they will be shitting out their mouths, dismissed!" They all started to go back to their regular duties, with cheers, laughter, and smiles.
During the day, I was advised that the ship was fully loaded and ready for sea, and had all officers notified we would be sailing on the next morning's tide, which was high at 0915.

The following morning, breakfast in the wardroom was finished by 0830, and all officers went to their stations, as I moved to the poopdeck, the day watch was already in place, and I said to Dan Culverhouse, "Away the gangplanks number one," as he relayed the order, shore men were already to carry out the orders, and the railing doors were shut, and locked once the gangplanks had been withdrawn. Then I gave the order for steerage sail, as I saw the ship start to move forward against the incoming tide, I raised my voice and called, "Away fore line!" As the rope ashore was untied and let go to be pulled onboard, the ships bow started to drift away from the dock, and when it reached the right angle, I called, "Away aft!" then Victory was moving forward and away from the dock, leaving the harbour my timing was spot on, as we reached the entrance, and swung into the Tamar, with the outgoing current. Once out in the Tamar and free to navigate, Dan called for the mainsails to be unfurled on all three masts. Going to the aft railing, I lifted my hat and waved it and my arm, goodbye to my house on the hill, not sure if anyone was watching as we left.

Clearing the heads and breakwater, we turned into the English Channel, as I called down to Ray Billings, who was beside the steersman at the wheel, "Bring her onto course number two."

"Aye sir," he replied, and I watched the wheel turn to starboard slowly, until we were on the correct course, a few hours later we left land behind, as we had moved far out into the channel, with the course set for Gibraltar.

Chapter 36.

Journal: Henry Robert Tolcher Captain RN.

July 7, 1803: Tonight, we slipped out of port on our way to Toulon, where Horatio and Hardy are blockading aboard the Amphion.
I found this out during our brief stay to provision, and reporting to headquarters. Robin and I caught up in the mess, and I told him of the crew that made up the Victory, as he remarked, "Then you have possibly the best sailors and gunners in the fleet, god, man, how did you wangle that?"
I answered with a smile, saying, "With my charm, dear cousin, no, honestly I don't know, I think they crewed her with any spare man they had, rather fortunate for me though. Now what's been happening out here while I've been away?"
There wasn't much that he could tell me, that I didn't already know, then talk drifted to what was happening at home, and I told him about my house purchase on Mount Wise, and about Joanna being pregnant again, he told me of his and Elizabeth's loss. After commiserating with him, over a few drinks, I told him I was sailing on the night tide, and we shook hands as we parted.

August 1, 1803: We arrived and joined the blockading fleet on the thirtieth of July, during the late afternoon, and I had the signals run up, to inform Horatio that his flagship had arrived, and would he care to come aboard?

I watched as his flag was struck, and he and Hardy and their possessions were on a longboat, heading toward us, I made ready to receive them aboard. As he walked through the railing door, all the crewmen on deck cheered his arrival. Handing his pennant to flags, it was run up in its correct position, as he and Hardy were being greeted by me and my officers.

That night, Horatio, Thomas and myself ate in the great cabin, as we drank a lot and mused over old times, and what was to become, the following night though, we all messed in the wardroom with all the other ships officers. With the main topic of conversation, being the political situation in Europe.

In 1803, the First French Empire, under Napoleon Bonaparte, was the dominant military land power on the European continent, while the British Royal Navy controlled the seas. During the war, the British imposed a naval blockade on France, which affected trade and kept the French from fully mobilising their naval resources. Despite several successful evasions of the blockade by the French navy, it failed to inflict a major defeat upon the British, who were able to attack French interests at home and abroad with relative ease.

When the Third Coalition declared war on France, after the short-lived Peace of Amiens, Napoleon was determined to invade Britain. To do so, he needed to ensure that the Royal Navy would be unable to disrupt the invasion flotilla, which would require control of the English Channel.

The main French fleets were at Brest in Brittany and at Toulon on the Mediterranean coast. Other ports on the French Atlantic coast harboured smaller squadrons. France and Spain were allied, so the Spanish fleet based in Cádiz and Ferrol was also available.

Vice-Admiral Pierre-Charles Villeneuve had taken command of the French Mediterranean fleet. There had been more competent officers, but they had either been employed elsewhere or had fallen from Napoleon's favour. Villeneuve had shown a distinct lack of enthusiasm for facing Nelson and the Royal Navy again after the French defeat at the Battle of the Nile in 1798.

During our blockading of Toulon for the following couple of years, and being relieved by Collingwood, when we needed provisioning, Horaito only maintained a loose blockade, as opposed to admiral Cornwallis with the Channel fleet up in the north. One morning while we strode together on the quarterdeck, I asked, "Horatio, you still wish to maintain this loose formation, may I ask why?" He smiled saying, "Hah Henry, haven't you guessed by now, I'm hoping to lure them out, so we have at them, that's why we've been having the action we've had, the bloody frogs foolishly think they can slip by us. Everytime they try, we inflict more damage, and that should be quite a strain on their resources." We both laughed, his thinking was full of merit, but I wondered how long it would be before some of them did slip by us, not that any had!

That night, in the mess, Horatio, announced, "I'm feeling in need of some English soil under my feet gentlemen, therefore, when Collingwood relieves us next, we will sail for home and have a spot of leave, I trust that won't spoil any of your plans." His announcement was greeted with cheers and anticipation for they all knew that Collingwood was due to relieve us soon.

Thomas Hardy enquired, "And where shall we make port sir?"

Horatio seemed to be thinking and soon said, "Plymouth is closest, so we'll have leave there, Hardy, three weeks should be enough I think, the men can have shore leave, and gentlemen anyone further away than a day by horse, please limit yourself to the port town."

While we were eating, I said to Culverhouse, "Dan have the course made ready for when its needed please."

He smiled and nodded, but didn't need to acknowledge any further.

A week later, admiral Collingwood's fleet arrived along with them was Robin on Majestic, and I gave him a wave as he passed by. Signals were sent to the Royal Sovereign, informing Collingwood what we were up to, then the course for Plymouth was acted on, as our fleet moved off station, toward the Straits of Gibraltar, and ultimately to Plymouth.

August 3, 1805: This morning, the fleet entered the Tamar, and all ships have moored to jetties in the harbour, both Hardy and Horatio, have left Victory.

I will soon hand duties to Dan Culverhouse, who has elected to remain aboard, while the ship's hull is scraped, while in port. I have shown him my house, and told him I would be there if needed urgently.

Someone at the house, must have been aware of the fleets arrival, because one of my house staff had driven my carriage to the ship, and were awaiting me. I left all my belongings onboard, thinking that if I needed anything, all I had to do was ride down to the ship.

As I arrived home, I was greeted by Joanna, and she flung herself into my arms, as we embraced and had a prolonged kiss, I noticed, that she wasn't alone, my family were with her, including my nan and pop.

After receiving kisses and hugs of welcome from my mother and nan, pop and father embraced me and shook hands with me, as I said. "Well this is a welcome surprise, let's go inside and you can tell me why you're all here."

We were all seated in the parlour, along with my wife's parents, and while the men had scotch in tumblers, the ladies had sherry. As I was told the latest news. My family had made the visit to have a look at their new granddaughter, and, in nan and pop's case, greatgrandchild. It was only by luck that they had arrived two days ago, and father had been in my study when the fleet had sailed into port. Using my telescope, he had enquired of Joanna, what ship I was on, and had announced that I was nearly home, and the whole family had gone into the garden to watch us tie up.

Then father asked, "So how long are you home for Robert?"

Looking around at everyone, I replied, "Just for a short time actually only three weeks, then we'll head back to the Med, I'm afraid."

He laughed as did pop, who said laughingly, "That's plenty of time to work at giving us another great grandchild, Henry!"

All the men laughed as he was chided by nan, and Joanna had blushed at his remark, but had a slight smile on her face. Then talk became general, and I was made aware of things going on in our country. After, half an hour I was interrupted by one of the house staff that there were two gentlemen to see me, going to the door, I saw Horatio and Thomas Hardy. Immediately inviting them in, I took them into the parlour, and introduced them to everyone as Ted handed them a scotch each. They both charmed all those present, and heaped praise on me to everyone, before I interrupted them, saying, "So Thomas, Horatio, to what do I owe the honour of your company?"

Horatio laughed and replied, "Hah down to business as always Henry, good man, Hardy and I have a bit of a problem, even though wherever I go people, want to do things for me, we can't for the life of us, rent any horses, and you'd told Hardy where you lived, so we were wondering if we could borrow a couple of mounts, so we can go home for our leave."

Laughing, I replied, "I don't think that will be a problem, you two, but there will be a price paid I'm afraid."

Hardy turned to me, and enquired, "Oh, and what would that be Henry?"
That you both stay the night and have dinner with us, and in the morning, you can leave when you've had breakfast."
Horatio laughed saying, "What a splendid idea! Done, good captain." Then he looked around laughing, put his hand to the side of his mouth saying quietly around the room to everyone, "He really is a stickler for the rules, but a damned fine captain, I hope you can put up with us two old reprobates?" Everyone laughed, and I looked at Ted, who gave me a nod, and left to organise the rooms and dinner. The rest of the day and night went well, Horatio entertaining the family with the tales of our actions, in between drinks and mouthfuls of food, he was most eloquent as he described in detail, my plunge over the rail during the battle at Cape St. Vincent to everyone's joy and laughter and of my leap aboard the Spartiate at the Nile.
Later that night, in our room, Joanna had jumped into bed saying with a smile, "Well I suppose you wish to have your husbandly rights, and make another great grandchild for your grandparents?"
I smiled replying, "Well it had crossed my mind, wife."
She laughed saying, "Not dressed like that you're not!" I laughed and shrugged off my nightshirt, as I moved toward the bed her gown came flying out of the bed, and I asked, "Permission to board madam?"
She giggled, and replied, "But of course dear captain, quickly now!" She sighed in ecstasy, as I

did as I was bid.

Next morning, we said our farewells to Hardy and Nelson, as they both galloped off, to their homes. In early September word reached England about the combined French and Spanish fleet in Cadiz harbour, and on the fourteenth of September both Hardy and Nelson galloped into the yard as my carriage was about to leave for the ship. My father and mother had gone home the week before, but my grandparents were still staying for a while longer. Leaving the horse reins in Ted's hands they bounded into the carriage as we set off for the naval yard, and once there to the dock where Victory was ready to leave, once we were aboard.

Onboard I had signals sent to all ships of the fleet, that we would leave on the morning hightide, which was at 0330, the next morning.

September 15, 1805: We slipped out of harbour, all ships in line astern of Victory, until out in the Channel, then sails were set as we make for Gibraltar. 0500: the ship is on course, and making good time, and I'm about to get some sleep before breakfast.
Napoleon's naval plan in 1805 was for the French and Spanish fleets in the Mediterranean and Cádiz to break through the blockade and join forces in the Caribbean. They would then return, assist the fleet in Brest to emerge from the blockade, and together clear the English Channel of Royal Navy ships, ensuring a safe passage for the invasion barges.

Collingwood like Nelson adopted a loose blockade in the hope of luring the French out for a major battle. Villeneauve's fleet successfully evaded Collingwood when the British were blown off station by storms. Villeneuve took his fleet through the Strait of Gibraltar, rendezvoused with the Spanish fleet, and sailed as planned for the Caribbean. Once Nelson realised that the French had crossed the Atlantic Ocean, he set off in pursuit. Villeneuve returned from the Caribbean to Europe, intending to break the blockade at Brest, but after two of his Spanish ships were captured during the Battle of Cape Finisterre by a squadron under Vice-Admiral Sir Robert Calder, Villeneuve abandoned this plan and sailed back to Ferrol in northern Spain.

There he received orders from Napoleon to return to Brest according to the main plan. When Villeneuve set sail from Ferrol on 10 August, he was under orders from Napoleon to sail northward toward Brest. Instead, he worried that the British were observing his manoeuvres, so on 11 August, he sailed southward towards Cádiz on the southwestern coast of Spain. With no sign of Villeneuve's fleet, on 25 August, the three French army corps' invasion force near Boulogne broke camp and marched into Germany, where it was later engaged. This ended the immediate threat of invasion.

As we sailed south, news reached us that Villeneuve had made a break for it and was headed towards the Caribbean, realising what the French and Spanish fleet were up to, Horatio had me, and the fleet go about (turn around), and we headed back to Cadiz. Villeneuve returned from the Caribbean to Europe, intending to break the blockade at Brest, but after two of his Spanish ships were captured during the Battle of Cape Finisterre by a squadron under Vice-Admiral Sir Robert Calder, Villeneuve abandoned this plan and sailed back to Ferrol in northern Spain. There he received orders from Napoleon to return to Brest according to the main plan.

Napoleon's invasion plans for Britain depended on having a sufficiently large number of ships of the line before Boulogne in France. This would require Villeneuve's force of 33 ships to join Vice-Admiral Ganteaume's force of 21 ships at Brest, along with a squadron of five ships under Captain Allemand, which would have given him a combined force of 59 ships of the line.

Had this have happened, we would have been up against it, but fate, and Villeneuve's fear of Horatio worked for us, it's a pity the weather didn't.

Chapter 37.

On 15 August, while our fleet was on leave, Cornwallis decided to detach 20 ships of the line from the fleet guarding the English Channel and to have them sail southward to engage the enemy forces in Spain. This left the Channel drastically reduced of large vessels, with only 11 ships of the line present. However foolish this sounded, it showed in the long run to be quite fortuitous for us, because this detached force formed the nucleus of our fleet that would fight at Trafalgar.
This fleet, under the command of Vice-Admiral Calder, reached Cádiz on 15 September.
After our chase of Villeneuve our fleet joined the fleet under Calder on the 28th September, and Horatio took over command of the combined fleets. Our fleet used frigates (faster, but too fragile for the line of battle), to keep a constant watch on the harbour, while our main force remained out of sight, approximately 50 miles west of the shore. Again, Horatio's hope was to lure the combined Franco-Spanish force out and engage it in a decisive battle. The force watching the harbour was led by Captain Blackwood, commanding HMS Euryalus. His squadron of seven ships comprised five frigates, a schooner, and a brig.
By this time, our fleet needed provisioning. On 2 October, five ships of the line, HMS Queen, Canopus, Spencer, Zealous, Tigre, and the frigate Endymion were dispatched to Gibraltar under Rear-Admiral Sir Thomas Louis for supplies.

These ships were later diverted for convoy duty in the Mediterranean, although we had expected them to return.

Collingwood in the meantime, having regathered his fleet, was at harbour in Gibraltar, when our ships under Louis, arrived there, needing to guard a convoy, he sent Louis to do that, and loading all the provisions we needed onto his ships, he made sail from Gibraltar, bringing us our much-needed supplies, and joined our combined force, with Horatio, making him, his second in command.

Other British ships continued to arrive, and by the fifteenth of October the fleet was up to full strength for the battle.

Under admiralty orders we also lost, Calder's flagship, the 98-gun Prince of Wales, which Hardy as fleet captain, after appraising Horatio of the orders, reluctantly sent home, because Calder had been recalled by the Admiralty to face a court martial for his apparent lack of aggression during the engagement off Cape Finisterre on 22 July.

I watched from the poopdeck, as the Prince of Wales departed, and I was joined by Horatio, as we both watched Calder's ship, then leaning on the rear rail said, "I hope you're a praying man Henry, I've never had much time for it myself, considering my family background that is, but Henry, start praying that Villeneuve decides to take a chance, and comes out, where we can finish them for good! Oh, and have some signals run up, inviting all captains to dinner aboard here tonight, please."

After a brief cough, he continued, "I think it's time to reveal my plans for the coming battle to one and all."

I replied, "Aye Horatio, I'll have it done, and inform the purser."

He smiled at me, saying, "Thank you, you're a good man Henry."

Meanwhile, Villeneuve's fleet in Cádiz was also suffering from a serious supply shortage that could not be easily rectified by the cash-poor French. The blockade maintained by our different fleets, had made it difficult for the Franco-Spanish allies to obtain stores, and their ships were ill-equipped. Villeneuve's ships were also more than two thousand men short of the force needed to sail. These were not the only problems faced by the Franco-Spanish fleet. The main French ships of the line had been kept in harbour for years by our blockades, with only brief sorties. The French crews included few experienced sailors, and, as most of the crew had to be taught the elements of seamanship on the few occasions when they got to sea, gunnery was neglected. The hasty voyage across the Atlantic and back used up vital supplies. Villeneuve's supply situation began to improve in October, but news of Nelson's arrival made Villeneuve reluctant to leave port. Indeed, his captains had held a vote on the matter and decided to stay in harbour.

Villeneuve then learned that some British ships had been seen in Gibraltar, and thought this meant that our fleet was not as strong as it had been before, he decided that this was the best time to leave Cadiz.

October 20, 1805: It is nearly 23:00, I write this in case it maybe my last entry, hoping this journal should make its way home should that prove to be the case. All the ships captains have made their way aboard for drinks and dinner, and I was about to join them, as my attention was drawn to the far sail of an approaching frigate, pulling my scope, I saw its signals being raised, and read the message, then the signals officer, John Pasco, passed me the message he had written down, it read: Villeneuve's fleet was sighted making its way out of harbour, by our patrolling frigates, heading west.

I took the message with me, as I joined the other officers in the wardroom, and made my way to beside Horatio, who was in the middle of telling a joke. After finishing the joke, as the laughter was going around, he looked at me enquiringly, and I passed him the message, he read it, and smiled as he nodded to me in affirmation. He moved to the main table, and turned a handmade map over for all to see, saying, "Gentlemen, it's now time to reveal my battleplan against Villeneuve, who has left harbour, and is heading west towards us! As you can see from my drawing, we'll not be forming line of battle, instead we're going to cut their line of battle in two columns, Cuthbert as my number two, you will lead your fleet in one column, while I lead the second. Ah, here's dinner, please sit and we'll discuss this over our meal."

Robin sat beside me, and we shook hands and said

hello to each other, as plates were placed in front of us by the serving staff.

Between mouthfuls, he took out a letter from his jacket, and passed it to me, saying, "I was hoping to see you before the fight, Henry, this letter authorizes you to access my funds in the naval bank, and is just in case, there's some prize money due to me, so give it to Elizabeth if I don't come through this one, don't worry about my pay, and incidentals, that's already been taken care of, but with luck you can give it back to me after the fight."
Reluctant to take the missive, I said, "Robin, my dear cousin, in that case I will be seeing you after the battle, and we can tear it up together, but don't even think, that I'm going to give you control of my money like this, you bloody pirate!"
We both burst out laughing, and the matter was forgotten, as I placed it into my jacket, and we turned our attention to what was being said around the table.

After further drinks and socialising, at about 22:00 I bid farewell to the captains leaving my ship, at the rail, as was customary as the convening authority, as they made for their own ships. When Robin took his turn, in the leaving procession, I wished him good luck as we shook hands, and said, "See you tomorrow night, or the one after that."
He smiled and replied, "I'll be looking forward to it cousin." Then laughed as he climbed down the side of Victory.

Now I'm alone in my cabin, but I fear there will be

no sleep for me tonight, so I may as well prepare myself for the battle ahead, and spend the rest of the night up on the poopdeck, I won't write again until after the battle, if I'm lucky to live through it.

The day was starting to lighten the sky, as Horatio, came and joined me, asking, "Can't sleep either, Henry?"

I smiled and replied, "No, Horatio, I just didn't want to wake up with a hangover, from all the wine we drank, I've stayed up here keeping my head clear."

"Just so," he said, as he took out his watch, and said, "Alright, its four am, time to go to work. Mr. Pasco run up the signals to turn the fleet toward the enemy, and go to battle stations! I'll return soon captain Tolcher."

"Aye Admiral," I replied.

Horatio had gone below to make his will, before he returned to the quarterdeck to carry out an inspection. Despite having 27 ships to Villeneuve's 33, Nelson was confident of success, declaring to me, that he would not be satisfied with taking fewer than 20 prizes. He returned briefly to his cabin to write a final prayer, after which he joined John Pasco again, saying, "Mr. Pasco, I wish to say to the fleet, England confides that every man will do his duty. You must be quick, for I have one more signal to make, which is for close action.

Pasco suggested that he consider changing, confides to expects which, being in the Signal Book, could be signalled using a single code (using three flags), whereas confides would have to be spelt out letter by letter.

Nelson agreed with satisfaction, and in a hurry, and said, "That will do, Pasco, make it directly."

As the fleets converged, Tom Hardy suggested that Horatio remove the decorations on his coat.
Horatio asked, "Why so, Tom?"
Hardy smiled and replied, "So that you would not be so easily identified by enemy sharpshooters."
Nelson laughed and replied, "It's too late to be shifting a coat, they are military orders and I don't fear to show them to the enemy."
Then as Captain Henry Blackwood, of the frigate Euryalus, came alongside, he called and suggested, "Admiral Nelson would you like to come aboard my ship to better observe the battle?"
Horatio refused, saying, "No, thank you Captain, I can observe better from here."
Then Hardy suggested, "What say you Admiral, to let HMS Temeraire come ahead of Victory and lead the line into battle?"
Horatio said, "Most certainly not Hardy, where I lead the fleet will follow!"

The twenty first of October dawned as a beautiful sunny day, but there was very little breeze. We were able to see the enemy fleet, and the position of both fleets were off Cape Trafalgar.
Villeneuve had reversed course in the early morning back toward Cadiz and as we watched the enemy fleet, there seemed to be a lot of confusion.
Pacing the quarterdeck with Hardy, Horatio would call to me when they neared the wheel, "Captain

Tolcher has Villeneuve shown his colours yet?
Because if he does, that's where we strike!"
I called in reply, "Not yet Admiral, when he does, I
will head for him sir!"

The main drawback of attacking head-on was that as
our ships approached, the Franco-Spanish fleet,
were able to direct raking broadside fire at our bows,
which we would be unable to reply. To lessen the
time the fleet was exposed to this danger, Nelson
had his ships make all available sail
(including stuns'ls), yet another departure from the
norm.
He was also aware that French and Spanish gunners
were ill-trained and would have difficulty firing
accurately from a moving gun platform. The
Combined Fleet was sailing across a heavy swell,
causing the ships to roll heavily and exacerbating
the problem. Nelson's plan was indeed a gamble, but
a carefully-calculated one.

Nelson instructed his captains, over dinner
aboard Victory, on his plan for the approaching
battle. The order of sailing, in which the fleet was
arranged when the enemy was first sighted, was to
be the order of the ensuing action so that no time
would be wasted in forming a precise line.

The attack was to be made in two lines. One, led by
his second-in-command Vice-Admiral Cuthbert
Collingwood, was to sail into the rear of the enemy
line, while the other, led by Nelson, was to sail into
the centre and vanguard.

The intention was to split the enemy line and engage in close quarter action, a form of combat in which, Nelson believed, the British fleet would have the advantage.

In preparation for the battle, Nelson ordered the ships of his fleet to be painted in a distinctive yellow and black pattern. this would make them easy to distinguish from any of the opposing ships, this later became known as the Nelson Chequer.

Nelson was careful to point out that something had to be left to chance. Nothing is sure in a sea battle, so he left his captains free from all hampering rules by telling them that "No captain can do very wrong if he places his ship alongside that of the enemy." In short, circumstances would dictate the execution, subject to the guiding rule that the enemy's rear was to be cut off and superior force concentrated on that part of the enemy's line.

11:00 With our entire fleet, which was visible to Villeneuve, drawn up in two parallel columns. The two fleets would be within range of each other within an hour. Villeneuve was concerned at this point about forming up a line, as his ships were unevenly spaced and in an irregular formation. The Franco-Spanish fleet was drawn out nearly five miles long as our fleet approached.

Drawing closer, we could see that the enemy was not sailing in a tight order, but rather in irregular groups. Nelson could not immediately make out the French flagship as the French and Spanish were not flying command pennants.

We were outnumbered and outgunned, the enemy totalling nearly 30,000 men and 2,568 guns to our 17,000 men and 2,148 guns. The Franco-Spanish fleet also had six more ships of the line, and so could more readily combine their fire. There was no way for our ships to avoid being "doubled on" or even "trebled on". As the two fleets drew closer, anxiety began to build among officers and sailors.

While waiting to go into battle, I thought: *During this momentous preparation, the human mind had ample time for meditation, for it had become evident that the fate of England rested on this battle.*

As the battle opened, the French and Spanish were in a ragged curved line headed north. As planned, the British fleet was approaching the Franco-Spanish line in two columns. Leading the northern, windward column in Victory was Nelson, while Collingwood in the 100-gun Royal Sovereign led the second, leeward, column.
The two British columns approached from the west at nearly a right angle to the allied line. Nelson led his column into a feint toward the van of the Franco-Spanish fleet and then abruptly turned toward the actual point of attack. Collingwood altered the course of his column slightly so that the two lines converged at this line of attack.
Just before his column engaged the allied forces, Collingwood signaled to his ships: Now men, let us do something today which the world may talk of hereafter."

Because the winds were very light during the battle, all the ships were moving extremely slowly, and the foremost British ships were under heavy fire from several of the allied ships for almost an hour before their own guns could bear.

Chapter 38.

While we waited to engage in the fight, Horatio,
Hardy and myself, observed what was happening.
from the poopdeck.
At noon, we saw that, Villeneuve send the signal
'engage the enemy', and Fougueux fired her first
trial shot at Royal Sovereign. Royal Sovereign had
all sails out and, having recently had her bottom
cleaned, outran the rest of the British fleet. As she
approached the allied line, she came under fire from
Fougueux, San Justo, Indomptable, and San
Leandro.
Villeneuve, had drawn up his fleet in the form of a
crescent, while our fleet bore down in two separate
lines, one led by us on Victory, and the other by
Collingwood in the Royal Sovereign. Having drawn
considerably ahead of the rest of the fleet, it was the
first engaged.
"See," said Nelson, pointing to the Royal
Sovereign as she penetrated the centre of the
enemy's line, "see how that noble fellow
Collingwood carries his ship into action!"

We watched as The Royal Sovereign closed with the
Spanish admiral Alava's flagship Santa Ana, before
breaking the line just astern of her, into which she
fired a devastating double-shotted raking broadside,
and fired her broadsides with such rapidity and
precision, at the Santa Ana that the Spanish ship was
on the verge of sinking almost before any other of
our ships had fired a gun.

Several other vessels came to Santa Ana's assistance and hemmed in the Royal Sovereign on all sides, the latter, after being severely damaged, was relieved by the arrival of the rest of his squadron, but was left unable to manoeuvre.

Not long afterwards, admiral Alava on the Santa Ana struck her colours, surrendering.

The next ship in line which was my cousin's ship, Dreadnought in the lee column, was engaged in battle with three Spanish first rate ships, L'Aigle, Achille, Neptune, and the second rate Fougueux. As I watched, through my telescope, I saw Robin directing his ship from the poopdeck, directly above the wheel, (the same place that I usually take when in action as captain), I smiled as I thought, *I'll wager Robin's enjoying every minute of this action!*

Then, I watched in horror, as his poopdeck was struck with a lucky shot. The shot from L'Aigle, struck one of the cannon on the poopdeck, killing the gun crew with the chain shot, the lighted wick and the firers hand with it, fell into the powder barrels behind Robin.

The resulting explosion, sent his body, minus an arm and leg, into the air, I heard someone yell, "Robin!" I had no recollection that it was me, as I followed his flying body in my scope, as his lifeless body hit the mizzenmast, and fell to the deck, and lay still, covered in blood.

Two hands rested on my shoulders, one from each side, that belonged to Horatio, and the other, Thomas, saying, "He was a very brave man, Henry."

Horatio said "Aye listen to Hardy, Henry, your cousin was a very brave man. Do not forget him, but come you have work of your own to do."
I nodded numbly, but looked back all the same, chain shot was pouring into the Dreadnought and soon she was completely dismasted, unable to manoeuvre and largely unable to fight, as her sails blinded her batteries, but kept flying her flag for 45 minutes until the following British ships came to her rescue.

Then my ship was in cannon range of the French flagship. Initially passing wide, but then with greater accuracy as the distance between us decreased. The flimsy forecastle was struck, and a lot of damage resulted, but the gunners there were still able to fire back at the enemy. A cannonball struck and killed Nelson's secretary, John Scott, nearly cutting him in two. Hardy's clerk took over, but he too was almost immediately killed. Victory's wheel was shot away, and another cannonball cut down eight marines. I yelled for the bosun, "Get below decks and steer with the tiller, and organize men for voice relay!" He answered, "Under way, and being done sir!"

Having had their walk interrupted, Hardy, standing next to Nelson on the quarterdeck, had his shoe buckle dented by a splinter. Bending over to look at the buckle Nelson calmly remarked over the cannon fire, "This is too warm a work to last long. We will probably get a storm tonight Hardy." Then he straightened up, saying, "I think we should anchor the fleet tonight, what say you Hardy?"

I smiled as I heard his comment, thinking, *we've been under fire for nearly sixty minutes now, and all he can think of is the weather, Christ Horatio!*
I never heard Tom's reply, because at that moment, we were about to cross the French line, I yelled, "Gunners double chain shot, and clear their decks, fire as you bear!" The length of Bucentaure shuddered as the broadside tore through her.
12:45: Victory had by now reached the enemy line, and Hardy asked Nelson which ship to engage first. Nelson told him to take his pick, and Hardy signed to me to take station on the Redoutable, I moved Victory across the stern of the French flagship Bucentaure, raking her again with my port broadside, creating death and mayhem below their decks. We then came under fire from Redoutable, lying off Bucentaure's stern, and the Santísima Trinidad. As sharpshooters from the enemy ships fired onto Victory's deck from their rigging, unperturbed Nelson and Hardy continued to walk about, directing and giving orders.
I passed by the Redoutable, before I swung the Victory over, I had the starboard broadside take them down the throat (firing at the front of the ship), the broadside smashed cannon and men as it tore along the gundecks toward the stern. Then I swung so my starboard side was in line with theirs, as we started to duel with our cannon, but we were also taking fire from the Santisima Trinidad, Neptune, and Héros. Leaving the Bucentaure to be dealt with by other ships following us, Temeraire, Conqueror, and HMS Neptune. Then a general mêlée ensued.

Having moved Victory, to lock masts with the
Redoutable, the crew of which included a strong
infantry corps, as we found out to our dismay (with
three captains and four lieutenants), they gathered
for an attempt to board and seize Victory. Seeing
this immediately as we closed together, I drew a
pistol, and my sword, and raced to the quarterdeck.
I yelled, "Marines, Gunners, standby to repel
boarders!" As the men and marines gathered and
drew cutlasses, two midshipmen, John Pollard and
Francis Collingwood, came from below carrying
muskets and pistols.
Just then a musket was fired from the mizzen top of
Redoutable, which struck Horatio's left shoulder,
seeing this, I yelled, "Pollard, Collingwood, kill that
frog," pointing upward at the mizzen with my
sword.
Then I turned my attention to Hardy and Horatio,
beside them, a marine lieutenant, Lewis Reeve was
seriously wounded and lay next to Nelson. Then I
knelt beside Hardy as Horatio said weakly, "They
finally succeeded doing for me, I am dead." Laying
a hand on Thomas's shoulder, I said, "Get him
below, Tom, there's going to be a fight here soon!"
Hardy turned saying, "He can't walk Henry."
Looking around, I called, then nodded, saying,
"Collingwood, help captain Hardy with the admiral,
young Collingwood will help you Tom, but get him
out of here now!" Looking at Reeve, I called,
"Pollard get mister Reeve below, then return."
I later learned from doctor Beatty that the ball had
entered Nelson in the left shoulder, passed through

his spine at the sixth and seventh thoracic vertebrae, and lodged two inches below his right scapula in the muscles of his back.

Grenades from the French were thrown at us from Redoutable, and marine second in command, captain Charles Adair, was killed, as one landed at his feet. The rest of us survived the grenades, and I got my men ready, for the coming assault, as I said, "They'll not take this ship men, she's our home!" As the French were preparing to board us, Temeraire, approached from the starboard bow of Redoutable and fired on the exposed French crew with a carronade, causing many casualties.

With a wave, and a smile to Eliab Harvey, thanking him, we were able to beat back the assault, about to yell another order to the bosun, I looked up to see Tom Hardy was back on the poopdeck in my place, and had the running of the ship in hand.

As Nelson lay wounded, my battle with Redoutable reached its height. The frogs repeatedly tried to board Victory, but we drove them back with heavy fire, and hand to hand fighting at the rails at 13:30 I called my men onto the offensive, and I boarded her with two hundred men at my back. Firing both of my pistols, I drew my swords once more, as I cut and slashed my way to the captain.

13:55, Captain Lucas, of Redoutable, with 99 fit men out of 643 and severely wounded himself, surrendered his ship and sword to me, and I had his colours struck, then looked across at Thomas, who gave me a smile and wave.

Moving away from the Redoutable, Hardy took us toward the Bucentaure, with Harvey on Temeraire we isolated her, as I said to my boarding party, "Well men, this is the one the admiral wants, so let's get it for him."

As Hardy moved us in close, my men were smiling and shouting, as the grapples were thrown, and I prepared my weapons, and myself to go into battle once more.

Having a quick look around us, while I had the chance, I saw HMS Neptune, Leviathan, and Conqueror similarly, to what Hardy and Harvey had done, engage the Santísima Trinidad, she was isolated and overwhelmed, surrendering after three hours.

As more and more of our ships entered the battle, the ships of the allied centre and rear were gradually overwhelmed.

14:15: Having swarmed aboard, the Bucentaure her crew completely demoralized, only put up a token resistance, and as the enemy officers were surrounded by my men Admiral Villeneuve, surrendered his sword to me, along with his command Eagle, Joe Dawson, gathered up the rest of the officer's surrendered swords. While I struck Bucentaure's and Villeneuve's colours, I looked at Hardy who was watching me, and I smiled and nodded. He smiled in return, nodded then said something to Charlie Denman, and walked below.

14:30: After giving me his parole, I left Villeneuve aboard his flagship, and returned with my men to the

Victory, carrying the flags and colours from the Bucentaure, while Dawson brought all the captured swords aboard behind me. I went below, to report to Horatio that 12 or 14 of the enemy were taken, and no British ship had surrendered. That last answer betrayed Nelson's anxiety about the outcome of the battle, but I couldn't linger, I was needed on deck. Back at my usual station on the poopdeck, I watched as, the lead enemy squadron was belatedly trying to join the battle, only to be bettered by Edward Codrington's brilliantly handled Orion, along with the Minotaur and the Spartiate.

Later, I signaled the ships nearby to support the flagship.

I visited Nelson again at 15:30, to confirm a glorious victory, but could not satisfy Nelson's determination to have 20 prizes. Nodding to me, he turned to Hardy, saying, "Anchor, Hardy, Anchor!" the dying man demanded, as the rising sea reminded him of his weather forecast.

At 16:30: As the battle was dying down, Tom Hardy came back to me on the poop, and said, "He's gone Henry, I kissed his forehead, as he asked, then he kept repeating: Thank God, I have done my duty as he died."

As he delivered the news, I removed my hat and hung my head, those that were watching me, started to do the same, as they all knew that Horatio had been wounded, and assumed rightly by my attitude that he had died. A silence descended over the Victory as the word passed around the ship.

Motioning to Pascoe to join me, I had him signal

We took 22 vessels of the Franco-Spanish fleet and lost none. Among the captured French ships were L'Aigle, Algésiras, Berwick, Bucentaure, Fougueux Intrépide, Redoutable, and Swiftsure. The Spanish ships taken were Argonauta, Bahama, Monarca, Neptuno, San Agustín, San Ildefonso, San Juan Nepomuceno, Santísima Trinidad, and Santa Ana. Of these, Redoutable sank, Santísima Trinidad and Argonauta were scuttled. Achille exploded, Intrépide and San Augustín burned, L'Aigle, Berwick, Fougueux, and Monarca, were wrecked in a gale following the battle.

Admiral Federico Gravina, the senior Spanish flag officer, escaped with the remnants of the fleet, he succumbed months later to the wounds he received during the battle.

After the death of Nelson, Collingwood assumed the command-in-chief, and transferred his flag to the frigate Euryalus. Knowing that a severe storm was in the offing, Nelson had intended that the fleet should anchor after the battle, but Collingwood chose not to issue such an order. many of our ships and prizes were so damaged that they were unable to anchor, and Collingwood concentrated efforts on taking the damaged vessels in tow.
In the ensuing gale, many of the prizes were wrecked on the rocky shore and others were destroyed to prevent their recapture, though none of our ships were lost.

That evening as the gale raged, I had invited Villeneuve to join us for dinner as a guest, in the wardroom, as he entered with Hardy, after receiving a glass of wine, Villeneuve asked, "I wish to express my sorrow to you, for your loss, and wish to honour such a formidable foe, gentlemen, I give you a toast, to Lord Admiral Horatio Nelson."

We returned his toast, then we sat down to have our dinner.

Conversation over dinner was about the battle, and admiral Villeneuve himself expressed his belief that Nelson would use some sort of unorthodox attack, stating specifically that he believed accurately, that Nelson would drive right at his line. But his long game of cat and mouse with Nelson had worn him down, and he was suffering from a loss of nerve. Arguing that the inexperience of his officers meant he would not be able to maintain formation in more than one group, so, he had chosen not to act on his assessment.

Chapter 39.

October 25, 1805: After the storms had abated, and a reckoning made, of the state of our fleet, and disposition of the prizes captured.

I sit here in my cabin, alone with my thoughts, and my cousins' personal effects, these had been brought to me on the Victory this morning, when a captain's conference was called by Hardy. Until this time, I have been too busy to dwell on the fact, that my cousin and good friend, was killed during the battle in the most gruesome way.

Running my eyes over his possessions, I have noticed his now familiar journal had been brought to me among is gear, and I sadly get up and carefully extract it, sitting back, I open it and make for the last entry I had read. From there I have read through to his last entry with tears in my eyes, as I wipe the tears away, I have decided two things: The first, being that I will finish his journal, with an obituary of the first order, and try to do him proud. Second, the very next time I am given shore leave in England, I will personally take his possessions home to his wife Elizabeth, instead of just sending them to her, as she has the right to know, how gallantly her husband had died, from one that witnessed his end during the battle.

Admiral Federico Gravina, the senior Spanish flag officer, escaped with the remnant of the fleet, he succumbed months later to the wounds he received during the battle.

Villeneuve attended Nelson's funeral while a captive on parole in England.

His sudden change to leave port, was prompted by a letter Villeneuve had received on 18 October, informing him that Vice-Admiral François Rosily, had arrived in Madrid with orders to take command of the Combined Fleet. Stung by the prospect of being disgraced before the fleet, Villeneuve resolved to go to sea before his successor could reach Cádiz. At the same time, he received intelligence that a detachment of six British ships (Admiral Louis' squadron), had docked at Gibraltar, thus weakening the British fleet. This was used as the pretext for sudden change. Towards the end of the battle, and with the combined fleet being overwhelmed, the still relatively un-engaged portion of the van under Rear-Admiral Dumanoir Le Pelley tried to come to the assistance of the collapsing centre.

After failing to fight his way through, he decided to break off the engagement, and led four French ships, his flagship the Formidable, Scipion, Duguay Trouin, and Mont Blanc away from the fighting. He headed at first for the Straits of Gibraltar, intending to carry out Villeneuve's original orders and make for Toulon.

On 22 October he changed his mind, remembering a powerful British squadron under Rear-Admiral Thomas Louis was patrolling the straits, and headed north, hoping to reach one of the French Atlantic ports. With a storm gathering in strength off the Spanish coast, he sailed westwards to clear Cape St Vincent, prior to heading north-west, swinging eastwards across the Bay of Biscay, and aiming to reach the French port at Rochefort.

These four ships remained at large, until their encounter with, and attempt to chase a British frigate, this brought them in range of one of our squadrons under Sir Richard Strachan, which captured them all on 4 November 1805 at the Battle of Cape Ortegal.

Only eleven ships escaped to Cádiz, and, of those, only five were considered seaworthy. The seriously wounded Admiral Gravina passed command of the remainder of the fleet over to Captain Julien Cosmao on 23 October. From shore, the allied commanders could see an opportunity for a rescue mission existed.

Cosmao claimed in his report that the rescue plan was entirely his idea, but Vice-Admiral Escano recorded a meeting of Spanish and French Commodores at which a planned rescue was discussed and agreed upon. Enrique Macdonell and Cosmao were of equal rank and both raised commodore's pennants before hoisting anchor. Both sets of mariners were determined to attempt to recapture some of the prizes. Cosmao ordered the rigging of his ship, the Pluton, to be repaired and reinforced her crew (which had been depleted by casualties from the battle), with sailors from the French frigate Hermione. Taking advantage of a favourable northwesterly wind, Pluton, Neptune, and Indomptable, the Spanish Rayo and San Francisco de Asís, together with five French frigates and two brigs, sailed out of the harbour towards the British. Soon after leaving port, the wind shifted to west-southwest, raising a heavy sea with the result that most of the British prizes broke their tow ropes, and drifted far to leeward, where they were only partially resecured.

The combined squadron came in sight at noon, causing Collingwood to summon his most battle-ready ships to meet the threat. In doing so, he ordered them to cast off towing their prizes. He had formed a defensive line of ten ships by three o'clock in the afternoon and approached the Franco-Spanish squadron, covering the remainder of their prizes which stood out to sea.

The Franco-Spanish squadron chose not to approach within gunshot and declined to attack. Collingwood also chose not to seek action, in the confusion of the powerful storm, the French frigates managed to retake two Spanish ships of the line, which had been cast off by their British captors, these were the Santa Ana and Neptuno, taking them in tow and making for Cádiz. On being taken in tow, the Spanish crews revolted against their British prize crews, putting them to work as prisoners.

Despite this initial success the Franco-Spanish force, hampered by battle damage, struggled in the heavy seas. Neptuno was eventually wrecked off Rota in the gale, while Santa Ana reached port.

The French ship Indomptable was wrecked on the 24th or 25th off the town of Rota on the northwest point of the bay of Cadiz. At the time, Indomptable had 1,200 men, but no more than 100 were saved.

San Francisco de Asís was driven ashore in Cádiz Bay, near Fort Santa-Catalina, although her crew was saved. Rayo, an old three-decker with more than 50 years of service, anchored off Sanlúcar, a few leagues to the northwest of Rota. There, she lost her masts, they had been damaged by shot earlier. Heartened by the approach of the squadron, the French crew of the former flagship Bucentaure also rose up and retook the ship from the British prize crew but she was wrecked on 23 October.

Aigle escaped from the British ship HMS Defiance, but was wrecked off the port of Santa María on 23 October, while the French prisoners on Berwick cut the tow cables, but this caused her to founder off Sanlúcar on 22 October. The crew of Algésiras rose up and managed to sail into Cádiz.

Observing that some of the leeward most of the prizes were escaping towards the Spanish coast, Leviathan asked for and was granted permission by Collingwood to try to retrieve the prizes and bring them to anchor. Leviathan chased Monarca, but on 24 October she came across Rayo, dismasted but still flying Spanish colours, at anchor off the shoals of Sanlúcar.

At this point the HMS Donegal, en route from Gibraltar under Captain Pulteney Malcolm, was seen approaching from the south on the larboard tack with a moderate breeze from northwest-by-north and steered directly for the Spanish three-decker.

At about ten o'clock, just as Monarca had got within little more than a mile of Rayo, Leviathan fired a warning shot wide of Monarca, to oblige her to drop anchor. The shot fell between Monarca and Rayo. The latter, conceiving that it was probably intended for her, hauled down her colours, and was taken by HMS Donegal, who anchored alongside and took off the prisoners.

Leviathan resumed her pursuit of Monarca, eventually catching up and forcing her to surrender. On boarding her, her British captors found that she was in a sinking state, and so removed the British prize crew, and nearly all her original Spanish crew members. The nearly empty Monarca parted her cable and was wrecked during the night.

Despite the efforts of her British prize crew, Rayo was driven onshore on 26 October and wrecked, with the loss of twenty-five men. The remainder of the prize crew were made prisoners by the Spanish.

The condition of our own ships was such that it was very doubtful what would be their fate.

Many a time I would have given the whole group of our capture, to ensure our own ships survival. I can only say that in my life I never saw such efforts as were made to save these prize ships, and would rather fight another battle than pass through such a week as followed it.

On balance, the allied counter attack achieved very little. In forcing us to stop our repairs to defend ourselves, it influenced Admiral Collingwood's decision to sink, or set fire to the most damaged of the remaining prizes.

Cosmao retook two ships of the line, but it cost him one French and two Spanish ships to do so.

Not fearing prize money loss, the British burnt, or sank Santisima Trinidad, Argonauta, San Antonio, and Intrepide.
Only four of the British prizes, the French Swiftsure, and the Spanish Bahama, San Ildefonso, And San Juan Nepomuceno, survived to be taken to England. After the end of the battle and storm, only nine ships of the line were left in Cadiz.

When Rosily Arrived at Cadiz, he found only five French ships, rather than the eighteen he was expecting. The surviving ships remained bottled up in Cadiz until 1808, when Napoleon invaded Spain. The French ships were then seized by the Spanish forces, and put into service against France.

The battle of Ulm, took place the day after Trafalgar, and Napoleon didn't hear about it for weeks after, as the Grande Armee had left Boulogne to fight Britain's allies, before they could combine a huge force. He had tight control over the Paris media, and kept the defeat a closely guarded secret for over a month, at which point newspapers proclaimed it to have been a tremendous victory. In a counter-propaganda move, a fabricated text declaring the battle a "spectacular victory" for the French and Spanish was published in Herald and attributed to Le Moniteur Universel

Vice-Admiral Villeneuve was taken prisoner aboard his flagship and taken back to Britain. After his parole in 1806, he returned to France, where he was found dead in his inn room during a stop on the way to Paris, with six stab wounds in the chest from a dining knife. It was officially recorded that he had committed suicide.

Despite the British victory over the Franco-Spanish navies, Trafalgar had negligible impact on the remainder of the War of the Third Coalition. Less than two months later, Napoleon decisively defeated the Third Coalition at the Battle of Austerlitz, knocking Austria out of the war and forcing the dissolution of the Holy Roman Empire.

Although Trafalgar meant France could no longer challenge Britain at sea, Napoleon proceeded to establish the Continental System to deny Britain trade with the continent. The Napoleonic Wars continued for another ten years after Trafalgar.

Following the battle, the Royal Navy was never again seriously challenged by the French fleet in a large-scale engagement.

Napoleon had already abandoned his plans of invasion before the battle and they were never revived. The battle did not mean, however, that the French naval challenge to Britain was over.

First, as the French control over the continent expanded, Britain had to take active steps with the Battle of Copenhagen in 1807 and elsewhere in 1808 to prevent the ships of smaller European navies from falling into French hands. This effort was largely successful, but did not end the French threat as Napoleon instituted a large-scale shipbuilding programme that produced a fleet of 80 ships of the line at the time of his fall from power in

1814, with more under construction. In comparison, Britain had 99 ships of the line in active commission in 1814, and this was close to the maximum that could be supported.

Given a few more years, the French could have realised their plans to commission 150 ships of the line and again challenge the Royal Navy, compensating for the inferiority of their crews with sheer numbers. For almost 10 years after Trafalgar, the Royal Navy maintained a close blockade of French bases and anxiously observed the growth of the French fleet. In the end, Napoleon's Empire was destroyed before the ambitious buildup could be completed.

Hardy and I have decided to take turns captaining the ship, because he is no longer a fleet captain and he has no ship, we sailed into Gibraltar for emergency repairs, before our return to England. Many of the injured crew were brought ashore at Gibraltar and treated in the Naval Hospital. Men who subsequently died from injuries sustained at the battle are buried in or near the Trafalgar Cemetery, at the south end of Main Street, Gibraltar.

With Horatio's body, it was preserved in a barrel of brandy and lashed to the main mast, with a twenty-four-hour armed guard for the trip home to a hero's funeral.

We set sail for home on December 4,1805, my orders were to make for the Nore, reaching there on

January 6, 1806. Horatio's body was unloaded, and Hardy left us there, as I turned Victory toward Portsmouth, making port two weeks later.

All crew members were given three months leave with full pay, and I made my way home on the daily service carriage, arriving three days later.

<u>Epilogue.</u>

January 3, – January 9, 1806: Nelson's body was
unloaded from the Victory at the Nore. It was
conveyed upriver in Commander Grey's yacht,
Chatham, to Greenwich and placed in a lead coffin,
and that in another wooden one, made from the mast
of L'Orient, which had been salvaged after the Battle
of the Nile. He lay in state in the Painted Hall at
Greenwich for three days, before being taken
upriver aboard a barge, accompanied by Lord Hood,
chief mourner Sir Peter Parker, and the Prince of
Wales. The coffin was taken into the Admiralty for
the night, attended by Nelson's chaplain, Alexander
Scott. The next day, 9 January, a funeral procession
consisting of 32 admirals, over a hundred captains,
and an escort of 10,000 soldiers took the coffin from
the Admiralty to St Paul's Cathedral. After a four-
hour service he was interred in the crypt within
a sarcophagus originally carved for Cardinal
Wolsey. He lies there still, one of England's greatest
Admirals.

Journal: Henry Robert Tolcher Captain RN.

January 25, 1806: My family were glad to see me
home, because they feared the worst upon hearing of
Nelson's death. Now their fears have been dismissed
with me at home. My homecoming was even better,
as I was informed I had another child. Within a few

days of my arrival home, I made the journey to see Elizabeth, Robin's wife, after I had everything of his washed and pressed, and gathered all his personal items together. Before I left home, I had gone to the naval bank and used Robin's authority, to withdraw the eighteen thousand five hundred pounds in his account, having the cheque made out to cash.

Now I was ready to fulfil my promise to Robin, I arrived at her cottage on the morning of my second day travelling.

Having been made welcome, I stayed for a day or two, during which time, I told her everything about Robin, and even though I didn't describe in detail how his death was, she knew that it had come quick, and he wouldn't have suffered. She was also pleased with my help getting Robin's money from his naval account, knowing how he felt about it.

Leaving her cottage, I told her "Elizabeth, anytime you wish, you and the children are welcome at my home in Plymouth, I'm off now to see Albert, and no doubt he will be in touch with you, until I see you again farewell, dear cousin."

My next stop was Taunton, and Albert was home, after returning from London and Nelson's internment at St. Pauls Cathedral, there he had seen Hardy and talked with him, so he knew I was alive, and of Robin's death.

He was pleased to see me as was the entire family, which had been reduced by not having Lady Elizabeth present, she had passed away, in 1803, but I had been informed of her passing by mail from him, soon after she had passed. He embraced me as I climbed from my horse, before we went inside. Over drinks in the study, we discussed Robin's death, and what I had done since, in looking after Elizabeth and her children.

Then he asked, "And what about you Henry, what are going to be doing, surely, it's time to retire while you're still young enough to enjoy life, after all you have a guaranteed income for life now?

I smiled, reached for the carafe of malt scotch, pouring us each another half tumbler full, then said, "Well now that you've mentioned that Albert, I was recently awarded more to my pension, parliament has increased the sum by another two thousand pounds, which means I'll be receiving ten thousand pounds per annum, so financially, I have all the money I could ever wish for, even if I were to retire from the service now. What with all my prize monies, and what not, and I still will be awarded more from the prizes taken at Trafalgar, but no, I won't retire just yet, after all I'm only thirty years old, much too young to retire, I was informed by the admiralty, that I've already been promoted to Commodore, and will be commanding a squadron of my own in the Mediterranean when Victory has completed repairs. Together with all the other captains and admirals, I will also receive, another gold medal, being my third, after those for the Cape St Vincent, the Nile, only Horatio, Ed Berry, and Collingwood, share that distinction of three gold medals for service during our wars against France. So, you see, I'm in good company."

Albert then asked, "When will you retire, Henry?" I smiled again, and replied, "Oh, I may give it some thought in about ten years or so." Then we both laughed.

After my quick overnight visit, I continued on to my next stop which was at my parent's farm. Where I was greeted warmly, after my father's question, "Are you staying for a couple of days Robert?" I shook my head, and replied, "I'm afraid not father, I've already been away from home too long, but I had to visit Robin's wife and family, he died at Trafalgar, and so I had to make sure his family was seen to. Then I went to see Albert, about the same thing, because he was holding monies in trust for Robin, but I only stayed overnight there also, and now I'm on my way home, I called in to let you know I was alright, and to give you all the news." Then later as we were all sat at the dinner table, I told them my account of the battle, in the correct sequence of events, which included how Robin was killed, the loss of my friend, Horatio, and of bringing Victory back to England, my award of another gold medal, my letters of thanks from the government, the increase to my pension for life, and lastly my new promotion.

The next morning, I left after breakfast, and rode to Plymouth, where Joanna, fussed over me, telling me that she had been worried about me, due to my longer than expected absence. That night she made love to me, quite a few times, before we drifted into sleep in each other's arms.

May 2, 1806: Whilst I was still on leave, I had my commodores uniform and pennant made, my newer frockcoats were gold laced with gold buttons. This had now become the standard wear of high office, and the only thing that changed was the gold epaulettes, and shoulder insignia, thinking that, *I'm a commodore now, next would be vice admiral, then full admiral. I could conceivably make admiral if I stayed for the allotted time I've given myself, so I may as well buy the extra sets now.*

Acting on my thoughts, I purchased, the extra sets of shoulder boards (as they were known), for vice and admiral, the difference being two stars for vice, and three for admiral.

I arrived in Portsmouth, aboard the service coach, and made my way to the admiralty office, dressed in my everyday commodore's frockcoat, that had my three gold medals embroidered in their correct place, on the left front shoulder. My orders were to make for Gibraltar, and report to the commander in chief, who was now admiral Collingwood.

Arriving aboard the victory, I passed my new captain, Dan Culverhouse, my pennant, and he passed it to signals, John Pasco, for it to be run up, as Dan and I made our way to the great cabin, which was now mine.

Placing my possessions on the double bed, I motioned for Dan to take a seat, and grabbing a carafe of wine and two glasses, we drank together as he gave me a report on the ship and new men. Otherwise, the crew were the same as I knew.

Smiling, I said, "Thanks Dan, that makes our life easier they all know us and what is required from each station. That's all for now, I'll see you and the others in the wardroom later, thank you."
That evening I reacquainted myself with the ships officers, as we talked of old times, and the newer ones to come.

After an early breakfast, the following morning, I was on the poopdeck as Dan took the Victory out of the harbour, then I glanced up at my pennant flying in the breeze, with the clan crest in the top corner of the red St. George cross on the white background (I had talked to Albert about using it on my pennant when I had visited him, and was given his blessing for my use of it), I smiled as I watched it, then directed my attention to all the crewmen I knew on the quarterdeck.
When we arrived in Gibraltar, Collingwood and I greeted each other, as comrades of old, as he gave me a squadron of seven ships to command. All their captains and I knew each other, and our brief was to relieve blockading squadrons at various French ports, we didn't have to worry about the Spanish now, because after Napoleon invaded Spain, they had now become our allies.
No great battles were fought, though several small French fleets would attempt to run the blockades. One fleet did successfully run the blockade, by then I was back in Gibraltar, and Collingwood gave me the job to go after them, we caught up with them in the Caribbean.

One of the ships was a troop carrier, and we caught them unawares unloading troops, we engaged them which resulted in sinking three of them. We hunted down the rest, and overwhelmed them in battle, capturing six of them.

They were taken back to Plymouth, and all my ships were given a month's shore leave, before we were to return to the Mediterranean.

In 1808, I was promoted to Vice Admiral, and made Collingwood's second in command.

His health began to decline alarmingly in 1809 and he was forced to request the Admiralty to allow him to return home, with me to replace him which was granted.

March 1, 1810: I was promoted to Admiral of the blue, and made Admiral in chief of the Mediterranean fleet.

On his way home Collingwood died because of cancer, aboard the Ville de Paris, off Port Mahon as he sailed for England, on 7 March 1810. He was laid to rest beside Nelson in the crypt of St Paul's Cathedral.

June 20, 1816: After faithfully serving in the royal navy for twenty-five years, I finally gave into my wife Joanna's requests, for me to retire from active service.

Having done so, I now spend my days in leisure, and in the raising of our ten children, though not all of them need my guidance. My youngest male child,

John, was the only one that was christened, due to the others being too old for such a thing, when Joanna and I got around to talking about having the children christened, I think in hindsight, that was something we should have discussed, back around the time we were married, but we did have other important things, like each other, to occupy our thoughts.

June 6, 1833: An admiralty post rider, called on me today, and after reading the despatch, it looked as if it was time to get my old uniform out again. Going into the house, I asked Joanna to join me in my study.

Showing her the despatch, I gave her time to read it, before I asked, "Well dear, do you think I should go?"

She replied with a smile, "Of course you must go my love, besides you'll not be happy if you don't."

I smiled saying, "That's if I can still get into my uniform."

She laughed, and said, "You will dear, you've still kept yourself fit, with all that walking and sword practice you do."

Resigned to the matter, I smiled asking lecherously, "Well, I could see if I can get into it again, would you like to come and help me?"

She giggled, and replied, "Alright, but you're not to try getting me knocked up again, ten years of that was enough."

I sighed, saying, "Ah, but you're past all that now my dear, now we can really enjoy it."

The smile that came to her face, beamed mischievously, as she giggled, and said, "Race you to the bedroom!" As she took off running.

I raced up the stairs behind her, and planted a smack on her behind, and she squealed and giggled loudly. She helped me to dress into my dress admirals uniform, with the three gold medals pinned on, and it still fitted like a glove, but when I went to put my weapons belt on, she chided me, saying, "You would be better, to wear your dress sword, my love." Shrugging my shoulders, I acceded to her request, asking, "There, how does that look?"

She smiled saying, "God, you still look gorgeously handsome, let me help you out of them now, and I might let you help me!"

Afterward, we went around the room picking all our clothes up, and she hung my uniform up again.

July 18, 1833: I have arrived aboard my old ship HMS Victory, to the welcome salutes and handshakes of many old familiar faces, at 11:00, we were all lined up in single file, around both sides of the Victory, as the guest of honour arrived. As being captain of Victory at the time, I had the pleasure of meeting and greeting them, as they stepped aboard, every person present saluted them aboard.

Then I was introduced to the queen in waiting, Princess Victoria, and her mother the duchess of Kent.

The princess (soon to become Queen), had come to meet all the surviving veterans of the Battle of Trafalgar, and she spent hours with us talking, and listening to our tales, as we all had lunch and drinks in my great cabin.

Before she left, we were all presented with a gold medal of appreciation from her on behalf of a grateful nation, on a wide ribbon that she personally placed over our heads, to all present.

After arriving home, a week later, I took my uniform off for the last time. It was time to sit back and enjoy the rest of my life, with my wife, family, and friends.

That dear family is my tale, I hope you have enjoyed it, as much as I am enjoying my life.

Henry Robert Tolcher, Admiral RN (Ret).

Authors Note:

Well that brings us to the end of The Ultimate Gamble, and the story of two members of the Fox-Davis/Tolcher clan that were present during that moment in history.

As always, any comments you have, or book enquiries can be expressed through my website http://timothydiamond.net

I can only hope you look forward to more Timothy Diamond novels in the future, as to what they will be, well I'm not quite sure yet, but I do have a couple of projects in mind, and will keep you informed through the blog page of the website.

Until we meet again with my next novel my thanks for reading, and do take care, cheers.

Timothy Diamond.

All Other books written by Timothy Diamond available from Amazon and his website:
http://timothydiamond.net

Playing with Fire: Book 1 of The Catalyst Trilogy Introduces Tom Davis, our main character and explores his early life.

Chasing the Sun, tells the tale of travelling to the Nullarbor Plain, and playing golf on the world's longest golf course.

Divine Retribution: Book 2 of The Catalyst Trilogy Back in action again with Tom, this time in S.E. Asia and other secret warzones.

The MV Eagle Star, tells the full story behind the magazine feature I wrote in 2009, and is the whole story, not an abridged version, as the article was.

Last Man Standing: Book 3 of The Catalyst Trilogy Tom's role has changed, and after thirty years of playing the game, it's time to quit...or is it?

The Other Side of the Coin, is a companion book to The Catalyst Trilogy, and focuses on Tom's business and personal life during a time of upheaval.

Set amid the backdrop of the life and times of William The Conqueror of England, we find his boyhood friend and ally Walter Tolchard, born into the nobility of French Normandy.
When Edward the Confessor died in 1066, Harold Godwin, claimed the throne of England for himself (despite an oath he made to William to support his claim). The Witan, a council of English lords, supported Harold. William, angered by the betrayal, invaded England to enforce his claim.
Walter survives the battles, and rises to prominence under William's rule, and founds a family clan that has been since, not far from the side of reigning monarchs.

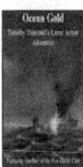

Timothy Diamond's new action adventure, introduces the exploits of another member of the Fox-Davis Clan. With Andrew Fox-Davis, and the eventual quest to go after what his cousin had found.

Back Cover of Book